Fudge Shop Mystery Series:
Series:
Deadly Fudge Divas

By Christine DeSmet

Writers Exchange E-Publishing
http://www.writers-exchange.com

A Fudge Shop Mystery: Deadly Fudge Divas
Copyright 2020 Christine DeSmet
Writers Exchange E-Publishing
PO Box 372
ATHERTON QLD 4883

Cover Art by: Aprampar

Published by Writers Exchange E-Publishing
http://www.writers-exchange.com

ISBN **ebook**: 978-1-925574-69-2
Print: 9798620879106

Dedication

To readers like Regina (and you know who you are), who love the mischief and mayhem I stir up in Door County, Wisconsin.

Acknowledgements

Many thanks for special support from the Writing Sisters group of published and aspiring novelists: Bibi Belford, Ceone Fenn, Julie Holmes, Blair Hull, Lisa Kusko, Martha Miles, Roi Solberg. Our wonderful retreats at Wisconsin B&Bs provided me with motivation as well as valuable plot and character advice for this novel.

Additional thanks for the support of the many writers I work with as a coach and teacher through University of Wisconsin-Madison conferences, retreats, and workshops. You never pause in your enthusiasm and interest in what I'm working on and I'm grateful to you all.

Novels are put together by a team that includes an editor as well as artists and technical people. The support I get at Writers Exchange Publishing means the world to me. Thank you to Sandy Cummins and the entire crew.

Thank you, Mary Clay, for being a superb beta reader.

As always, thanks to Bob Boetzer for endless support and for cooking while I write!

Chapter 1

I should have been happy.

Why wasn't I happy? Five reasons. They called themselves the "Fudge Divas".

This was the first week in April and tourists would soon clog our two-lane, picturesque, winding roads. I hoped many would stay at my newly renovated, historic Blue Heron Inn.

In the middle of the kitchen sat the new giant, white marble countertop, perfect for loafing fudge so joyfully delicious that angels would strike up a chorus. Instead, yelling and arguing echoed from the divas.

Nasty thoughts of them stumbling off the bluff came to me more than once.

The Blue Heron Inn sat atop a scenic outcropping of rock that was part of the ancient escarpment stretching from Wisconsin to Niagara Falls. Cedars and sugar maples dotted the B&B's hilltop perch. My parents and grandparents had just tapped the maples a couple of weeks ago after the daytime temperature kited into the fifties for a few days with the nights in the teens and twenties Fahrenheit.

The inn overlooked Lake Michigan's big bay on the western shoreline of Door County, known as the Cape Cod of the Midwest. The powder blue-and-cream inn's past may have included housing some of my Belgian ancestors when they'd immigrated to fish, farm, and work in the forests. Many immigrants in the 1800s made wood shingles for a living. The shingles were sent via steamer ships down to a bustling, growing Chicago. My parents were now farmers, but Dad and Grandpa still wielded an axe often to create firewood.

It was ten o'clock on this chilly Saturday morning, a good one for a fire in the fireplace, and so foggy it appeared white cotton candy pressed against the windowpanes.

Ordinarily springtime ushered in as quietly as a yellow daffodil sneaking through the last remnant of a snowbank on the south side of a building.

The fudge divas's zumba music and raucous exercising and voices--arguing again--had the wood floors rumbling, the antique chandeliers swaying, and my mind muddled.

The dark fudge ingredients in front of me were a primordial pool jiggling to the shock of earthquakes. The sweet confection had no chance of hardening into anything I could cut and serve as fudge.

The divas, all in their fifties, included and were invited by my former mother-in-law Cathy Rivers. She lived in Fishers' Harbor these days, but the rest of them had arrived early Wednesday from various cities and parts of the country. They dubbed their girlfriend vacation the "Freshmen Fudge Frolic".

The women had attended the University of Wisconsin-Madison where they'd met as freshmen in the early 1980s.

Their first "fudge retreat" day in Fishers' Harbor included cocoa bean-jalapeno-spiced facials at the new local spa called the Glass Slipper, owned by Cathy. She was also staying in an upstairs room, though she had a condo nearby.

My grandpa Gil--whom I'd called Gilpa since a toddler--didn't trust Cathy.

"Ava Mathilde Oosterling, she's pushing that darn son of hers on you again to get your fudge business," he'd said many a time.

Just yesterday while in the kitchen I'd responded, "How is inviting her friends here pushing Dillon on me? I'm going to be making gobs of money."

"Exactly. And then you'll become too busy and you'll ask Dillon to help out more, and then his mother will be here all the time, and pretty soon she'll offer to buy this from us. That will leave you with nothing except a paid-off mortgage."

Grandpa had helped me out by co-signing on the mortgage papers to buy the Blue Heron Inn several months back.

Grandpa feared for himself, too. He and I shared Oosterlings' Live Bait, Bobbers & Belgian Fudge & Beer, a small shop that sat on our village's harbor. That's where I got my start, just a year ago when I'd moved back from the West Coast.

It was true Cathy liked to take straw and spin it into gold. But Cathy also loved our quaint area. Originally from Milwaukee, she'd visited here last year and ended up staying, admiring the historical significance of this area of the country. Cathy bought an old mansion on Main Street and turned it into the Glass Slipper. Since Wednesday, Cathy and her friends visited the spa every day, then returned to the inn to nosh on different fudge flavors paired with local wines. But instead of reminiscing about English lit classes and cheerleading in college, they debated return-on-investment ratios. They still looked like cheerleaders, though. Exercise was part of every morning and afternoon.

Diva Jackie Valentine--a tall redhead and sometime voice of reason among them--said on the first day, "We're not letting menopause cause a meno-plus in pounds. We eat fudge with impunity."

I was thirty-three and played basketball with friends over at the school playground, but these health-conscious divas could probably beat us in a game.

They'd brought along a couple of twenty-somethings--Zadie, the daughter of Pepper Elliott, and Zadie's friend, Yola Wooten--but those two disappeared day and night. Couldn't blame them. They had freaked out after hearing there'd been a murder upstairs last year; I accommodated their request not to stay in the dead woman's room.

The fifty-somethings, on the other hand, loved the drama of murder. They declared that every inn had to have a murder and a ghost. It's just how it's done, right?

Grandma had assured me the high energy level and constant kibitzing was their manner of communicating. "They're like puppies," Grandma Sophie said, "that constantly gnaw on each other's tail. It's playful."

Puppies? The women struck me as sharks.

I was praying the April fog would lift soon so the divas could go on another of their adventures and leave me in peace to figure out my fudge. The boards under my feet in the kitchen continued to reverberate. Jackie's voice wafted in, "And again!"

Groans resounded. A strained voice sounding like Pepper's said, "Kim, stop it!"

Yes! Kim, Pepper, Jackie, Eliza, and Cathy--stop it!

Jackie bellowed, "Pepper, for goodness sake, pick up the pace!"

Another voice--Eliza's with its hint of gravelly tone--ground out, "Jackie, you're not the boss of us."

"You got that right." Cathy's sweet voice had chimed in. "If this were a TV show you might not last the night, Jackie."

I gasped at the threat, listening hard from the kitchen.

"Cathy," Kim's voice joined the fray, "that was not called for at all."

Jackie laughed heartily. "No offense taken. I guess we've all imagined doing each other in at some point, right?"

"Shhhh, she might hear," Eliza said as the music hit low notes.

I shuddered. I did not want another murder in the inn.

I leaped from my morbid thoughts when the back door to the kitchen banged open and shut.

Best friend Pauline Mertens skidded to a stop on the other side of the kitchen island, flipping her long, black hair behind her shoulders--an action she did a lot when it was time to one-up me or hold something over on me. "Ava, I have big news."

Though it was only morning and on her day off at that, she wore a new, red blouse fit for our county's five-star dinner restaurants. I groaned inwardly. New clothes usually meant another misadventure with her so-called beau.

Regaining my bearings by focusing on the fudge problem, I kidded, "You're taking my guests for a long hike into Peninsula State Park right now and then losing them?"

She rose to her six feet to look down. She enjoyed having two inches on me. "If you're going to run an inn, you have to take charge like I do. Tell them, 'If you don't behave and sleep in on Saturdays, you won't get your chocolate milk after recess or your fudge.'"

Pauline was a kindergarten teacher.

I turned to the cupboards behind me to retrieve antique plates featuring yellow roses. It was only a coincidence, but the women loved them because yellow roses were their signature flower. They'd asked about the collection's price, which I thought rude. Fortunately, I'd inherited the plates so I had responded with a toothy smile, "They're priceless."

With a sigh for Pauline, I said, "You know I can't give these particular guests any rules to follow."

Pauline plunked her giant apple-green purse on the white island top next to the pan of fudge. "Didn't you hear me? I have news. And it's from John."

"Can't we take my problem first? I have about ten minutes tops before those divas rush the dining room expecting yet another new fudge flavor for brunch. And this--" I pointed to the jiggling ooze. "--Makes me a nervous wreck."

"Tell them it's pudding. They'll brag about it on social media and you'll be rich with a whole new line of desserts. Oh woe is you."

Huh. Honesty. It hurt. "So I'm whining. I'm a millennial wienie who needs 'mommy's' help."

"At least you have a mother who actually responds to you." She sniffed the fudge pan.

Pauline rarely allowed herself or me to mention her mother, so this alluding to the woman surprised me. I suspected we'd talk about it later. When she was ready.

She said, "Put on decent clothes and come with me. I need your sleuthing skills. I received a surprise from John."

I was intrigued. Her boyfriend, John Schultz, was traveling the state gathering video stories for a public television show idea he'd sold last fall. So it was odd she wore makeup and the new red blouse with a dazzling infinity scarf to match. Her black hair was lustrous. In contrast, my brown hair was tied in a ponytail sagging against the back of my heated neck. The customary, long-sleeved white blouse and Cinderella Pink Fairy Tale Fudge pink apron were dotted with egg yolks that had splashed during a zumba-induced tsunami in a mixing bowl.

Giving in, I turned to the warming oven behind me to retrieve omelets. "So John finally texted you?"

With dark eyes sparkling, she said, "He texted me an address. To a *place*."

Her emphasis on "place" was ominous. I plated an omelet atop antique yellow roses. "These smell heavenly, don't you think?"

The omelets were redolent with winter onions that had popped up after the snow melted in Grandma's garden. The egg dish was also filled with organic cheddar cheese delivered yesterday by Mom from her cheese factory on my parents' dairy farm south of our village of Fishers' Harbor.

To further put off talking about John, I said, "I only have to put up with the divas for one more day. They leave tomorrow."

"Good thing. I couldn't get in your front door," Pauline said from behind me. "I think the latch is jimmied from those women knocking the floor off-kilter."

"Or slamming the front door in each other's face. There's something odd about the way they relate to each other, especially for a college reunion."

"I bet they have some secret."

I blinked at her. "Grandpa thinks they have a secret, too."

"Maybe they robbed a bank together. When my kindergarteners do something bad, they do the same thing."

"They argue over money? And rob a bank?"

"No. But they love to argue over secrets. I had to stop one kid from dunking another in the janitor's scrub pail the other day."

I forced an uneasy laugh. "If something bad happens, you and I can handle it. Our instincts have been pretty good in solving a murder or two."

"Or three." She fussed with her infinity scarf. "There won't be a murder. Life, Ava, is about secrets and who holds and owns the secrets. We all want power. Women have egos just like men, you know. But, in the end, all the fighting tires my kindergarteners and they become friends because that's easier than fighting. Those five women are going to be tired by the time they leave tomorrow and they will fall into crying hugs because they'll miss each other."

I plated another mouth-watering, onion-cheese omelet from the warm oven. "So the arguing equals bonding." At least we weren't talking about John, though the mysterious "place" had now teased my brain's curiosity juices.

Pauline was shaking the fudge pan as if it were an Etch-A-Sketch. "Why aren't they exercising over at Jane's bookstore? I thought they'd taken over her great exercise room in back."

"They broke the stripper pole yesterday. Jane texted me. She's furious and wants to be sure my guests pay for it before they leave."

"All this trouble because you couldn't say 'no' to a fudge frolic set up by Cathy."

Cathy Rivers had been my mother-in-law nine years ago for all of a month. Dillon and I--in a silly, libido-driven, not-very-grown-up time after college graduation--had driven to Las Vegas and gotten married. Then, because of revelations about Dillon's past misadventures, I got our mistake annulled. But after eight years, people mature. We'd met again last April when both of us returned to Door County. Dillon and I tiptoed into being friends again. Over this past winter during pleasant evenings in front of the fireplace at his place or mine, it had deepened to something more, though we weren't sure what it might mean yet.

Pauline pulled me from the blast of troubling thoughts. "This fudge has bacon in it!" She grabbed a serving spoon from the utensil holder then dredged straight through the middle of the pan, slapping a glob into her mouth.

"Pauline?!"

She swooned, got off the stool, then pirouetted. The melodrama came from acting out picture books with her kindergartners. After sitting again, she smacked her lips. "Dauntingly delicious delicacy to die for."

I rolled my eyes at Pauline's penchant for alliteration.

"Can't you see it's not setting up?"

She winked. "This would be terrific with beer, Ava. Try a Belgian ale for breakfast perhaps? What will you call this fudge? What fairy tale lends itself to bacon? The *Three Little Pigs*?"

"That's awful." But she'd made me smile, which is why she was my BFF. I relented again. "What's this about John giving you an address to a place?"

She rose to dance with arms raised. "I thought you'd never ask!" She sat again, hugging her green purse with a smile the size of a half-moon. "He texted that he wanted me to look at a place. You know what that means!"

"No, I don't."

With two plates of omelets, I headed across the trembling wood floor into the dining room. The fudge divas were exercising two rooms away in the parlor beyond the foyer. Where we were, the pink tablecloth's skirt swayed.

Pauline followed with two plates, setting them next to delicate china cups rattling in their saucers. "A 'place' means he's picked out a place for us to live. As in 'together'. After we're married."

Shock burned my cheeks. "Did John propose?"

"Not yet. But he must be going to." She toggled up and down on the toes of her sexy black riding boots. Her dark eyes sparkled.

In my opinion, John Schultz was not interested in marriage in the near future. I could never hurt her feelings, though. "Did John say anything more about this 'place'?"

I hiked back into the kitchen. Pauline hustled behind, stomping her boots.

"He gave me an address and no other information. He wants me to look at it without him first because I suspect he wants me to feel the impact of seeing 'our place' for the first time." Her face exuded dreaminess. "He wants me to say 'yes' to the place and to, well..."

I grabbed the last omelet plate and delivered it to the dining room table. "Did you go online to look at a satellite image of this so-called place?"

"Of course not. John would want me to see it in person first."

Back in the kitchen again, I grabbed goblets from a cupboard and set them on the island. "Maybe you should wait for him to come back and go together. Dillon and I could go with." To help assuage the disappointment I was sure would happen.

"That's not John's way of doing things." Pauline was fussing again with the infinity scarf, as if it were choking her. "He's very shy at his core."

"Shy? He wears Hawaiian shirts and sandals to funerals."

"He has to stand out. He works in TV. Now listen, Ava. I'm going to find this house, open up the front door, and there on a table will be romantic red roses with a ruby ribbon revealing a ring."

"Will your class be studying 'R' this coming week?"

"Yes." She beamed. "It's like John knew. R for romance, R for ring--"

"Enough, Pauline. He's over in Rhinelander--"

"Another R!"

I let my shoulders sag. "He's hours away in the north woods of Wisconsin chasing a hodag. He's not thinking about marriage. He's chasing a mythical monster and you're chasing a mythical-ever-after."

"Why can't you admit John is the real deal?"

From the refrigerator I grabbed the orange juice to make mimosas, though serving juice spiked with champagne to my rockin'-and-rollin' fighting guests was probably not a good idea. "So real that you bought your own engagement ring--then lost it in the woods."

"I knew you'd bring that up. Can we not go there?"

While we'd been running for our lives from a murderer in the woods of southern Door County last fall, Pauline had lost her purse. In it was a diamond ring she'd bought, thinking John had wanted her to choose her own ring. We never found the purse. Now some raccoon probably wore a shiny bauble.

Pauline said, "No man asks a woman to look at 'a place' unless he means they're moving in together. Come with me. Please?"

"After I go down to check on the fudge shop."

Pauline hugged me carefully, wary of my messy apron. "Thank you! I'll say hi to Jane at the bookstore. I want to see if she has any wedding planner books. I'll meet you at the fudge shop."

As we finished pouring mimosas, a frowning Pepper Elliott strode into the kitchen. The short, petite woman was dressed in pink as usual, this time in a leotard and exercise shoes. Her blond bob was perfect, as always. She hadn't been exercising.

She whiffed a mimosa, then set it back down without a sip. "You have to do something. Kim is driving all of us nuts."

"The white gloves again?"

"She's exercising in those stupid white gloves. And cleaning at the same time. Kick, dust a vase, kick, dust a table. This is your place. She already broke one of your lamps the other day. Maybe you can say something."

I couldn't because my ex-mother-in-law who wanted to again be my mother-in-law loved Kim's idea for the magical white gloves that could clean anything.

Pepper said, "She's dusting again to convince Jackie to invest in a television shopping network spot for the white gloves."

Pauline picked up the pan of failed bacon fudge. "I'm so sorry, Pepper, but we have an emergency down at the fudge shop. Ava's Grandpa Gil isn't feeling well."

A best friend's lie to the rescue! *Thanks, Pauline.*

Pepper's wan face paled more. "Is Gil all right? What's wrong?"

Already pushing Pauline toward the back door, I said, "I'm sure it's just a spring cold. I need to go take over for him. Your brunch is ready. Enjoy."

Pauline and I trotted out the back to avoid drawing more attention from the other ladies.

We hiked down the steep, narrow blacktopped street. The feathery fog was turning into a golden haze with the late-morning sun smiling on it.

On the corner of Main and Duck Marsh Streets, Pauline handed me the fudge ingredients (a.k.a. the primordial pool) and we split. I headed down my old street toward the harbor, wending by the cabin where I used to live. Dillon now rented it. From there I cut across the cabin's lawn to head east to the shop.

After I came through the back door with the pan of wiggling fudge, I skidded to a stop, wrinkling my nose. "Grandpa? It smells like an oil tanker in here. And what's that on your face?"

Chapter 2

Crouching in the center of our shop as if he were being hunted, Grandpa Gil swiveled his head to and fro. "Are those crazy fudge divas behind you?"

Motor oil smudged his frayed, gray sweatshirt. His silver hair was sticking straight up with dark smears. He looked like a grimy Einstein.

I set the bacon fudge aside on my register counter. "What's going on, Gilpa?"

"This is to ward off the fudge divas."

He stepped to his register counter on the bait-and-tackle side of the shop. His hand plunged into an old coffee can that contained oil for soaking rust off bolts and screws. Then he dabbed motor oil on his cheeks.

"Gilpa! Stop that." I grabbed a hand towel from under the counter and offered it. "What's wrong?"

He stuffed the towel into a back pocket. "Ava Mathilde Oosterling, those fudge divas texted me just now about a boat ride for eleven o'clock." He hauled out his phone. "Look. That nutso Pepper asked if she might bring me soup. Why does Miss In-the-Pink think I'm sick?"

I gulped. "Pauline and I sort of lied and escaped them by saying you weren't feeling well and needed me."

He stomped to his coffeemaker where he began filling a thermos. "I don't care how much money they flash under my nose."

"But they like you, Gilpa." I sneezed from the oil smell at war with the redolence of fudge making--sweet chocolate, cherries, luscious caramel, maple syrup and flavoring, and now bacon. I had to get Grandpa out of the shop before the fudge began absorbing the oily odor. "They'll be leaving tomorrow. What is that oil on your face supposed to do?"

He screwed the cap onto the thermos. "I didn't want to tell you, but, well, they keep kissing me! Motor oil will get rid of that bunch of evil crows."

"They like to be called fudge divas, Gilpa." A chill slithered down my back. "A bunch of crows is called a murder."

"Just what I'd like to do to them!"

"Watch your tongue, Gilpa. Our track record with dead bodies isn't so good."

"Balderdash. What a mess they left for me yesterday. Dirty wine glasses and wine spills and crumbs all over the deck on *Sophie's Smile*. That deck's teak, dontcha know." *Sophie's Smile* was the boat he'd refurbished over the winter with Dillon's help. It had helped the two of them patch their relationship, though I had the feeling the patch was unraveling because of Dillon's mother and her friends.

I headed over to the glass cases to check the fudge inventory. "Wasn't Kim along? Certainly she would have wanted to demonstrate her miracle cleaning gloves."

"Of course Miss Kimberly Olkowski was along." He spat the words. "She wouldn't miss a chance to soften up her friends. Kim even hit on poor Eliza again for money."

Eliza Stefansson had lost her husband recently. She'd taken over his farm implement dealership in southern Door County, not far from my parents' dairy farm. It was true the business hadn't been faring well, though its inventory of tractors and other farm equipment had to be worth a couple of million dollars. Heck, my dad had bought a new tractor a couple of years ago from Eliza's husband for over three-hundred thousand dollars.

Grandpa picked up the oil can again. He peered with wide-eyed anxiety toward the big picture windows flanking the front door.

I had to reassure him. "They love your boat rides. Just one more can't hurt, Gilpa. Maybe you should go outside. You'd feel better on your boat. We can get through one more day with them."

Grandpa pointed at his face. "My cheeks are sore from those women planting kisses on this kisser!"

I giggled as I readied my register. "Now there's a line I bet you haven't said to Grandma."

"You best not tell your grandma anything. Sophie's all up and worried about that village flower committee meeting. I can't bother her about my popularity with the ladies." Grandpa yelped, his body hopping in place. "Crapola. Here they come."

The divas--all decked out in an expensive rainbow of coats, boots, and scarves flapping in the breeze--were flocking next to Grandpa's touring boat. The boat had emerged in the dissipating fog. Pepper's daughter, Zadie, and her friend, Yola, had now joined the older women. Not finding Grandpa out on the dock, the women turned in unison and then flew toward the shop.

Grandpa swiped an oily hand across his lips. "If you find out tomorrow they don't show for breakfast, it's because I've drowned them in the harbor."

His words inked my soul with fear. Grandpa had a way of predicting his own trouble.

I stood between my grandpa--who looked like he'd swam through an oil spill--and the open door where his troublesome "crows" were flying through. The five fudge divas plus the two twenty-somethings chattered and laughed as they sent the cowbell to clanking.

Grandpa grumbled, "I'm out the back door."

"Gilpa, no you're not," I hiss-whispered to him with my back to the women. "The divas are our social media street crew. Think of all the touring business and fishing equipment you're going to sell because of them talking you up. Think of my fudge sales." My heart was racing, but I added the *coup de gras*, "You're responsible for me coming home from California and starting this fudge business."

My implication was clear: These divas were Grandpa's fault. I was miserable already for having said it. "I'm sorry."

"Grrrrr." He held up his thermos of coffee like a battering ram. "You'll find me on my boat."

With his head tilted down like a buffalo's, he stomped into the flock of fudge divas. They fluttered and flapped their coats like wings, letting him through.

The door hung open in his wake, held back by a sun-drenched breeze popping in off the bay. Flags snapped on poles along the piers. Seagulls screeched, some toddling about near the door looking for fudge handouts.

The women surged toward the door. A chorus rent the air, "Yoo hoo, Gilsen! What happened, Gilsen? Gil, can we help?"

Jackie trotted outside in the lead. "Gil? Will you be ready to take us up to the ferry later? What time should we be here?"

Petite Pepper turned back inside the shop, sagging within her pink designer coat. "I was so looking forward to visiting Washington Island today and the lavender farm boutique. Lavender is utterly soothing."

Eliza pulled her coat tighter over her exercise clothes. "Soothing for what? You didn't lift an arm or foot during today's exercises."

Pepper's daughter, Zadie, said, "I don't think we have to exercise every morning. Isn't this supposed to be a vacation?"

Eliza snapped, "I suppose you can sleep in. Your life is a dream. Some of us can't sleep. Some of us need exercise to keep our minds off things like death!"

I rushed to close the door with a *clankety-clank* to keep them separated from my grandfather. He was now talking to a possible customer on the pier near his boat. "Ladies, today it might be best to drive to the ferry on your own for your Washington Island sojourn."

Washington Island was a famous landmass off the northeast tip of Door County. Only accessible by a ferry, for decades the island had been home to wheat farmers, a Coast Guard station, and a church or two. It'd been re-discovered by tourists who loved to bike its flat roads and visit new features including the lavender farm, vodka distillery, and the ostrich ranch. Artist enclaves had sprung up as well.

Jackie's long red hair settled back into place in the wake of the door closing. "Of course we can drive. I'll pay everybody's ferry ticket for the cars."

Cathy said, "We agreed we'd do things together, including riding together wherever we went. We can't all fit in your car or mine." She turned to me, finger-combing her shoulder-length brown hair which had a distinctive white stripe at her widow's peak. "Do you think Gil will be ready to take us in his boat anytime soon?"

All seven women stared at me, though Zadie and Yola were rolling their eyes, unseen by Zadie's mother, Pepper, or the other women. We were likely down to five women who wanted to take the ferry ride. Five rich women. Who wanted to boost my fudge sales.

"I'll make a phone call or two." My mind was racing to figure out who to call in the off-season and who might have a mini-van large enough for five passengers, possibly seven with big purses and eventually bulging shopping bags. I also wondered if word had gotten out across Door County already about these women. I suspected I'd get a lot of turn-downs.

Cathy, in her gentle way, gave me a lovely smile. "Ava, thank you so much for making this girlfriend weekend a wonderful adventure for us. Perhaps Dillon can drive us in a construction company van."

The ladies in one of those dirty things? Perhaps not. Dillon was also busy working on a fancy house somewhere and had said the refurbishing was urgent with a close deadline. "I can certainly give him a call, Cathy, but I'm sure I can come up with somebody to take you to the ferry and then drive you around the island. I'll also need to check to make sure the ferry is running. The ice didn't go out too long ago in Death's Door."

Eliza began sniffling. "Death," she muttered. "Everything is death."

I said, "Sorry. I didn't mean anything by that word. That's what it's called."

Death's Door was the treacherous area between the tip of Door County and Washington Island where Lake Michigan met the bay. The lighthouse on Plum Island helped guide ships through the churning waters of the strait. Yet many ships had gone down with great loss of life. We all knew the tales about boats laden with Christmas trees or lumber heading to Chicago in the 1800s and never making it.

Jackie withdrew a hand from a pocket of her coat. She flashed a wad of cash. I'd noticed since their arrival on Wednesday she seemed to have money stuffed everywhere in her clothes--pockets, belt, sleeves, bra. She enjoyed pulling it out on a whim. "I'll pay for the transportation. My treat."

Pepper piped in, "No, you won't. My daughter and her friend are along, so that makes three of us, so I need to pay more."

Zadie said, "Sorry, Mom, but Yola and I are going shopping in Sturgeon Bay."

Sturgeon Bay, a half hour's drive away to the south, was our county seat and sat on the canal that split our county. Its downtown boasted a thriving mix of shops and a beautiful, peaceful marina where world-renowned yachts were built and repaired. I yearned to escape there today with Zadie and Yola.

I suggested, "Ladies, how about we plan on a noon trip to the island?" That gave me an hour or so to figure out their transportation.

The women were rushing out the front door when a huge column of water plumed into the air. They screamed.

A few fishermen, including Carl "Moose" Lindstrom, were hollering as well. Moose owned the Super Catch I, a rival fishing rig at the other end of the harbor.

I raced out, not seeing much but the backs of all the women.

Rocketing into the fray was Dillon's American water spaniel, Lucky Harbor, a curly brown whirlwind. He wove through our legs, then--Sploosh!

Lucky Harbor landed next to what appeared to be a fisherman and my grandpa in the icy water next to our wood pier. Fortunately the water was only about four feet deep. Grandpa and the fisherman were flailing about for their footing. The fisherman appeared disoriented. I would be, too, if I'd fallen into this ice cube-like water. At this time of year hypothermia could set in within a few minutes.

Lucky Harbor paddled hard for Grandpa who was flailing and gasping in the icy water.

The women were dancing about yelling, "Ava! Help! Ava!"

Moose bellowed, "Grab the net!"

"Got it!" I hustled to the outer north wall of our shop where I grabbed the rescue pole with the net on its end. We used it to dip for tourist belongings and kids' toys that slipped into the water. "Excuse me, ladies." I squeezed through the throng. A few more people had come running from Main Street to see the excitement.

By the time I reached the water's edge, Grandpa, Moose, and Dillon's dog had rescued the poor fisherman. Grandpa climbed out of the water with help from Moose.

Everybody lay waterlogged on the wooden pier, in shock and shivering. Grandpa was face-down, exhausted.

Cathy offered her expensive, fur-trimmed coat to my grandfather, which he waved away. She gave it to the fisherman, who gladly accepted it.

"Gilpa, are you okay?" I kneeled down but didn't know what to do. He was still face down, breathing hard, a slimy mess of oil and water, his silver hair now an ugly storm cloud on his head.

Moose rolled him over and helped him to a seated position. "Let's get you inside. What were ya all doin' in there? Bobbin' for apples?"

Grandpa growled, "None of yer durn business, Moose."

"I'll get some towels," I said.

I replaced the pole on its hook then raced inside and into the back room for towels. By now the seven women were inside. They peered out the front windows.

Moose had paused the men outside to help them wring out the water in their shirts and jackets before coming inside.

Lucky Harbor shook spirals of the water, then sniffed wet footprints, as if trying to figure out what had happened.

I was about to take a stack of towels outside when I saw Eliza crying. Pepper had an arm around her shoulders as they viewed Grandpa and the men.

With my heart beating notes of sorrow, I said in a light voice, "Eliza and Pepper, could you taste-test the mint fudge for me and tell me what size pieces to cut for the samplers. It seems awfully rich."

Pepper said, "I'd love to."

Sniffling, Eliza followed her to the counter.

The men outside were making their way to the door. I slipped behind my counter, put down the stack of towels, then hid the pan of failed bacon fudge on the shelf beneath the register. I shuffled inventory papers over the top of the pan.

Outside, Moose was steadying the fisherman with one arm around him. Grandpa rejected an offer of help with a flail of his own arm. He had his pride.

Zadie and her friend Yola were now leaning against Grandpa's register. Zadie motioned me over to her, whispering, "That was Eliza's fault. I saw it."

Zadie Elliott was a carbon copy of her short, pretty mother Pepper in looks, but with much longer blond hair. She wore mostly black and white instead of pink. Zadie had been a teenage model, something Pepper had told us many times in the past few days. Zadie ran a cosmetics store in Milwaukee called Blush Rush. For entertainment, she took the train into Chicago. I hadn't really gotten to know Zadie because she and her friend went out every night, coming in after midnight often and then sleeping in. They requested I re-heat their breakfast every day.

I said, "I doubt it was anybody's fault. The fisherman slipped somehow. It happens now and then if you're not careful on wet wood. I think we had frost this morning."

Yola left us to head for the fudge counter. I signaled Zadie to follow me over to Grandpa's register counter for more privacy.

Zadie shrugged. "I saw Eliza. The others must not have noticed. Eliza's acting weird."

"Of course. She's grieving."

"Maybe she's suffering some mental condition because of it. I heard her say, 'That's him,' and she rushed down the dock to Gil's customer and suddenly they were in the water. I swear she tripped the man on purpose. I think she thought the man was her husband."

"I'm sure she didn't do such a thing. Or say such a thing. Her husband is gone."

"She said it. 'That's him.'" Zadie shrugged again.

Yola returned with a pink sack. Chocolate notes assailed the air, making my mouth water. A glance back showed Cathy behind my register ringing up purchases. I mouthed a silent "thank you" to Cathy.

Yola said, "This has to be the most fun I've had in a long time. Sure beats my dull life over in Green Bay. There's nobody in my garden center yet at this time of year. Glad you invited me along, Zadie."

Gardening in this area didn't get into full swing until May because the ground was too cold this far north. Yola's garden center in Green Bay was a good hour's drive away. She'd had a makeover this past week, going from a mousey braid down her back to an auburn, shoulder-length swishy do. Her nails were the nicest they'd look all year for a gardener in a sky blue gel application sporting yellow flower decals.

Zadie waved Yola over to Grandpa's register. She said to Yola, "You heard her, too, didn't you? Eliza thought that man was her husband."

Yola winced. "Purely creepy." She bit into a piece of dark Belgian chocolate fudge, a smile curling onto her face. It was a flavor that included a local porter beer for a special ingredient. Cooking with beer meant the shelf life for the product was just a couple of days, but with these women that wasn't a concern.

Jackie interrupted us, diving with a hand into Yola's fudge bag. "Thanks, kid. This fudge has been alleviating my hot flashes. Does it have hormones in it?"

"No, none of my fudge has hormones," I responded for the tenth time since Wednesday. "My parents' farm is all organic."

"Oh, that's right. With cows that get classical music in the barn. It's too bad your mother wouldn't entertain thoughts of my investing in her creamery."

Zadie and Yola evaporated to some other part of the shop.

This topic had come up two nights ago over wine at the Blue Heron Inn. "She's happy with the way things are," I said. Yet again. "She doesn't want the business to get too big or busy."

"But people in Door County need jobs. Your parents' farm is the perfect way to create jobs and be a hero, or is that heroine? Oh, dear, that sounds like a drug." Jackie laughed. "I'll talk to my husband about drawing up a business plan for you and your mother. Your mother likely doesn't understand high finance."

Gee, thanks. I went back to my register to pick up the towels.

Cathy chimed in. "Oh, Jackie, we want Door County to stay quaint. Small is beautiful, too. Like this bait-and-fudge shop. It's unique and Fishers' Harbor is lucky to have this."

Pepper-in-Pink joined us with the bundle of new pink purses I'd put in stock. "Maybe my daughter could start a boutique here, too. Blush Rush is doing so well in Milwaukee that she's been traveling to Chicago all the time lately looking for more unique products, like these cute clutches. Door County has its famous cherries and apple orchards. What do you think, Zadie?" She turned to call out to her daughter who'd taken up a post near the marble table by the window. "Maybe you'd like to open a Blush Rush in Fishers' Harbor?"

Zadie reached into Yola's bag and popped my famous pink fudge into her mouth. "Definitely worth thinking about." She savored the fudge. "When I'm out and about tonight, I could scout a location."

She was lying. Zadie would never be happy here.

Kim popped up from behind an aisle of bobbers. "Remember I'm trying to branch out from my Madison base. Maybe you could all invest in a satellite shop for White Glove Cleaning here in Door County."

The group chorused, "No, thanks."

Kim's face grew dark--as if she wanted to swear at them all-- and then she laughed. "Okay. You'll be sorry when I do it without you and become richer than all of you combined." She practically skipped over to the fudge case.

Pepper followed her, putting the pink clutches they were buying on top of the glass fudge case where the lighting was designed to shower sparkles like pink sequins over the top of the fudge. Kim and Pepper were laughing together, helping each other arrange the silly purses in various sparkly displays.

I would never figure out these women friends.

I grabbed the towels then went outside. "Are you guys all right?"

Grandpa harrumphed. "Don'tcha know I always require anybody boating with me to prove they can swim first?"

Moose laughed. He and I shuffled Grandpa and the forlorn fisherman into the shop. I closed the door.

Pepper said to Moose, "I like your name, Carl. Carl Lindstrom. It's a solid name. Nobody's named Carl anymore."

Zadie winced, obviously embarrassed by her mother. Yola rolled her eyes.

Jackie said, "If my Victor weren't the world's handsomest man, I'd get it on with you, Moose."

Kim said, "He sure knows how to do a load of laundry the hard way, though."

To that, everybody laughed.

Zadie opened the door for a soggy Lucky Harbor. He shook, showering everybody with water, making them gasp.

I said, "Watch the floor, ladies. The wood gets slippery when it's wet."

Lucky Harbor trotted over to Pepper, stabbing his wet nose between her knees. He looked up at her and whined.

Pepper patted the dog in her usual confusion, then backed her petite frame away from him. He'd been doing that routine since the moment she'd arrived. I grabbed him by the collar. "Lucky Harbor, be polite. No nose on people."

When I let go he took a couple of steps toward her again, whining.

Zadie said, "He's in love with my mother."

Pepper grimaced.

The dog shook another time. Arms flew up to cover faces.

Grandpa said, "Can you ladies clear the way, please? It feels like my niblets have frozen. I'd like to head to the shower in back."

Amid giggles, they parted, but as he took a bold step across the wet floor he landed flat on his back. His eyelids blinkered shut.

"Gilpa!" He was out cold. "Call 911!"

Chapter 3

Grandpa Gil lay splayed out on the shop floor like a dead fish. I was on my knees putting a towel under his head.

"Gilpa! Wake up!"

With shaky hands I reached for my phone, but it wasn't on me. I'd left it on the register counter as was my habit so it wouldn't fall into a copper kettle or in the harbor.

"Somebody call 911!"

The panicked women had surrounded us on the floor. One of them spilled the contents of a purse while looking for her phone.

To my relief Cody Fjelstad wandered in from the back, his short, red hair like a signal flag breaking through the crowd. "Miss Oosterling, what the--"

"Call 911. Grandpa slipped and fell."

Cody handed me his phone. "You call while I go into action. I'm trained, ya know."

Last fall Cody--fresh from high school--had become a volunteer firefighter. He'd coped well with his Asperger's symptoms, which manifested itself in his brand of perfectionism, including his hate for dust and dirt, and his love of shiny things--

like fire trucks and my sparkly Cinderella Pink Fairy Tale Fudge with its edible glitter on top. Dillon had told me Cody had been top-notch when they'd completed CPR training side by side.

Cody was checking all of Grandpa's vitals and shaking him gently. "He's breathing. Come on, wake up, Mister Oosterling. I think you just had your breath knocked out of you."

Grandpa's groans emanated from the floor as my best friend Pauline shoved open the shop door. She barely missed Grandpa's head but dropped her huge purse in shock. The purse exploded, spewing crayons, glue bottles, and animal-print bandage strips across Grandpa and the floor around us.

"What happened to Gil?" Pauline knelt down to pick crayons off my grandfather's chest. She wrinkled her nose. "Why is he covered in oil and all wet?"

"A long story," I muttered, sponging with towels around my grandpa.

Cody said, "His eyes are open, Miss Oosterling."

I said, "The crayons spiking his head probably did the trick."

Pauline sneezed. "Don't tell me he was working on an engine again. I thought he and Dillon had installed a new one on *Sophie's Smile*."

Cody and I each took an arm to help Grandpa to a sitting position on the floor. "Gilpa, take it slow. I called for an ambulance."

Grandpa wheezed out, "No ambulance. Give me an invisibility cloak."

Jackie said, hovering above us on the floor, "What's he talking about?"

Eliza said, "Harry Potter magic. Toss a cloak on him and he turns invisible."

Kim said, "What a great line for my business." She held up the white dusting gloves she wore. "Like magic they make dust disappear."

Jackie said, "Would you stop with the gloves already!"

"Now, now." It was Cathy, ever the peacemaker.

Jackie said, "Come on, gals. Romeo needs to get cleaned up for our boat ride, and so do we. Give us a call, Gil." She puckered up and threw him an air kiss.

Cathy patted one of my arms. "He's going to be fine. He has such a good sense of humor."

After the women left with Lucky Harbor by Pepper's side, a sudden and pleasant hush filled the shop. For a moment, we stared at each other in relief. Moose was standing there, too.

Cody was still crouched next to Grandpa, who remained seated on the floor. "Take it slow, Mister Oosterling."

"Help me up. If I hurry, I can take my fisherman customer out on the lake and escape those darn women. Don't count on me coming back anytime soon."

Cody and Moose picked up Grandpa and settled him onto the stool behind his cash register. His wet fisherman customer excused himself to go back to a rental cottage to change clothes.

I poured chocolate-laced coffee from Grandpa's thermos for him. He slurped as he shivered. Moose took off his bulky insulated sweatshirt and draped it over Grandpa's shoulders.

"Drink up, Gil. I'll come back for the sweatshirt later. You sure do get yourself into trouble."

"It's those dames. They're bad luck."

Moose laughed. "It's hell to be popular, you old Belgian buffalo. Wait 'til I tell Sophie about you steppin' out with a gaggle of dizzy dames." He walked out, hooting with more laughter.

"Dern him," Grandpa muttered.

I asked Cody to go over to my grandparents' place for a new set of clothes for Mister Oosterling.

The clock over the door said it was half-past lake trout or ten, and going on coho salmon, or eleven. "Gilpa, maybe you should take it easy today. Go with Grandma over to Saint Ann's for the Saturday senior meal. She's taking pies over. You can play cards with the guys. Cody can handle questions here about your fishing guide business and Moose can take your fisherman customer this time."

Grandpa growled. He never liked Moose horning in on his business. "But I'm doubling-up on my payments for that Grand Banks boat. Gotta pay it off."

In reality he was behind on payments. I was covering his half on the boat loan through the modest increase in my fudge shop business. Online sales had picked up in the Christmas season and had come back again for Easter. My fudge eggs were a hit.

Gilpa hated me covering his bills, especially for a boat--a necessary attachment for a man in this county. Dillon had bought the used boat online last fall, suggesting they share ownership, but Grandpa's pride demanded he own the boat outright eventually. Grandpa had gone along with Dillon's co-ownership deal at first to please me, which warmed my heart. The co-ownership was Dillon's secret plan to patch the rift in their relationship. But the closer Dillon and I got, the more Dillon's mother Cathy seemed to be around the shop, too, and the more Grandpa had gotten surlier about the Rivers family taking over our lives. What Grandpa hadn't yet said out loud was that he didn't want me falling in love with Dillon or marrying him a second time. Sometimes, like now, my insides felt dead as old concrete as to what to do.

The best way to deal with Gilpa was to distract him. I retrieved the goopy fudge under the register counter.

"Gilpa, I need your help. Figure out something to do with this."

He sniffed it. "Bacon and chocolate." He dipped two fingers in then tasted it. "Gee, perfect skunk bait. Give it to Al Kvalheim. He's always got a critter to haul out of town."

"Gilpa!"

He chuckled. "Gotcha, Ava, honey." He dipped in another finger's worth of bacon-chocolatey goodness and hummed. "This would be perfect on top of one of your friend Laura's big cinnamon rolls. Bacon-fudge-topped cinnamon rolls. Makes my mouth water just thinkin' about 'em."

Pauline and I shared wide-eyed discovery.

"Brilliant, Gilpa. When Laura gets here with her fresh-baked goods later this morning, we'll try it out on her. Maybe we've created a hot new thing."

The back door banged shut. Cody appeared with new clean clothes for Grandpa who hustled to the shower in the back of the shop.

I said, "Thanks, Cody. Why are you around? I gave you the day off."

"Gotta study for an exam." He hefted a backpack he'd obviously ditched by the door when he first came in. "This fudge shop is about the quietest place I could find."

"My guests said they'd be back within the hour for a trip to the big island." I flashed him a sly smile. "You wouldn't want to earn big bucks driving them up to Washington Island in one of the fire department's warming buses, would you?"

He guffawed as he settled on my stool behind the cash register with his books.

"I guess that's a 'no'."

"Yeah, and illegal. Can't use those buses for joy rides. Could be a fire and a whole family would need to sit in that bus to watch me and Dillon douse flames."

"Don't mention fire around me and Pauline."

We both shivered. Then we headed for the kitchen. I had to wash my hands. They smelled like crankcase oil.

Pauline said, "Jane gave me a bill to give to you to give to the women for her broken exercise pole."

She flashed it from her purse.

Drying my hands, I sagged, bracing my backside against the counter.

"What's wrong?" Pauline asked.

"I don't think I can do this, Pauline."

"What? Dry your hands? Make more fudge? You're upset because that batch of fudge didn't set up right."

"No, silly. Okay, sort of. But speaking of fudge, I haven't even started thinking about what to make for the upcoming Sweets, Suds and Buds festival next weekend. Why did I volunteer to hold a grand opening at the inn? I must be nuts. If those women make me exhausted, what will I do with a couple of hundred people coming to taste new craft beers and fudge at my inn?"

"So you don't think you're cut out to be an innkeeper. You've never failed at fudge. You always think best when you create new fudge flavors. Why don't you create 'Diva Devil's-Food Fudge'? It'll make you feel better."

I gave her a hug. "Thanks. They are devils, but that could be too pointed."

"Hah. You never used to be worried about your reputation. You married a bigamist, after all."

"He didn't mean to be a bigamist." Dillon had married another woman before me in a youthful mistake he regretted immediately. He'd filed for a divorce, but somehow the woman had failed to properly sign and file the right papers. Thus, Dillon ended up married to two women at once. "That was in the olden days, girlfriend. College-graduation-do-something-stupid days. I'm thirty-three now and mature. So is Dillon. Give him a break."

To escape her imperious look, I tidied the kitchen counter.

Pauline laughed, twisting her long black hair into a knot on top of her head. "No worries there. That man loves you. No need to trip him and haul him to the altar again like a buck during deer season. He's tripped himself and is just waiting for you to pick him up."

That's what bothered me about Dillon and myself--we seemed to be waiting for the other to make the first big move. Can true love hatch out of limbo? Shouldn't there be more than just a spark? Shouldn't an explosion happen, thrusting us into the future? We'd experienced a spark long ago, and that didn't sustain us. I'd dumped him before, but was I strong enough to pick him up now? Carry him with me into the future? I hated this confusion within my heart and head. Hated it. Watching Pauline be so sure of herself made me feel jealous of her. Ach! Not good!

To ward off Pauline's need to talk about her own possible wedding--or my feelings for Dillon--I told her Zadie's words about Eliza perhaps pushing or tripping Grandpa's customer into the water.

She said, "You're making too much of it. Wouldn't Gil have heard the man say something about being tripped?"

"I guess you're right. Zadie's bored, always looking for some extra entertainment."

"Let's get going. This place John has picked out will get your mind off all of this mess with the divas and the inn."

I hurried to place paper coffee cups ten in each stack across the back of the counter. It made it easy for Grandpa or me to rush into the kitchen and grab a manageable amount for customers out in front. "Pauline, you have a house. What is wrong with you living in that with John?"

"A tiny little ranch house? John hates it because whenever we, well, you know, anyway he hits his head on the wall just getting out of bed. And I only have room for a double bed, nothing roomy enough for fun."

"Ewwww. Too many details."

"You're just jealous because you and Dillon live apart and you can't have him over at the inn with guests around, and you can't stay overnight at his cabin because it's straight across the street from your grandparents' and they'll see you sneaking in and out."

I flicked a towel at her thigh. "When was the last time John stayed over at your place, Miss Romance?"

She grabbed the towel from me. Her face turned red as the raspberry jam in the jars nearby that I used in creating my Rapunzel Raspberry Rapture Fairy Tale Fudge. "John will change soon. You'll see. He'll become a homebody. You're just jealous."

We walked back into the shop where I grabbed a jacket on a hook next to my aprons on the wall behind the register.

Cody was straightening goods on the shelves. "Those women sure do mess things up around here. They're like your kids, Miss Mertens."

As Pauline and I walked to the door, I said, "Whatever the 'place' is all about, it must have to do with John's show. Maybe it's a shed to keep his equipment in and he wants you to sign for it."

"Pffft. He wouldn't have me sign for a shed."

"Spring is here and summer is coming. He's going to be gone. As in gone, gone, gone filming in tiny towns. He's not buying a house and he's not going to propose."

"Want to put money on it?"

"No, because I'd win. June is coming and you'll be sitting around. Instead, you could go along with John this summer. Have fun traveling."

"And leave Door County? In summer? When I finally have time off to enjoy the most beautiful spot on the planet? Besides, I doubt I'll be leaving. I sneaked a peek at John's calendar on his phone and found out he's going to be videotaping a segment about all the famous churches in this area of Wisconsin in June. That could be code for picking out our church for the wedding."

Her eyes sparkled.

"Hold on, Pauline. First of all, you realize you sneaked into your man friend's phone, which isn't good. And second, this is April. There's no time for you to put together the kind of June wedding you deserve."

She hugged me. "You're so sweet."

I ventured, "You're feeling pressured by all the advertisements about June weddings." Door County's businesses and media did a good job touting our natural beauty as a place for weddings.

"I can make it work. If John and I are to be partners, I have to show him I can hold up my half of the partnership."

That made sense. As in a bad television dating show sort of way. We headed toward her gray, nondescript car. "It's not a partnership if you don't talk about things and decide on them together."

"You and Dillon talk all the time, but where does that get you?"

"We talk because we want to be sure this relationship is good for both of us."

"You two were married before. In Vegas. Then you annulled that. What's to discuss? You're a soap opera."

"We acted in haste."

"You know Sam still thinks he might have a chance with you. He wants kids."

Sam and I and Pauline had gone to high school together, though Sam was two years older. He had been a football jock. I was as starry-eyed about athletic men as Pauline was right now about a short, stocky guy who loved to wear Hawaiian shirts and sandals even in winter.

But I adored Pauline. She had a good heart. She'd needed me from the time she was in kindergarten. She'd grown up with parents who'd argued a lot. She'd spent considerable time with me on our farm, staying overnight frequently when we were young. She had a sister, but they weren't close. The sister was finishing a master's degree out East. Pauline was the sister I never had. I hoped that maybe I was the sister she had always really needed.

We were almost to Pauline's car when a red Mustang zoomed into the harbor parking lot next to us. Out popped short, petite, red-haired Fontana Dahlgren. She was nine month's pregnant, big enough for twins though the doctor told her she was having only one. We girlfriends felt she would pop a boy football player fully formed. The baby shoes would have to come with spikes and the bonnet would be a Green Bay Packer helmet.

Fontana and I had been in grade school together. She was older and had bossed me around. It was borderline bullying, though we didn't use that term. She'd been my rival last fall when I had opened a farmer's market roadside stand in the countryside in southern Door County near my parents' farm. She felt I was invading her territory. We'd resolved that tiff which was based mostly on her insecurities about becoming pregnant out of wedlock. When the father of her unborn child had been murdered, she'd come undone. Pauline and I figured out who murdered her lover, though we'd come close to losing our lives in that fiery misadventure. I shuddered thinking about it.

"Just the very person I wanted to bump into," Fontana said, her bright red-orange lipstick shiny as polished apples in the sunlight. Her lips almost matched her hair color, which was natural, unlike Jackie's. "I have a favor to ask."

I was admiring her car, laying my hand on the warm hood. "I don't need to order any more of your sheep's milk soaps. We've got plenty for the upcoming festival and beyond."

She rubbed her belly protruding from under a light jacket. "The kid sometimes kicks things over the goalpost." She recovered, breathing in big draughts. "Silly, this isn't about soap. I wanted to ask you a favor. And if you do it, I'll take you over to the Glass Slipper right now and pay for a manicure. You really should do something about those nails."

"I bake and work hard. I don't want long nails. Nor do I want polish that can come off in fudge."

"The new polish doesn't come off. You're behind the times, Ava. Did you know Bethany is working at the spa today? That girl does the best manicures." She flashed her fingernails. Purple with white stripes down the middles.

Bethany Bjorklund was Cody's girlfriend.

A crisp wind smelling of the icy water whipped about us. I said, "Thanks, but no time for manicures, Fontana. We're on an errand."

"If you come with me, I'll put the top down. And let you drive."

Fontana knew I loved fast cars. I looked from Pauline's mousy, drab car to the sleek, red sports car.

Pauline shrugged at me. "It's officially spring when our tops are down!"

Pauline squeezed into the convertible's back seat. Fontana took the shotgun seat--barely fitting. I slid into the driver's seat and then put the top down. The wind tousled our hair--a freeing, powerful feeling. I didn't care what Fontana's favor was. Maybe she'd forget about it.

I backed out of the parking spot in the harbor lot, then headed up a backstreet to Main Street. With nobody around, I roared onto the street, fishtailing.

Pauline yelled from the back, "That's not funny!"

I laughed. "But it was fun!"

Fontana laughed, too. "The baby loves it, but let's be careful. Sometimes my stomach doesn't stay down. Which reminds me of the favor I wanted to ask. You know how I love fudge."

"Yeah." With few tourists around, I was pushing us toward thirty-five miles per hour, ten over the speed limit. The breeze cut at our faces. I felt like a filly let out of a stable after a long winter.

Fontana turned in her seatbelt toward me. "I want you to be my birthing partner in the hospital when the baby is born."

My hands slipped on the wheel and hit the horn.

Pauline guffawed behind me.

I eased through an empty intersection. "Don't you have Sam and Jonas at-the-ready?"

Jonas Coppens farmed across the road from my parents' dairy farm. He'd been a childhood friend. Last fall, he'd help shelter Fontana at his farmhouse when it was feared the killer might want to harm her and the baby. She'd been living with him ever since, though it was common knowledge they were just friends and not in love. Sam Peterson, being a social worker, had helped her, too, by meeting over coffee a few times to give her advice on how to handle the trauma and grieving. We'd all been concerned about her unborn child. Pauline and I had hopes that Sam and Fontana might fall in love.

Fontana's flame-red hair whipped in the cold breeze. "Sam and Jonas are so nice and I don't want to play favorites. The doctor said I could only have one person in the birthing room as my coach."

"I don't know what I'd say to you during the process. I can recite recipes and the history of the inn. It was built in the eighteen hundreds about the time fudge was invented by the Vassar college women students. That's the extent of my talent. Is that what you want to listen to in the birthing room? Mix two bars of chocolate with cups of cream, breathe harder, add sugar and now push?"

"Actually, yes. And you grew up on a farm. You saw calves being born. I know you won't faint on me."

Pauline was howling with laughter behind me. "Take the next turn south."

As I roared around a corner, Fontana said, "I love your fudge, which is made with organic ingredients. You know I love organics."

"What does organics have to do with childbirth, Fontana?"

The wind was twisting my hair as we emerged from the cocoon of the small village. We headed southeast into the countryside.

Within a couple of minutes Pauline had me turn onto new a blacktopped stretch called Sunflower Road. Tall cedars lining the road swayed like sentries in the spring air, waving us on. Leaves hadn't yet busted out on the maple trees, but the air smelled springtime sweet so I opened my mouth to taste it.

Fontana said, "Fudge has everything to do with childbirth. You see, I don't want to give birth using any chemicals. No shots or intravenous chemicals for me. I'm so addicted to your fudge that I think a sugar high is all I'll need. Sweetness is what I want in my birthing room."

Again, Pauline was splitting a gut in the backseat.

I glanced at Fontana, incredulous. "You want to use my fudge as a painkiller?"

Fontana never blinked. "Well, yeah, okay?"

Pauline yelled, "Slow down! We're here! This is the place!"

I slammed on the brakes, flying into a gravel driveway a little too hot. The Mustang fishtailed toward a white board fence.

Chapter 4

ravel flew and peppered the white board fence as I hit the brakes, but the fancy red Mustang found purchase on short grass.

Anxious about Fontana's condition, I uttered an "I'm sorry" her way. She was gape-mouthed and pointing at the scene in front of us.

I kept the motor running, thinking we'd ended up at the wrong address.

With white board fences on both sides, the lane drew our gazes straight ahead about fifty yards to a new, sprawling stone and cedar house. Yellow daffodils bloomed next to the foundation. Low-growing purple-blue hepatica--a flower that loved winter snowmelt--inked areas around some of the lane's white posts.

The house seemed ethereal out here in the countryside. Several peaks and cupolas in the red steel rooftop indicated high ceilings within. Arched windows marched one after the other along the tan front that flared away from a grand entrance arched in stone. A big round window looking like an eye stared over the portico and front door. I imagined a chandelier behind that window, lighting the way at night as limousines delivered guests.

To the left of the house hunkered a three-car garage of the same character; it augmented an attached two-car garage on that side. To the right, a matching, wood-and-stone barn or stable nestled in front of tall cedars getting cozy with a few maples and white birches yet to leaf out.

Door County was known for hiding mansions and estates in its rural environs. A sense of awe--as if we'd happened upon the Emerald City--silenced us.

Fontana muttered, "I didn't know John was this rich or I'd have made a play for him. This looks like a damn nice place to raise a kid."

I said, "Pauline, are you sure this is the right address?"

"Yeah. You just missed hitting the post with the fire number."

She repeated the address on Sunflower Road. We weren't far from Fishers' Harbor, maybe four miles. We'd made a couple of turns off Highway F. A red-winged blackbird newly arrived from down south called "wheet-wheet" from his perch atop a white board near us.

I pressed the Mustang onward, stopping in a circular driveway by the front door.

We got out, with Fontana grunting as she heaved herself up.

The breeze hummed like a base cello through the cedars, a signature sound in Door County.

I still hesitated, doubting John having anything to do with this manse. "I'll knock and ask directions. This can't be the right place."

A knock on the door brought nobody.

Pauline appeared behind me holding up a key. "This was right where his message said it would be. Under the angel's butt."

A gray concrete angel maybe ten inches tall sat on a miniature stone bench a few yards away amid the remnants of a winter-weary flower garden. Somebody had been here long enough to landscape last summer.

Pauline was shaking so with excitement that she couldn't get the key in the lock. I took it from her and shoved it into the keyhole.

"Thanks," she said, blinking several times. "This feels like Christmas."

How had John swung this place? In his fifties, he had lost a job in Milwaukee before moving to Door County. He'd started over with the benefit of money he'd won in an age-discrimination hassle, now becoming a videographer. He'd only landed the TV show gig last fall. A show about interesting places and mythical hodags in Rhinelander, Wisconsin, likely didn't pay enough to buy this place. Perhaps he'd done better in the discrimination suit than I had first thought.

Inside, the finest white marble flooring with striations of caramel color led from the foyer to a massive formal dining room straight ahead. A sleek Scandinavian-style dining table and chairs for eighteen people seemed to float in the airy space. Beyond the table, two sets of French doors framed a back yard that appeared from this distance to have a pool.

We ventured in, our shoes smacking on the hard floor. The open concept flowed to our right, where creamy carpeting took over in a living room with a two-story ceiling and enough room to handle a hundred people. A massive stone fireplace dominated the far wall. Built-in stone shelves here and there held delicate statues depicting wildlife including a heron and swan. With little imagination, the heron and swan could take flight, soaring under the skylights and sparkling lights crafted in Scandinavian simplicity.

I muttered, "This place makes me feel ten pounds lighter, as if I can fly."

Fontana waddled to one of two white sofas near the fireplace and reclined, resting her puffy feet in their sandals on a tufted sofa arm. "Not me. I'm staying right here to have the baby. I'm sure this is heaven and in heaven there is no pain, bloat, or aching backs."

The living room smelled lemony clean and surfaces gleamed. "Kim Olkowski would be the one in heaven here. She'd go crazy testing her white gloves in this place."

Pauline wandered about the living room, turning, twisting to look at things as she headed toward a corner to our right with a white piano. Pauline plunked a key, a C, D and E, but then a C-sharp. The sour note registered on her face. "Something's wrong about this. John can't afford this."

"Duh," I said.

Fontana moaned, "Who cares. I'm comfortable."

Pauline used both hands to toss her hair about in high-level thinking. "It must be for some party he's planning for his crew. It's not about us living here, that's for sure." She growled. "Why am I so desperate? Let's go."

She must have shrunk six inches before my eyes. The fresh lemony brightness and fairytale airiness of the place dulled.

"Pauline, don't feel bad. He wanted you to take a look for a reason. And if it's for a party, he wants you involved or he wouldn't have asked you to check it out."

Fontana pushed herself up and off the sofa with a grunt. "Not all of us can compete with Ava for having an outstanding life of luxury, Pauline."

I blinked at her. "What's that supposed to mean?"

"Listen, I'm no dope. I'm also older and wiser than you two."

"Not that much older."

"I'm the one who taught you to love the finer things in life. Your mother sent you to school without matching clothes and without makeup."

"I was in grade school, for cryin' out loud."

"My point is that you loved me dollin' you up at school. You never forgot it because the first thing you did out of college was elope to glitzy Vegas and after that you ended up in glamorous Hollywood."

"Glamorous? I was a struggling writer living in a motel efficiency apartment who worked with an all-male production team who kept me from doing much beyond going for donuts."

Fontana rubbed her rounded belly. "Oh for heaven's sake, suck it up and quit whining, Ava Oosterling. That writing gig is where you learned to make fudge and other candies and desserts that you brought to the studio and sold for big bucks to the actors and crew. I taught you to yearn for the glitz and glamour and therefore I'm the one responsible for you starting your fudge shop. I should be getting a cut of the profits, not Gil."

"Take it all back, or I'll..." This was how it always was with Fontana. She loved controlling me or at least trying to. I grabbed Pauline's arm. "Let's go."

Pauline sighed. "And leave her here?"

"Sure, why not. She's homeless."

Heat came to my face and weighed on my heart in an instant. I faced Fontana. "I'm sorry. I didn't mean to mock you for living with Jonas. That's not my business. But you have to stop baiting me." I gave Fontana my best burning glare.

"When pigs fly."

Then--

Fontana burst into laughter. "You are so easy to rile up. I gotta pee."

As Fontana waddled away toward what appeared to be a bedroom wing past the left side of the fireplace, I looped an arm around one of Pauline's and led her back to the dining room and foyer.

Pauline said, "She's right, you know."

"About what?"

"It wouldn't be a bad thing if you wore a little makeup now and then."

I hissed at her.

She winked.

Then we laughed. I hugged her.

Pauline peered back at the magnificent living room, wistfulness rippling across her face. "Maybe this wasn't meant to be, but it reminds me that I've never really done much of anything in my life. I mean, why can't I have all this?"

I paled with a realization that came like a lightning bolt. "Pauline, you're a teacher, the best and most exciting thing anyone can ever do in the world. You've helped dozens of kids read and--"

"Learn to tie their shoes." She sighed. "But I want to be Cinderella and have somebody help me into new shoes."

"Tell me this obsession to be with crazy John isn't because I did a bunch of crazy stuff and traveled and you didn't?" I grabbed her by the forearms and made her look at me. "Tell me that wishing you were married to John isn't because of me."

For a moment she stared back, then blinked, looking away as she let out a big breath. "So what if it is? You're my best friend. Hearing Fontana talk about you just now made me realize how adventurous you are, and I'm not. I've never gone anywhere, done much of anything. Even my sister went East on her own and who knows where my mother is. I certainly haven't allowed my heart to lead me into big adventures."

I shook her arms. "They're called my mistakes, Pauline, not adventures. Don't repeat my foolish mistakes."

"But what do I do with this feeling of being dull? We're thirty-three. Look at me. Wearing red so I don't feel dull. How did I come to this state of being?"

"You're not dull. Change the letter in that word and you're a 'doll'. Okay, doll?"

"I've been teaching kindergarten for a decade already. We're in our thirties, Ava."

"Stop reminding me of our age. Are you feeling a ticking biological clock?"

She stepped back from me. "How can I not feel it ticking? I'm with darling kids every day. And when Laura named one of her twins Spencer Paul for me, I could feel my womb doing flip-flops."

"Clara Ava was named after me and I'm not checking the time on the clock. There's plenty of time to find a good guy and have children, Pauline."

"Not really."

Panic was welling up inside me because of the misery on her face. "Look at me. Dillon and I agreed to take things slowly. Look how happy we are." An odd discomfort wormed its way into my psyche. Dillon had said he wasn't ready for kids yet. What did "yet" mean? How long did one wait for "yet" to ripen and become the right time? I realized I hadn't said anything back to Dillon in that conversation we'd had last summer. I had nodded after he'd said, "Not yet." I'd agreed to "not yet".

As usual, Pauline was starting to make me think more deeply than I ever liked to. "Let's look at the kitchen," I said. "Maybe there's something we can taste-test."

"You mean steal."

"May I remind you that John gave you access? I'm hungry. I never ate breakfast."

"Those guests of yours have something wrong with them, you know, if you of all people forget to eat."

"I can't ask what's going on with them because they're all Cathy's friends."

Pauline shrugged. "We women are too complicated. Men would just go have a beer and forget their worries."

As we wandered in to gawk at the gorgeous appliances, we spotted at least two dozen red roses in a vase on a table in another dining area in an entertainment room beyond the kitchen.

Pauline raced to the bouquet. "They have to be from John. See? You were wrong, Ava."

I didn't bother mentioning she was the one who had just given up on John. She pulled an envelope from the bouquet.

Pauline withdrew a note and read, "'*What do you think?*'" Her dark eyes sparkled. "What do I think? He means it, Ava. He wants to know if I want to live here. John wants to marry me!"

As was her habit, she twirled and danced while I took the note she'd dropped on the table.

"Pauline, asking you what you think doesn't constitute a marriage proposal."

She inhaled the scent of the roses as if her life depended on ingesting the perfume. "Can't you be happy for me? John is different. This is his way."

She moved each rose aside, looking, looking. She was searching for a ring. My gut said she wouldn't find one. It made me sad. And feel lost and inadequate. My friend was in a sorry state and I didn't know what to do about it.

Pauline nabbed her phone from her purse. She began texting. As her thumbs did a dance, she crowed, "Yes, yes, yes!" She stuffed the phone back in her purse.

Fontana joined us. "Yes for what? Those sure are gorgeous roses. Ava, maybe you could make some of your rose-petal fudge for the birth, too. Roses are for love."

Pauline hugged Fontana. "I'm in love, Fontana."

Fontana gave Pauline a cockeyed look. "Your aura isn't right. There's a black fog pushing in from one side, crowding out the aqua."

"Now I have the wrong aura?" Pauline slung her purse over a shoulder and grabbed the vase of roses. Petals fell to the floor at our feet. "What is with everybody? You're determined to split up me and John." Tears bubbled in her eyes.

I hastened to take the roses from her before she tossed them at us. "That's not true, Pauline. Even you said that something is off about all this. Even you don't trust John, or yourself. You just won't admit it."

Pauline glared at me for a full second, then snatched back the vase of roses. She marched to the foyer, her boots pounding. Soon the front door banged, making Fontana and me lurch.

Unease slaked my mouth dry. "I don't believe in auras, but I did get a bad vibe about Pauline. She's gone around the bend."

Fontana dismissed that with a wave of the hand. "Happens to most of us after a long winter. We're all like bears here in Door County at this time of year, crawling out of our caves. We're grouchy and hungry. Sort of like me all the time lately."

I headed for the front door. "She wants a baby. There are babies all around her these days and it's affecting her."

"I'm sorry." Fontana appeared close to tears.

"It's not your fault you're having a baby, well it is, but... Never mind." I opened the front door to get fresh air.

It struck me that I was in the middle of a maelstrom where every woman in Door County was not acting normally. I wondered if it had anything to do with the ice going out on Lake

Michigan and our bay. Were we all breathing in too much fresh air? Was it possible to get high from spring?

As she stepped onto the front portico, Fontana said, "You're right, Ava. John's up to no good with this place. It doesn't use organic anything. You should have seen that bathroom. Cheap soaps you'd find in any low-rent motel room. Not that I would know anything about such rooms."

I gave her a hard look as a cool breeze teased hair across our faces.

"Okay," she said, holding onto her stomach, "I might have been in a cheap room once or twice because I like a bargain. Heavens, I conceived this kid in Cherry's car and it didn't cost me a dime that night." She giggled.

The now-deceased Professor Tristan Hardy had been known as "Cherry" because he was a horticultural cherry tree specialist. Because he was a staid university-type, it had come as a surprise to everybody to learn he and the flamboyant Fontana had been secretly dating.

As the gravel crunched under our feet, Fontana said, "Cherry was fun. That's all that mattered to us. We had fun. Maybe that's what Pauline sees in John."

"But John is never around so she's not having fun. She just explained a bunch of gobbledy-gook to me that tells me she wants fun and that's what he represents to her. But he's her opposite and I believe he's using Pauline. He asks her to do things like check out this house. She's what Grandma would call his 'Girl Friday'."

"What do we do about it? She's not listening to me or you, and you're her best friend."

We paused to turn back and look at the house and keep our conversation private. I said, "I have to come up with a plan."

"What sort of plan?"

"I don't know yet. I'll make fudge and figure it out. She has no family to rely on. I'm it."

"You're a pretty nice 'it'."

"Even if I don't wear makeup?"

She tisked. "I'll wear you down eventually. As we get older, our lips begin to thin. Lipstick helps."

Fontana waddled away fast on purpose. She didn't want to hear me growling at her.

My phone buzzed as we reached the Mustang. Fontana had already squeezed into the driver's seat while I read my message. It was from Eliza. The fudge divas were at the fudge shop, but nobody had arrived to take them to Washington Island. Apparently my grandfather had escaped them somehow. Eliza wanted to know what I'd arranged for transportation. Weary of the women, I didn't text her back.

With a sigh, I plopped into the passenger's seat. Fontana's words, "He was fun," echoed in my head. Maybe that's all love was supposed to be: fun. Maybe that had to be the nature of my plan to help Pauline find happiness beyond John. I had to find fun things for her, fun alternatives to John. But what?

I turned to Pauline in the back seat. She was half hidden by the two dozen roses in the vase centered atop her knees.

"Pauline, I'm sorry. I apologize. I think it's wonderful that John is unconventional."

"Cross your heart and hope to die if you don't mean it?"

"Cross my heart," I said, with hidden fingers crossed. John was unconventional. I hadn't lied about that part.

Fontana put the car's top up. We were shivering in a sudden brisk breeze that smelled like a spring shower could be in the offing.

When we arrived at the harbor parking lot near the fudge shop, the divas were engaged in a loud discussion next to a short yellow school bus. In the center of the group stood a stout woman with a curly mop of blond hair and wearing a gray bus driver's uniform.

"Oh no," I groaned. "Mercy Fogg is here."

Mercy loved trouble--especially if it bugged me.

Mercy yelled, "Nobody gets on my bus with a gun!"

Chapter 5

My guests had circled Mercy Fogg. She was blocking the door to the yellow school bus. She'd parked it in the first spot next to the fudge shop.

Pauline said to me, "That's the kindergarten bus. She's not an approved driver for the school."

"Mercy probably hot-wired the bus so she could use it to make a buck off my guests."

While Fontana hung back, Pauline and I hustled from Fontana's Mustang toward the bus. The chatter from the divas crescendoed like a gathering flock of blackbirds.

I asked, "What's this about a gun?"

Mercy spotted me. "Your guests are packin'. I'm not taking any weapons onto this bus."

Pepper lifted a holster on a belt--all in pink, of course. The pistol within had a pink handle. "We're allowed to carry in this state."

"Not on my bus," Mercy repeated, her blond curls flopping about her round face in the breeze.

I shook my head at Mercy. "This isn't even your bus to drive. You stole this bus."

Jackie pulled into her tall height, her hair whipping about like a warning flag. "This is quite rude, Miss Fogg. What do you believe Pepper will do? Shoot you if you don't use your turn signals?"

The group laughed. Zadie and her friend Yola were texting like mad. I cringed. This would be all over the Internet with the headline: "Gun Fight at Oosterlings' Fudge Shop".

Kim, putting on a white cleaning glove, said, "Let me hold the gun during the ride so you can see we're not using it. I can clean it for you, Pistol-Packin' Pink Pepper."

The group howled again, which only made Mercy sport an angry frown.

Eliza pushed away Kim's proffered arm. "You're the one who broke a lamp in the Blue Heron. No way in hell am I letting you handle a gun. Give it to me."

"Eliza Do-Gooder. That's what happened that night thirty years ago," Kim said in a stern voice that blew me back a step.

Cathy held up her arms. "Girls, please stop."

Eliza said, "Stop? Stop trying to play the peacemaker, Cathy. You treat Pepper like she's a child. You feel she should be grateful and lucky you let her onto your foundation board. You're like a parent allowing her child to do something. Your need to hush everyone is why Dillon got the hell out of here for years. Let Pepper defend herself."

Everybody paused. I had sympathy for Cathy. Dillon had confessed to me last year that she had suffered with severe post-partum depression when he was born. She had relied heavily on her husband Edward's parents to raise Dillon the first year of his life. To my knowledge, Cathy had done everything she could to make it up to Dillon.

But now I wondered: What secret had to be hushed?

Jackie grabbed her flyaway hair. "Eliza--dear friend, Dillon's back in Wisconsin now, so your point is moot."

Eliza snapped, "For how long? The only reason he's in this town is to finish a few carpenter jobs for his mommy."

I wanted to point out that maybe he was sticking around for me, though again I felt my life was built on ice as thin as that forming overnight on local ponds.

Cathy skewered Jackie then Eliza with a pinched look. "Both of you can go jump in the lake."

Mercy growled, "This is the bay, not the lake. People around here don't call this the lake. That's the other side of the peninsula. If you want to tell somebody to jump in a lake, we have about a half-hour's drive from here if I use my lead foot."

The group of women appraised her as if she were an alien with horns.

Cathy said, "So now I don't belong here? After the investments I've made in the downtown and in preserving the old Victorian on Main Street?"

This time I had to speak up. "That's not what Mercy meant, I'm sure."

Cathy said "Thank you" to me, then pointed to Jackie and Eliza. "All our troubles would be over if you two would get along. We promised to get along."

Why did they need to promise to get along?

"Ladies," I offered, "you're all best friends from college, right? You're here for a fudge frolic girlfriend vacation. I can take the gun to the inn and hold it there while you go on your trip."

Mercy stepped to Pepper, snatched the pink holster, then shoved it into my arms.

The women all talked at once, some agreeing to my holding it while others said it was unfair of Mercy to take action. Jackie brought out a fistful of bills and ruffled them under Mercy's nose. Zadie and Yola were capturing the ruckus on their cell phones.

A tall shadow striped across us all, shutting down the flurry.

I never thought I'd be grateful to see the sheriff.

Jordy Tollefson appeared next to me on my left. His tall, runner's figure and broad shoulders from years of being on the Green Bay Packer's practice squad wore his tan uniform well. The sun was strong and he'd left his jacket behind, so his badge on his pocket drew our attention. An official Door County sheriff's department baseball cap covered his hair and shadowed his face that sported aviator sunglasses. He removed them, folding them with a sigh, then placed them in his front shirt pocket. Brown eyes widened with what I'd learned over time signaled disgust.

"Ava, it appears you're fomenting trouble again." Jordy removed his cap, revealing trimmed dark brown hair with a perfect side part that always made me feel like reaching up and tousling it--just to mess with him.

Nervous giggles emanated from the women now standing arm-in-arm as if no arguing had ever happened, though Zadie and Yola were behind them. Probably texting in secret.

Jordy's eyes read me up and down before his gaze landed on the pink holster and pink-handled pistol in my hands. "A new purchase? Could I see your permit?"

"It's not mine. It's Pepper's."

Pepper raised her hand like a schoolgirl, but said nothing.

Zadie said, "Mom bought it for this weekend." She was using the gravelly vocal fry voice every woman under twenty-five used, particularly when annoyed. "Mom doesn't like being in a backwater place without protection."

Backwater? My insides took umbrage.

Jordy perused the group. "Huh. Are these the divas who exercised over at the bookstore?"

The group didn't speak, so I had to. "Yes. Why?"

Jordy put his cap back on and then took a piece of paper from a breast pocket. "Which one of you broke the stripper pole?"

Again, nobody spoke.

Jordy grunted. "I have a complaint about a broken stripper pole. If it's not paid for today, I'll have to file the charge Jane made about vandalism, and if that happens, it's official court business and I might have to arrest the person or persons who busted the pole and ran."

The fudge divas remained mum. Mercy Fogg climbed into her bus, as if to leave. The women wore panic on their faces but they didn't give up the guilty party.

Pauline edged next to my right shoulder, whispering, "I gave you the bill. Tell him."

I muttered, "This isn't my problem. I didn't break Jane's pole."

Across from us in the circle, Cathy's plaintiff gaze snagged mine. Only because I was dating her son did I relent. "I guess I could pay for the pole and add it to your bills."

The women hooted then clambered onto the bus.

Mercy Fogg engaged the engine with a roar. The bus took off from the parking lot.

Jordy shook his head in derision.

I handed the pink holster and gun off to Pauline.

She said, "I don't want the thing. What if one of my students happened by and saw me?"

She handed it off to Fontana, who promptly checked its chamber for ammunition like a pro. She found a bullet, which she let lay in her palm. "How about that! It was loaded."

My heart skipped a beat. "It was loaded?"

Pauline said, "The way they were arguing, it's a good thing we ended up with it. Jordy could have happened upon something messier to solve than a broken stripper pole."

Jordy took the holstered pistol and bullet. He put the bullet in a pocket. "What's your guest doing with a loaded pistol?"

Pauline said with a cheery smile, "They're planning a heist, though Ava hasn't had a murder on her hands for a while."

"Pauline!" I yelped.

Fontana said, "I recall something about a diamond heist involved with a murder at the inn a year ago. Perhaps Ava could have an anniversary crime."

Jordy chuckled. "Come to think of it, Ava, I kind of miss sparring with you down at the jail in Sturgeon Bay." He winked, which unnerved me. Heat climbed to my earlobes. He handed me the holster and pistol. "Put that somewhere safe until the ladies are ready to leave town."

Fontana fluffed her red hair, making it flare in the breeze under Jordy's nose. "They're not leaving until tomorrow. Plenty of time for trouble. Maybe you and I can tail them tonight and get into a little trouble ourselves?"

Fontana flirting with her big round, pregnant belly made us all laugh. Jordy included. In the back of my mind I wondered if Fontana wished things could get serious with Jordy.

Pauline and Fontana left, leaving Jordy alone with me.

An uncomfortable moment passed in which he grinned at me and said nothing.

"Did you want something else, Jordy?" I regretted the way that sounded. Like an innuendo. I was starting to worry about myself.

"I thought I'd buy a pound or so of fudge to share back at the office. Do you have anything with bacon?"

I hooted. "Follow me."

We headed for the shop but paused as a tan SUV pulled to a stop in the parking lot. It was Brecht Rousseau, probably with my delivery from his wife's bakery, the Luscious Ladle. Laura Rousseau's bakery was a few miles north of us along the bay's shoreline in a community called Sister Bay.

I stuffed the pistol in my back pocket and went over to the vehicle. "Hey, Brecht. How ya doin'? And how are these cute kids?"

From the front passenger seat he handed me a giant box of frosted cinnamon rolls. "I'm better now that the kids stopped crying. Riding in the SUV is the only way to get them to quiet down sometimes. That and coming over to your fudge shop to see the dog."

"Lucky Harbor is with Cody, but he always seems to know when Clara Ava and Spencer Paul come to visit. He can't miss licking food off their faces."

The twins were ensconced in the back in their safety seats.

I asked, "Do you need some help?"

"Sure." He was already out and leaning into the back trying to unbuckle the adorable, nine-month-old babies.

Jordy helped Brecht unload the twins. Somehow watching Jordy handle babies and with such tenderness caused me to pause.

Embarrassed, I headed into the shop before either man caught me staring.

Cody was stocking shelves with new pink fudge logo aprons when I walked in with the cinnamon rolls in the giant box. I set them on the counter next to my register. Cody came over.

"These are big, Miss Oosterling! Big as my head."

"Yeah, Cody. Now all I need are customers."

Grandpa charged in from the back door. It slammed as I went to greet him. Lucky Harbor galloped into the back hallway, then paused for me to take off the message tube I saw clipped to his collar. Dillon and I sent love notes that way on occasion. This note said, "Miss you. Stacking a stone wall today. Wishing for something soft. Like your lips."

I blushed in front of Grandpa. Lucky Harbor galloped on to the front of the store to see the Rousseau twins.

As Grandpa and I walked into the shop, he said, "Never thought I'd be glad to see Mercy Fogg, but thank goodness she agreed to take on the divas."

I asked, "What do you mean she 'agreed'?"

"I hightailed it over to Main Street earlier to escape the divas and climbed into a county dump truck to hide from them. I thought I was hiding out with Al Kvalheim at the wheel, but there sat Mercy Fogg, dammit all." Grandpa grabbed his coffeepot from behind his register. It was empty. "I wasn't about to tell her I didn't know what I was doing. I begged her to take the divas up to Washington Island."

"Whew. You begging your enemy has me thinking I'm in a different universe."

Grandpa came over, plunged a finger into the frosting on top of a roll and slapped the sugar into his mouth. "Al Kvalheim showed up and he had spare keys for the school buses because he'd just changed the oil."

Al was our village's handyman. He fixed broken water mains, potholes in the streets, and leaning street signs that had been hit by the snowplow Mercy drove during the winter.

"Did you pay her? What do I owe you?" I asked, grabbing a pink apron from the wall hook behind the counter.

"Not a dime! When I told her who the women were and how rich they were, she laughed in a maniacal way. She muttered something about 'soaking them' for the ride."

Cody and I chuckled as Grandpa scooted back to the kitchen to fill his coffeepot with water.

The cowbell on the door banged. Jordy held the door open while Brecht pushed a stroller through the opening. Clara Ava sat in the front seat, with her twin brother Spencer Paul snuggled down in the rear. Lucky Harbor circled the stroller, tail wagging. The brown, curly American water spaniel wiggled all over, his tongue lapping each child's face and hands. They squealed happily in response.

Brecht's shoulders relaxed. "I always get to see their best side when we visit the fudge shop, Ava. Can I move in?"

I was tying my apron in back. "Only if you grab one of these pink aprons and pitch in to make fudge." I nodded to my left where six copper kettles stood waiting for action.

"Not a bad idea. Can't find any other job, it seems."

Cody came out from the back with quarts of cream from my parents' farm in his arms. "We can always use another volunteer fireman."

Brecht clung to the handle of the stroller, watching his little ones pull Lucky Harbor's ears. "No fire for me. I... I still have nightmares."

Cody and I exchanged a glance.

Grandpa toddled out to the shop with his coffeepot filled with water. He proceeded to assemble his thick brew. "That PTSD stuff ain't fair, Brecht. Take things easy. Your wife's holdin' down the fort for now, and that's okay. No shame in that. If it weren't for Ava makin' a little bit over the winter with her fudge business, I'd be in the bad soup myself."

Jordy knelt down to ruffle Lucky Harbor's ears. "My department does school visits. No money in that, but maybe that's a way to get out and about in the community, Brecht.

People will get to know you and maybe job offers will find their way to you."

Brecht straightened. "You mean trot me out for show-and-tell?"

A sad chill shot through the air and through my core.

Jordy rose. "I didn't mean it that way."

Cody hollered over from a copper kettle in which he was pouring cream, "Hey, I have a touch of Asperger's, but the more I tell people about it, the better I feel. I think talking about it helps me cope with it."

"I don't have Asperger's." Brecht turned the baby buggy around to head toward the door. "I don't have a disease and I don't need to be cured."

It was hard to breathe.

I grabbed a full pan of peanut butter fudge from the glass display case, then rushed to him. "We're sorry. We're trying to help you. Would you take this back to Laura? She wanted to make chocolate cupcakes with fudge chunks baked into them."

His shoulders sagged. "I'm sorry." He turned back to us.

Then baby Spencer Paul giggled at Lucky Harbor. The giggle seemed to loosen something warm in Brecht's eyes and face.

I said, "Please stay and help me for just a few minutes. Jordy said he was in the mood for bacon fudge. I was thinking of combining bacon fudge with Laura's cinnamon rolls. We need you to help judge. Laura will want to know if it works. If it does, we've got a whole new line of products."

For a second, he looked as if he'd march out the door. "How can a guy resist bacon?"

Everybody laughed, which made Lucky Harbor bark several times and wag his tail. I wished with all my heart that Brecht would find peace and a job soon. He'd been out of work since his return from duty and honorable discharge late last fall.

I found the pan of goopy, failed bacon fudge from the morning and we all dug in with spoons and knives to taste test the sugary combination with the cinnamon rolls.

To mollify Lucky Harbor, I tossed him goldfish-shaped crackers. Chocolate could poison a dog, and sugar wasn't good for dogs or babies. Brecht gave a bottle to each of the babies. Cody, who loved shiny things, crinkled colored cellophane into balls for the babies to play with.

To my surprise, big tall Jordy knelt down in front of the baby carriage to play a form of catch with Spencer and Clara. Jordy's hands were clumsy but gentle as he rolled the makeshift balls up their short arms. Both babies squealed and giggled.

One of the babies reached out and grabbed Jordy's hair, mussing the part. Again, that odd, warm stirring of confusion.

The divas returned at around four in the afternoon from Washington Island loaded down with purchases made at the lavender farm shop. The inn soon smelled of lavender soaps, lotions, perfumes, and bedding sprays. They gifted me with edible lavender buds they knew I used in making my divinity fudge.

When they asked for a final boat ride up and down the coast, Grandpa surprised me and agreed with gusto. He obviously was glad to say farewell. I suspected he also looked forward to their generous tips for the last ride.

They took off at six o'clock. Heaven for me. My ears only detected the creaks of the historic place adjusting its wood bones as it settled into night.

Dillon and I went to the Troubled Trout bar and restaurant for steak and fried cheese curds and a nice bottle of Door County red wine made with cherries. I told him about the strange day.

He fixated on the pink pistol. "Why would she carry such a thing here in Door County?"

I put down my wine glass. "It does seem wacky. There's nobody much around, and this is paradise."

Dillon stopped mid-bite on a piece of steak. "Your instincts have never been wacky."

I warmed to the compliment. "The women have some secret. And they fight about money. Then there are jealousies, it seems, about every little thing."

"So the pistol is to protect herself from her friends?"

Dillon's question made me pause.

The women stayed out late that night. With the wine and good meal, I headed to bed, knowing they could lock the front door whenever they chose to stumble in.

At eight o'clock the next morning, Sunday--when the women were due to leave--Jordy gave me a call on my cell. I was enjoying coffee in my bathrobe in my apartment. Breakfast at the inn on Sunday wasn't until nine-thirty.

He said, "I'm standing outside your front door."

My nerve endings zinged. I cinched my robe around me and left my apartment to trot through the parlor. I tugged extra hard as usual on the sticky door.

Behind Jordy, and down the hill and from the area of the harbor, red and blue flashing lights strobed the misty morning. Ice pooled in my gut.

"What...is it, Jordy?"

This time he wore his regulation hat, and a leather jacket. He didn't blink. "We got a call. About one of your guests. I found her."

"Found her? Who? Where?"

"In the harbor. The water. Alongside your grandfather's boat."

I swayed.

Jordy caught me with both hands securing my shoulders. "I'm sorry, Ava. There's blood on your grandfather's boat. We'll be testing the blood, of course. My deputy's at Gil's house now."

"My grandfather? No!"

Chapter 6

In disbelief, I tried to bolt past Jordy but he held me fast on the verandah of the Blue Heron Inn.

"Maybe change your clothes?" Jordy said.

A breeze bustled about the calves of my legs where the white terrycloth bathrobe fluttered. All I had on underneath it was a sleep T-shirt. Barefoot, the cold dampness of the verandah boards registered, adding to the chill already racking me. My heart and head demanded I go to Grandpa Gil and Grandma Sophie.

"Jordy, what's going on? Who did you find in the harbor?" *Please say it's not Grandpa.*

"I was hoping you could tell me. I recognized the woman as one I had seen in your group yesterday."

A woman. A relief. Not Grandpa. Wait. The relief was horrible of me. "Who?"

"She had no identification on her when we pulled her out. But I'm pretty sure she was your guest with the red hair."

The news blew me back inside the inn. "Jackie Valentine drowned?"

Jordy pushed hard on the door to close it against the spring chill. "I need you to wake your guests. I'm going to have to question them. And you should double-check on Ms. Valentine's room first. Just in case she's there after all. But don't touch a thing. I need to look for prints, blood, that sort of thing."

I drew my robe's collar up around my neck. The word "blood" flashed like a neon sign in my mind. Jordy had mentioned blood on my grandfather's boat. "What about my grandpa? He obviously didn't do anything."

Jordy shifted his stance. The leather jacket scrunched in response to his movement. The amber overhead light of the double entryway cast a shadow from his hat brim across his eyes. "I'm sorry, Ava. With the blood on his boat..."

"Is he under arrest? He better not be!" I pivoted then marched through the parlor, heading for my apartment to change clothes.

Jordy stalked behind me, his boots stomping on the wood floor then getting muffled intermittently by his walking on rugs. "I'm sorry, Ava."

"It's a mistake." I turned to him as I opened my door. "You know how he is. Grandpa gets into things but he means no harm."

Even I recognized how weak that sounded knowing what the sheriff had found. A body. A dead woman. Potentially one of my guests. Blood.

Too horrible to digest.

The bay of Green Bay was one-hundred-twenty miles long, and ten to twenty miles wide--over sixteen hundred square miles of water--but disaster chose to happen here at my shop's little harbor, of all places. Why? Why!

I entered my apartment and closed the door in Jordy's face, not caring if the sheriff thought ill of me.

This had to be the worst Sunday morning of my life. Tears sprang to my eyes. I could barely see to dress myself. I thought about calling Dillon, but when I snatched up my phone and turned it on Dillon's text trumpeted: "At Gil's. Come quick."

I called his number. He didn't pick up. My heart fibrillated. I hit the button for Grandpa. No answer. They were likely prevented from calling me. Hadn't I seen flashing lights in that direction? *Remember--Dillon is with my grandparents, calming them.* A deputy was likely with them and asking horrible questions. Ach!

I threw on clean undies but for expediency I slammed on the same jeans and plain white sweatshirt with the shop's pink logo and peanut butter fudge smudges on one sleeve that I'd worn yesterday. I'd give anything to be making my Fairy Tale fudge flavors now with not a worry in the world.

Slapping away tears, I slammed my feet into my work shoes with the steel toes. Jackie was dead? I wanted to kick something, anything. One of my first guests was dead!

Trembling, I stuffed my phone into my jean's pocket. I recalled the arguments escalating over the past few days. Then the pink pistol had appeared. I'd placed it on the top shelf of the china hutch in the dining room.

As I rejoined Jordy in the foyer, I glanced into the dining room. The pistol was missing.

That meant nothing, I told myself. Pepper, who was short, must have spotted it atop the hutch as she'd climbed the stairs or come down them, then retrieved the pistol easily enough by standing on a chair. She then took the pistol upstairs with her after the women had returned sometime late last night. Jordy hadn't said anything about a gunshot wound. Why was there blood? It was a drowning. An accident. It had to be. A knock on the head. Jackie must have fallen.

Jordy's tall figure watched my every move in silence, which gave me more heebiegeebies. Fontana's words echoed. She'd said I was due for an "anniversary crime". Prescient of her. She'd been that way in grade school. She always knew what the bullies had planned for me before I did.

I turned toward the carpeted staircase. Gripping the railing, I headed up to wake my guests.

Jackie's room proved to be empty, her bed undisturbed.

Could she really be dead? Maybe she was out for a stroll in the morning's calm.

Cathy, Eliza, Pepper, and Kim were dressed and downstairs and standing in the parlor to the right of the stairs within a couple of minutes. While dabbing their eyes with tissues, they hugged each other repeatedly in a round robin affair.

Yola and Zadie, not used to waking early--though it was now eight-thirty--made their way down the stairs one bleary-eyed step at a time. They, too, had red-rimmed eyes and tissues at their noses.

Jordy waited for the women to settle into a semi-circle.

Zadie, fashionable in the latest designer tights and top ensemble, went to her mother, Pepper, and cried into her shoulder, "Mom, this is horrible. Has anybody called Victor?"

"I don't know." Pepper sobbed. "One of us will."

Yola, in her usual casual earthy top over ripped jeans, leaned back against the staircase's end post and finial. Her new auburn haircut was a snarly, unkempt mess, uncharacteristic of her. She used the hem of her top to swipe at tears. The action exposed her front but fortunately she wore a floral T-shirt underneath.

Cathy was passing around a tissue box she'd grabbed from a parlor table.

Jordy, stony-faced, stiff in his leather hat and jacket, held a small recorder in one hand. "Ladies, what happened last night?"

Pepper sagged, and the women had to help her petite frame to a nearby powder-blue sofa. The women floated about her, flowing into seats. Zadie sat beside her mother, with Yola next to Zadie. Everybody stared down at the floor at their feet from where they sat, though giving each other furtive glances. Their demeanor sent my antennae into the air.

I was still standing and eager to get to my grandfather, but I was compelled to hear what they had to say. Maybe they would exonerate my grandfather and a nightmare would be averted. I edged my butt onto a chair near the foyer facing them.

The sheriff stayed standing.

Eliza muttered, "This isn't real." She sat on another blue sofa across from Pepper. Eliza sniffled, stony-faced, so stunned that she had no tears streaming down her cheeks. She had to be suffering, what with the death of her husband. "Jackie was the strongest of us all."

Kim, sitting in a chair to Eliza's right, said, "She was the most opinionated, that's for sure."

Pepper sighed in her daughter's arms. "Don't blame her, Kim, for thinking it wasn't wise to invest in your White Glove Cleaning venture."

"That's not what I meant," Kim said, frowning.

Cathy, sitting on this side of Eliza, said, "Kim, Jackie wanted the best for you."

Kim rolled her eyes, which I felt was pretty bold what with the sheriff watching her.

Jordy had pulled a chair from the dining room and now settled next to me. He removed his hat and hung it on the back of the chair. "Ladies, where did you all go last night? Hour by hour? With Jackie?"

Cathy sat up. "We went for the boat ride with Gil. We got back around eight."

"It was closer to nine," Eliza said. "We were all hungry by then."

The sheriff asked, "Had you been drinking during the boat ride?"

Kim said, "Of course. Jackie did. We all did, but Jackie liked her wine."

I blinked at this because it seemed Kim was pushing a conclusion about Jackie onto the sheriff. The others in the circle exchanged glances, though it was such a quick thing I almost missed it. Zadie covered one of her mother's hands with hers.

Cathy brushed her dark hair off one shoulder. "We went to the Troubled Trout for the prime rib and perch special."

Jordy asked, "What did Ms. Valentine eat?"

They all looked at each other in confusion. Something was amiss.

"Was there something odd about what she ate?" Jordy looked about the circle.

Pepper said to him, "You think she was poisoned?"

"I'm only after facts. I have no conclusions. What did she eat?"

Cathy said, "Erik's new fish-and-cheese balls. A whole plate of them."

Erik Gustafson was the bartender and new owner of the Troubled Trout. Last year at the age of nineteen he had beat Mercy Fogg in the election for village president. He'd hired chef Piers Molinsky--a Chicago transplant who'd come to Door County for a fudge contest I'd offered last summer to help get my business known. At first, Piers had proven a troublesome contender, getting into silly arguments with the other chef contestant. In the end he admitted he loved making muffins more than fudge. He'd also fallen in love with Door County and last autumn had been looking for a steady gig here.

For the fish-and-cheese balls, Piers took white fish from Lake Michigan, wrapped the small bite-sized fillet around a cheese curd, rolled it all in seasoned flour and cornmeal, then deep fried the balls into golden sinfulness. For a tiny moment, I reflected on how good things were usually in our Lake Michigan bay of Green Bay: native lake trout, brown trout, a few Coho or Chinook salmon. Water should give life, not take it away.

The women were smiling, which seemed odd under the circumstances, except I couldn't blame them for savoring the taste of those cheesy fish delights.

Jordy noticed, too. "You're amused. Why?"

Eliza said, "Jackie said she was pretending those were her husband's, well..."

"Cojones?" Yola offered.

Zadie elbowed her friend.

The women cringed, but nodded.

Jordy said into the recorder, "The women nodded at that." Then he addressed the group again. "Is her husband staying here?"

Cathy said, "No. He's in Chicago, at home. This was our girlfriend vacation. A fudge-and-wine getaway."

I offered, "They call themselves the Fudge Divas."

"We're helping Ava with her business," Cathy said.

Kim ground out, "How long do I have to wait in line for help with my business?"

Everybody gasped.

Kim shrugged. "Sorry. I'm in shock over Jackie's death. All of us were in the middle of talking about our business investments."

"Or divestitures," Eliza said in a notch above a whisper.

Jordy went on. "So you went to eat at the Troubled Trout. Jackie ate a plate of fish-and-cheese balls. Then where did you all go?"

Cathy leaned back, scratching her forehead where her white stripe began in her hair. "It had to be around eleven-thirty or more. We came back here."

"And Mrs. Valentine was with you?"

"Yes." Cathy chewed at her upper lip as others gave her furtive glances.

Jordy skewered her. "And?"

Cathy's countenance grew grave as she connected with me. "Oh, Ava. I'm so sorry." She switched her gaze to the sheriff. "Jackie said she'd noticed a light on down at the harbor when we walked back from the restaurant. She, uh..."

Cathy had gone so pale I thought she might be a ghost.

My heartbeat had gone into overdrive.

Cathy continued, "Jackie said she remembered she'd left a bottle of wine on the boat. While the rest of us headed up to our rooms, she went back to Gil's boat."

The sheriff asked, "You saw her come back to the inn after that?"

Cathy swallowed visibly. "No."

With terror striking me, I launched from my chair, struggled with the stuck front door to get out, swearing under my breath, then ran as fast as I could down the hill to get to my grandfather.

Chapter 7

Deputy Maria Vasquez sat at the kitchen table across from Grandpa Gil. He had his back to me.

Lucky Harbor wriggled from under the table to wag his tail and sniff my hands for treats.

Dillon got up from a chair, a strong arm gathering me to his side. "Hey, Ava. We're trying to convince Maria to try a Belgian waffle."

Grandpa huffed. "Instead of trying a Belgian in the court of this kitchen."

"Gilpa, don't say anything," I said, leaving Dillon's arms to give my grandpa a hug.

"Hell, no reason to lie that I was on the boat," Grandpa said.

Grandma Sophie tisked. She stood by the stove, her usual spot. She was still in her powder blue fuzzy bathrobe, now pouring coffee for everyone. With her fluffy white tresses floating about her head and shoulders, she moved like an angel around us, belying the tension. A stack of Belgian waffles stood in the middle of the table; nobody was eating despite Grandma's homemade cherry preserves begging us to plop them on the thick waffles.

I slid my backside into a nearby chair and then covered my grandfather's hands with my own. "You need an attorney. A really good one."

Grandma and Dillon echoed that.

Grandpa growled, "Don't need any damn lawyer. I didn't do anything."

And yet, the deputy sat there.

"Maria," I said, "my grandfather didn't do anything."

She typed on a computer device.

"Maria, stop that."

Dillon came to me and placed a hand on my shoulder. "I offered to call an attorney but your grandfather wouldn't let me."

Gilpa raked his hands through his silver hair, which was sticking up in all directions. He had on only a white T-shirt over his denim jeans and it had holes in it. He hadn't yet donned his usual plaid flannel shirt for the day.

Dillon edged from the group, slipping into a jacket. "I'll go up to the inn and take care of your guests, Ava. Including Mom. She's devastated by Jackie's sudden death."

"Gilpa, what were you doing in your boat at eleven or something last night? Did you see Jackie?"

Grandma Sophie patted my shoulders from behind while setting down a plate of waffles. "Honey, let's not talk until Maria leaves."

Maria began to say something but Grandma sat across from me with a hand held up to halt the deputy. "Gil was in his boat for a brief time. That's all he knows."

I tore off a corner of a waffle and fed it to Lucky Harbor. He settled on the floor next to my feet.

Maria, in her crisp tan uniform and with her dark hair in a neat bun at the back of her head, closed her computer notepad. "Your grandfather's not being accused of murder at this time."

At this time.

I stuffed a wad of waffle in my mouth to keep from screaming. Maria didn't know what I knew. I'd just come from the inn where the women had implicated my grandfather in Jackie Valentine's death. A light had been on in the boat after eleven o'clock last night. Grandpa had been present.

Maria gathered her things.

Grandma Sophie said to her, "You're sure I can't send some of these waffles home with you? They warm up fine in the microwave. I've got homemade cherry jam, too. From last year's orchard harvest near Juddville."

Maria took two steps to the doorway then stopped. "Those orchards were darn good last year. I wouldn't mind taking something with. My mom's back from a visit in Mexico, and she caught a spring cold. She loves waffles."

"Big, tall Belgian waffles and cherries cure a lot of things." Grandma hustled to get a paper plate and plastic wrap.

I helped transfer the giant "mattresses", as we called the waffles, onto the paper plate.

Grandma said, "Are your cousins back for the season?"

"Yeah. They'll be working the orchards again and one of them got hired by a big dairy down near Brussels to milk cows."

"My parents' neighborhood," I said.

Maria was originally from New York, but she had relatives from Mexico who were seasonal workers. Door County's many inns, motels, resorts, and restaurants also hired college students from European countries. Our summers were so robust with tourists that there was no way business owners including dairy farmers could find enough help among the local population of about twenty-eight thousand. The summer population sometimes swelled to two-hundred-fifty-thousand people.

Grandma put extra waffles on the plate before securing the shrink wrap around the load. "Say hello to your mother for us."

Maria said, "Thanks."

I handed Maria the wrapped waffles and a jar of homemade cherry jam from the cupboard.

After we escorted Maria through the living room and out the front door, Grandpa grumbled, "The sheriff always has it in for me. There was no reason to send that sweet Maria to our door."

Grandma heaved a big sigh, raising her eyebrows at Grandpa.

"Gilpa," I said, "this is serious. Jackie Valentine was found in our harbor next to your boat. I'll get you a cup of coffee."

To my surprise, he obeyed me though he stomped to the sofa, sitting next to the arm on this end, mumbling swear words. Grandma settled next to him. They whispered as I went to the kitchen.

After carrying three mugs of coffee to the living room, I took the only chair. My grandparents' place used to be a one-bedroom rental cabin, much like the one across the street where I used to live and where Dillon now resided. Grandma and Grandpa had added a sunroom and an extra bedroom toward the back that served as their office. They had moved to Fishers' Harbor a few years ago from our family farm near Brussels area in Door County.

Grandma Sophie put an arm around my grandfather's shoulders, then laid a cheek on his. "Maybe I'll cook up a big batch of booyah today."

Her hair reminded me of a giant halo. The angel in this family, she could cure anything with her cooking, especially with her Belgian pies and booyah. Booyah was a red tomato stew made with chicken usually and every vegetable within reach.

I set my mug aside on a folding table. As soon as I did that, Dillon's dog hopped up next to me, wedging himself between my hip and the chair arm. He'd always been sensitive, trying to comfort me. I put an arm around him brown, furry body and we mirrored Grandma with her arm slung around Grandpa.

"Grandpa, the truth now. Was Jackie with you on the boat last night? Or on the dock? Either one?"

Grandma said, "It's not his fault. And they both left at the same time."

So Grandpa and Jackie had indeed been on the boat together. "My guests said Jackie went to get a bottle of wine. True?"

Grandpa slurped his coffee, spilling a little when he plopped the mug on the side table. "The lady wasn't nice to me."

Grandma Sophie's face went as white as her hair.

I must have whined because Lucky Harbor licked my cheek. "What do you mean, Gilpa?"

"The darn woman kept grumbling about her friends, how they didn't respect her, how nobody respected her."

"She was drunk?"

"Not sure. She wasn't wobbly. She stomped about my boat as if she owned it. Darn her, she came right at me inside the cabin and hugged me!"

Grandma Sophie kissed his cheek. "You're huggable, Gil."

Grandpa's shoulders hunched to his earlobes. "I found her damn wine bottle and handed it to her and told her to get off my boat."

"Did she leave then?"

"No. So I did. I had my keys on me by then. That's the only reason I was there at that hour."

Grandma said, "We'd gone to bed, and he woke up remembering he'd left the keys in the boat."

"So maybe she tripped as she climbed off the boat and her horrible death was an accident. Did you tell Maria any of this?"

Grandpa shook his head. "Well, no. Dillon told you. He told me to zip it. He was correct. I'm no dummy. Right away I got the impression from Maria that the sheriff is sure this lady was murdered."

"That's not what Maria said, Gilpa. Maybe because of the blood they found on your boat they have to speculate and check all angles. That's their job."

My grandfather's clasped hands fell apart. He appeared stunned. "Blood? On my boat? Maria never mentioned blood."

"The sheriff mentioned it to me."

"Those darn fudge divas spilled everything else in *Sophie's Smile*, so I guess they figured blood was okay, too." He shook his head in disgust. "They should be called the deadly fudge divas. Jackie Valentine's death has to be their fault somehow."

Grandpa's face had turned red, always a sign he was about to explode and take things into his own hands. That always turned disastrous.

Grandma patted his arm closest to her. "She must have hit her head. We'll know by tomorrow and that will be the end of the speculation, Gilsen Oosterling."

Grandma always used his full name when she was about to tell Gilpa to stuff it and calm down.

I said, "Grandma's right. The sheriff will get to the bottom of this fast."

Grandpa rose with a grunt. "I need to clean my boat."

He hurried into their front porch, grabbing a jacket, and then he was gone. The outer door banged shut.

Grandma Sophie got up, biting a corner of her lower lip as she gathered their mugs. "Well, isn't this the biggest pickle we've ever been in."

She paused, giving me one of her looks of entreaty, confusion maybe.

"What is it, Grandma?"

"Your grandfather spoke in his sleep last night. About a dress."

"Odd. Maybe he's buying you a dress?"

Grandma winced, her shoulders scrunching up. "He mumbled 'Jackie,' then I think he said 'give her the dress, dammit'."

My breathing had stopped. "And?"

"That was all."

For a moment, we just stared at each other, ingesting the portent of this. "I'm sure Grandpa wasn't arguing with Jackie on the boat about a dress. That would be preposterous."

Grandma finally took a big breath and lowered her shoulders. "Yes, of course. It has to be nothing. He's just tired. And those guests of yours do tend to shop a lot and talk about clothes."

She hurried with the coffee mugs to the kitchen.

After going back to the inn's kitchen, I checked my phone.

Pauline texted me about John coming back to Door County tomorrow, Monday. She wanted to know if I thought it would be okay if she lied and called in sick to her school--so unlike her. I called her and filled her in on what had occurred.

Pauline gasped. "I'll skip Mass. I'll call Laura. We'll come right over. You shouldn't handle this alone."

"I'm okay. I have Dillon with me. He's in the parlor now with his mother and the other women."

"Laura and I will be there to make sure you don't get involved with trying to solve a murder again which can only lead to you irritating the sheriff again or getting yourself hurt or hunted down by a killer. If you were a student in my class, your achievement board on the wall would have several crossbones on it instead of stars."

"That's not funny, Pauline."

"It wasn't meant to be funny. You need me, Ava Mathilde. Dillon is not enough."

I hugged Pauline fiercely when she and Laura showed up a half hour later, coming through the back door to the kitchen loaded down with food.

Dillon and Lucky Harbor were still in the parlor with Cathy Rivers and the other women. The sheriff had left. It was nine-thirty, the usual time for the Sunday breakfast to be served, but I was moving like a robot with its battery almost drained.

Laura, a bakery chef, dove in. She'd brought cinnamon rolls. Pauline set out dishes in the dining room, then came back to help me cut melons into bite-sized pieces.

Pauline had on more new clothes for the Mass she missed, but all of us wore pink fudge-shop aprons that tied around the neck and waist for full frontal protection. Her long, dark hair sat atop her head in a neat, prim bun, so unlike her.

The inn was eerily quiet, except for our chopping atop the wood cutting boards. We stood side by side at the white marble island, our backs to the stove and Laura.

Pauline, to my right, said, "Do you think one of them killed her?" Her voice was low.

"No, Pauline. It was an accident."

"The way they were always fighting makes me wonder."

I paused with the knife in my hand. "I thought you didn't want me involved in this. Your speculating only whets my curiosity and makes me worry for Grandpa."

Laura said, "If she was murdered it has to be by some stranger, some person passing through. Though don't tell Brecht that."

"Why not?" I asked.

Laura walked around to the other side of the island to face us, wiping her hands with a towel after stirring eggs in a bowl for scrambled eggs. Hair clips held back her blond bob. "Because Brecht will go into commando mode, try to call his buddies, then he'll get in our mini-van and cruise the roads nearby looking for the enemy."

Pauline and I stared across at her with concern.

I set down my knife. "His PTSD kicks in." Post-traumatic stress disorder.

Laura nodded.

"Is he getting worse?"

Her eyes shimmered as if she might cry. "I don't know what to do to help him. He's frustrated about not having a real job."

"That's not PTSD," I said, trying to sound hopeful. "Anybody out of a job feels frustrated."

"I suppose. He needs to feel worthy. He needs a meaningful job and we can't find one that doesn't involve pressure or too much stress. Even small deadlines or being told he has to be somewhere by a certain time can frustrate him."

Pauline said, "Something will come along."

"I hope so. It was a long winter, but luckily twin babies are a lot of work and they kept him busy. But he talks about moving."

"No," Pauline and I chorused.

I added, "Our little namesakes simply cannot move away from us. Nothing doing. Clara Ava and Spencer Paul stay."

"I don't want to move. The quiet here in Door County and the parks and being in nature are exactly what the doctor ordered for Brecht. But he's used to hard physical labor and creating plans of action that mean something."

"Planning which diapers to use doesn't quite fill the bill," I mused.

"Not at all."

Pauline said, "He wants to be a good man for his family. For you. He loves you very much, Laura."

She nodded, a tear slipping out. She ducked back to the stove and began scrambling eggs in a cast iron skillet.

Pauline and I finished chopping the melons. Their fresh aroma swirled into the air. As we finished putting the colorful wedges in china bowls, Pauline said, "Were there any witnesses to Gil getting off that boat and leaving her there alive?"

We took the bowls into the dining room. I lowered my voice. "You'd think some or all of those other divas witnessed something?"

"Yes."

"But they don't seem to know what happened. Grandma knows when he got up to go get his keys, so we know the time frame."

As we re-entered the kitchen, Laura turned from the stove. "Eleven o'clock or so is an early time on a Saturday night for young people and anybody without kids. There had to be people on Main Street. Doesn't Erik stay open until bar time?"

Bar time was two o'clock in the morning. "That's brilliant, Laura. Main Street is usually rolled up by midnight at this time of year, but if anybody might know something it'd be Erik at the Troubled Trout."

"The bar is down at the other end of the harbor. He may have seen the lights on Gil's boat and paid attention to people wandering down that way."

I gave her a big hug. "I'll go over there when he opens for lunch." I wasn't about to text or call him now. He'd still be sleeping after closing up the bar and restaurant at the wee hours of the morning.

We were about to finish setting out breakfast when Pepper wandered into the kitchen. Lucky Harbor stuck by her side, watching her expectantly.

Pepper had a tissue in one hand. "Dillon said to bring his dog in here for you gals to keep. He won't leave me alone."

"I'm sorry, Pepper."

"I like him, but you understand I am not in the mood at the moment."

"Of course." I addressed the spaniel. "Lucky Harbor, if you want fudge, stay here."

He responded to the code word "fudge" with a doggie smile. I tossed a handful of goldfish-shaped crackers on the floor near the back door. He leaped on them. I'd mop the floor later.

Zadie came in then. "Mom, are you okay? You left the parlor in a hurry."

"Yes, honey, I'm fine. For goodness sake." The words came out with a sharp edge. "Please stop asking if I'm okay. My friend just died." Pepper left, leaving her daughter behind looking bewildered.

To my chagrin, Lucky Harbor galloped after Pepper before I could catch him.

Zadie winced. "She's in shock."

"We all are," I said. "Do you remember anything about last night that seems odd? Such as seeing anybody weird on Main Street?"

"Weird? When? What do you mean?" Zadie plucked a melon wedge I'd left on the wood cutting board. The model and owner of her own skincare and makeup shop in Milwaukee had changed into designer sports gear. She appeared ready for a photo shoot.

Her toned body was a perfect replica of her petite mother's physique. Zadie's long blond hair swished about with her every move, as if she were in a perpetual shampoo commercial.

I asked, "Did you see anybody head toward the harbor after you all came out of the Troubled Trout?"

"No."

"Was Jackie drunk?"

Zadie shrugged. "Everybody was drinking, but I didn't count drinks. Yola and I don't pay much attention to my mother's friends. I'm assuming Jackie was drunk if she ended up in the water."

As I turned back to the refrigerator to pull out the orange juice and milk, I asked, "She said she was going down to the boat, and you actually saw her going there alone? Nobody following her?"

"I didn't look. She just walked away while we came inside. Yola and I headed upstairs. Everybody was going to bed."

"You heard her come in later?"

"No. I must have gone to sleep." She shuffled back from the marble-topped island. "I better go be with Mom."

After she left the kitchen, I exchanged a look with Pauline and Laura.

Pauline asked, "What's wrong?"

"What she said doesn't make sense. She and Yola have always stayed out late every night. And they always split up from the older women."

"Last night was their last night here. Maybe they felt obligated because Zadie's mother was among the group."

"Oh, they had dinner with them and came back here, but then they snuck out again as they usually do."

"So she's lying?" Pauline asked.

"No. She left before I could ask the right questions."

My phone buzzed. I pulled it out of my jean's pocket, then groaned. "It's Mercy Fogg."

Laura said, "What does she want on a Sunday morning?"

Rolling my eyes, I answered the phone. "Hi, Mercy. The women aren't going anywhere this morning."

"I didn't call to scare up business. I'm standing here with your grandpa outside your fudge shop. He told me to call you because he's been arrested."

Chapter 8

I trotted down the hill from the inn for the second time that Sunday morning. With purse over her shoulder, Pauline matched my long-legged stride.

Grandpa's harsh voice mingled with that of the sheriff's as we rounded the corner of the bait-and-fudge shop. Spring sunshine sparkled off the water in the harbor, almost blinding us. I regretted not donning sunglasses. Pauline dug hers out from her purse.

The sheriff stood blocking the pier next to *Sophie's Smile*. Grandpa was in Jordy's face with a string of words that curdled the air. I didn't see any handcuffs.

Mercy was on her phone, pacing back and forth a few feet behind Grandpa. When she saw me an embarrassed look washed over her face and she shoved the phone in a pocket.

I growled out the side of my mouth to Pauline, "Who could she possibly be calling about this?"

"Let's ask."

"After we rescue Gilpa." I hustled to Grandpa. "What's going on?"

"The sheriff refuses to let me onto my own boat."

Despite Grandma's prediction, it wasn't wrapped in yellow tape. Yet. Two seagulls landed on the wood pier beyond the sheriff and began their lurching gait to hustle handouts. Another seagull swooped in but landed atop the bridge on the boat.

"Maybe he hasn't finished checking it for evidence," I said, imploring the sheriff, who stood with arms crossed.

Jordy's aviator sunglasses reflected us standing there, including Pauline at my side and Mercy hovering behind us.

"Jordy, he's not under arrest, right?"

"I've threatened."

Mercy said, "Good thing I was here to call you or he'd be in the back of that squad car by now."

"Thanks, Mercy," I said, not bothering to turn to her. I focused on my grandfather. "Gilpa, this is a crime scene. You have to stay away."

"I need to get on *Sophie's Smile*." His dark eyes flickered in agitation.

The sheriff said, "Nobody gets on the boat. I was about to bring yellow tape across this pier and the slip around the boat, but Gil seems to disagree with my actions. If he continues to disagree I'll need to arrest him for obstructing."

"Grandpa, he's just doing his job. You probably won't have any business today anyway."

Grandpa growled at me, combing his wild silver hair with a hand and blinking rapidly, as if he were a lighthouse keeper signaling with the light in Morse code. "Now is when I like to do all those extra things on the boat. Get it spiffy for the season."

He'd been getting it spiffy every day, so his silly words made me suspicious. What was he hiding on the boat?

Grandpa edged in front of me, with his back to the sheriff, and he kept blinking.

I accepted the signal with return blinks, then stepped around my grandfather to talk with Jordy. He had six inches on me, so I was looking up into those aviators and his pursed lips.

"Jordy, do you really need a second look? Poor Jackie came out here to retrieve her wine bottle last night and fell in. Is there any real reason for you to hold off on allowing my grandfather to get his boat ready for business?"

Jordy licked his lips, as if I were carrion and he a hungry wolf. "Nobody gets on this boat until after the autopsy. Please take your grandfather and move on, Ava."

He dug into a pocket of his leather jacket and pulled out a roll of yellow crime scene tape. All I could see was myself in his aviator's, but I imagined his brown eyes holding steady on me, which was as effective as holding his weapon on me. I'd had enough dealings with Jordy in the past to know when to back down.

I said in an even voice, "There are seagulls on the boat walking around and picking at things. Are you going to arrest them, too?"

Jordy pointed behind me. "Go. Before I arrest you, too."

"How soon will we know results from the autopsy?"

"I hope tomorrow. We don't have other cases at the morgue at the moment. As soon as the doc calls me, I'll call you."

That was fair. I flashed a bright smile to my grandfather. "We need to leave the sheriff alone. And, Gilpa, don't you and

Grandma need to head to church? If you hurry, you can make the eleven o'clock mass."

"Hmmph," he said.

Pauline and I escorted Grandpa into the bait-and-fudge shop. Mercy followed, unfortunately. Once inside, I walked with Grandpa toward the back door alone.

Once we were out of earshot of the front area, I said, "What was the blinking about? Why do you need to get on your boat so desperately?"

Grandpa ran a hand over his face, wincing. "They're going to find my blood on it with that woman's."

I rocked on my feet. "Your blood? With her blood? Gilpa, what happened?"

"Oh, Ava honey, this isn't good. I'm so sorry. Look here." He showed me the palm of his right hand. A scratch crossed his lifelines. "I told you she was hugging me and well, you know."

"She was trying to kiss you?"

He nodded with a beet-red face.

"So you had to fight her off? She scratched you in the hand?"

"It wasn't that I had to fight her off. It was more that I had to stop her from harming herself. I didn't want to say all this in the house with Sophie there, but that Jackie woman was so upset that she picked up a knife in the galley. That scared me. I asked her for the knife, but she refused, said she had an idea how to use it."

"She was mad at her husband, my guests said."

Gilpa leaned against the back door, looking through the glass into the back yard and across to his home. Grandma Sophie was outside and dressed for church, talking with a neighbor.

Grandpa said, "I had no idea what was going on. I just knew I had to take the knife from her. I got nicked in the hand, but so did she."

A bad feeling wriggled up my spine. "You were trying to get back on the boat to clean up the blood, weren't you? Before the sheriff found it inside. He already found blood on the outside. Some of that could be yours, too, right?"

Grandpa nodded. "They're going to find that cut on her hand. Then come looking for me. Ava, you know I love you. I want you to be proud of your gramps, but nothing I do turns out right."

"Don't say that--"

He bolted out the door then strutted across the lawn toward Duck Marsh Street.

I steeled myself to return to the front of the shop where Mercy was perusing the glass case. Pauline was sitting on Grandpa's stool, hugging her purse and looking lost.

Mercy mused, "Not much for fudge at the moment."

"This is not the tourist season, but I'm about to get busy and stir up new batches of Fairy Tale Fudge. My guests are going to need a bit of magic after the death of their friend."

Pauline slid off the stool. "I'll help."

"Thanks, Pauline." I grabbed a couple of aprons from the hook behind the register and tossed her one, hoping Mercy would leave.

She said, "Can I help?"

I gave her a cross-eyed look, to which she responded, "Hey, I'm sad, too, about Mrs. Valentine. I made more money in the past four or so days than I did in the past two months. I'm going to miss those ladies. Jackie was the biggest tipper of them all, too. She liked how I drove. Fast."

Somehow her appreciation of Jackie softened my heart a little, though I had to be wary with Mercy.

"I guess you could help us haul ingredients from the kitchen out to the copper kettles," I said, though Pauline rolled her eyes.

I'd never allowed Mercy into the back area before, so it felt odd seeing her stout frame taking up a lot of room in the small kitchen. I loaded her arms with cream and sticks of butter.

Once she left the room, Pauline hissed at me, "She's trying to get information out of you. Probably selling it to online news sources."

I hefted kilo bars of Belgian dark chocolate from the cupboards into Pauline's arms. "I don't think so. Mercy's lonely. She's got nobody but her dad and he resides in a nursing home."

"She has a dog. Tell her to go home."

"She saved John last fall when he got knocked out and suffered amnesia. She took him in not even knowing who he was."

"Yeewww. Don't remind me. She had him sleeping in her bed."

"Mercy's complicated. If she's up to something, then all the better to keep her close."

"She's driving that yellow bus illegally. The school district did not hire her. She stole that bus and is running on the school district's gas instead of her own car."

"So now we have stuff to hold over on her."

"You're brilliant."

"I know."

Pauline headed out of the kitchen.

We didn't get to find out much from Mercy because Cody and his girlfriend Bethany showed up, loaded with laptops and books in their backpacks.

"Hey, Miss Oosterling," Cody called out as the cowbell clanged on the closing door. "Sorry to hear what happened. Bethany and I came over to watch the shop. I know you'll want to be up at the inn for the day."

Not really. Making fudge was my escape. The physical activity of creating something sweet and sublime had always helped me not only think, but it soothed my soul. But the two first-year college students appeared so eager to help me that I couldn't deny their kind gesture.

"Thanks. You two are lifesavers."

Mercy came over after distributing her load near the copper kettles. "I'll be on my way then. My bitch was off her feed this morning, so I better head on home."

After Bethany winced, I informed the timid nineteen-year-old, "She means her female dog."

Mercy was out the door with a clang. The bus engine roared.

Bethany set out her computer on Grandpa's register counter.

Cody hopped over to inspect the copper kettles and the supplies. "Is it okay if I teach Bethany how to make Rapunzel Raspberry Rapture Fudge?"

"Sure. I believe we still have raspberry jam in the cupboard."

"And can I make some of the guy stuff? The Worms-in-Dirt Fudge? I want to take that to my paramedics class."

"Sure." He loved the manly fudge made with Oreo crumbs for dirt and gummy worms poked into the top of the fudge for effect.

"And can Bethany and I dream up a new fairy tale flavor?"

"Sure." Their enthusiasm and kindness warmed me. "I need a new flavor for the festival next weekend."

Pauline said, "Just don't do anything with the Three Pigs and bacon, please."

Cody hooted. Bethany laughed, too. We left the shop at around ten-thirty.

Outside, as we walked across the flattened grass still brown mostly from its winter hibernation, I recounted Grandpa's information to Pauline.

She muttered, "What're you going to do?"

"There's nothing I can do but wait. Dad's on his way."

We passed my old cabin and hit Duck Marsh Street, where I looked across the way to my grandparents' home. Their vehicle was still there.

Pauline asked, "Did your grandpa tell your grandma about the knife and blood on the boat?"

"I know him well enough to know the answer. No, he didn't."

"You have to make sure Sophie knows about that stuff before the sheriff calls on them again. Shouldn't she know everything?"

"We have to give Grandpa time to tell Grandma."

"Tattling is bad for kindergarten kids, but not us, Ava."

Unease caused me to chuckle at that. I was thinking about the women panicking yesterday about their secret.

Pauline and I made the turn onto Main Street and mounted the steep grade up the hill to the inn.

When we came up the front steps of the verandah, Kim was outside smoking a cigarette, of all things. "Don't you think this calls for a smoke?" she said, her tone raw.

I must have appeared judgmental. "It's just that you're all so health-conscious."

"Screw it," she said. "Jackie's not here anymore. We can do what we want. I need a smoke to cope, okay?"

I reached for the door handle. "Her sudden death is hard on everybody. I'm so sorry. I understand."

"No, you don't. Do you know they all think I'm a loser?"

My hand stayed on the door handle. "I doubt that."

"I bet you think that. I broke your lamp." She puffed again on the cigarette and ran a hand through her short-cropped hair.

"It's just a lamp."

"I looked around on the internet. It's an antique. It cost a lot."

"It came with the place. I didn't have to pay for it directly."

"Oh." She puffed on the cigarette again. "You're more honest than Jackie or any of them would be about such a thing."

"Even Cathy?"

She chortled, surprising me. "Cathy is the innocent one of our group. Every group needs one."

"Why do you say that?"

She shrugged, then walked away from us to blow smoke into the air.

Pauline and I turned our attention to going inside. It took extra effort again to pull open the jimmied door. I made a mental note to ask Dillon to fix it.

Once inside, the place appeared empty. Nobody sat or exercised in the parlor as usual. The dining room was devoid of people or plates. We found Dillon in the kitchen with Laura. She was drying the china plates while Dillon was placing them in the cupboards.

Dillon looked good enough to eat. He gifted me with his quirky smile. I went into his arms for a much-needed hug.

He said, "You never do anything without drama, do you, Ava Mathilde?"

I sighed against his shoulder. "I guess we were made for each other."

Pauline sighed from the other side of the marble island. "Maybe we could have a double wedding?"

"Whoa," Dillon said, chuckling. "Have you heard from Mr. Video? Did he finally get down on one knee?"

"No, but John is coming back tomorrow and his message was very mysterious. And you should see the house he has picked out for us."

Something odd registered in Dillon's eyes. He grabbed a sweatshirt slung over the back of a chair and pulled it over his head. "Take it slow, Paulie girl. Ava and I are taking things slow this time around and it's mighty fun courting." He doffed a Green Bay Packer cap. "Now I gotta go drag my dog away from Pepper Elliott and get him outside for his hunter exercise. She must be slippin' him extra treats."

He dropped a quick kiss on my lips before heading through the dining room to retrieve his dog, who had to be upstairs somewhere.

After he left, Laura turned to Pauline and me. "The breakfast was horrible." She slumped back against the counter, a hand running through her blond bob.

"What happened?" I asked, taking over the stool Dillon had vacated. The seat's warmth felt good.

"Your guests kept talking about who was to blame for Jackie's death. Eliza even said young Yola was to blame, and that made her friend Zadie mad at Eliza."

"Why would they want to blame Yola Wooten?"

Laura shrugged. "One of them said Yola wanted Jackie Valentine to help her make connections in Chicago for her garden center in Green Bay."

"Yeah, I knew about that. But how could that harm Jackie?"

"Eliza Stefansson contended Yola was pressuring Jackie too much. Eliza accused Yola of making trips to Chicago with Zadie to visit Jackie and her husband to ask for assistance."

I popped to attention. "Did anybody hear from her husband yet?"

Laura reached for a crumpled dishtowel on the counter and folded it. "I believe Cathy said she'd heard he'd be here by early afternoon. They seem to have been in touch a few times this morning."

I couldn't imagine driving almost four hours knowing you were coming to collect your dead wife's body.

"So," I asked, getting up to pour myself coffee, "did the ladies believe the pressure caused her to commit suicide? Jackie didn't seem like someone who'd crumble under pressure. And I don't understand why they were arguing again."

Laura came over to the island and sat. "Those things were said when Cathy had left the dining room on her phone with Victor. When she came back, the women hushed a little. I was here in the kitchen, but I heard somebody go 'shhh' and then Pepper said in a low voice, 'We have to keep Cathy from knowing. We've kept the secret for almost thirty-five years already.'"

I almost dropped my coffee cup.

Pauline leaned over the top of her purse sitting in front of her on the island. "I knew it! I told Ava they had some big secret when they first got here."

"Actually, I suspected it. You just told me about your kindergarten kids not being able to keep secrets." I eased onto the stool on the island's end.

Laura said, "Whatever the secret is, it sounded serious and I don't think these women like the secret."

"So it has to be a big one," I said, "if they've kept it that long."

Pauline took a notepad and pen from her purse and handed them to me. "I can see you can't resist playing detective. You want to write all this down."

I snatched the implements. "They had to be college freshman or sophomores. I wonder what they did? What was the worst thing we did?"

Pauline said, "We papered the trees around the chancellor's house on Halloween. And it was also your idea to let the cows loose from the dairy science department barn. They ended up on State Street in Madison the next morning."

Laura laughed. "You got caught?"

"No," I said, giggling. "Nobody ever found out."

Laura said, "You're both laughing, but the women weren't laughing earlier. I could tell they were panicking, as if Jackie's death was tipping the balance and they were afraid somebody would find out what they'd done. They were blaming Yola for bugging Jackie. Do you think Yola knows about their past? And if she does, her friend Zadie must know. You don't think there's something odd about all this? I might be reading more into it than I need to, but I have a husband who went on secret missions in bad places and dealt with conspiracies. Maybe you haven't noticed, Ava, but these women are acting like a secret army in the way they control what they say and do."

That sober thought quieted us.

Thumping the pen on the notepad, I said, "Maybe we're imagining things. They're grieving. They are a bit wacko, but I thought it was because of menopause. My mother's not handling it so well herself."

"And thus the vacuuming she does all the time," Pauline added.

My mother found vacuuming as soothing as I found fudge-making. "Vacuuming is harmless. Pepper had a gun, and Jackie was so mad she wielded a knife, endangering my grandfather."

Pauline said, "So this is serious."

I kept feeling sorry for Dillon's mother. She'd never be involved with danger. She was fragile. "It's none of our business what their secret is."

Pauline gave me a cross-eyed look. "Since when? Aren't you intrigued?"

"Of course. But somebody died, and my grandfather's in the thick of it. If I ask too many questions, all it will do is make it look like I'm trying to protect Gilpa--as if he's guilty. And if he's guilty of something, it would be assumed a murder. It was an accident. Grandpa tried to save Jackie Valentine from herself. Repeat after me. It was an accident."

Laura and Pauline bit their lips.

I deflated like a balloon. I had to act. "Come on. We have an important errand."

"No," Pauline whined, hugging her purse. "Your ideas always get me into trouble."

I hopped off my stool and grabbed her hand. "Since when have I ever got us into trouble?"

Their laughter was loud.

Chapter 9

rik Gustafson always opened for lunch on Sunday at eleven o'clock. I wanted to know what he'd overheard last night when the women came for dinner. Pauline and Laura agreed to tag along with me.

To our chagrin, Mercy Fogg sat atop a barstool.

I had no choice but to greet the nosy woman. "Hello, Mercy. I take it your dog checked out okay?"

"No. I'll have to take her into the vet tomorrow."

"Sorry to hear that." I was genuinely sorry for her dog. If anything happened to Lucky Harbor I would fall to pieces. He wasn't my dog, but he'd brought Dillon and me back together and the dog loved the word "fudge."

Erik strolled in from the back. "Hey, Ava. Ladies."

Mercy chortled. "I noticed he called only Laura and Pauline 'ladies'."

"That's not funny," I said, though it was sort of. Old-style kidding worked around here.

Erik handed Mercy what appeared to be her credit card. She said, "Thanks. Glad you found it."

"You're welcome," Erik said.

Erik, who'd just turned twenty, was tall and had neat-clipped brown hair that gave him an air of boyish innocence. He had broad shoulders and had played on the high school football team, a guy much like Jordy Tollefson but younger. In the tourist season, Erik attracted his share of repeat business in the restaurant area from the young set.

Mercy gave him a wave as she slid off her stool. She nodded to me. "Your grandpa get off to church okay?"

"I assume so. Grandma never lets him miss."

"He's such a funny guy. I told Erik about Gil trying to get on that boat. How's Dillon feel about a bloody fight on it? Was he there, too, when the woman got dumped in the drink? Well, enjoy your lunch."

She left just in time--before my hands might have encircled her throat.

We three friends took a stool and asked for colas.

I told Erik, "I guess Mercy told you about Jackie Valentine's death."

"Yeah," he said, placing bar napkins in front of each of us before setting the beverages in place. "That's too bad about Mrs. Valentine. Do they know yet who did it?"

Pauline piped in, "It wasn't Dillon Rivers or Gil Oosterling. Maybe it was Mercy Fogg!"

I said, "We're pretty sure it was an accident."

Erik said, "Mercy said your grandfather is a prime suspect, but you know I don't believe her crap."

"You can't blame her. She's probably going to go head to head with you next spring. That is, if my grandma doesn't enter the race."

"Sophie's running for office?"

"She's mentioned it, but she's busy with the Main Street flower committee at the moment. Lots of arguing over how many marigolds to plant versus geraniums next to the sidewalks in the terraces. And don't even mention the hanging planters for Main Street's lamp posts."

Erik nodded. "Flowers are what we're famous for in the summer in Door County. That and parks and lighthouses and boating and fishing and golfing and art fairs and summer theater in the park and Cinderella Pink Fairy Tale Fudge." He took a big breath.

We laughed.

I asked, "Do you remember anything odd about the women last night? The fudge divas were here for dinner."

"They were nice. They laughed a lot. I only had a few other customers at the same time, so they got their food fast and they liked that."

"You were their waiter?"

"Oh, yeah. I don't hire extra help until May. It was just me and Piers. He stayed in the kitchen. I ran all the food. Serving five women isn't a big deal."

"Only five?" I sipped my cola.

"Yeah. Yola and Zadie didn't come in until just before the women were done. They sat right here on the corner of the bar. They passed Mercy on her way out."

Pauline said, "So they didn't eat anything? Your prime rib and cheesy fish balls are great here."

Erik leaned stiff-armed against the bar. "Yola and Zadie came earlier and got take-out. They came in then about the time Mercy did. They bought her a beer."

"So Mercy was here the whole time the women were eating? A couple of hours?"

He nodded. "She ate her prime rib at the bar. After the women left, she followed them out. It wasn't a few minutes later Zadie and Yola trotted in with her credit card. They said she dropped it just outside the door."

"That's when they all came home." Nothing seemed amiss, though it must have bugged Mercy to lose her credit card. She was all about money right down to the value of a penny. It struck me she was similar to the fudge divas with their money obsessions, only different.

Pauline let Erik refill her glass. "The women are sort of secretive, and have a lot of funny stories. Did you overhear anything odd or interesting last night?"

Erik shook his head as he set down her refilled glass. "Jackie had the fish balls and made a big fuss about her husband's you-know-whats. It wasn't the kind of joke we men stick around to listen to."

I grimaced on his behalf. "My grandpa said she was upset about something but not coherent evidently."

Erik nodded. "Mercy said Jackie was on Gil's boat last night after they left here."

Pauline said, "To get a bottle of wine she'd left behind after a happy hour excursion."

Laura spoke up from the other side of Pauline. "Jackie Valentine was upset about her husband, though does anybody know for a fact that's the man whose precious jewels she wanted?"

Erik held up his hands. "Ladies, this is beyond my scope. Bartenders don't get involved with spreading gossip."

I speared him with a look.

"All right," he said, "When Eliza Stefansson and Cathy Rivers passed by the bar on their way to the ladies' room, Eliza told Cathy that Jackie had just told her she was going to file for divorce, that she'd learned her husband had drained their bank accounts."

"Wow." A chill rattled through me. "No wonder Jackie didn't want to invest in Kim's White Glove Cleaning."

Laura piped up. "When did she learn that? It must have been before she came here. It's why she was so irritating from Day One, don't you think?"

Laura's fingers tapped the bar as she thought. "The fudge divas have been at your inn since Wednesday jabbering away about their money. Jackie refused to invest in the cleaning business all along. She knew all along about her money problems but why did she wait until last night to tell Eliza about it all?"

Pauline said, "What if Eliza murdered Jackie?"

"But why?" I asked, stunned at their calculations.

Pauline sipped her drink. "Jackie kept her money problems a secret from everybody. Yet she told Eliza about filing for divorce last night. Eliza lost her husband not long ago, and she's in big trouble and needs money. Eliza's known Jackie and her husband a long time. There could be something going on behind the scenes with Eliza and Victor."

My stomach grumbled. I frowned at my BFF. "You say that with such finality."

"Because I made it all up." Pauline shrugged. "Remember the way my students make up stories? Everything the women talked about this past week could be made up. You and I used to do that in college all the time. We pretended we were people we weren't." She got off her stool. "Only thing was, back then, just like now, you started believing some of that stuff. It's how you ended up eloping. You've always believed in fairy tales."

I wasn't offended. "Coming from the woman who believes she'll live in a mansion soon?"

"Hah." She slung her purse over her shoulder. "Come on, Laura. Let me take you home."

Pauline stomped out of the Troubled Trout.

Laura shrugged. "She's my ride. See ya later, Ava."

"Thanks, Laura. Don't worry about it. Pauline's troubled about John and his actions or lack thereof, as usual."

Sighing, I got up to go.

Erik said, "I'll never understand women. Pauline's your best friend, right?"

"Best Friend Forever. Yeah."

"But you just had a fight?"

"No. That wasn't a fight. That was an agreement. She's always right about me. I'm right about her, too."

"You know what I think?"

"About Pauline and me?"

"No, about Mercy Fogg."

"What?" I was back to being curious.

"She might know something about the murder. If it's a murder. I was here alone around midnight when Mercy came back in."

"Looking for her credit card."

"No. You saw her earlier. She just picked that up. No, last night she left when Yola and Zadie came in, but it was after midnight or so and all the women had left when Mercy blew back in the door huffing and puffing, like she'd been running. She was glancing through the windows as if watching for somebody. She didn't wait long before she took off."

My blood was boiling. "Darn her. She knows something important. She loves messing with me."

"Why is that?"

"Erik, you have a lot to learn about women and their relationships."

"But why does she mess with you?"

"Because she likes me and she wants to have a reason to visit with me again. She needs juicy gossip to tell me. No woman worth her salt comes for a visit without gossip to share with another woman."

Erik shook his head, blinking in confusion again.

Since it was around noon, I took off for the inn. I was eager to eavesdrop on the women.

Before going to the inn I took a detour to the fudge shop. Grandpa's boat bobbed on the shallow harbor water. With the yellow tape wound from post to post on the pier in front of it, the boat appeared lonely, shunned.

I wondered what the sheriff had found out this morning.

Cody was loafing a batch of dark Belgian chocolate fudge on the marble table near the front window. The sugary vanilla and chocolate aromas in the shop made my mouth water and relaxed me.

Bethany was taking care of a mother and young daughter of maybe eight years old. They were stocking up on pink prize gifts for her birthday party that afternoon. Several Cinderella Pink coin purses sat on the register counter. Bethany promised the mother and daughter she'd deliver Cinderella Pink Fudge as soon as the sparkly new batch of cherry-vanilla had set up.

With the shop operating in its fairy tale bliss, I hiked up the hill to the Blue Heron Inn. It was after lunch time and I felt guilty for being late.

Cathy met me at the front door, stopping in the double-entry area. She wore an expensive, powder blue designer angora sweater that matched the color of the inn. Black denim skinny jeans and ankle-length leather boots made me jealous.

The white stripe in her hair above her forehead moved as she raised her eyebrows. She grabbed my arms. "I need to tell you something. Quick. While they're all still upstairs."

"I just heard about Jackie wanting a divorce and Victor's financial trouble."

She dropped her hold on me. "Eliza said those things, but I've known Jackie and Victor for years. I doubt Victor's in financial trouble. I would have heard about that. Eliza said those things to me because she was trying to convince me to intercede with Jackie and Victor so he'd help her with the farm implement dealership. But now Jackie is dead. It's all moot. What I wanted to tell you is that I saw Kim snooping through Jackie's room. I had cracked my door, about to come out of my room when I saw her slip inside Jackie's room and shut the door quietly behind her."

"Is she in there now?"

"I think so."

"Cathy, why didn't you knock on the door and ask her what she was doing?"

"And embarrass her? What kind of friend would do that?" Cathy stepped back and into the foyer, pausing under the lit chandelier. Its sparkle warred with the bleak and strange goings-on.

"What should I do, Cathy?"

"None of the rest of us can confront her. I was hoping you could before Victor showed up."

I yearned to return to the fudge shop and pretend I had never bought this inn. An inn was a great place if you didn't have guests. "Maybe she's experiencing a sadness that is profound and she needs to touch Jackie's things as a reminder of her."

"You're a kind person, but she was sneaking in and didn't leave the door open."

"It's past noon. Why don't I make sandwiches and a salad for everybody?"

Cathy sighed. She led the way through the dining room. "Victor loves Door County cherries. Do you have cherries?"

I trailed her like a duckling after the mother duck, curious now. "This is Door County, Cathy. The biggest producer of cherries in the country. My cupboards are filled with jars of cherries."

"I haven't made bread in ages and I need something to do besides obsess over Kim upstairs."

"Cathy, are you scared of her?"

She marched into the kitchen with a hand waving off my question. "Don't be silly. Forget what I said about Kim. You must be right. She's grieving. Nothing wrong with visiting Jackie's room. Let's make fresh bread with cherries in it."

I turned on the oven. "How about a loaf of cheesy cherry bread?"

"I'm drooling already." Cathy whipped on a pink apron over her angora sweater.

Cathy was acting oddly, rare for her. In the past she'd been the cool, calm one in Dillon's family. She was making a racket retrieving baking pans--another sign that she was upset.

"Cathy, is there anything you want to tell me about Dillon? And the boat?"

She gasped, hugging a bread pan. "He lives right there in your old cabin. He had to witness something, hear something what with all the noise those women made, and your grandfather tromping to his boat, yet my son hasn't said a thing." She took a deep breath. "He's protecting us, isn't he?"

I hadn't thought about this angle. Her words gave me pause.

Several loaves of bread sat on cooling racks on the kitchen island by the time Victor Valentine arrived at around two o'clock.

Victor was older than I expected, maybe in his early sixties, but was breathtakingly handsome with thick, wavy white hair groomed to perfection above his collar. His tan looked real. He had a physique that said many hours were spent in sports or exercising. A tan sport jacket over a black cashmere turtleneck and tan pants and light brown shoes all seemed Italian perfection. He didn't appear to be on the verge of financial difficulty, though keeping up appearances was likely important.

The women greeted Victor in the parlor with hugs, tears, and condolences. Zadie and Yola, perhaps because of being younger and not of the circle of older friends, stood apart from the group, but Zadie offered to bring in his suitcase.

"Thank you, Zadie, but, no," Victor said, swallowing back his emotions. He sat down on one of the parlor sofas.

The women clustered in other seats and in the sofa across from him, though Zadie and Yola settled near Victor on the floor rug. He peered down at Zadie. "I found a condo not far from here where I'll stay tonight."

"Okay," Zadie said. "If you need help collecting Jackie's things, Yola and I can help. I realize that might be painful for you."

Pepper, swathed in her signature pink and with Dillon's dog at her feet, offered, "Maybe it'd be best to let Victor have some space before we rush to pack up Jackie's things."

"Of course, Mom."

I sat in a chair near the foyer where the sheriff had stood that morning. Victor turned his attention to me. "Jackie had texted and called me several times over the past few days to express what a wonderful experience this was in Fishers' Harbor and at the Blue Heron Inn. Thank you."

Startled by the compliment, I fumbled and said, "She loved fudge."

The women appeared relieved to have something innocuous to talk about. They chattered away, telling Victor about all the Door County wines they and Jackie had tasted and the different flavors in the Fairy Tale fudge line that they'd tried, plus several others I'd made.

Victor asked, "What was her favorite flavor of fudge?"

I didn't hesitate. "With her long red hair, of course it was Red Riding Hood Fairy Tale Fudge. I'll stir up a batch in her honor today, Victor."

I explained to him the fudge ingredients included those for red velvet cake.

The talk of food carried us naturally into the kitchen where everybody made their own sandwiches with the fresh, warm cherry-and-cheese bread. Zadie and Yola stuck around to swoon over it, too.

We ate in the dining room with my finest elegant antique table settings. The women told more tales about their Door County travels, about the ferry ride in the freezing wind to Washington

Island where they visited the lavender farm's shop and a bitters distillery.

Victor said, "One of the ingredients of Wisconsin's best cocktail--the brandy old fashioned. Jackie and I were in Vegas once and I asked for the drink, and the bartender looked back at me and said, 'You're from Wisconsin.' I told him Illinois but we flatlanders drive north to Wisconsin just for the booze."

We laughed. We talked about how it was true that Wisconsin not only hoisted its share of great Belgian and German beers, but its cocktails focused on brandy. Recently, distilleries began making other spirits. Door County's wheat from Washington Island was a major ingredient of vodkas made in Wisconsin.

The discussion felt like we were toasting to Jackie's memory.

For dessert I served chocolate cupcakes with cherry frosting.

Victor asked, "No fudge?"

"I'm afraid I've run out of fudge but my helpers down at the fudge shop have been whipping up new batches. I'll be sure we have Red Riding Hood Fairy Tale Fudge for our afternoon tea time. I hope you'll join us."

Victor nodded. "I'd like that. I'd like to take a stroll around town before tomorrow, too."

Kim said, "I'd be happy to give you a tour. I'm already packed."

"I can give him the tour." Eliza gentled the dainty cup in her hand into its saucer. "I've decided to stay longer, since I don't live that far away."

She looked at me, asking a silent question.

Flustered and embarrassed because I hadn't offered already, I said, "Of course all of you can stay overnight. Free of charge.

This is a trying time for all of you. You were all such good friends of Jackie's."

Victor looked into his cup. "I was informed that the autopsy should be complete tomorrow. I'll be taking Jackie home then." He cleared his throat, eyes downcast.

A moment of silence followed. All of us stared into our cups or plates.

Eliza said, "Jackie and I were particularly close lately."

I exchanged a look with Cathy.

Kim said, "Because you two both refused to believe in my expansion of White Glove Cleaning."

Nobody gasped. Silence sufficed.

Eliza clung to her china cup. She said to Victor, "I'd love to escort you to her favorite places along Main Street, Victor."

Cathy said, "Why don't I do that? I know Fishers' Harbor very well."

Victor said, "You and Jackie were always a force together on the foundation board."

Zadie raised her hand, a gesture left over from college classrooms probably. She said to Victor, "Yola and I can escort you so that you ladies can be together at this time."

Victor nodded yet again. "You're all so kind."

Victor went off with Zadie and Yola. After a couple of hours, I found the three of them in the parlor chatting with the other women, except for Pepper. She wasn't feeling well and stayed upstairs in her room.

The group bided their time with walks, reading, and chatting.

I went to the shop that afternoon where I made Red Riding Hood Fudge. As I loafed it on the table with the wood paddles, working the sugar crystals until the red fudge began to set up properly, I wondered why Kim Olkowski would choose to chide Eliza in front of Jackie's husband about refusing to invest in that silly cleaning company. It was just as Pauline had said--they were like kindergartners who never forgot a slight. Investing in a cleaning service probably wasn't the issue among them at all. So what was the issue? Victor had said nothing about a divorce or business problems, though he probably wouldn't admit to those things now.

The questions lurked as I served the fresh fudge in the inn.

Then Victor went back to his condo early.

Zadie and Yola went out as usual, while Jackie's friends chatted and toasted Jackie before retiring.

A morbid quiet pervaded the inn on Monday morning.

Nobody exercised, argued, laughed, or teased as usual.

I set out brunch omelets, French toast, and fruit, along with pieces of sparkly Cinderella Pink Fairy Tale Fudge that Cody and Bethany had made for me.

Early afternoon on Monday, Jordy Tollefson called while I cleaned the copper kettles to get ready for new batches of sweet candy. The effect of Jordy's words made me drop my phone into a copper kettle. I must have screamed.

Grandpa came barreling in from the back. "What in tarnations is wrong, Ava? You sick?"

I plucked my phone out of the empty kettle then put it on speaker.

"I wanted you to know first," Jordy said. "The water in her lungs didn't come from the lake. She was drowned somewhere else, then put into the lake. I'd like to know if you or your grandfather know more than you're telling me."

Chapter 10

I hung up on Jordy.

Unnerved, confused, I hiked up the hill bearing fudge and the bad news about Jackie for the ladies. The sheriff had requested they stay until he'd talked with them one more time and one at a time. He'd be at the inn by three o'clock.

By two o'clock, Jackie's friends gathered in the parlor, all of them distraught.

Rain drizzled a gray wash over the day.

Victor was inconsolable and returned to his condo upon hearing the news of his wife's evident murder.

Pepper looked wan, still not feeling well. She sank into my parlor's tufted, Victorian-style chair that made her appear child-like. Skinny fingers clasped the wooden curl at the end of the chair arms. She peered down at Lucky Harbor, who laid on the floor next to her feet. "Does he have to follow me constantly?"

Pepper's bad mood startled me. That wasn't like her.

Cathy winced from where she sat on the nearby sofa. Maybe Pepper's sharp tone came out of her sorrow and shock.

I led Lucky Harbor outside then returned to the parlor. I texted Dillon about fetching his dog. Dillon was still working on a big house somewhere, insulating and finishing its garage, he said. I figured his spaniel would wait for him or Pepper on the verandah just fine. The sun broke out and the temperature dallied with the sixties, plenty warm for the hunting dog that had reveled playing in the snow all winter.

By the time the sheriff and Maria arrived at three o'clock, Pauline was off school. She came charging into the inn's kitchen, skidding to a stop across from me at the island. I was putting together a snack plate that included Wisconsin cheeses, three of my signature Fairy Tale Fudge flavors that Cody had made, and homemade crackers drizzled with olive oil and dressed with a pinch of red pepper flakes. Sweet and hot went together well, and cheese moderated everything.

Pauline asked, "Are you okay?" She huffed to catch her breath. She was in her usual garb for kindergartners--washable navy blouse and black slacks. What looked like green finger paint and chocolate milk striped the bottom of the blouse.

I asked, "Don't tell me you ran all the way from the school?"

"I did. My car has a flat again."

"The same high school kid?"

"Probably. But never mind him. Murder? How? When? Why? Who? I can't believe I was thinking about murder before--just like you. And I tried to deny my intuition, and I told you off, and well, I apologize."

"Don't worry about it. I'm glad you're here."

As I turned to the stove to create homemade cocoa with Belgian chocolate, I explained what I knew. "And so the sheriff is talking with each woman privately upstairs, one at a time. Those not being questioned wait in the parlor."

We could hear them muttering, though Maria was with them so they likely weren't talking about anything of significance to the murder case.

Pauline whispered, "Jordy can't really think one of them did it?"

"Of course not," I replied, stirring the milk and chocolate, watching the latter melt. "I'm sure those savvy women wouldn't be talking to him if they thought they were suspects. They want to help. They might have some clue as to what happened. Maybe they saw somebody."

My own words made me freeze in place.

"What's the matter?" Pauline asked, coming around the island to stand next to me at the stove.

I resumed stirring the milk and chocolate. "Something Erik told me yesterday after you and Laura left the bar. He said Mercy came in after midnight looking as if she were watching outside for somebody or something. She didn't stay long. She hurried right back out."

"Mercy is odd. And strong. She certainly wouldn't be hiding from anybody. That woman hunts and drags deer from the woods on her own in the fall."

"Exactly." I kept stirring, my insides beginning to feel hot, too.

"Strong enough to haul Jackie?"

I nodded. "She wouldn't be pleased to have me sic the sheriff on her. Mercy would do everything in her power to cause trouble for me and my family if I fingered her and she turned out innocent. She could ruin Grandma's run for village president next year, not to mention complain about this year's flower choices. Grandma loves variety, but Mercy is a staunch supporter of sturdy and cheap marigolds."

"But you have to share this with Sheriff Tollefson. Murder is serious."

"Mercy would not be involved in a murder." I was trying to convince myself more than Pauline. "She wants to run for village president again. She loves a battle, and my grandmother is a worthy opponent."

"You should run next year. What cups are you using?" Pauline asked.

I pointed to a section of cupboard.

"Me? Village president? Dillon says I'm too competitive and take on too many things at once. But if Erik decides to go to college and give up being president, I'd hate to see Mercy Fogg slip back into being village president. She was bossy and downright unpleasant and unpredictable. She wanted to paint all the garbage cans with polka dots. And she would try to pass ordinances to allow condos right on the harbor."

In the past Mercy had supported razing Oosterlings' Live Bait, Bobbers & Belgian Fudge & Beer. Because Duck Marsh Street was so close to the harbor, she'd made no bones last year about favoring selling the cabins there, too, to developers. My grandparents would have to move from their pleasant, quiet street, and so would Dillon.

"Do you really think I'd make a good village president?"

"Yeah, I do," Pauline said while setting blue cups onto the countertop. "Look what you've done with your fudge business.

It's given Cody a great job. A person with Asperger's can have a hard time finding the right job, but not here because of you. You gave him the courage and willpower to push on and study to be a volunteer firefighter and now he's studying to become a forest ranger."

"I guess that's a good thing."

"You believe in people. Except Mercy, but that's another matter. You believe in the goodness of this community. Your fudge shop--and now the inn--have become a hub of activity and pride for the community."

"But Grandpa and I are in debt up to our eyeballs."

"So life isn't always what we want or imagine it should be. Heck, because of a historic fudge recipe right here in our county, you got the prince of Belgium to fly here last fall! And he gave a huge donation to the Belgian Heritage Foundation to help restore the historic church it's in. All because of you and your decisions."

I stood a little straighter. "Thanks, Pauline. Usually you tell me my decisions are wacky."

"So we've reversed roles for today. You've been telling me lately I'm not acting right. We're here for each other. It's what BFFs do. It's what women do for each other."

I was going to tear up if I didn't watch out.

Staring into the pot, I said, "I'm really feeling sad, though, and I don't know if I can run an inn, much less run a village. Look at the trouble surrounding me again. Guests should not go through this. Last year when I debuted my fudge at a party here in the inn, another woman was murdered. What good is friendship among women if I keep killing them off?"

"Stop that thinking!"

"It's true. I feel as if I keep this place somebody else will die or be harmed." A shiver--like a premonition agreeing with me--rippled through me. I had to pause in stirring the fresh cocoa. I stared at the bits of chocolate swirling in the milk.

Pauline sighed. "Now what's wrong?"

"I'm wondering if chocolate can be like tea leaves and foretell my future."

Pauline peered into the pan. "All I see are chocolate swirls with no faces of anybody about to succumb to anything. There is no death in that cocoa. It's called killer cocoa because you're a whiz when it comes to chocolate."

Pauline retrieved the last of the chunky, powder-blue ceramic mugs from the cupboard. A local potter had made the mugs for me to match the inn's color scheme. Pauline held one up, then turned it over to read the inscribed name in the pottery. "This guy is really talented. How do you know him?"

"My grandfather knows his grandfather."

"What about your grandfather? Jordy can't possibly think..."

"As soon as the sheriff is done here, he'll be talking with Gilpa. And me. As soon as I pour this cocoa, I'm going down to Duck Marsh Street to be with Grandma and Grandpa. Mom and Dad are milking cows right now, but Dad said he'd drive up ASAP."

"Your grandfather needs a lawyer, not his son."

"Gilpa doesn't think so."

"Not good."

I nodded. "You can say that again."

The sheriff's questioning of my grandfather didn't go well. Maria was there again. My grandparents' kitchen was crowded with my family and Pauline. I hadn't told Dillon about this for fear he'd be pegged as a suspect by virtue of owning the boat with Grandpa.

We were sitting around the table at around five-thirty in the afternoon. Grandma was serving fresh coffee and pie as she always did for company but nobody was eating. Grandma was the quiet thinker in this family. My father took after her. I wished I could be like them, but I was telling everybody to not say a word as Maria and the sheriff walked in.

Jordy said he'd needed to take pictures of Grandpa's hands, of all things.

"No way!" Pain struck to my core. I held up my hand. "Jordy, he didn't do anything."

Grandpa hooted. "Let him take pictures. I'm innocent." He slammed a big forkful of pie into his mouth.

Jordy said, "I have a job to do, Ava. I must collect all evidence, even insignificant things like a cut on a hand which evidently happened on the boat in a disagreement with the woman who is now deceased. The cut will be healed within days, so I need to photograph it now and log it into my evidence collection."

Pauline, sitting beside me, pulled down my hand that was still in the air.

Grandpa flopped his palm up and stretched his arm over the middle of the table.

My dad said, "We need a lawyer."

The cut could be seen plainly. I imagined my grandfather in a jail jumpsuit. The sheriff snapped photos.

Then Jordy asked Maria to swab Grandpa's cheeks for DNA.

My mother freaked and left the room.

I snatched Jordy's camera. "He refuses to give a DNA sample until he has a lawyer by his side."

Grandpa chuckled. "It's okay, Ava. This won't prove a thing. My DNA is all over town already. I live here. I've even spit on the street once."

Grandma spouted, "You didn't?!"

"I did, Sophie. The street has my spit on it. It has my DNA, too." He pointed at Jordy. "Maybe you think I wrestled Jackie Valentine down on Main Street with people watching?"

Oddly, I thought about Mercy. What had she seen outside of Erik's bar after midnight Saturday night?

With a deadpan countenance, Jordy said to Grandpa, "Did you?"

I almost tossed Jordy's uneaten piece of pie in his face. Pauline jiggled my arm again to keep me from doing so.

Grandma handed Grandpa another piece of chocolate chiffon pie. She shut up people the smart way--with delectable food. I was sorry I hadn't gone over to the fudge shop and brought back a big batch. Jordy had a weakness for my fudge.

"Sheriff," I said, "remove Grandpa from your list of suspects. He would never murder anybody."

Jordy finished swallowing a bite of pie. "You don't listen very well. It's my job to make a list."

I snatched his pie dish again and before he could take the last bites I got off my chair with it. "It's my job to protect my grandfather."

My dad said, "Honey, that's my job."

Grandma Sophie appeared next to me with the coffee pot. "Ava, honey, your father is right. Your protesting like this only makes your grandfather appear guilty. The sheriff will think you're trying to cover up something."

Grandma was always the voice of reason. I shut up.

Grandpa said, "She's right, A.M. and P.M." He knew I always melted for him when he called Pauline and me by the initials he loved. Ava Mathilde and Pauline Mertens. "You are my sunshine day and night. Thank you for being that." He also said that a lot, too, particularly when he wanted me to agree with him. How could I be filled with bluster when he called me his "sunshine"?

Across the table, Pauline nodded at me.

From the living room a vacuum cleaner started.

I gave Jordy his pie plate back and then stomped outside to wait for him.

A chill speared the air. I rubbed my arms and wished I'd grabbed my jacket. Deputy Maria Vasquez came out first. She patted me on one shoulder, but didn't say anything. Probably wasn't allowed to say much. She left in her squad car.

When Jordy marched out, I followed him to his car. "I think Mercy Fogg knows something." I relayed what Erik had told me about Saturday night.

Jordy put on his aviator eyeglasses, a sign he was intrigued and wanted to keep things official. The sun had lowered in the sky and was lasering orange-gold beams through the tree limbs that highlighted the cragginess of his face. "Thanks, Ava. But somebody ducking into a bar then leaving again doesn't give me much."

His dismissal of me was infuriating. As he folded his tall frame into the front seat of the squad, I asked, "Did you find out anything new from talking to the fudge divas?"

"Fudge divas?"

"My guests. That's what they call themselves."

The corner of his mouth tugged. "Maybe they know how to fudge."

I blinked a few times. "You mean they're lying? About what? What did they say? Who told you what?"

"I've said too much."

"Jordy, we know each other pretty well." I still wondered if he had the hots for me. I wasn't above using that in this case to help protect my grandfather and guests. "I apologize for my behavior earlier. You know I respect you. You've helped save me in the past and I appreciate it." A stretch, but so be it. "You noticed something about my guests or one or two of them. What is it?"

"What did you notice?"

He was playing games. I could play, too. "They argue a lot. Don't you think that's odd for old friends? Most women on retreats have fun. I think they have secrets. Maybe they learned something about someone in Fishers' Harbor while they were out and about."

"You think they're hiding something?"

"You think they're hiding something."

The corner of his mouth twitched again. Bulls-eye.

Sudden regret came over me like a fever. What the heck was I doing? I didn't want him thinking the women killed their friend. Heck, Dillon's mother was among the fudge divas. "Pauline said something about them acting like kindergartners who get mad when a couple of them have a secret they don't share with the others. Maybe the women know about some enemy of Jackie's. Somebody who was out to get revenge. But they can't say who for some reason."

"Mercy Fogg?"

"I don't know. I thought it was your job to make a list of suspects."

He flashed me a hard look from where he sat inside the squad car. "I'll catch up with Mercy. I want to know about your fudge divas. You say they've been here since Wednesday and whatever troubles them didn't come out?"

I shook my head.

He shook his head. "You're slippin', Ava Oosterling. I'm shocked you don't know their secret."

That hurt my pride, but I swallowed it. "All right. Here's what else I know. They talked mostly about money troubles. They disagreed on what to invest in, mostly each other's stuff, though Kim Olkowski's White Glove Cleaning company came up a lot. That's all I heard. But a friend of mine at the inn said they agreed to hush around me. There's something they didn't want me to know."

He laid an elbow on the window frame of his squad. "Money can be a motive for murder. What about Kim's business? Did

Jackie Valentine want to invest in it and somebody else didn't like that?"

"Jealousy could be the ultimate motive. But I don't fully believe one of them could murder the other."

He shrugged his noncommittal answer, waiting for me to say more.

"Jackie didn't want to invest in Kim's business. I also know that Eliza Stefansson wasn't excited to do so either. The rest of them didn't care, so I doubt they'd murder Jackie so that they could then support Kim."

"Are you sure?"

"I thought you asked each of them questions already."

"I did," he said, "but I always like your take on things."

Was he were using me or complimenting me? I said, "I don't know what to think except that with Jackie's death they've been quiet for the first time since they got here."

"Quiet? What do you mean?"

"Before her death they talked loudly, argued or debated-- whatever you'd like to call it about their companies. They also exercised every morning to loud music. Overall, they were loud. Big loud."

"Huh." He savored that as much as the taste of Grandma's chocolate chiffon pie. "They told me they used to be cheerleaders in college. Maybe they're just reliving old times by being loud." He nodded to himself. "Loud noises cover up crimes, too." He started the car's engine. "Do you know where Mercy Fogg lives?"

I gave him directions. Her house was only a few blocks away on the other side of Main Street.

He said, "That's not far. What do you think of her relationship to your guests?"

"She drove them around. She told me Jackie was her biggest tipper. And Mercy wants to run for village president. She'd have no reason to kill Jackie. Mercy loves her dog, too."

"But does the dog love her?"

Jordy left me with that strange question. His squad rumbled away on Duck Marsh Street.

Pauline came out of my grandparents' house, hefting her green purse over a shoulder. "Your grandpa turned on the TV and his picture was on the local news. He's furious about the photo they used. It's one with a tie."

I was relieved to be able to smile at something. "Must have been taken from the church photos on Facebook."

"You sure have a mess on your hands. What'd you talk about out here with Jordy?"

Robins were squawking to defend new territory. Their fighting reminded me of the women. "Jordy found it interesting the women were so loud. He also wonders if they were covering up something."

"People get loud when they're nervous. I've told you about my kindergartners."

"And secrets. I have to find out what their secret is."

"Just ask them. Ask Cathy."

"I guess I could." It all seemed simple somehow when Pauline said it. "Thanks, Pauline. What if the whole retreat idea had been a ruse by one or more of them to do in Jackie for some reason?"

"Stop. Those women are friends. Be logical."

Again Pauline made sense.

It dawned on me this was Monday. John was supposed to return home to Door County today, which meant Pauline would learn all about that fancy house out in the countryside. Yet, she hadn't said a thing earlier and here she was with me now, not racing off to be somewhere with John. Pauline was a true friend.

The robins were still cussing and tumbling in a flutter of brown feathers across the lawn next door.

With trepidation, I said, "I could use some good news. Do you have any?"

She beamed. "Aren't you proud of me holding in my excitement? John asked me to meet him for dinner out at that new house."

I smiled for her sake. "I'll give you a ride to your car and help you change the tire."

"That'd be great."

We walked across the street to my yellow pickup truck parked in front of Dillon's cabin. I kept the truck there because the inn had a small parking lot.

A minute later I was driving north along Main Street when to the right I saw a familiar person walking along on the sidewalk. "Isn't that Zadie?"

She had just turned the corner and didn't see us. She was heading at a rapid pace away from us and away from the lake.

Pauline said, "Yeah. Out for a walk, I guess. You said she and Yola went out a lot together."

"That's just it. Together. I wonder where she's going alone."

"Gosh, going out for a walk alone isn't a big deal."

"Maybe in Fishers' Harbor it's not, but why wouldn't she have asked her friend Yola along this time? She seems in a hurry, too."

"So now you think Zadie is suspicious? Because she's alone? Why?" Pauline dug her phone out of her purse. The hour popped up on her screen. "We don't have time to follow her on a goose chase, Ava. I have to meet John at seven."

"Okay, okay. Onward to the school and your flat tire."

Seeing Zadie alone niggled at me. Those young women had always gone out together. Yet on the very day we had found out her mother's friend had been murdered, Zadie had taken off on her own. Wouldn't she stay around to console her mother? It struck me as odd.

Chapter 11

When I returned to the inn, Yola was also gone.

"She left with Zadie," Kim said. Kim sat at the dining room table making notes in her ledger. She'd been making notes every day.

"I saw Zadie alone earlier by herself walking along Main Street." I was fishing for information.

Kim shrugged. "They must be meeting up somewhere then."

"Everybody else is upstairs?"

Kim said Cathy had gone back to her own condo for the evening and that Eliza was taking a walk along the harbor.

"That seems morbid." I recalled Zadie said Eliza had perhaps tripped Grandpa's customer, dumping the poor man in the lake.

Kim shrugged. "Eliza said she wanted to see if she could get rid of her bad feelings."

"About what?"

"About Jackie. Eliza's always been jealous of her, and she feels bad. She said she should have apologized the first day of the retreat. Retreats are for clearing the air, she said."

I leaned over the back of a chair across from her. "You mean 'always' as in since you were in college together?"

"Uh, yeah." Kim didn't look up from her business notes. "Eliza used to be quite attractive, but a nobody compared to Jackie. When we were on the cheerleading squad, guess which of us ended up on TV the most with game-day coverage?"

"Jackie."

"When we would waitress at events together, guess who got the most tips?"

"Jackie. What kind of events did you all work at?"

"Nothing special really. Just parties around Madison." She flipped her ledger shut, then rose. "I have to finish packing. And I should catch up with Eliza."

Her muffled footsteps on the stairway carpet faded soon after.

The women apparently had no plans for dinner. I could understand why they had no appetite. In case they needed to nibble, I made a homemade pizza and put it in the oven.

After Kim left the inn, I realized Pepper had to be upstairs yet. She hadn't been feeling well, so I made a pot of tea and took it up. I knocked on her door.

"Pepper? It's me, Ava. I have hot tea for you."

A moan ebbed through the wood door, concerning me.

"Pepper?" I knocked again. "Pepper? Are you all right? May I come in?"

After no response, I opened the door to find a pile of pink sprawled on her back on the floral rug. I set the teapot on the nearby dresser and rushed to kneel beside her. "Pepper!"

Her eyelids fluttered, but blood was seeping out from under her head.

Before I could hit 911, Pepper revived herself. "Don't call anybody."

"You're hurt. There's blood."

"Oh," she said, groggy. "I must have fainted."

She tried to rise from the rug, but I stopped her with a gentle hand. "Stay there, Pepper. I'll get a cool washcloth."

After a rush into her bathroom and back, I had her sit up and away from the blood. She insisted on holding the washcloth herself. The red spot on the rug was the size of the palm of one hand.

Pepper said, "I'm so sorry about this. I must have been in too much of a hurry."

"Did you trip on the rug? I'll get rid of it."

"No," she said in a subdued voice. "I think I was almost to the door. We were all going for walks to follow in Jackie's footsteps. To feel her spirit and all."

So that's why Eliza was at the harbor.

"It wouldn't do well to join her spirit."

Pepper chuckled. "No, indeed. I suppose we'll all be there sometime with her."

"I'd feel better if we took you to a clinic to check for a concussion."

"No, I'm fine. Headachy, but I'm seeing straight. Maybe you can help me up and we'll see how I do on my feet."

I put the rag aside on the rug. I gentled her short, sparrow-like frame to a standing position. Pepper wore pink walking shoes and a pink jogging outfit with plaid highlights at the collar, cuffs, placket, and pockets. Blood hadn't touched any of the cute attire. If this had been me, I'd look like roadkill.

To make small talk while she assessed herself, I said, "Your makeup is impeccable as always. You should do commercials for the brand."

"Thanks. My daughter and I offer quality products at Blush Rush. They might cost more, but everything in life worth it costs a lot more."

"Not my fudge," I said, kidding with her. "It's cheap so it can be enjoyed by the masses."

"Your fudge is way underpriced, Ava." She peered down at her outfit, then up at me standing next to her. I still had an arm firmly around her narrow shoulders. She said, bright-eyed, "Why didn't I think of this before? Pink is my favorite color, and pink and lavender are the accent colors at our shop in Milwaukee. I'm sure Zadie would agree to selling your Cinderella Pink Fairy Tale Fudge at Blush Rush. We'd be the first cosmetics store in the country that also sold fudge, I bet. Are you game?"

Heat bloomed on my face. "I wasn't fishing for compliments about my fudge or trying to use you and Zadie to sell more of it. Really. You girls have had enough trouble over business dealings in the past few days."

Pepper took a few steps. "Thank goodness for your very cushy rug. I'll pay for the cleaning."

"No need. I have my own rug-cleaning machine. And maybe I can use Kim's white gloves."

Pepper chuckled. "You're sure I can't pay? I feel terrible about this."

"It's just a rug, Pepper."

"You people in Door County are mighty generous. The world needs more kind people like you, Ava Oosterling."

Pride bloomed inside me the first tulip of spring. "Thank you, Pepper."

She went into the bathroom to clean up, then declared she needed to get outside with the rest of the girls.

Pepper headed out the open door of her guest room and into the hallway. She appeared steady enough, but I escorted her down the carpeted staircase. I helped with the front door that was always catching. From there she refused assistance. She toddled down the steep driveway.

I watched, worried. My instincts said something was definitely wrong with what had just transpired. She had to be hurting but she didn't want me making a fuss or helping her, not even touching her.

Back inside the inn, I trotted back up the stairs and to her room. There wasn't blood or hair on the edges of her dresser, or the nearby decorative table, or in any odd places in the bathroom. Did somebody clock her over the head and clean the room before they left?

When I peered behind her opened door, I discovered a bloody smudge on the round, antique brass door handle.

I couldn't detect a fingerprint.

After getting a paper towel and cleaner, I stared again at the bloody door handle, wanting to be sure I hadn't found a fingerprint. Maybe this was all just an accident. Pepper hadn't been feeling well. She could have fainted against the door handle. But...she fell away from the door.

Who would want to harm Pepper? Was a killer lurking in my inn?

I called Dillon.

He came over with Lucky Harbor. He set the dog to sniffing and inspecting every inch of the inn, even the back stairwell originally built to lead from servants' quarters on the second floor down to the kitchen. It also accessed the back of the inn and yard.

Outside, in the dimming light after seven o'clock, the American Water Spaniel was particularly interested with the gazebo. It was big enough to house a small band for entertainment or a dozen people in a wedding party. Dillon had built it for me last fall. He'd designed and cut a decorative wood valance around the top depicting mother ducks and their ducklings to reflect Duck Marsh Street and the many ducks that inhabited the marsh at the end of the street. Up here on the cliff overlooking the harbor, we enjoyed a view of the duck's reedy marsh, too, as well as the expansive bay. A freighter--its night lights blinking--was drifting by in the distance.

Dillon pulled me playfully into the semblance of privacy that the gazebo's lattice structure provided. He kissed me soundly. Electricity sizzled to my toes.

I admired how he'd changed over the years. He wanted to be known as an ordinary man. He worked construction, a far cry from the olden days of his youth when he prided himself on gambling and living a high life frought with the odors of glitz and risk. Now, he always smelled like clean wood shavings because of his construction jobs, or of the land and forests where he trained his hunting dog. This Dillon Rivers was the opposite of the man I dated in college. This Dillon Rivers created earthquakes in my heart. Which confused me, too. Was he real? Can people change that much?

I asked, "Do you think I'm being paranoid? Maybe Pepper just fainted and fell on something, as she said she did."

The dog's snuffling noises increased. He whined. He was a blur of brown, curly fur going over the gazebo.

Dillon hooked his thumbs in the waistband of his jeans as we watched his dog. "Lucky seems to have gotten lucky about something."

The dog began following a trail through the wet, winter-weary brown lawn grass of the back yard. We tracked in his wake with me clicking on the flashlight I'd brought along.

Lucky Harbor headed toward the side of the house opposite the kitchen's back door. An open verandah stretched across the rear of the house.

Lucky Harbor then snuffled his way to the northeast side of the house. A new section of verandah added on by Dillon wrapped around to where new French doors allowed guests to step outdoors directly from the parlor.

The whining dog led us to the small parking area in front of the Blue Heron Inn where he appeared to lose the trail. He circled back to the grassy area and wiggled all over again. He growled low in his throat.

I flashed the light on the ground but didn't see anything. "What does that growl mean?"

"Don't know. He's never growled before."

His face revealed concern, which made my imagination take off. Had somebody been sneaking around the inn? I didn't want to worry. I had too much to do. I needed to go inside and bake pizza and set out pies Grandma had brought up to the inn to serve the fudge divas. The women would be back from their walks at any moment. Darkness seemed to spook them. Which seemed odd, now that I thought about it. An involuntary grunt came out of my throat.

Dillon said, "What's wrong?"

"The women friends staying here were always determined to go everywhere together. Although they said that was what a retreat was about for them, I assumed at times they were afraid of the dark. But why did Jackie go out alone, even if she were drunk? Why did they let her go out alone? I hate to say this, but something about the way they insisted on being together all the time feels odd."

The night was the color of violets now. It had to be around eight o'clock.

I peered down the hill and onto the twilight shrouding Main Street. "The pure darkness here at night was perfect cover for somebody intent on doing harm and not being seen. What had Jackie been up to the night she died? She'd eaten dinner with the divas. She'd argued with my grandfather on the boat. What happened in the dark between the time she'd bloodied her hand with the knife on the boat and when she'd drowned somewhere? We know somebody had to have put her in the lake. Where would she have gone next after being with my grandfather?"

Dillon petted his dog and made a fuss over him as a reward for tracking whatever it was. "Maybe she said something to your grandfather that he doesn't realize is a clue."

Lucky Harbor snuffled into my hands, looking for treats. I offered him a couple of cheesy fish-shaped crackers from my pockets.

Dillon and I settled our backsides on the front steps. Stars were blinking to life above in the twilight. Dillon put an arm around me and drew me against his warmth.

I said, "I'm worried about Pauline, Dillon."

"Like you don't have enough going on already?"

"John Schultz concerns me."

I told him about us finding the roses at the lavish house in the countryside on Sunflower Road.

Dillon's body jerked.

I asked, "You know that place? White board fence? Angel statue in the front yard?"

"With the key hidden under it." He sighed. "Where I've been doing construction on the garage."

"What do you know?"

Dillon got up from the steps, thumbs hooked in his jean's pockets, the stars above sprinkled around his head and shoulders. "John wants his proposal to be a surprise for Pauline."

"He's proposing for real?" My insides flipped. "When?"

"Whenever he finds that ring she lost last fall. He knows she feels really badly about losing that."

"He better feel bad. After she paid for it herself. Because John gave her all kinds of mixed signals about her picking such things out, as if that's romantic to go alone and buy your own ring. What a beast..."

A slow burn was catching fire inside me. Lucky Harbor sat next to me on the step.

Dillon settled next to me on my other side. "He's really sorry about that. He told me he wants to make it up to her."

"By buying her that big house?"

"No. He can't afford that. But the next best thing. He wanted her to know about the house and approve it."

I sighed. "He's got another plan?"

"A party really. For her thirteen kindergartners."

That brought me to attention. "What kind of party?"

"You know that John's been in touch with your old Hollywood manager since last fall."

"Marc Hayward. This has to involve making lots of money for Marc."

"John tells me Marc fell in love with Door County's picturesque, rural atmosphere, and the innocence of the place."

"Innocence? A woman was just killed under my watch." It was my turn to rise to my feet. I rubbed my arms against the chilly night air. "What are John and Marc up to?"

"Marc wants to do a reality show in which kindergarten girls take over a mansion, along with their toys--that come alive. The little girls would be part of a fundraiser for local charities. That would entail them being filmed making cookies from scratch--no, I'll make sure it's your fudge. John wants pony rides and games, too."

Ponies? Little girls in charge of a mansion? My fudge on national TV? I stared in disbelief. "So he wanted Pauline's approval of the house because she's going to be involved with her thirteen butterflies for a television show?"

"National PBS show. He got people interested because of his local series."

I chuckled. "He's done a show on the trolls and trollway in Mount Horeb, and another spot about Seymour, Wisconsin, being the birthplace of the hamburger, and the most recent one is about the mythical hodag creature living in caves around Rhinelander. Now, based on that experience, National Public Television wants him to be responsible for thirteen little girls making a mess of a mansion? I don't buy it."

"There's a catch. You can't tell a soul, especially not Pauline. I promised John it was his deal."

I spun in place. "No way am I keeping a secret from Pauline. Friends don't keep secrets."

Dillon grabbed one of my hands. "What about your women guests? You've told me they have secrets from each other."

Lucky Harbor hopped from the steps to the ground, then sat, panting, his eyes reflecting starlight.

"Your dog is always following Pepper. It's like he's watching out for her. Why would he pick her? There are too many odd things going on lately in my life."

Dillon lifted our entwined hands and kissed one of my knuckles. "I hope that doesn't include me."

"Never." Or did it? Why did doubts about us as a couple plague me?

"Maybe Lucky Harbor realizes she's not feeling well. Some dogs detect seizures before they happen."

My senses jerked awake. "You don't suppose he knows something serious is wrong with Pepper?" We sat again on the verandah's lower step.

"It would explain her fall if she fainted because of some illness she's going through. Dogs are keen on detecting our moods, even changes in our health."

"Pepper's health isn't my business."

"Try again. You wouldn't give up on Pauline or me so easily, would you?"

"Of course not."

I snuggled into the side of him, thinking about the issue of keeping secrets. We women used secrets like currency. Sharing a good secret helped us develop friendships. Not sharing certain secrets with a girlfriend could destroy the friendship. Did I dare keep this secret about John from Pauline?

Dillon and I sat sharing the starlight until the fudge divas became silhouettes off in the distance at the bottom of the hill walking in our direction.

Lucky Harbor took off, his nails scrabbling on the blacktop as he loped down the grade straight for Pepper.

I muttered to Dillon, "You're right. That dog knows something."

Dillon kissed my forehead. "Promise me you'll be careful with your curiosity. I don't want you harmed."

He left me to lope down the hill, saying good night to the divas as he passed them.

I implored the stars overhead. Why would Dillon think I'd be harmed?

Chapter 12

On Tuesday morning, wind stirred the thick fog coming off the bay as if it were whipped cream being nudged by a spatula onto a cake.

The women--including Pepper--came downstairs at eight-thirty. Some made wistful glances toward the parlor as if in homage to Jackie and her usual morning loud exercise commands.

The women seemed to have replaced their need for exercise with hunger. I was ready with pancakes made with fudge chunks and served with homemade Door County maple syrup I'd bought at a farmer's market along Highway 42.

Cathy had come from her condo where she'd stayed the night. "I know the exact trees where this syrup came from."

Eliza said, "Me, too. Maybe we should all go on a trip into nature."

Young Yola said, "Nature heals. It's amazing that research keeps finding how important being among plants can be for humans. Everybody needs plants."

She sounded like a commercial, still trying to press her case to start her pop-up gardening shops in Chicago. But Jackie wasn't here to refuse her money for the venture anymore. And Yola's friend Zadie, curiously enough, wasn't at the table to support her friend. Yola had told us Zadie had taken off early for a run. Zadie's mother, Pepper, was at the table eating the pancakes as if nothing had happened to her yesterday. I ached to ask questions but kept my mouth shut.

Kim chattered across from Pepper about a new idea for advertising her white gloves, something about starting smaller than a shopping channel debut and instead finding a local press person who would interview her for a Facebook campaign.

Eliza, next to Pepper and across from Cathy, was talking about her hope that the spring planting season for farmers might help the sales at her deceased husband's farm implement dealership. Some farm tractors sold for six figures.

Nobody was talking about Jackie.

Zadie came through the front entryway, struggling with the creaky front door that still stuck within its doorjamb. I reminded myself yet again to ask Dillon to fix it. Zadie was breathing hard from her run when she plopped into a dining chair next to Yola.

"The fog is thick out there. I love it."

I said, "We call it pea soup. It's dangerous to be out running or biking in this."

"I only go on the sidewalks. I know my way around now."

"What's your route?" I was still curious after seeing her yesterday out alone.

"It varies. These pancakes look divine."

Everybody chattered about the pancakes containing Fairy Tale Fudge.

Then sniffles came when they talked about packing and how hard it would be to part.

Eliza said, "There comes a time for everything, including good-byes to our loved ones." She dabbed a tear with her napkin.

Everybody paused out of respect for her deceased husband and for Jackie.

Cathy suggested they go to her spa after breakfast for one last round of chocolate facials.

I mentioned Victor had called about having a short service in honor of the fudge divas and the friendship they had for his wife.

Zadie said around a bite of fudge pancake, "That's nice of him."

Yola finished chewing. "Victor needs us all at this time."

Eliza nodded. "Indeed. It's very hard when one loses a spouse."

Previously that morning, and before the women had trundled down the stairs, Victor had called me to say he'd finally been given permission to claim his wife's body. He'd made arrangements with a funeral home in Sturgeon Bay. Victor wanted to have a brief ceremony in Door County before he took his wife's body back to Chicago for a formal funeral for family, friends, and the many colleagues the Valentines knew in the construction industry.

Victor had said over the phone, "I'm sorry I haven't taken the time to gather her things. I just can't seem to make myself move."

"That's understandable, Victor," I'd said. "Packing her things will make it feel real. I'm so sorry."

"I know I have to do that later today. Thank you for your patience." The gurgle of maybe coffee being poured had come over the phone.

"If it makes it easier for you, I'll put together her suitcase and bring it downstairs for you. You can pick it up at the inn anytime. Or can I drop it off? Where's the condo you rented?"

"No worries. I'll stop by." He slurped something, coffee I presumed. "Thanks for doing that. I don't know when I'll get back this afternoon. The funeral home and I need to talk about arrangements. Is that okay if I don't make an appointment?"

"Like I said, anytime, Victor. Whatever I can do to help."

"Thanks," he said on the other end. Then came another gurgle of something being poured. I'd made a note to make sure I had Grandpa's formula for coffee percolating in my kitchen all day. Victor would appreciate the strong brew mellowed with Belgian chocolate.

That phone conversation had been almost an hour ago. Now, as I sat with the women in the dining room I realized Victor might stop by at any time.

I pushed back my chair from the table. "While all of you are eating, I'll go upstairs to gather Jackie's things, but..." Against my better judgment, I looked across the table at Kim, who'd been quiet. "Kim, maybe you already packed her things?"

"Me? No. Why do you say that?" She sipped from her cup of hot chocolate.

"I..."

My stomach went acidy. I realized I had put myself into a pickle. Cathy had told me she saw Kim sneak into Jackie's room on Sunday. I had to lie to protect Cathy. Near the other end of the table Cathy was pouring more maple syrup over her pancakes, a smooth move so others wouldn't notice her wincing because of me.

I finished with, "I happened to be coming up the stairs with towels and thought I saw you go into her room."

"Me? No," Kim repeated. "Touching Jackie's things is the last thing I'd do."

The table waited for me to make everybody even more uncomfortable. I cringed inside at my ineptness.

Kim looked about the table at her friends. "Can you imagine me in Jackie's clothes? She loved those caftan tops, all those flowing things. I don't see myself cleaning a house in my white gloves and wearing her crazy caftans."

She giggled. It seemed forced to me.

The table of guests joined her in light-hearted banter about Jackie's unusual clothing choices.

Yola said, "If you have that much money, you don't care who cares what you wear. I just wish she would have agreed to invest in my garden pop-up stores in Chicago. Now there's a city that needs the healing powers of plants."

Zadie, next to her mother, said, "Mom, maybe we could talk with Victor about something we could do in Jackie's name in Chicago that could include Yola's garden pop-up idea. Instead of putting them in malls, they could go inside of the buildings he builds? Wasn't he working on a children's hospital wing? Didn't Jackie help with designing the interior? Kids love plants. Don't they need plants? I go to Chicago a lot. Would it be okay if I stopped by to see Victor sometime soon?"

The babble made Pepper smile in a genuine way for the first time in a couple of days. She wiped her mouth with a delicate touch of her cloth napkin. "Zadie, what an intriguing idea. I don't see why not."

"Great, Mom."

Yola's face flushed with delight. "Thank you!"

Kim plunked down her antique china cup a bit too hard. My head dinged like a cash register, hoping she hadn't put a crack in it. She said, "Wait a minute. If anybody is waltzing down to Chicago to ask for money for their business, maybe we should all go. Give Victor some time, then all of us go down there as a sort of reunion in the name of Jackie for him."

Eliza coughed, putting down a forkful of pancake. "I'm not going down to Chicago to try to sell farm equipment." A huff eschewed from her like an exclamation point.

"We can't talk to Victor here. It'd be rude," Kim said. "What's wrong with setting up a Chicago meeting?"

Zadie jiggled in her chair like a school kid. "Yola and I could approach him here about setting up a meeting at least. He treats us differently. We're younger." Off the scowls around the table, she added, "We're like his..." She seemed confused.

Eliza snapped, "His children? That's a bit presumptuous."

Zadie blinked several times, her face returning to the red hue it'd worn when she'd come in from her run minutes ago. I felt sorry for her trying to help. She was out of her league with this older generation of practiced sharks at the table.

Yola said, "Not children. We're like his *daughters*. That's what Zadie was trying to say. He won't get mad at us if we ask him something about money for you guys. It won't affect Zadie or me or our relationship with him. We have no relationship. I mean, we know him, but that's all. He'd look kindly on us. We'd have a better chance of persuading him than any of you."

It was the most Yola had spoken since she'd arrived last Wednesday. I could feel a possible new round of argumentative financial discussion brewing. I excused myself and went upstairs. Straight to Jackie's room.

Where I found a bloody hammer tossed on the bed.

Chapter 13

The ordinary hammer lay in the middle of Jackie's bed, which was still made. The white chenille spread with pink roses had nary a wrinkle. Two nights ago she'd been found dead in the harbor; Jackie hadn't even come upstairs to her room. The sheriff had gone over this room during his visit and had found nothing of substance, as far as I knew. Now this. After yesterday. When I'd found Pepper with a blood coming from the back of her head.

Previous to that, Cathy had told me she'd seen Kim sneaking into this room. Kim denied it. Kim was lying. Had we found the murderer of Jackie? Had Pepper threatened to turn her in? It was obvious the way they had all acted at the breakfast table minutes ago was a charade. They shared a secret.

I called Jordy about the hammer. I didn't tell him about Kim yet. It was all too involved for a phone conversation.

The sheriff told me not to touch anything.

Listening to orders was not my forte. I was pleased events were unfolding in a way that would get my grandfather off the hook, though it was sad to think Kim Olkowski was a murderer--

a bit frightening, too. She had broken my lamp downstairs last week, but was that proof she was a violent person? No. I even liked her white gloves; those five-fingered friends practically picked dust motes out of the air on their own. I'd be the first to order a box.

The hammer looked new, the ordinary kind of claw-shaped tool everybody bought at any number of hardware stores. Would Kim be so stupid as to pitch it in this bedroom in plain sight? She might if she were in a hurry. Maybe she'd heard me coming yesterday with the tea. Now I wish I'd checked on Jackie's room last night or at least had locked the door after the sheriff had finished going over the room.

My phone alerted me to a text. Pauline. I'd texted her several times last night to no avail to tell me about her date. Actually, I was aching for her to tell me anything John might have said about the big surprise. I had promised Dillon I wouldn't tell, but keeping this secret was killing me. Her text said she'd called in sick and got a sub for school today; she wanted to come right over. My heartbeat skipped into gear at what this might mean-- juicy information coming my way! It was only nine-thirty. The women would still be downstairs finishing breakfast before heading over to Cathy's Glass Slipper spa.

When Pauline arrived I let her in via the servant door and stairwell at the back of the kitchen. We tiptoed up to Jackie's room. I closed the door.

I filled her in on what was unfolding.

"Kim did it? She killed Jackie?"

"It looks that way, though she's playing it cool downstairs. She lied about being in here to my face, but she might have a reason. It's odd she'd lie in front of all her friends."

"Not odd at all if they vowed to cover for each other. Maybe more than one has been in here. Stealing things from Jackie. Everybody getting a souvenir?"

"Gruesome, but could be." I moved off toward the closet in the far corner. "Tell me more about last night while we look around."

"Ugh. Last night. What are we looking for?"

"Anything we know the sheriff will miss or not consider important, and anything important he'll want to keep secret but we need to know, too."

"Why do we need to know stuff he should know but doesn't know?"

I turned to give her the kind of look she usually gives to me, eyebrows hiked high on my face. "Jordy's still suspicious of my grandfather."

"Your grandfather's been known to lie."

"Pauline, whose side are you on? Did you know the ladies tipped him for the boat rides, but they haven't yet paid the full bill for all the excursions since Wednesday?" I went back to embrace the closet. "Why the 'ugh' about last night? You met John at that fabulous house and then what?"

"John's doing a story on the house. He wanted to know if I'd be willing to host a party there with my kindergartners so he could film them having fun."

Finally, the secret was out. "That sounds nice. Is that all?" My fingers were going through all the flowy caftans lined up in the closet.

"Yeah. That's all he said. I guess he thinks it'll make a cute episode for his local series. I'll have to get permission slips from all the parents. It seems like more work for me with nothing much in it." She was opening and shutting drawers of a dresser.

I turned to look at my friend. "No proposal of marriage?" I wanted to say, *No explanation that this will be a national show? With Hollywood involved?* Had John been embellishing things with Dillon? Probably. I wanted to dump John in the bay.

Pauline had donned plain jeans and a sweatshirt, unusual when John was in town. The choice of attire spoke to me. Her hands and fingers weren't even messing with her hair, which also said a lot about her mood.

She said, "No marriage proposal. It's just as well. You were right about him. And me. It's just my biological clock is all. I should have been happy with the roses he gave me. I mean, I'm happy. John's happy with the way things are. We're both happy. He's just not marriage material. I'm going to break things off."

My heart sank into my stomach for her. I couldn't blab about what John had told Dillon. What if it were true? John intended to propose to her?

I turned to the closet again. "It's not a bad thing to be just dating. You and John sort of skipped that stage. You met last summer, then he gets his show deal and he's traveling while you're teaching school. You hardly know each other."

She didn't answer.

From the closet I picked out a caftan top in paisleys of varying colors. It made me a little seasick to look at it. I had to agree with Kim about Jackie's clothing choices, though I hadn't paid attention to her clothes because she was so loud. I had mostly avoided looking at her directly, as if that would have lessened the decibels.

I returned the top and its hanger onto the bar in the closet. I checked all the clothing for pockets and found nothing in them.

Pauline said, "Come here. What's this?"

We gathered in front of the antique writing desk. Pauline had lifted up the blotter on top.

"Looks like a receipt. For clothes from a shop here in Fishers' Harbor. The little one next to the book store. Oh that reminds me I need to drop off that check to Jane for the broken pole."

"But why is the receipt hidden under the blotter?"

"Good point. Does it have any personal information she didn't want stolen?"

"No. It's dated Thursday."

"Rapunzel Raspberry Rapture Fairy-Tale Fudge day. I made a big batch."

"And she bought a new dress."

"Which she never wore." I went back to the closet and pulled out a bright short-sleeved dress with a tulip skirt. The colors of spring splashed within the fabric in a tasteful way. "This looks new. It has to be this dress. I'm suddenly realizing this dress doesn't look like her. More like something the twenty-somethings are wearing now. More Zadie and Yola."

"Maybe it was going to be a gift. Does Jackie have kids?"

"No."

We couldn't figure it out and time was wearing on. The sheriff would be here within the half hour. I thought about what Grandma had said about Grandpa dreaming about Jackie and some argument over a dress. I worried Grandpa would get into trouble with the sheriff--yet again--if I didn't handle this myself and find out the information for the sheriff, thus excluding Grandpa from the mix. With another sandwich-sized clear plastic bag and the pen again, I nudged the receipt inside the bag.

Pauline noticed. "You're going to get in trouble hiding evidence."

"Jordy had his chance earlier. It's not my fault he didn't lift up the blotter."

"What if he did when he was here? What if that was put in here *after* he left?"

I mulled that over. "So maybe Kim hid the receipt in here. Why? It's just a receipt for a dress."

I turned toward the bed behind me.

Pauline said, "I don't think we should disturb it."

"What if something is under it or between the mattress and box spring?"

"Crap. Good thing I wore old clothes."

We found the loops on the sides of the mattress and heaved it off the box spring, keeping the hammer in place as best we could. The room had just enough space for us to take the mattress toward the closet and set it down.

There in the middle of the box spring sat Pepper's pink pistol.

"What the heck?" I mused.

Pauline flapped a hand at me. "Don't touch it. You'll get us in trouble."

"That's Pepper's. What's it doing here?"

"Obviously Jackie took it. Or Kim."

"Or Cathy." I gulped. She'd pointed the finger at Kim for coming in here. But she was the mother of Dillon. "Scratch Cathy."

"Why would Jackie or Kim have done that?"

"Maybe Kim thought Pepper was going to use it for some reason. Those women were mad at each other all the time. You said so. "

The thought of having a shoot-out right here in the inn made me quake worse than a rabbit facing hounds. "That clinches it. I'm not cut out to be an innkeeper. Fudge is a lot safer. I'm going to tell Grandpa we have to sell this inn."

"For once you're making sense. Getting involved with you always gets me in trouble. I could lose my job over this."

I plunked my hands on my hips and looked across the box spring at her. "How so? It's not like you're wielding the gun."

The pink gun seemed to pulsate from the center of the covered bedsprings.

Pauline tossed her hair about her shoulders. "You're about to pick up the pistol, aren't you? I'm a witness. And if we find out Pepper used it to threaten Jackie, and you keep this pistol, then we're some kind of an accessory."

"Accessory to what? Nobody shot anybody. It sounds like you're talking about barrettes for your hair. A barrette is an accessory."

Pauline seethed audibly through her teeth. "Leave this to the sheriff."

"Of course, but we might be preventing someone using the pistol. Give me one of your plastic bags and a pen."

Pauline's purse always held plastic bags for saving anything for her students. This time she'd save this pistol from possibly harming somebody. With the pen and bag, I crawled to the middle of the box spring, used the pen to nudge the pistol into the clear plastic bag, then crawled back.

Pauline ducked.

I said, "Kim had to have been in here, now that I think about this. She was either hiding this pistol, or would have been looking for it. Jackie was bossy. She might have taken it away from Pepper, for Pepper's own good."

"It doesn't have blood on it, does it? Was it used to hit Pepper over the head?"

I looked. "No blood. It could have been cleaned up."

"With white cleaning gloves."

I walked to the desk and put the pistol in Pauline's purse.

"Oh no you don't."

"Too late. It's in there amid the crayons." I pointed toward her end of the bed. "Pick up your side of the mattress. You get to keep the gun for now in case we encounter the sheriff as we run some errands. We'll put the pistol back later when we know he's about to show up here. The sheriff will want to frisk me, not you."

"Lucky you. He has the hots for you."

"Pauline, a sheriff never has 'hots'. It's not dignified," I said, grunting as we heaved the heavy queen-sized mattress.

"You think I'm stupid? Haven't you noticed how he stands straighter when next to you?"

A knock came on the door. The doorknob rattled.

With a zing-zing of a zipper she closed her purse as I opened the door to the sheriff.

Sheriff Jordy Tollefson was his usual grumpy self, not appreciating that somehow the door to Jackie's room had been left unlocked by me and somebody had deposited a hammer in the bed.

While he questioned all my guests again, Pauline and I escaped. My phone time said it was nearly ten in the morning. We headed to the book store where I handed Jane Goodland the check for the broken stripper pole, as everybody called it. The bent silver metal pole lay on the floor in the back of the store. The ceiling had four holes in it where the pole's screws had ripped away.

Jane was tall, blond, curvy, a former lawyer who had studied burlesque in college. Photos of her on the Internet were mighty sexy, though she was always clothed in discreet ways.

She knew about Jackie's death of course. I updated her. As we looked at the bent pole, she responded to my comment about the women being secretive and what my mother described as "clique-ish."

Jane said, "They sound like burlesque dancers instead of strippers."

Pauline and I exchanged a look. I said to Jane, "You'll have to explain that."

"Burlesque is not the same as stripping. Being a stripper is about unveiling all your secrets. Burlesque is about the art of keeping your secrets. There's more allure if you keep what's important to you a secret. If your guests are keeping secrets--such as one of them killing Jackie and then the whole group trying to make it look like an accident--they've taken it to a fine art."

Pauline muttered, "The burlesque of murder?"

Jane shrugged, then petted her big Bernese mountain dog, Barkley, that had loped amid us. He sat on each of our pairs of feet in turn, begging to be petted. He got pats all around, then trotted back to sit at the front door in a heap. He preferred cool weather. Jane let him out, then we gathered around her front cash register area. She sat on a stool while we leaned against the counter.

I worried my lower lip with my teeth. "You live upstairs, right?"

"Yeah. It's an okay apartment but I'd love to find a house."

"Did you happen to look out your windows on Saturday night past midnight or so?"

"I was just coming home on a date, but I don't recall seeing anything out of the ordinary. Al Kvalheim was emptying garbage bins into his truck up the street. I recall hearing a rattle outside and looked onto Main Street and saw him. There wasn't anything else going on that I recall."

"And nothing at the harbor behind you?"

"I didn't look. Sorry. I usually love looking at the harbor and seeing boat lights at night, but there's not much out there at this time of year. The view is the best thing about the upstairs apartment, but I was tired. Sam was, too. He left and I went to bed."

"Sam Peterson?" I raised my eyebrows.

Pauline explained to Jane, "Her ex. They were engaged once."

Jane paled. "Oh. Sorry."

I said, "Don't be. That's over. We're still friends. But I thought, oh, cripes, sorry--"

"Just say it," Jane said, chuckling.

"I thought he might care about a friend of ours. But I guess not."

Pauline again interjected. "The friend is pregnant." Off Jane's disturbed blink, Pauline added, "Not by Sam. By a professor, but he's not around anymore."

Jane said, "It's sure complicated around here."

Pauline laughed. "That's because of Ava. Nothing is simple around her."

"Hey," I said, "that's not true."

"One of your guests was murdered and your grandfather's being looked at as if he's a suspect and you're hiding evidence in your pocket."

Jane got off her stool. "What evidence?"

I produced the receipt from the clothing store next door, handing it across the counter.

Jane read the receipt. "For a dress. I remember the women coming in here after making purchases next door. On Saturday. They had the audacity to buy some magazines but said that they would take care of the exercise pole later."

"Who bought the dress?" I asked. "Was it the younger ones? Or Jackie? The tall one with red hair?"

"The younger two of the group hung out over in the romance novel section. The other women were at the magazines here near the counter. I'm sure it was the short one in pink who bought the dress. I overheard her whispering to the more plain-looking one that she'd bought it as a surprise for her daughter. But the plain-looking one was carrying the bag, probably to keep the secret that the mother had bought the dress for the daughter. A surprise gift sort of thing."

This seemed innocent to me and didn't add up to requiring a gun or hammer. "The plain one was probably Eliza Stefansson and the other was Pepper Elliott. Pepper must have bought the dress for Zadie and later asked Jackie to keep it in her closet." Where it still hung.

I muttered more musings to Pauline. "Why hadn't Pepper claimed the dress? Why hadn't Eliza mentioned it? She seems upset with everybody enough that she'd love spoiling a surprise."

"Maybe they were scared to say anything since the sheriff had searched the room."

"Once. And hadn't found a hammer or pink pistol."

Jane handed back the receipt. "What's going on? You're finding weapons in the inn?"

"Yeah, Jane. Under odd circumstances, too." Jane Goodland was a friend and former lawyer who had my back, as we said here, and she knew my reputation for digging into the details of anything suspicious. She kept my secrets because she knew ultimately I was helping the sheriff, my guests, and of course protecting my trouble-making Grandpa. "Victor is due any minute, so I better get back. Thanks for the tip about the secret surprise dress." I put the receipt back in my pocket.

Jane looked at her phone, checking the time. "Have you been at your fudge shop yet this morning?"

"No."

"Well," Jane said with a lilt in her voice, "you better check it out. A customer came in a few minutes ago and told me there's quite the crowd over there and some reporter from the state capital showed up."

I checked for texts and emails. To my shock, there were several urgent messages from the local group of church ladies who took over my shop at will at times under the guise of helping me.

Dread filled me like icy harbor water spilling into my waders. Now what had Grandpa done? Why were the ladies there?

Chapter 14

Pauline and I had to wind our way through a throng of cars clogging the harbor's parking lot.

Trotting along, I puffed out to Pauline, "Dotty and Lois have been at it again on social media."

"They mean well."

In the past, the Door County women's group--without my permission--had set up a rummage sale in my shop and card games and gambling all for the sake of helping my shop prosper. Retired Dotty Klubertanz and her friend Lois Forbes, along with a hundred of their closest friends, had taken it upon themselves to be my guardian angels or social media street team. No matter what I said or did to discourage them, they would not be thwarted. They looked upon me as their project that would help them skip happily through the Pearly Gates someday.

Pauline and I skidded to a stop outside the door to the fudge shop as several customers came out carrying big cloth bags. Their arms over-flowed with wrapped fudge and matching Cinderella Pink Fairy Tale aprons, coin purses, dolls with hand-made dresses, and more. Husbands and dads and grandfathers were along with boys. They carted out cartons filled with Fishermen's Catch Tall Tale fudge flavors like Worms-in-Dirt and Big-Fish-Lie Fudge, along with fishing equipment.

The locals, with a couple of lost-looking but party-ready tourists, greeted me with cheery hellos and hugs. Support for me rent the air. "This, too, shall pass," some said, "like all the other murders!"

Cringe.

"Gil isn't a killer and neither are you, Ava."

Cringe again.

"The autopsy must be wrong. That woman was drunk and landed in water too cold for polar bears."

Sadly, I wished that were true.

People milled about the dock to view my grandfather's boat and the harbor. Grandpa was yapping away at the crowd.

I wended through the throng then tugged on one of Grandpa's elbows. "The sheriff told you to stay away from this area." The yellow crime scene tape still wrapped *Sophie's Smile*.

Grandpa wore a dapper red-and-black checked flannel shirt. He'd combed his silver hair back, though it stood up in the wind giving him the look of a cocky rooster. He pulled me aside to show off a side pocket in his denim jeans filled with cash.

I gasped. "Give that back. You can't make money off a woman's death."

"Ava, they're lovin' the salty tales from this old sea captain. And if you haven't noticed, you're benefitting from a woman's demise as well. Those cash registers inside are smokin'." His eyes sparkled under silver brows.

Pauline caught up to me, grabbing an arm. "Ava, that reporter Jane referred to is none other than that pesky Jeremy Stone."

Ugh. The reporter from Madison had exploited me a year ago when the inn had been in the middle of trouble--because of a dead movie star.

I was heading back toward the busy shop but Pauline hung back.

I turned to her. "What's wrong now?"

She hefted her purse. "The pistol. Jeremy is the kind who can sniff things like that. I don't want this pistol in my purse because he'll find it."

"It's not like he can get a search warrant for your purse."

But my friend grimaced in a way that said she was right. I shouldn't have taken the pistol in the first place.

We trotted up to the inn. In passing by the women in the parlor I merely mentioned that I had to check on the thermostat after my electrician called just now wondering if his installation was working. A lame lie, for sure, but we got upstairs, replaced the pistol under the mattress in Jackie's room, then headed back down the hill to the busy shop.

Dotty was ringing up purchases. Cody was wrapping and bagging fudge and other Fairy Tale gift items as fast as his arms and hands could work.

Grandpa's register was manned by Sam Peterson, to my surprise. The social worker visited often because of Cody. Sam had helped Cody as a young teenager connect with others coping with life's challenges, too. They remained friends.

My nose twitched with the sweet smells of success.

After a couple of customers passed, giving me a hug and patting my shoulders, I shut the door. The bell clanged. Everybody in the shop whooped and clapped.

Dotty waved from the register counter. She was just shy of my height by an inch, a plump lady with a pink sweatshirt bedazzled with pink sequins. Her short, white hair was spiked with gels--a new doo for her.

She crowed, "There she is, folks, Ava Oosterling, the proprietor of all things fudge and felonious."

The crowd roared.

I grew hot.

Cody waved with a big smile on his freckled face. "Miss Oosterling, everybody's here to make sure you don't lose the inn."

Instead of making me feel good, that set my stomach to churning. Did everybody staring back at me--my good supporters--think I was a loser? Did I have such a bad reputation for bad luck?

Pauline muttered, "I don't see the reporter."

Sam wiggled his eyebrows several times from across the room, a clear signal he had something of importance to tell me.

I thanked the crowd then grabbed Pauline by the elbow.

Sam left the register, leading us back to the empty minnow tank where the space was free of customers.

When Sam was worried or scared, he got a nervous tic. His forehead and scalp moved as he blinked his blue eyes and moved his eyebrows. The movement drew attention to his blond hair, always in the latest style.

I whispered, "What's wrong?"

"Jeremy Stone is in your kitchen in the back waiting for you. He wanted to head up to the inn but I told him you weren't home. I guessed."

"I was at Jane's. Can you get rid of him for me?"

Sam jerked back in shock.

I said, "Gee, Sam, I didn't mean kill the guy."

Pauline chuckled. "It sounded like that, and with your track record..."

"Stop it, you two." I said to Sam, "I'll leave by the front door. Tell him I have an emergency."

Pauline said, "Your whole life is an emergency."

This time Sam smiled. "Good thing we never married. I'm not good with too much drama." His scalp and hair moved back and forth as if to punctuate his words.

"And yet," I said, feeling a volcano's magma bubbling inside of me, "you're dating a stripper."

A flinch struck the corner of his mouth. "Jane Goodland does burlesque."

"Don't go technical on me. I thought maybe you and Fontana might be getting together. You were dating last fall. What happened to you two?"

"It's just that...I'm not sure I'm ready to be a dad."

"You're a social worker and you don't like kids?"

"That's not what I said, dammit."

Both Pauline and I gasped. Sam never swore.

I apologized. "Of course being a social worker doesn't equate with having kids. I'm really sorry I said that, Sam. I haven't been myself lately."

His face grew stern, unforgiving maybe, uncharacteristic of him. "I came here to see Cody, not get involved with you judging me. Cody's girlfriend Bethany had called me. She said they were supposed to go out on Saturday night, but he canceled, said he forgot to study for his yesterday's exam. Bethany said he never showed up at their required English lit class yesterday over at the technical college center."

"Have you talked with him?"

"Not yet. It's why I'm here, but then your grandfather asked me to take over his register and I was happy to help you out. Cody's been too busy for me to talk with him." He took a deep breath, misery scoring his handsome face. "This was bad timing on my part. The shop is usually dead."

"Gee, thanks. Don't you know it only hops when somebody is found dead?"

He hurried out the door.

Pauline shifted her purse to the other shoulder, frowning. "That's not like our Sam at all."

"I know. Dating a stripper? Afraid of kids? He's all mixed up."

"Do you think he still has feelings for Fontana?"

"I don't know. We'll have to figure out a way to help him."

"Oh no you don't. If it's like the way you're helping me with John..."

"When will you learn I'm more experienced than you in matters of love?"

She hissed at me.

The noise in the shop battered my eardrums, but it was good noise: the old-fashioned cash registers dinging, people laughing, the crinkle of the stiff cellophane Cody liked to use to wrap fudge purchases, and kids asking a million questions of moms and dads. Cody appeared happy and normal enough. I made a mental note to ask him about his classes and Bethany. Love trouble abounded, it seemed.

Taking a deep breath, I trotted back to the kitchen where Jeremy Stone was going through my cupboards.

"Get out of my kitchen, Jeremy."

His hooked nose was raised as usual into the air. "Now, now, Ava Oosterling, my stories weren't that bad last year. You ended up with an increase in business that probably saved this little shack."

I crossed my arms, glaring at him.

He resumed opening cupboard doors. "No hidden diamonds this time."

"Snooping is not nice. I could call your editor to tell him how you operate and then guess who would be living in a shack?"

His hands patted a covered kilo brick of imported Belgian chocolate, making me shiver. "My editor is the one who asked me to do an anniversary story about you and the re-opening of the inn. Last year I had the good fortune to report on the unfortunate death of one of your guests. How ironic that the story seems to be repeating itself."

"Last year's death didn't happen in my inn technically. I did not own it then."

"But your fudge was the murder weapon. Was fudge involved this time, too?"

I pointed toward the door. "Leave."

Jeremy held up a hand. "I drove four hours to get here from Madison because my editor remembers your guests from his time in college. This wasn't just my idea, so hold your hatred for me in check."

He'd intrigued me. "He knows the women?"

"All of them went to the university in Madison during the same years he was there. Frat boys notice the cheerleaders. He dated Jackie Valentine once."

Jeremy took out a notebook, flipped to a certain page. "Same age. She wasn't Valentine back then. She was a Baumgartner. Pretty. Popular. Always part of the college fundraisers, helping other students. She created a food pantry for poor students who barely got by, some even going homeless or living in crappy old firetraps of houses near the campus. From that time onward she was part of many nonprofit organizations, lately being part of a construction industry board that gave money to disadvantaged women interested in the construction trades. I interviewed one young woman on the street crew in Madison who got her job because of the scholarships Jackie Valentine bestowed on her. Jackie's life meant a lot to a lot of people. She's why I'm here. Trust me, I have no interest in writing about the bad luck of a small fudge shop operator."

He'd effectively silenced me. Jackie's death was a horrible tragedy. She sounded like a wonderful human being and all I'd done since last Wednesday was complain about her noise level.

Pauline said, "This shop isn't small. Ava has Internet sales now."

Jeremy handled another kilo of sweet perfection, sniffing it. "How big are those sales? I heard your former mother-in-law arranged this special women's retreat to help boost your sales. You must be struggling online and off line."

He was baiting me, his usual journalism tactic. "Did you see that crowd out there, Jeremy? That's success however you want to paint it."

"Is that every day?"

Pauline dropped her purse on the floor with a big plop and stepped toward him. Pauline towered over the reporter. I enjoyed his flinch. She balled her fists but then relaxed. "I play basketball and I'm good at it, Mr. Stone. Do you want me to bounce you out of here? Your head would just fit my palms. It's not polite to talk down to people. Now say you're sorry."

"Pauline, wait. No head bouncing. Jeremy might be able to help me."

Jeremy backed away. "Listen, I'm after facts. I can't help boost your fudge sales or take you out on a date."

Pauline stepped toward him again.

Jeremy stepped back further. He fiddled with his notebook while keeping a sharp eye on her.

I said, "We could use your help. There's something strange about the women that we can't figure out. They're very secretive."

"Is it about the fire?" A wormy smile crawled across his face.
"What fire?"

Pauline and I exchanged a glance because we'd almost been killed last autumn in a fire at the hands of an evil person.

Jeremy consulted his phone. He appeared to be looking through electronic notes. "There was a fire at the home of the vice chancellor at the time they were in college. I found a connection to the cheerleaders, who apparently were working for the catering service at a party there just prior to the fire."

"They caused the fire?"

Jeremy closed his phone. "No evidence of that. The fire happened later, it seems, after the party was over and the catering service and the cheerleaders left."

"How extensive was the damage?"

"The place burned to the ground. They never found the cause. Authorities could only guess that maybe a candle tipped over, but the report I dug up about the investigation showed the cheerleaders said they'd snuffed out the candles before leaving as part of their duties."

I sank my backside against the counter. "I noticed they don't talk about college days much at all, as if that's verboten. Instead, they talk about money a lot. Maybe money is a safe topic, though they argue about investments. It's very confusing."

Jeremy's expression brightened again. "I'm a journalist and know when people are avoiding talking about something. They make a point of talking about something else. Could it be that they focus on money talk because it's painful to remember that fire? I find it interesting that they've never said peep about it. That fire was a big deal, front page stuff. When people get together for a reunion, they eventually circle around to events that had to have affected them emotionally somehow."

"No," I said, thinking this through. "Maybe they blame themselves for the fire?"

Pauline said, "But after over thirty years? It obviously wasn't their fault. Did you find anything else in your research?"

"I've only started. There could be more to find."

I said, "Maybe you can go back again into the archives at the university communications department and your newspaper to see what more you might find out? Research each name and not just Jackie Valentine. I recall that Kim Olkowski, one of the group, said to Eliza Stefansson 'That's what happened thirty years ago.' But they didn't elaborate. Eliza also said once that Yola was responsible for Jackie's death."

Jeremy scribbled fast across his paper notebook. "Sheriff know about that statement?"

"I didn't tell him yet but I will and soon. I'll have to tell him I think the statement was in reference as to how drunk Jackie might have been. Yola is in her twenties and a friend of Zadie, who's the daughter of another woman friend in the group, Pepper Elliott. I felt that maybe Yola had encouraged her to drink or bought her an extra glass of wine or something of that sort."

Jeremy took out a chair at the small table and sat. "The autopsy showed that Jackie had been drinking. I already looked at the report."

I nodded.

"Who's Yola again?"

"One of the younger ones, a friend of Zadie who's the daughter of Pepper Elliott. Pepper was one of the cheerleaders. She came with the group and is staying at the inn."

He scribbled in the notebook again. Then he scowled. "Why are you helping me?"

"Do I have a choice? I know you'll stick around no matter what I have to say."

He laughed.

"Also my grandfather is in trouble. I'd do anything for him. His name is on the bait-and-fudge shop papers as part owner and the mortgage papers for the inn. The sheriff thinks my grandfather had something to do with Jackie's death."

"Gil? That codger? With his temper? No surprise."

"Don't repeat that." I sat down across from him while Pauline recovered her purse from the floor and hung by the sink across from us.

I explained the cut on my grandfather's hand, the blood on the boat, the argument my grandfather admitted to with Jackie.

Jeremy grimaced. "Man, you sure know how to get yourself in trouble up here in bucolic Door County."

"It's not my fault."

It felt like it though. Why couldn't I keep my life together? Pauline had said once that my fatal flaw was that I had no restraint. I didn't think enough before I acted. Maybe it was time to accept that this mess was my fault. I had to try harder to rectify things, to make order out of my life's chaos. Now I felt good about returning the pistol to where we'd found it under the mattress in the inn. Later, I could "discover" it and call Jordy.

Doing what as logical and right would be a start for changing my life.

"My grandfather and I are partners. If I lose, he loses. If he's arrested, I'll die. Even worse, he might lose his boat. Jeremy, he can't lose *Sophie's Smile*. That boat is why he gets up in the morning. If he has to sell it to afford a lawyer, I'll never recover. My grandfather saved my life by helping me re-start here in paradise after a lot of mixed-up years of wandering. When my grandmother broke a leg, he asked me to come back and help her for a few weeks. But it was part of his plan to help me. He found most of the equipment you see around you in this shop. And now, to have one of my guests found dead next to his boat, with her blood in his boat... It makes me cry."

Pauline sniffled. "That was beautiful."

Jeremy stared at me so long I thought cobwebs would form over him. "You love him." His voice was barely a whisper.

He closed the notebook. "My grandfathers both passed away several years ago. Both served in a war. One worked the rest of his life in a car factory and built his own house with his own hands. The other went to college at forty because he wanted to be the first in his family to graduate with a degree. Their tall, long shadows still follow me."

He darted off his chair and out of the kitchen before I could comment.

Pauline slid into his chair opposite me. "You and Jeremy Stone? Your enemy? Working together?"

"I should never have said all that to Jeremy."

"You told him stuff that came straight from your heart instead of your addled brain. You weren't lying for once. You seemed alive with the heartfelt truth just now with Jeremy."

She made me smile. "Maybe I'm changing for the better, Pauline."

She got up and came over to my chair and threw her arms around my shoulders. "At last!"

"Maybe it's just a spring cold coming on."

She laughed harder. "Being a better person will be hard. But I'm here to help you get through the rough patches. If you help me through mine."

I rose and hugged her. "Deal, girlfriend."

A hoary hunch inside me, though, feared a rough patch was ahead. "Whoever killed Jackie must have heard that she'd argued with my grandfather on the boat that night. The killer might think he knows something vital."

"Like what?"

"Something about that fire? About who burned down the vice chancellor's house?"

"I just got a chill."

Chapter 15

Pauline and I had just missed my grandfather. The church ladies said he'd headed to the bank with the donations he'd collected.

The ladies were in the middle of a contest to name my next fudge flavor that I'd introduce at the festival next weekend. I realized how much I'd been forced to neglect the one thing that calmed me and helped me think straight--making fudge.

Evidently Cody hadn't come up with a new flavor. I still needed to know why he'd skipped his date with Bethany and his college English class and exam.

Pauline and I headed out across the damp lawn behind the shop to go to my grandparents' place. An angry crow cawed in a bare maple tree, as if warning me.

Pauline and I collected Grandma's big picnic basket of goodies for lunch for the fudge divas and headed up the hill. It was after eleven this Tuesday morning. So much had happened already this morning that it felt as if a week had gone by instead of mere hours.

Victor Valentine's rental car sat in my driveway. The sheriff's squad was gone.

Once inside, Pauline and I discovered Victor entertaining the women in the parlor with tales about his wedding day with Jackie.

Cathy told me they hadn't gone to the spa, but had stayed here once Victor arrived. I wanted to ask about the sheriff, but their pleasant reminiscing made me swallow the words.

Lucky Harbor sat on Pepper's feet, his back lined up against her legs. His piercing brown eyes seemed to signal me about something. He probably wanted his cracker treats. I tossed him one, which disappeared with a snap of his jaws. He kept staring at me, though. What did he want? Victor was resuming his story, so I didn't interrupt.

Zadie was still in her running clothes, sitting on the floor next to Victor. Dishes were on the dining room table yet. It appeared Victor had arrived shortly after my departure earlier, which would have been while Sheriff Jordy Tollefson had been going over the room upstairs again.

Curious about their visit with Jordy, I waited for Victor to end his tale about him and Jackie performing a salsa dance at their wedding reception.

"Can I get you all coffee or tea? What did the sheriff say?"

Cathy waved me off. "He found a hammer, but none of us knew about it. I told him it was likely left behind by my son. Dillon is here so often fixing things. The sheriff left. And I helped myself to your kitchen and made coffee for us just minutes ago. But thanks."

I took note of a few dainty antique cups sitting around the room. "I'm glad you did. I want everybody to feel comfortable. What about lunch? I brought sandwiches my grandmother made."

Zadie spoke up from the floor. "I think it'd be good for us to go out. Victor should visit places that Jackie liked. Though, I guess I better change clothes and we should help Victor pack Jackie's things."

I had this sense of déjà vu about the room and realized everybody was sitting in the same spots as before when we had gathered, as if they had assigned seats. Or a pecking order like hens in a coop. Kim sat next to the multi-millionaire, her hand dangling off the chair arm close to his hand. Was there an intimacy I hadn't noticed before? Was she making a play for him, for his money? Why was Zadie at his feet? Was this a blatant play for Victor's friendship and thus a gift of money from him in the future for her business or her friend's business?

Shame came over me. Jeremy's quiet words about loving my grandfather pulled me together. I glanced at Pauline for support. She stood beside me, purse over her shoulder.

Feeling uneasy, I said to the group, "If you're thinking of a trip to Sister Bay and Al Johnson's Swedish Restaurant, allow me to give you a gift card I won in a raffle at Christmas."

Pepper said, "We couldn't do that. That's yours."

"Not anymore. I gave it to Jackie to use as a surprise for you all. It'll be in her room. I'll get it for you. I need to check the towel closet upstairs anyway."

Pauline followed me up the carpeted stairs.

In the upper hallway, she whispered, "What raffle? The only raffle here at Christmas was at Erik's bar and that was a meat raffle for the snowmobile club."

Meat raffles were about the biggest draws for bars in winter in Wisconsin. Guys in particular loved them. They bought tickets to benefit charities or their clubs. Winners got donated bratwursts or packages of venison steaks or hams and other carnivorous items.

"Okay, I lied. There is no card, but I wanted to see Jackie's room again. After Zadie mentioned nobody had been up here since the sheriff arrived, I had to have another look."

"You don't believe her?"

"Of course not." We stood in the hallway, pondering. "I don't believe any of them. Cathy's lying, too, to cover for her friends. She says that's Dillon's hammer, but I swear we saw blood on that hammer."

"We did see blood, but we didn't touch it or get that close. And it could be Dillon's hammer and it's his blood on it from a construction accident. It's just that Cathy didn't realize it had blood on it."

My body chilled with the implication. "Cripes. The sheriff is probably questioning Dillon right now. Let's hope what we saw on that hammer was just paint. But Cathy had told me Kim was snooping earlier, remember?"

All the bedroom doors hung open. I muttered to Pauline, "Looks like Jordy had himself a look in all the rooms."

I peeked in the other rooms before venturing to Jackie's. All were in ordinary stages of messiness with clothes, jewelry, and makeup strewn on dressers, chairs, and beds. Pepper's bed was made. The only other tidy beds were in the room belonging to Zadie and Yola at the end of the hall on the right.

Pauline said, "What's the matter?"

"I didn't expect those young women to be so neat."

"So this is like a version of the fairy tale 'Goldilocks and the Three Bears'. Who's been making my bed? Zadie and Yola? Zadie takes after her mother."

"I suppose. But there's something I'm missing here. Zadie and Yola dash out most of the time, always in a hurry. Zadie goes out very early for a run every day. Do you ever remember making your bed in your early twenties?"

"No, but mostly because I didn't want to hang around my mother. She was usually yelling about something from the moment I woke up."

Concern lurched into me. "No word from your mother?"

Pauline shrugged. "Like I care?"

I knew she did, but I didn't pursue it. I didn't know what to say or do to help my friend. The conundrum of her missing mother created a dark hole in my heart. My own mother did so many things for me, including supplying my fudge shop with fresh, organic cream. She called almost every day with something funny to tell me about herself or Dad on the farm. I couldn't imagine life without Florine Oosterling.

I closed the door on the room shared by Zadie and Yola. It was next to Jackie's room as we turned to go back the other way in the hallway.

We went into Jackie's room. The hammer had been taken by the sheriff, of course. The pink pistol wasn't around, to our shock.

Pauline asked, "Who do you think took it?"

I still wondered why Kim would have whacked Pepper over the head. I still believed she did it. I was living among guests who did such things and then lied about it. "Probably Kim."

Pauline said, "Everything else looks in order."

The bed was made. "Too much order. Jordy would not have paused to tuck in sheets and a blanket. Which means one of those women did this."

"So maybe Pepper came in here. She's Mrs. Neat."

"I'll have to ask. When the others aren't around."

"Check the closet and see if that gift dress for her daughter is still there."

I did so and it wasn't. "Maybe Pepper was in here. No dress."

Pauline nodded. "So that much is solved. What are you going to say when we go back downstairs? You don't have a gift card."

"I'll just say I can't find it."

"I thought you were turning into a better person? Lying is not a good way to start over."

A horrible racket downstairs drew our attention. I rushed out of the room and then trotted down the stairs.

Mercy Fogg was rapping on the front door, yelling, "Open up, Ava!"

I struggled with the stuck door. "Mercy? What's going on?"

The breeze whipped her blond mop about a scowling, red face. Deputy Maria Vasquez stood behind Mercy.

The women and Victor crowded behind me.

Taking in the faces, Mercy sputtered, as if she'd forgotten her purpose. "I've come for that dog of yours."

"I don't have a dog."

"Don't play dumb with me or the deputy. That dog that's always here. Dillon's dog."

"Lucky Harbor?"

"He's not so lucky now."

"Maria," I said in my sweetest voice, "what's going on?"

She grimaced. "Lucky Harbor is being charged with a paternity suit. He allegedly impregnated Mercy's golden retriever, Queenie."

A merciless grin slid across Mercy's face. "Queenie is registered with the American Kennel Club. Somebody owes me a bundle for the damages. That somebody is you, Ava, because you're responsible for allowing him off his leash."

She quoted several thousands of dollars she expected from me. And Dillon.

When Deputy Maria Vasquez and Mercy Fogg stepped into the parlor, Lucky Harbor leaped into Pepper's lap. The petite woman was barely visible behind the curly brown fur. It was clear Dillon's hunting spaniel suspected something was wrong. Oddly, he gave the appearance of protecting Pepper. A tiny growl, and then a whimper issued from his throat.

I stepped into the middle of the parlor, between Mercy and Pepper and the dog. "Is this really necessary? You can't have a dog arrested."

Maria said, "I'm afraid I am authorized to collect the dog. I can see he's not wearing a tag, and Mercy's lawyer has asked for a blood test."

"You have a lawyer?! Because two dogs had a romance?" I glared at Mercy. Then I looked at Maria. "He's always losing his tags. I'll find it. I'm sure it's in the inn somewhere."

Victor's handsome visage smiled at Mercy. "This dog appears to be well-trained and I've only seen him here with the women. Could it possibly be that your golden retriever was visited by some other dog?"

Pepper's head popped out from behind the dog. "He's been with me since last Wednesday."

Mercy's forehead furrowed. "The romance had to happen a couple of months ago, when you weren't here, Pepper. The vet confirmed her pregnancy and the timing."

Victor took out a wallet. "How much will it take?"

Mercy made her way to the front door. "No amount of money from you, Mr. Valentine. This is between me and Ava."

I spouted, "Because my grandmother's on the flower committee for the village and you're not. You lost your post as mayor last year and you're still mad about it."

"This isn't about stupid flowers." Mercy turned to Maria. "Deputy, please do your duty."

Mercy stomped out. She tried to slam the front door, but it stuck so all it did was screech against the wood under it. I closed the door and returned to the deputy.

"Maria, this is silly. Dillon's dog is neutered."

Everybody laughed, including Maria, who left within seconds.

The rest of us turned to the dog panting and smiling atop Pepper's lap.

Zadie leaped to her feet. "Let's all go to lunch and celebrate saving Lucky Harbor."

Eliza said, "A dubious thing to celebrate in the middle of Victor's sorrow."

Victor held up a hand. "Jackie must have cared about the dog. She had a good heart. Let's caravan up to Sister Bay and take the dog along, just to keep him away from that Fogg woman's sight, if it's okay with Ava."

The offer was such a nice surprise. "I'll get his leash."

Cathy was on her phone. It appeared she was texting Dillon about the dog's brush with the law.

Eliza put on a wan smile and walked across the parlor to hug Victor. "As long as it's okay with you, Vic. You're a generous man. Sorry I tried to speak for you."

"No harm at all." He kissed her lightly on the forehead. It was one of those friendship kisses but I noticed Yola and Zadie exchanged a wince, and Kim narrowed her eyes a bit.

All of the women except Cathy went upstairs. Victor went outside to move things around in his car, he said, so that he could accommodate riders in his back seat. Pauline put her purse down in order to help me and Cathy pick up cups and saucers in the parlor. We carried them to the kitchen where we set them on the counter.

I took advantage of having Cathy alone with Pauline and me. "Cathy, I lied about that card thing so that I could look around upstairs. Did you also lie about the hammer being Dillon's? What did the sheriff say when he was here?"

She sat on a stool at the island, folding her hands in front of her. "It could certainly have been my son's hammer."

I exchanged a look with Pauline. "We think we saw blood on it. I think Kim used it to hit Pepper over the head, though Pepper denies anything of that sort."

Cathy blinked at me. "I don't know what to say."

"What's going on, Cathy? Your friends are hiding something. What is it?"

"I don't know."

"You mean you don't know what the secret is or you don't know what I'm talking about?"

She paused in such a way that I knew it was the former. I said, "There's always been something between or among them all. I thought this fudge fantasy weekend would be a good way to bring it out in the open and be done with it or solve it, whatever it is. We've gone our separate ways for years because of something between each of them."

"Besides jealousy over money?"

"I don't know."

"You never asked Jackie about any of this? You had many meetings with her over the years."

"We kept it businesslike. Jackie gave the scholarship fund well over a million dollars over the years. You don't question somebody who does that."

She had paled, unlike Cathy. This was disturbing her.

Pauline rinsed a few plates behind me and put them in the dishwasher.

I said to Cathy, "You saw Kim come out of Jackie's room. She denies it." My stomach felt like it was churning gravel. "Sooner or later the sheriff will need to know that."

Tears began to stream down her cheeks. Pauline grabbed a paper napkin and gave it to Cathy.

I sat down across from her, whispering, "I'm sorry. I won't tell. That's up to you, Cathy."

"I feel horrible," she muttered, dabbing her face. "This is all my fault. I thought this would be a great retreat for women friends. Some friends we all turned out to be. All of us were drinking, of course, though not Zadie and Yola."

"You're talking about Saturday night?"

She nodded. "I didn't have that much, but enough to know better than go by the water. I was dizzy. I should have asked Zadie and Yola to stay with Jackie. But then if I'd done that, Eliza would have accused me of treating them like children. Zadie and Yola probably went out later anyway on their own. If only they'd checked on Jackie."

I recalled the tiff between Eliza and Cathy over Cathy acting motherly. "Did Zadie and Yola go out? Do you recall? Or did everybody go on up to bed? I heard a lot of racket and assumed you all went to bed, though Zadie and Yola usually go out late."

"Why is this important?"

"Maybe they saw the killer and didn't realize it."

"They're sharp young women. Why wouldn't they say something if they had seen someone?" Cathy put down the napkin. "You can't possibly think they killed Jackie?"

To tell the truth, I hadn't given it serious thought until this moment. I exchanged a glance with Pauline and could tell she thought the same thing. She sat down next to me in the kitchen.

The other women would be down any minute. "I don't know what to think, Cathy. I want to believe it was a stranger, but Zadie and Yola might have been out there at the time of this happening. They could have heard my grandfather arguing with Jackie. Then Jackie must have gone somewhere nearby and somehow drowned in a tub."

Cathy said, "It's quiet here in Fishers' Harbor at night. They could have heard something. But then you know how girlfriends are. Their conversations consume them and they're oblivious to the world."

"Jane said she heard Al picking up garbage after midnight. That would have been around the time of the murder, which could have covered up the noises from my grandfather and Jackie arguing."

"If what you're saying happened, somebody had to bring Jackie's body back to the harbor and your grandfather's boat. Poor Pepper. If her daughter is involved it will kill her." Cathy grabbed the napkin again to staunch new tears. "Pepper knows something is wrong. That's why Lucky Harbor sticks to her. That dog has always been sensitive."

That was true. He was an excellent bird dog with a good nose. He also knew how to play me for treats. But this? Could a dog detect a murderer in our midst?

Cathy was shredding the napkin, staring at her motions. "I think Pepper hit herself over the head to make it look like Kim did it. To save Zadie."

Chapter 16

I sat at the kitchen island confused and in shock at Cathy's words. "You're sure? Pepper is protecting her daughter by trying to make it look like Kim killed Jackie? And you think Pepper hit herself? Knowing you were downstairs and would know Kim was upstairs?"

Cathy's face was chalky white. She kept shredding a paper napkin.

The kitchen felt chilly, the coffee's aroma mocking us. Pauline and I sat on our stools at the marble island like statues. It was a little past noon. Two of the women trundled down the staircase and headed outside for their trip to Sister Bay.

Pauline said, "That sounds far-fetched, Cathy. Sorry."

My former mother-in-law finished shredding the napkin. She scooped it into a neat pile atop the countertop island. "I know it does. Women's intuition is always crazy."

"Zadie and Yola stayed in, though. That's what they've said."

Cathy shrugged, rising. "There's something Pepper is holding in. And she did suffer that cut on her head. If she didn't do it to herself to protect her daughter, then Kim did it on purpose." She shuddered.

"So you think it's possible Kim murdered Jackie? She snuck out after everybody went upstairs on Saturday night?"

"Ask the sheriff what he found on the hammer."

"He likely didn't find Kim's fingerprints. She's always wearing those white gloves."

I didn't say another word because the rest of the women came down the stairs. Eliza came into the kitchen to collect Cathy, then off they went on their trip.

Pauline got off her stool. "I know that look. You think Cathy's right?"

"She's a shrewd businesswoman. Why didn't I think of this before? We need to be looking for a pair of white gloves, preferably finding a pair doused with Pepper's blood."

"Can I eat first? I'm starving?"

"Sure. They'll be gone for a couple of hours. I have leftover pizza."

"Perfect."

We gobbled down a piece each, then hurried upstairs to scour Kim's room.

We found no white gloves covered in blood in Kim Olkowski's room, nor did we expect to. If Kim were the murderer, she'd be smart enough to do away with the gloves.

I said, "We could go up and down Main Street and look for the gloves in the garbage cans."

Pauline headed for the staircase. "No way. I'm not going to be caught by parents in this school district dumpster diving on a Tuesday afternoon. I'm supposed to be sick."

I followed her down the staircase as she added, "Call Jordy about this. Have him and Maria go through the cans."

On the way to the kitchen I took out my phone.

"For once you've listened to me?" she asked.

"Heck no. I'm calling Al Kvalheim. Jane said she saw Al collecting garbage at around midnight on Saturday. Al had to have noticed something.

But Al hadn't. I asked him where the garbage was now.

"Gee, let me think. That was so long ago," Al said, his voice thick from the cigarettes he was trying to quit smoking. "I was out late that night because the truck had broken down on Saturday so I had to fix that and then I found out the tires were low so I had to get my tire pump and I wasn't close to a plug-in. My truck's plug-in doesn't work for some reason. So I had to go back on low tires--"

"Al, I just need to know where the garbage is now, particularly anything you took from the harbor and between there and my inn and Erik's bar."

"It's all in the shed just outside town. I won't be taking things to the dump until Friday when I get ready for the Sweets, Suds and Buds Festival. What're you looking for?"

I was losing my patience. "A white glove with blood on it."

"You mean I can help you solve that lady's death? I'll meet you over at the shed and unlock it right away."

"Thanks, Al."

When I got off the phone, I grabbed another cold pizza slice and chomped.

Pauline laughed. "You're happy. We find a white glove and your grandfather will be cleared. Life will be back to normal."

"Yes." I savored how quickly I had gotten my life back together.

"Except you forgot about the dress in his dreams. That seems like your grandfather is concerned about those divas. He saw or knows something but doesn't realize its importance."

"Maybe it's just a dream about my grandmother and we're making too much of it."

"I suppose. I need to head home before school lets out."

"But first we have to scour the ladies' cars sitting in my parking lot."

Pauline groaned. "Why?"

"Because."

She followed me outside.

The vehicles were unlocked. Nobody locked anything when parked on top of this cliff at the inn. We went through a couple of cars not finding anything out of the ordinary until we got to Pepper Elliott's small, red sports car. To our shock, under the front passenger seat and on the floor we found gobs of new receipts for clothes bought over the past week in various shops around Door County. I counted two dozen receipts from our best shops in Sister Bay, Egg Harbor, and Fishers' Harbor.

Pauline said, "We didn't see all of these clothes upstairs in the inn. There are enough receipts here for two walk-in closets full of new stuff."

There were no clothes in the small trunk of the car or back seat.

"For some reason," I mused, "Pepper hid these."

"What if somebody else hid them in her car? Nobody hides their own receipts."

"They do if a husband or somebody isn't supposed to see them. But yeah, you could be right."

"Of course I am. Give me credit. I'm a teacher with kindergarten kids who hide stuff all the time inside their pants and underwear. You'd be amazed what drops out of their shorts on the warm days in fall and spring. One little boy a couple of years ago tried to hide candy bars but they melted and began running down one leg."

"Okay, I get the picture. So you're right. Pepper probably wouldn't bother hiding receipts in her own car."

I stood with Pauline in the sunshine dappling through the bare maple tree limbs fat with red spring leaf buds. Warm air wafted around us as it rose off the blacktop. Shrill robins kited past in an aerial fight for nesting grounds.

The receipts plagued me. "So, my grandfather talked about dresses in his sleep. Do you suppose some of this clothing is hidden on the boat? Maybe he encountered this stuff."

"Jordy and Maria went over the boat a couple of times."

I called Jordy and asked if he had confiscated dresses or women's clothing off *Sophie's Smile.*

Jordy growled back, "Is this some kind of joke?"

"It's not like I asked if you were a cross-dresser, Jordy."

"Stay off that boat. Don't cross the yellow tape." He clicked off the phone.

I relayed the conversation to Pauline, who said, "I'm heading out."

"Wait! You're not going to help me go through garbage or inspect the boat?"

"I have more important matters to take care of."

"Like what?"

"I'm going back to that house south of town. I want to be sure the grounds are safe for my kindergarten girls. Who knows when John will want to start filming the show with them."

My instincts flinched. "You really think it's on the up-and-up about a TV show using that house?"

"I trust him."

"So you're taking things slow with him?"

"Yes. You were right about him all along. Are you happy I'm not going to marry him after all?"

She didn't want my answer.

After Pauline drove away, I needed Dillon. In the worst way. A quick call got me an invitation to my former digs on Duck Marsh Street.

Dillon would help me figure out this mess. Jackie was dead, and Cathy wondered if Zadie did it, but maybe Kim was involved, as Cathy said. Cathy was Dillon's mother, but he had to be told about her suppositions. But if Kim didn't murder Jackie, and Zadie did it, that meant Pepper might be protecting her daughter Zadie. And it would be likely Zadie's friend Yola knew. If Kim were involved, that left only Eliza who maybe didn't know anything going on but that didn't seem to work since Eliza was in serious competition with Kim for money to save Eliza's dead husband's farm implement dealership. So, were they all in on it? Had the murder been orchestrated by the entire group?

I wanted to be wrong. There had to be some stranger who'd wandered through town, did the deed, and took off. If so, what was his or her motive?

I needed a kiss and hug from Dillon to set my mind straight.

To my surprise and disappointment, John Schultz was at Dillon's cabin. I gave Dillon a quick kiss but more amorous moves would have to wait for later.

John was reaching into the refrigerator. He sported a Green Bay Packer long-sleeved T-shirt instead of his usual Hawaiian shirt. Despite the chilly spring air, he wore shorts and sandals that showed his dimpled knees and hairy legs and crooked toes. He was a man in his fifties but he dressed like a college student.

"Hello, Ava!" he bellowed, looking up at me as I came through the front door. "Just the woman I wanted to see."

Dillon was putting catsup back in the refrigerator. He gave me a wink. "Just the woman I always love seeing. What's up, honey?"

I helped Dillon clean up the table that used to be mine. "Mercy insists your dog had sex with hers and that there are puppies on the way."

Dillon laughed heartily. "Does she know Lucky Harbor is fixed?"

"Not yet. I thought I'd let her stew for a while."

"You're wicked." Dillon leaned his backside against the kitchen sink, laughing.

John grabbed a can of cola from the refrigerator and popped it. "Mercy deserves a bit of a joke on her. I still shiver about her hauling my unconscious body into her bed last year." His shoulders flinched.

I asked, "What brings you to town, John? I hardly ever see you." It was my way of saying, *Why don't you visit my best friend Pauline more who loves you, you lout?*

As we all stood around in the kitchen, he exchanged a look with Dillon. "I suppose I should tell her since you're involved."

Dillon shrugged his assent, crossing his legs at his ankles and folding his arms. "I don't know if she can keep this secret. She and Pauline are like sisters."

Protective, I piped up, "What's going on? What about Pauline?"

John put his cola down on the table then went to the living room area where he picked up a long tool by the fireplace. He brought it back and said, "A metal detector. A super-duper one. Got it from a geologist friend up in Rhinelander. He says he uses it to check for Hodags." John bellowed boisterous laughter.

Hodags were mythical creatures, of course. I smiled at his lame joke.

I sat down at the table. "What's going on with you two?"

"Dillon and I are going into the woods to look for that ring that Pauline lost last fall."

I blinked hard, looking up at Dillon.

He nodded. "We're going to give it a try."

John handed the metal detector to Dillon, then went back to the couch that sat in front of the fireplace. He brought back a colorful scarf and a pair of shoes I recognized.

I said, "Those are Pauline's."

"I sneaked over to her house and got these. They're for the dog."

"Lucky Harbor's going to wear a scarf and shoes?"

Dillon laughed. "This afternoon we're going to take Lucky down to that woods where Pauline lost her purse last fall and see if he might sniff out that ring. The snow should be gone now in that ravine."

The horror of what had happened in that woods near Brussels in southern Door County flashed a memory filled with red flames that I'd never forget.

John was all smiles, even in his twinkling eyes. "I want to ask Paulie girl to marry me, but I know darn well any ring I give her will only remind her of losing that ring she bought last fall for herself. I don't want my Paulie feeling embarrassed or not feeling good enough for me. I want her to say 'yes' to me with no regrets."

My mouth was hanging open and I couldn't shut it to speak. It occurred to me John might love to find that ring because it would mean he wouldn't have to buy one. However, evidently Dillon was on board with this. It had to mean John was going to do the honorable thing.

I said, "I suspect you don't want me telling her you're doing this?"

John whooped, high-fiving me with his big hand. "You got it, Ava Oosterling. Lips sealed. Okay? You tell and I'm not invitin' you to our wedding."

This was rushing ahead too fast for me. "Has a date been set by you two? And what about Pauline's opinion?"

Pauline had decided to adjust her feelings about marrying this guy. Because of me pushing her to be wary of John. I was now feeling sick and confused. Again.

While Dillon hauled the metal detector back to the fireplace, John slid into the seat across from me at the table. "I know you think I'm crazy, Ava. And I am. I'm crazy to think Pauline might be able to love me. Paulie's been down in the dumps lately and I don't know why. This surprise will cheer her up."

She'd been down in the dumps about John and about her mother not being around. Now I wondered if Pauline was afraid John would ask her to marry him? And that there'd be a wedding without her mother present? Or, depending on the condition of her mother, maybe Pauline was fearful her mother would appear and cause a huge scene? It was coming together now in my heart and head what was going on with Pauline. She wanted to marry John, but not until she'd found her mother.

I got up and kissed Dillon, then forced myself to hug John. His whiskers scraped my right cheek. "I'll keep the secret for now. But, John, you better come through for Pauline with a proper ring that you pay for or there will be another murder in Fishers' Harbor."

John let out a big breath. "You're a good woman, Ava."

After leaving the men I trotted over to the fudge shop.

The only people in the fudge shop were Brecht Rousseau and his twins in their stroller. Brecht sat on the stool behind my cash register.

"Where is everybody?" I asked.

"The church ladies? I sort of yelled at them." His craggy face wrinkled in pain.

"Sort of yelled? About what?" Why was my life seemingly filled with men in trouble?

Brecht was straightening the money bills in my register. "They were all being so nice to me and the kids. They were offering me fudge and asking my opinion about twenty pieces and marked as many score sheets. They kept giving me pats on the back and cheeks. They were holding the kids and making them giggle. The ladies were being so damned nice. As if they pitied me."

He was staring toward the window now. The flags at the harbor whipped in the wind. Nobody was out there. Waves plumed over the concrete piers. The yellow-taped *Sophie's Smile* rocked in its berth.

"So you raised your voice because they were nice to you? Are you all right?" I glanced at the babies asleep in the stroller in the middle of the shop.

"My life has been reduced to babysitting and fudge tasting. The maple flavor is outstanding, by the way." He eased his tall frame off the stool. "Now that you're here, I better get going."

I headed to the stroller and knelt in front of the sleeping cherubs. "Where did Cody go?"

Brecht shrugged. "He said he had stuff to take care of."

"That's not like him. Thanks for being here."

I rose from my haunches, perusing the shop. The women had stuffed the shelves with homemade quilts, tablecloths, doilies, and other items I didn't ordinarily have for sale. I was used to their over-zealous kindnesses after a year of such gestures, but Brecht was a former army soldier suddenly dropped into this quiet place where kindness was our weapon. He didn't know how to "shoot" back yet.

I got out my phone. "Brecht, I need your help. I need you to go on a mission."

At the word "mission" he perked up. "Yeah? What?"

"Cody hasn't been himself lately. He suddenly skipped class and canceled dates with a very sweet girlfriend here in Fishers' Harbor. Do you think you could be sneaky and see what's up if I ask you and Cody to go shopping for special ingredients I'll need for the fudge for the upcoming festival?"

"Sure."

"I'd love it, too, if you and Cody could come up with new flavor possibilities. He promised me he'd create one, but he's seemed to drop it, again not like him. Cody loves making fudge, or used to, and he's creative. He'll take that bait."

Brecht smiled finally. "We could have used you in the army. You're sneaky."

I rushed to wrap fudge samples. "You'll need these when you stop at the stores. If you find new places that will stock my fudge, all the better, and I'll stock whatever they want to feature here in my shop for the festival weekend."

He tucked a blanket around the sleeping twins. His tenderness toward them made my heart split open.

Cody answered his phone but sounded upset, which knocked me off-kilter. He rarely got moody. He was at his parents' house but didn't elaborate. Still, he agreed to let Brecht pick him up.

After Brecht and his twins left, I had the shop to myself. I did my best thinking by making fudge. It was around two o'clock in the afternoon now, and I knew the women and Victor might be descending on me soon.

Fudge carried history with it. Making fudge made me feel like I could time travel on a magic carpet. Various types of fudge were likely made by most or all cultures around the world right back to the ancient Egyptians or before. Fudge didn't melt in the sun or in heat like plain chocolate, so I liked to imagine that sometime scientists might open a tomb somewhere and find fudge had been an offering to gods upon a famous queen's or king's death. Or maybe somebody would take fudge to Mars because it wouldn't melt in its heat.

What would be my new Fairy Tale Fudge flavor for Saturday? What went with local craft beers? What fairy tale reflected the goodness of Door County in spring, and the goodness of my life?

And how was I to help Pauline? Why did I want to stop her from loving John?

Ach, I gave up.

Nothing seemed good right now. Murder? Secrets? John proposing to Pauline soon?

Ach, ach.

I peered about the shop. Grandpa wasn't around. I ventured to the window. Aha! His figure passed by the interior of a boat window. Of course he would flout the sheriff and ignore the yellow crime-scene tape.

I hiked fast to the pier, lifted the tape, and boarded.

"Grandpa?" He had gone below evidently.

The topside cabin was empty. I opened cupboards looking for dresses. Insane, I knew, but Pauline and I had found all those receipts and Grandma had told us about Grandpa mentioning a dress in his dreams. Nothing out of the ordinary appeared topside, so I went below.

"Grandpa?"

Nothing.

"Grandpa? It's just me. Ava."

I looked under the bunks and in the cupboards. No dresses. No grandpa.

Back next to the stairwell I knocked on the door to the head, or toilet. "Grandpa?"

No answer, but he had to be inside. Panicked, I hollered, "I'm opening the door!"

He was crumpled over the stool lid, out cold.

"Gilpa!"

In one fist he held what looked like a yellow floral sundress.

I took out my phone to call 911 but in the next instant the phone was smacked out of my hand--hard.

Chapter 17

I woke up in the emergency room of the hospital in Sturgeon Bay.

My back ached. My left wrist and hand felt like a hammer had come down. Had it? The back of my head sported a goose egg.

A disembodied female voice said, "You're lucky I came along looking for fudge or you'd a been a goner. Your grandpa, too."

Fontana. Her red hair flickered like strobe lights in front of me.

My mother hovered next to me, too. I could make out a dizzy, blurry visage of her long dark hair and a bib apron with her signature Holstein cow black-and-white motif on it. "Honey, be still."

A mumble managed to come out of me as I sat up. "What happened? Where's Grandpa?"

Mom said, "Your grandfather came to in the ambulance and insisted he didn't want to be admitted to the hospital, but your dad insisted. He's in a room not far from here."

Fontana said, "And grumpy. The fudge divas arrived, fresh lipstick and all."

I managed a chuckle, though it hurt my head. "I need to see him."

Mom stopped me from rising on the gurney. "You stay put, dear. I'll go see how he's doing and report back."

A nurse in a pleasant outfit with blue bunnies on it for the Easter season showed up. She wrapped a cuff around my arm and took my blood pressure. "You'll be free to go soon. Just sit there for a while. You probably have a very mild concussion. I'll check back in a half hour."

After she stepped out, Jordy Tollefson in full uniform marched in. He carried his official hat, both hands fingering the brim. "What the hell?"

He blinked several times, his gaze sweeping over me.

Fontana told him, "She already knows she wasn't supposed to be on the boat."

He sidled closer to me on the opposite side from Fontana. They had me surrounded. "You weren't supposed to be on the boat," Jordy growled.

To avoid his steely gaze, I turned to Fontana. "Where's Grandma?"

"In the hospital chapel. She took one look at you and Gilsen and set up a prayer vigil with anybody who'd join in. She was busy on her phone earlier, too."

I sank within myself. "Contacting the holy street team, I'm sure. They probably thought we were in danger of meeting Saint Peter at the Pearly Gates."

Jordy grumbled, "And you would have found a way to sneak through the Gates without Peter's permission, I'm sure."

"Jordy, can't you ever congratulate me? I found my grandpa and probably took a hit meant for him. I get points for that, don't I?"

"He's not so smart either," Jordy said. "What were you two doing on that boat?"

The star on his chest burned the reflection of the overhead lights into my retinas. I reached out and covered his star with a hand before giving it a second thought. Jordy's hand enveloped mine. Warmth poured through me oddly, in a satisfying way, like when I enjoyed Grandma's Belgian waffles. I felt calm, as if I'd come home, as if I could rest and ignore the world. Startled by that, I pulled my hand away.

"I'm okay, Jordy."

He set his hat next to me. "No, you're not. I don't want you falling off this gurney, not when I have a mile-long list of questions for you."

So he was just doing his duty. I had thought maybe... The hit on my head was making me think crazy things. "Where's Dillon?"

Fontana's big pregnant belly crowded me on the other side. She fluffed the tiny pillow behind me. "He's on his way. He was out in the woods with his dog and a friend. Took them a while to walk back to their car. He thanked me for finding you."

"Thanks, Fontana. Were my guests at the harbor when you found me?"

"I'd stopped at the inn first and all those ladies and Victor Valentine were there and wondered where you were."

"What time is it?" I asked.

"Past six now, but I found you around five."

"Five. I remember it was around two when I was about to make fudge."

Jordy asked, "How soon after that did you go onto the boat?"

"Maybe a half hour or hour after that."

"Who would want to harm you and your grandfather?"

My mind spun with color wheels as it pulsated with pain. "It could be anybody, Jordy. I've been looking into things, trying to find out who might have killed Jackie."

"Maybe somebody doesn't like you snooping." Jordy said it with a wry tone. "Do you have a suspect in mind?"

The antiseptic smells of the ER assailed me. Off in another area a little boy was crying about a cut on his foot. Instruments clinked in some pan. A machine beeped. Nurses and aides exchanged orders and moved people about. The urgent cacophony of it all acted like truth serum.

"Kim Olkowski," I said. "Everything points to her so far." I felt instant shame, though. "Couldn't it have been a stranger going through town?"

Jordy said, "Could have been. We're looking at everybody we can. We don't have many cameras pointed at our streets and roads, so it's tough. Erik has a camera over the doorway to his bar and restaurant. We saw Mercy Fogg and the women going in and out, but that's all."

Fontana huffed by my side, her breath tickling my face. "Ava needs to rest. You can't possibly think anything she says at this moment is reliable? Those women did not kill one of their own. Maybe it was Al Kvalheim. He lies about his smoking habit."

She spoke directly at my face now, her ruby lips flapping and glinting in the light of the ER. "Didn't you say he was out at midnight collecting garbage? He could have toted that woman in a garbage sack and plopped her in the water without anybody thinking a thing. Ouch." She took a deep breath. "That was the baby kicking. He or she wants out." She looked down. "Damn. Nothing. Why can't my water break while I'm in the E.R.? Free health care."

My eyesight was clearing. I tried to get up but met with Jordy's chest. He pushed me back.

"Hey," he said. "Just sit there, Ava." He handed me a glass of water from a table nearby.

I accepted the water and drank, looking into his soft, brown eyes. "Jordy," I said, clearing my throat, "I don't think Al is the kind to murder somebody. What would be his motive?"

"He doesn't have one. He's not high on my list. Did you see anybody else out and about?"

"I know that Jane Goodland and Sam Peterson were out at the same time."

"I've already talked with them."

"Dead ends." I sighed. "What about the dress found on the boat with my grandpa?"

Fontana said, "That was a cute sundress. I swear I saw that on sale in Egg Harbor."

Egg Harbor was south of Fishers' Harbor.

I said, "Maybe Jackie pissed off the clerk?"

Jordy said, "I have the dress in evidence. I'll check out the clerk. Know anything more about it?" He addressed both of us.

"Gilsen said he found it stuffed under the engine hood of his boat. Maria and I must have missed it in our search." He coughed.

I noted, "Embarrassing for you to miss something that big. You should work with me and Grandpa more."

Jordy huffed.

I told him, "Grandma said he mentioned a dress in his sleep. Did he tell you that?"

"All he said is the dress was stuffed into the engine."

Fontana tisked. "Those women are clothes hogs. Could've been any of them hiding that dress. It strikes me somebody was jealous of another. Nobody ruins a nice dress like that unless they're trying to make a statement."

Jordy and I stared at her. Fontana made sense. What it meant, I didn't know.

Panic hit me like a cold brick alongside my head. "Anybody call Pauline? Where's my phone?"

I slapped the pockets of my jeans. Nothing.

Fontana had her phone out. "I didn't think of her. She's going to be so mad at you."

"Me? I was knocked out. I couldn't call. You could have called earlier."

"Me? I was riding in the ambulance, too, because they worried about my baby because of all the excitement. You know, finding you two looking dead took a lot out of me."

"I'm sorry. Thank you, Fontana. Maybe somebody has my phone?"

"Your phone's gone, honey. Went in the drink probably." I heard Pauline's voice on Fontana's cell phone, then Fontana said,

"Ava's in the hospital after almost dying but I saved her. Same ol' same ol', right?" Fontana clicked speaker phone.

Pauline's "What the hell happened this time?!" erupted into the ER.

Jordy laughed. Nurses giggled. The little boy in the corner muttered, "Those ladies are loud."

My parents came in with the doctor, announcing they were taking me and Grandpa home for the night.

Dad was shaking his head over everything. "We gotta get going. Your grandpa is having a fit about his popularity with those guests of yours."

That made me smile. "Dad, you and Grandpa are handsome. It's an Oosterling curse."

He hugged me with strong arms. "Kiddo, thank God you're all right."

Jordy gave me a curt nod before exiting the ER.

Grandpa, Grandma, and I stayed overnight at the farm. Grandpa had a mild concussion, too. He didn't know who hit him on the boat. I was nursing a pretty good goose egg on the back of my head but my vision had returned.

My father was worried about me in his quiet way. "It's good to have you here tonight."

He left the house to milk the cows. He had a hired hand, but it took two of them to milk the three hundred cows in a timely way, even in the modern dairy parlor where eight cows stood at once with machines on them. It was after seven-thirty at night already, past the normal milking time. The cows would be bellowing for him.

Mom decided to vacuum the living room, telling us to go upstairs to bed and rest. I wished I could vacuum my worries away. What I needed to be doing was making fudge, but fudge making was frustrating me lately. What was happening to me?

Pauline showed up with Fontana a half our later. We met in the farm kitchen with its table for twelve. Mom was still vacuuming in some distant room.

Pauline and Fontana made toasted cheese sandwiches. Mom had made coleslaw earlier and that came out of the refrigerator to be plunked on the big table after a tablecloth had floated into place. Plates and silverware clinked and clacked. Salt and pepper shakers in the shape of cows appeared. We giggled. Being with my friends was restorative.

Pauline had stopped by the inn before racing here. She had left notes in the kitchen about the spaghetti pies and brownies for my guests.

"Ava," Pauline said, retrieving small bowls from the cupboards, "you can't be alone anymore as long as those women are around. They're bad luck. Except for Cathy of course."

Fontana said, "One of them tried to kill you and your grandpa."

Pauline said, "Cathy saw Kim go into Jackie's room. We saw the hammer. She probably bought another one."

I let go of my sandwich to sit back in my chair at the table. "Jordy never mentioned finding a weapon on the boat."

Pauline said, "Because it's in the harbor, along with your phone."

Fontana was slicing a banana-peanut butter pie in front of me.

The aroma had me drooling. "Jordy probably went back and found those things by now."

The vacuum stopped. I got up--slowly. "I'm going to talk with Grandpa. Grandma needs a break."

Pauline said, "Can we come with?"

"Of course."

Grandma was glad for the break. "He keeps wanting to know what's for supper. He gets beat up and all he can think about is food."

I giggled, peering at him lying atop the bed cover fully clothed and with his work shoes still on. "How long did it take to get the lipstick off his face?"

Grandpa shook a fist at me playfully. "I'm handsome. Get over it."

Grandma said, "Bah! You Belgian buffalo." She left for downstairs.

The farmhouse bedroom was small. It only had room for one chair on one side of the bed and the dresser on the other. I sat on the end of the bed, while Fontana eased into the comfy chair. Pauline stood by the door.

Grandpa's silver hair was combed. Grandma must have done it. He was in a fresh, red-checked flannel shirt and denim jeans.

"Your darn grandma won't let me move from this bed."

I patted his nearby ankle. "You better listen to her."

"I suppose you're wondering about that dress."

"Yes, we are."

Fontana echoed, "We think maybe the dress was bought in Egg Harbor."

Fontana was thrilled to be part of this.

I exchanged a smile with Pauline, then said to Grandpa, "You told the sheriff you found the dress under the boat engine cover."

"Found it Sunday."

"And you didn't tell me?"

"I have to protect you, Ava Mathilde. I sneaked back on the boat after the sheriff and Maria left. I didn't know what to do with the dang thing. Couldn't take it to the house because Sophie would have a fit. I felt stupid with a dress in my hand. I knew it was important."

"Why didn't you tell the sheriff?"

"Because he'd arrest me! I was on the boat when I wasn't supposed to be."

I patted his leg again. "Why put it on the boat?"

"So you didn't find it. At first I hid it in a fudge shop cupboard."

"Our shop? My shop?"

"It worried me, though, that those women might find it and involve you or the fudge shop, so I took it and put it back on the boat."

I remembered that Jeremy Stone had been going through the cupboards on his visit. Had he seen the dress? Grandpa seemed confused about the dress. An unreliable witness, Jordy would say. Grandpa had just said he found the dress, but he then took it, brought it to the shop, then put it back in the engine, then retrieved it to put it behind the toilet on the boat. Screwy.

"Is Grandma mad you never told her about the dress?"

"She'll get over it. I'm a handsome bugger, remember? I didn't want Sophie thinking I had naked women on the boat. So I tried to stuff it behind the sink in the head. That's the last thing I remember." He swiped a hand over his face. "This mess is all my fault. I should never have agreed to haul those ladies up and down the coast in my boat. Heck, I had to dodge ice floes yet, but I never felt they were as dangerous as those women's kisses." He gave me a wink. "You feelin' okay, A.M.?"

"Sore and I need to take it slow, like you. I'll be fine."

"You won't be fine until you get rid of those women in that inn. They're not just fudge divas. They're *deadly fudge divas.*"

He silenced us all for a moment.

I said, "They're waiting for the body to be released. Then they'll leave. They're all friends."

Grandpa huffed. "Friends? One of them probably tried to kill you and me, and one of them had to be responsible for dumping their friend in the harbor, probably doing it because they wanted to blame me and get off scot free."

Pauline said, "But Jackie was a big, strong woman. We're all talking as if just one person did the deed. Wouldn't it take two people to carry her? And do it swiftly enough so nobody saw her or him?"

I asked. "I've certainly thought about that, but they were in the inn that night."

Pauline leaned back against the doorjamb. "You don't. You went to sleep. And you snore. If they heard you snoring, they would know they could sneak out and do anything."

"I do not snore."

Grandpa was chuckling. He insisted on getting up.

We escorted him downstairs so he could have the pie.

Dillon showed up without John, to Pauline's disappointment, to make sure I was okay. His hugs felt good, but my mind went back to Jordy's warm hand holding mine. It was as if Jordy wanted something from me. I didn't think it was romantic. Jordy wanted to talk to me about what I knew and about my theories on the crime.

We ate our sandwiches and coleslaw. Dad and our hired hand came in two hours later when we were watching a popular show about a true-life veterinarian. The vet saved a goat having its first kid, which made Fontana weepy. She went home to the farm nearby where she stayed with our friend Jonas Coppens. He raised goats and sheep.

Pauline and Dillon left soon afterward.

Dad and Mom and my grandparents insisted I sleep under their watchful eyes.

The next morning Mom was driving me back north to Fishers' Harbor when her phone rang. I answered it for her. To my surprise it was Jeremy Stone.

"Hey, Oosterling, it's taken me a half hour to track you down."

"You found out about the dress?" Anticipation seized my body.

"What dress?"

"One that caused a lump on my head."

"Forget a dress for a moment. I had a conversation with the wife of that vice chancellor whose mansion burned down after their party back in your fudge guests' college days. It wasn't a pleasant conversation. Mighty short. She remembered those 'damn girls', as she called them. She'd caught one of them with her husband in a lip lock that night."

I looked over to my mom, who was listening as she drove up Highway 42 toward Sturgeon Bay. I asked Jeremy, "So?"

"It's plausible the vice chancellor's wife was the arsonist. She wanted to get rid of the memories of being cheated on in her own house. Want to guess which of your ladies was the heartthrob cheerleader doling out more than a shake of her pompons?"

Did he have to make this sound so sleazy? "Jeremy, just tell me what you found out."

"It was Pepper. She wasn't Elliott back then. Pepper Neuendorf, from Milwaukee. She married Quincy Elliott later, but it seems Mrs. Ex-Vice Chancellor doesn't think Pepper forgot about the vice chancellor."

The mostly brown spring scenery was sliding by as Mom drove. Muddy ditches morphed into spots of green grass and gray fence posts and split rail fencing and Holstein cows and then commercial buildings as we entered Sturgeon Bay, passing the intersection that went to the county justice center.

"I'm not sure I understand, Jeremy. What does any of this have to do with the murder of Jackie Valentine?"

"The ex says Jackie showed up once looking for money on the behalf of Pepper. Jackie accused the woman's husband of getting Pepper pregnant. After Pepper was married to Quincy Elliott."

"A soap opera."

"It could be, but I'd like to ask your guests some questions."

"Stay away from Pepper and all my guests, Jeremy." He was returning to his past sleazy ways. I should never have agreed to have him help me.

"Don't have regrets."

The darn journalist was reading my mind.

He continued, "What if it's true that Pepper carried on an affair with the former vice chancellor? What if her daughter isn't Quincy Elliott's at all? What if Quincy has no idea? What if Jackie Valentine was the only one who knew about this and Pepper was afraid Jackie would expose the secret? Maybe Jackie had asked for big money. Extortion. And Quincy Elliott might disown his daughter Zadie and divorce his wife. Do you know how rich that guy is? He owns stores all over the country. Pepper and Zadie may run their own little shop in Milwaukee, but that's a hobby. It's Quincy who enables them to have their hobby."

I gulped. A mother-daughter murder team? Under my roof? "But what if none of it is true? You haven't proven a thing, Jeremy."

"There's one way to try and find out."

Acid came to my mouth. "Ask Pepper? No, Jeremy. You leave my guests alone. All you have is rumor to go on."

I thought about how odd Pepper had been acting during her visit, and how Lucky Harbor always went to her. Had he been trying to tell me something? Had he also witnessed the murder because he always followed Pepper? Maybe Dillon had let him out for a potty break at midnight that night?

I got off Mom's phone feeling sick at heart and sick in my stomach. I rolled down my window a couple of inches. The brisk spring air needled my face. My hair whipped about.

Mom asked, "What's wrong, honey?"

It took a moment to collect myself. "That journalist. He makes up stuff."

"Journalists have ethics. It's not like he's Pavarotti."

"That's the deceased opera singer, Mom. I think you mean paparazzi."

We chuckled, which eased the stew swirling within me. Had Jeremy just uncovered the secrets the women were tired of keeping? Had Pepper killed Jackie? If so, the others had to suspect it. Or were they willing to keep this a secret, too? Pepper could not have hauled Jackie's body to the harbor alone.

I dreaded going back to the inn to face those women who claimed to be friends.

Chapter 18

om and I got back to Fishers' Harbor at around ten that Wednesday morning. We had promised Dad we'd check on Grandpa. Grandma and Grandpa had left the farmhouse earlier than we did. Grandpa was used to getting into our shop no later than five a.m. to help serve fishermen and women who geared up for Lake Michigan excursions.

Grandpa wasn't home.

Grandma was in a hurry gathering papers and notebooks for a Main Street flower committee meeting coming at her within the hour.

"Your grandpa is over on his boat, I'm sure." Grandma was pushing her white halo of hair away from her face as she gathered a different jacket for today's warmer weather. The sun was spangling everything; the brave daffodils lining Grandma's front porch glowed and waved like yellow angels.

Grandma grabbed a scarf and used it to tame her hair in a ponytail at the back of her neck. "Gil is determined to do everything possible to get himself arrested. If I were a smart woman I'd just call up Jordy Tollefson and tell him to pick Gil up now on charges of wifely neglect."

Mom chuckled, helping Grandma Sophie knot the scarf. "You'd miss him eventually."

Grandma stepped to me and cupped by face in one warm hand. "Ava, honey, you let the sheriff do his job. I'm glad you found your grandpa, but there's some awful person out and about in our village and I advise you not to be alone anymore, not even along in your fudge shop. Can Pauline join you?"

"She can't skip too many school days. I'll call Fontana."

"Your guard is a woman nine months pregnant?" She shuddered, letting go of me to pick up her papers and notebook. "What's wrong with that man of yours? He needs to be by your side."

I gave her a hug. "Dillon has to work, too. He texted me about repairing a storefront door and some steps before the weekend, and I believe he's part of the crew assembling the stage at the beach behind Erik's bar for Sweets, Suds and Buds."

"Good enough, but don't be alone until this murder is solved."

"All right, Grandma."

Mom said, "I'll make sure she doesn't get into trouble."

"Florine," Grandma mused as we all headed out the door, "that surely puts my worries to rest."

She was being sarcastic. My mother trusted me too much. She didn't know how to help me when I was in trouble except to vacuum up the dust in life that I left behind. I knew she loved me. The whir of a vacuum was her way of saying it.

Mom and I drove in her delivery van around the block to the harbor parking lot where we found Brecht Rousseau's minivan.

Inside Oosterlings' Live Bait, Bobbers & Belgian Fudge & Beer, the cheery cowbell clanged, announcing us to Cody and Brecht. They were stirring batches of fudge in tandem over at the copper kettles. The aromas of peanut butter and Door County maple syrup suffused the air in the shop.

Grandpa wasn't around. A glance out the big bay windows made me and Mom slump in place. Grandpa was inside the cabin of his boat, illegally behind the yellow tape.

"What do we do, Mom? Do you have a vacuum big enough for him?"

She went outside to retrieve dairy products from the van.

"Hey, Miss Oosterling," Cody called, making me turn back to the two men pushing ladles about in the copper kettles. "What would you think of a fudge that was like a peanut butter and jelly sandwich? That's what I'm making."

I hadn't tried that previously. "PBJ fudge? Sounds good."

It was good to have him back in the shop and acting like his old self.

Mom came in carrying cartons of cream and milk. "With a glass of cold milk, I think you've got a winner. Do you have a name for it?"

"Not yet. Brecht said we should get Pauline's kindergarten butterflies to come up with a name from a fairy tale for you."

I hooted, putting on a pink apron. "Brilliant! I'll call Pauline. Maybe she can bring them over here for a field trip today for a taste test."

While Mom took the supplies back to the kitchen, I opened up my cash register, readying it for any customers that might wander in before lunchtime. "Cody, would you be able to go to the bank for some rolls of quarters for me?"

"Sure thing." He took off his apron, hung it up, then headed out into the sunshine. The lack of fog off the bay this morning made me happy because fudge set up faster in drier weather. It also helped not to have too many customers opening the door constantly, letting in the humidity that rolled in off the lake.

My asking him to go to the bank was a ruse. Mom was still in the kitchen in the back. I rushed over to Brecht. "So, did you find out anything yesterday about Cody and what he's up to?"

"He apparently feels he'll be a better ranger if he doesn't have a girlfriend right now." Brecht lifted the wood ladle from the fudge. "Taste test?"

I grabbed a plastic spoon off a shelf. The peanut butter flavor was intense and delicious.

Brecht lifted the heavy copper kettle by himself, walking it over to the white marble loafing table by the window. He poured the luscious, tawny peanut butter mix onto the marble.

Cody's decision worried me. "He broke off a date with Bethany because he's studying to be a forest ranger? She's a big reason he's been doing so well coping with his Asperger's. Is he afraid he can't juggle too many things?"

"I didn't get the idea this is about his Asperger's." Brecht returned to the other copper kettle and began stirring the maple fudge mixture while I picked up loafing tools and scooped the mouthwatering peanut butter fudge in front of me by the window. We conversed across the room and over the tops of the shelving units.

Brecht said, "He talked a lot about the murder."

I paused with my wood loafing tool. "But he didn't know about the murder until after Saturday night and he broke up with Bethany that night."

"True enough, but he felt it was time to focus on his law enforcement classes, and I guess geology and geography. He's studying the history of Door County's parks, about the glacier reaching us thirty-thousand years ago and he said something about an ocean of water covering this area as high as the dolomite rocky cliff where your inn stands today."

"So dolomite rock trumps his girlfriend?"

"He feels the coincidence of Saturday night confirmed he'd done the right thing by breaking up with Bethany."

"He's superstitious? Maybe there's no chance of them getting back together."

"Beats me. He's young. He's fascinated that Wisconsin had volcanoes up north, and people lived here in Door County eight thousand years before he did." Brecht shrugged. "You talked with Bethany?"

I scooped fudge back and forth on the cold marble. "I suppose they'll work it out. What about you?"

"What about me?"

"How's the job hunt going?"

"Somebody needs a motel manager up in Jacksonport, but that doesn't appeal to me. I need to be home at night for the twins so my wife can get some sleep. Bakers get up at three or four in the morning."

Being a motel manager didn't seem to fit Brecht anyway. I couldn't see this robust, strong, ex-Army Special Ops guy being happy handing people room keys and changing light bulbs.

As Brecht brought over the maple fudge to let it flow on the other half of the marble-topped table, I got an idea. "You know Mercy Fogg, right?"

He laughed.

"Her father is a veteran. He's in a nursing home a few minutes from here. I wonder if you might stop by her house and see if she'd be okay with you visiting her father."

"Of course I'll be happy to talk with a fellow vet, but I'm suspicious of anything involving Mercy Fogg, on your behalf. Is she up to something again?" Brecht picked up loafing tools and started massaging the lava-like fudge. Working the mixture always pleased the sugar crystals and made for a smooth fudge.

I told him about Mercy coming to my door with the deputy sheriff and asking for the outrageous amount of money for the dog romance.

Brecht straightened across from me. "Sounds like she was making it all up as a way to get inside the inn or confront you. When we were protecting villages and property overseas we always had to discern fake versus real reasons used to gain entry."

"I had the same reaction about her. But why?"

"She needed a look around? She wanted to check on one of your guests? Did she want to ask them something?"

That sparked an idea. "She'd met the ladies before but not Victor Valentine. Maybe she wanted to get a good look at him."

"Maybe she's playing detective, too."

"If you stop by her house to ask her about visiting her father, you could chat her up about the murder and what she knows."

A smile spread across his handsome face as he paused in his loafing of the maple fudge. "I can do this, General."

I laughed. "You like going on missions, don't you?"

"Yes, Ma'am, General, sir."

With enthusiasm he left soon afterward.

Mom came into the shop from the back. "You should have plenty of cream for enough fudge for maybe a hundred people. Do you have any old fudge for the cows?"

Sugar helped cows with digestion. They had a sweet tooth. Fudge treats helped them process their feed efficiently and that meant more milk and healthy cows. Many farmers bought truckloads of rejected, imperfect candy from candy factories to feed to their cows. In our case, if I had any fudge that was getting too old for sale to the public, which sometimes happened during this slow time of year, Mom would take it. The fudge treats were used as rewards to help train the cows on halters and leads for the dairy shows my parents frequented. We had a few award-winning Holsteins at the farm, and my fudge had contributed to the trophies and ribbons that filled the den in the farmhouse.

After Mom left with a package of fudge, I called Maria Vasquez. I needed to know what she'd discussed with Mercy Fogg during the whole dog-romance issue, if anything.

Maria didn't have anything to tell. "She thought she'd seen some of your women guests sneaking around in back of Erik's bar on Saturday night."

That wasn't news, but I played along. "Which ones?"

"She wasn't sure. She described several of them and pretty soon I had counted all the women in my notes. But she said she'd know who she meant if she were face-to-face with them at your place."

So the stuff about the dog really was a ruse. Poor Jordy and Maria. They were probably obligated to do paperwork and waste time with Mercy's complaint just so she could play detective. If she solved the case for them, she'd use it as propaganda in next year's election to win as village board president. Hmm. But if I figured this out, that would put the Oosterlings in the driver's seat, and Grandma had half a chance of becoming village president. The competitive streak in me bubbled over like champagne being poured in a glass.

Maria and I ended our conversation.

While the fudge set up, I decided to check on my grandfather.

The meaningless yet menacing yellow tape flapped about the boat in the breeze. A seagull had perched on the bow. He picked at the tape in a mindless game.

I went inside the cabin, then below deck. Grandpa was bent over the toilet in the head, working with a screwdriver and wrench. My heart lurched remembering finding him here yesterday. The bump on the back of my head was still mighty tender.

"What's wrong now, Grandpa?"

"One of us with a hard head did damage to the toilet lid."

"I believe that would be you."

"Hah." He got up, red-faced from the strain of being practically upside down over the fixture. "There. Ready for guests." He winked at me. "Just not your guests."

"Tomorrow is Thursday and that means more tourists will be coming for the long festival weekend. You'll have plenty of business if this weather holds like this and if the sheriff releases this boat back to you. You realize you can't use this boat yet?"

"Balderdash." He returned his tools to a small toolbox sitting on the nearby counter. He plucked something out of the box, handing it over.

It was a single, brownish hair, though the exact color was tough to discern in the dim light. I laid it in one palm. "What do you want me to do with this, Grandpa?"

"Whoever thumped us on the head lost a hair. I found that on the floor and it's not yours."

"But those women have been on this boat many times. Shouldn't there be hairs all over the place?"

He waggled an index finger. "The sheriff and his crew were here twice going over this boat. They vacuumed even more than your mother. They would have picked up every hair."

"True. Mom says Jordy vacuums with a special make of machine she admires."

The hair was about three inches long. Yola, Eliza, and Kim all had light brown or auburn hair. Zadie and Pepper were blond. And Cathy had almost black hair.

I peered across at my grinning grandfather with his messy silver hair. "Wow, Grandpa, maybe you just narrowed our list of suspects."

He took the hair from me and put it inside a plastic sandwich bag he pulled from a drawer. "I want the honors of taking this down to the sheriff's office. That Tollefson fellow won't be disrespectin' me anymore."

"Jordy means well, Grandpa. We shouldn't be violating his yellow tape."

"We found the hair, didn't we?" He pocketed the bag.

"I'll go with you. Grandma doesn't want either of us being alone. And you shouldn't be driving. Your goose egg is much bigger than mine."

"Sophie hovers too much."

"She loves you. Let's call Jordy and let him come pick up the hair."

Grandpa growled, turning to check his navigation instruments. "I suppose I'm pretty busy. I could use a nap anyway, I suppose."

"Me, too."

I left Grandpa on *Sophie's Smile*, but stayed vigilant through the shop window.

The peanut butter fudge and maple fudge had turned out divine. A tiny slice of each put in my mouth at the same time turned on the juices. Creating a layered fudge with the two flavors was a definite "do".

The ladies had gone out for a quick sandwich for lunch, so I worked in the fudge shop that afternoon. Dread descended on my shoulders when it was time to head back up to the inn at four o'clock to prepare snacks and dinner. This emotion worried me. Again I wondered if were cut out to be an innkeeper.

I closed the shop and locked the doors early, trudging over to Duck Marsh Street.

Pauline caught up with me in her car as I hit the intersection of Main Street. The temperature had kited to seventy degrees, an unusual blessing in early April. Geese were migrating in V-shaped skeins above. White pelicans and swans--back from wintering down South--floated in the open water of the bay not far off our shoreline.

I got in Pauline's passenger seat. "Thanks for the ride."

"How's the bump on your head?"

"Still solid as a rock."

"Maybe you're growing a horn. You could visit my classroom. The butterflies would love talking with a unicorn."

I told Pauline to turn her gray sedan left onto Main instead of heading up the hill to the inn.

"Where are we going?"

"To look around. How could Jackie be accosted and hauled somewhere then back again to the harbor without anybody noticing, even at night?"

Main Street had only a handful of vehicles on it. It was hard to believe our peaceful hamlet would soon be choked with bumper to bumper cars and tourists crowding the sidewalks. Money was needed and wanted, but the peace was nice, too.

Pauline thought Grandpa's discovery of the hair was brilliant. "So maybe Kim did murder Jackie? It's Kim's hair? Did you call Jordy?"

"Not yet."

"You're like his best deputy."

"What's that supposed to mean? *Best* deputy?"

The sight of Zadie on a sidewalk distracted me. We had passed her before I could speak. "There she is again, Pauline. By herself. She turned that corner back there, on foot. Turn around. We have to find out where she's going."

Chapter 19

Pauline parked her car so that it was hidden from Zadie around a corner, but the engine and muffler's rumbling and pinging made me nervous.

"You really should get a different car." It was something I'd said to her repeatedly for the past year since I'd returned to Door County.

"So you can sneak up on people and involve me in even more of your wild-hair sneaking around? No way."

"But you're with me now and you love it."

"Hah."

"Hah."

Pauline and I got out of her rust bucket, which was parked only a block off Main Street. We trotted along a narrow, uneven sidewalk broken by maple tree roots until we got to the next corner where Zadie had turned right.

We sucked up behind a tree trunk. Yards ahead of us, Zadie flounced along like a colorful, high-heeled parrot in a flowery dress. Much like the one found on Grandpa's boat? It gave me the shivers. She carried a large, red purse.

Pauline muttered, "That's a great bag." She glanced at her own worn purse. "And great shoes. All the young teachers wear three-inch heels so easily."

I whispered, "Who goes for a long walk in three-inch heels?"

"You're sounding old. And you could improve on your shoe choice sometimes."

I peered down at my serviceable brown work boots with the steel toes.

Pauline whispered, "We need to go shoe shopping."

I sighed. Deeply. The lump at the back of my head was throbbing. "We're sneaking through somebody's back yard tailing a possible murder suspect and you're thinking about shopping?"

"I have to buy something new for John's show taping. I want a color that will pop on screen."

"Pauline, nobody will see your damn shoes. The show is about the little girls holding a tea party. I didn't think you were even going to be in the show. The way John described it, it's supposed to be just the girls and the whole idea is to see how soon they get into trouble. Throwing ice cream at each other or something of that sort."

Pauline thumped her bag on the ground. "You do not understand romance."

"What's romantic about your kindergartners tossing food? It's not like John will pop out of a cake and propose to you." I clamped my mouth shut. I was having trouble keeping John's secret. It would be just like him to do the cake thing.

Fortunately, Pauline ignored me. "Come on, we're losing her. She went around that next corner to the left, off toward those refurbished condos."

We hiked fast, but it was uphill and I wasn't feeling well. We were barely catching a glimpse of Zadie's colorful dress in the distance. She stopped near a doorway, turning around as she waited. We ducked behind a thick pyramidal cedar.

Pauline said, "Do you think she saw us?"

"Shhh."

We waited for the sound of a door opening. After a click and thump, we stood. Zadie had disappeared, presumably inside.

We gaped at the condos, resplendent in blond rock and golden-colored wood siding. The rehab had been done by Cathy Rivers and her husband last fall, though they didn't own this development. It sat on a rise so that the upper story condos enjoyed a harbor view. Dillon had worked on installing the balconies.

Pauline said, "So who do you think she's visiting?"

"Beats me. We need to get the number off the mailbox out front. We can look up the address online and see what or who pops up."

I ran over and came back. My head drummed.

Pauline clamped two hands on my shoulders. "You don't look so good."

"I shouldn't have run."

"What was the number?"

"Uh..." I couldn't conjure it. "Crap. Maybe it started with a six? Or was it a nine? There was a roundness to the number."

"Eight?"

"No."

"Zero?"

"Addresses here don't start with zero."

She filched an aspirin from her purse and stuffed it into my mouth, then handed me a small bottle of water. "You're pale."

"I'm fine."

"No, you're not. You just lost it and couldn't remember numbers you saw seconds ago."

A car passed by and pulled in a few doors down.

Pauline said, "We better leave before were caught. We can come back another time for the number."

I was scared. Not about forgetting the number so fast. "Pauline, what if I forget other things, too? Like how to make fudge?"

She said as we rounded the last corner before reaching the car, "You'd forget my name before you'd forget how to make your precious fudge recipes."

"I suppose you're right, Hazel."

She shook her head at my joke as she started the car.

When we got to the spa, Bethany greeted us with unexpected news. "Cody's trying to find you, Ava."

"Oh. Yeah. I lost my phone. Do you know what he wants?"

"He said you shouldn't go back to the inn alone. He said you shouldn't stay there alone in your apartment."

Bethany's eyes continued to grow wider as she talked. "Are you in some kind of danger, Ava? I mean, is it true those ladies were trying to kill you on the boat to cover up their crime? Cody talked with that reporter and Jane in the bookstore. They found out stuff about Pepper and her daughter Zadie."

Bethany's string of insights made me dizzy. "I already know about the rumor about Zadie maybe not being her daughter. I don't think that's true, Bethany."

She winced. "Cody researched it. He's thorough."

I sank into one of the cushiony chairs, exhausted. She started a shoulder massage.

I must have fallen asleep because suddenly I was in the car again and felt much better.

To our surprise, we spotted Zadie again a few blocks ahead of us on Main Street, this time presumably returning to the inn.

"Pull over," I whispered.

Pauline did so.

"Now she's dressed in her running clothes and not carrying the red bag."

We waited until Zadie trotted up the steep hill toward the inn.

A minute later, Pauline drove into a space in front of the inn. We walked around to the back, intending to go in through the kitchen. We halted, though, before touching the knob.

Through the screen and glass we witnessed Zadie and Eliza hug, then Zadie left the kitchen.

Eliza took out a notepad and made notes.

There wasn't anything strange about a hug in this part of the country, however Zadie had never struck me as being chummy with the older women in the group. In fact, Zadie and Yola were city women, not enamored with Eliza and her farm implement dealership woes.

I turned the latch, pushing open the door before Eliza could escape.

"Eliza," I said, shutting the door behind me, "how are things here?"

Eliza shoved the paper and pen in her pocket too quickly, it seemed.

Her dishwater-colored hair, as we called it here when blond had let brown tones and a bit of gray take over, was messy. The hair Grandpa had in his pocket could match.

Eliza turned to set the teakettle on the stove. "We just heard that Jackie's body has been released and Victor arranged for cremation tomorrow."

So Zadie was hugging her to express compassion? I asked, "Will there be a ceremony? A life celebration? I believe we talked about something before Victor returns to Chicago."

"I don't know yet. We're going to go to the Troubled Trout bar tonight. We'll all be leaving tomorrow, I guess." She went into the dining room.

I muttered to Pauline, "If they all go home it means somebody's hoping to get away with murder."

Pauline whispered, "You have no proof of any of these guests doing anything to Jackie."

"You're right. But gee, Pepper gets hit with a hammer at the inn, and Grandpa and I get hit over the head on the boat. There's a pattern here, Pauline."

Eliza returned with an antique rose teacup and saucer.

I handed her my tea box with its assorted teas. "I know this sounds odd to say, but it'll be a little sad when you all leave, Eliza."

Pauline rolled her eyes at me from behind Eliza's back.

While Eliza picked out a teabag, Pauline made a big commotion of plopping her purse on the marble countertop. She sat on a stool next to it and across from me, giving me the stink eye.

Eliza was sniffling, dunking a bag of lemon tea in the yellow rose china cup.

Now I felt like a heel. "I didn't mean to make you cry."

"It's okay," Eliza said, picking up her cup and saucer. "All good things come to an end. I guess, good people, too. Poor Jackie. You've been a gracious hostess. I'm so sorry our visit was such an awful downer."

I couldn't hug her because she held the steaming cup in front of her, but I wanted to. I wanted to hug them all and make this horrible visit evaporate for them. "Maybe remember all the good times with Jackie and the others while you were here. You were all able to reconnect. You were all cheerleaders back in college. It must be fun to think back to those fun days."

A small twitch appeared at one corner of Eliza's mouth. "As they say, we were young and foolish then. We're no longer either." She put down the cup and saucer on the counter next to the stove. "I better go up and change clothes for dinner."

I said, "You're dressing up for the bar?"

"I guess, a little bit."

"You're wearing dresses?"

She gave me a strange look. "I doubt it. But we want to dress up for Jackie's memory. She loved Erik's cheese curds." She laughed. "Jackie made us pay for eating them. I still hurt from all the exercising we did last week."

She headed through the dining room for the staircase.

Pauline and I waited to hear the creak of the stairs as she ascended to the second floor.

Pauline whispered, "What is wrong with you? Asking her about dresses? And their past? A tad obvious."

I set the wooden tea box to the back of the counter by the stove. "Well, I failed at finding out anything."

"Because there's probably not anything to find out. Some stranger hit you over the head. You know, Jackie was dumped next to your grandpa's boat, and both of you were hit over the head on the boat. It feels like somebody wants to steal that thing or make a statement about it. Maybe this is about the boat."

Sometimes Pauline made stunning and brilliant statements. "The boat? Why would the boat be significant?"

My head needed help to think. Somebody had brought fresh peanut butter fudge from the shop and put it on the island counter. It was wrapped in my shop's pink cellophane that Cody loved to work with because it crinkled and sparkled. I dove in for a bite of fudge. Peanut butter aroma filled the kitchen. Another pink package held my lost phone. Thank you, Cody!

"The women all loved the boat rides with my grandfather, correct?"

Pauline nodded, munching on a tiny piece of fudge. "Correct. Who loved the boat the best?"

"I don't know. You're thinking envy over the boat could be our culprit? So the boat was targeted because the person hates the boat? They're jealous of me and Grandpa?"

"This has to do with making a statement about money."

I slipped another piece of peanut butter fudge into my mouth. It exploded on my tongue like friendly sunshine. "The women argued about money the whole time."

Pauline stood taller in some realization, her dark eyes flashing. "Didn't ancient Vikings say good-bye by sending dead people off into the ocean on burning ships?"

I put down the cutting tool I was about to use to slice off more fudge. "So you're saying what?"

"The fire at the mansion long ago--think about this. Maybe one of the women is so upset about that fire that she wanted to set Jackie off into the bay. Maybe Jackie caused that fire and it's been weighing on their minds all these years."

"So the murderer wanted to send her body off into the bay in Grandpa's boat on fire? You're nuts, Pauline. This is something I'd think up."

"Hear me out. It'd be easy enough to wear an extra dress and use that to start the fire."

She was intriguing me now. "Women shoplift by wearing a second dress under another dress. We know there's been a strange obsession with buying clothes, which we can't seem to find in any of their closets or things, except for that nice dress with the tulip skirt in Jackie's closet, which was never her style."

"But Zadie's and Yola's style. And there was a sundress hidden on *Sophie's Smile*. Your grandpa discovered it."

"Together, those two girlfriends could have hauled Jackie's body to the boat."

"We just saw Zadie at somebody's condo. The murder could have happened there."

A chill sullied the taste of the fudge, leaving my mouth dry. "Everything does seem to point to those young women. But why would Kim hit Pepper over the head with a hammer?"

"We don't know for sure if she did. Cathy thinks so, but Kim denies it."

"But would Zadie hit her own mother over the head? For what purpose?"

Pauline sank back to the stool. "To blame Kim? Yola could have done the hammer deed, too, to save Zadie the trauma."

"There's only one thing for me to do. I have to talk with Pepper. And the sheriff."

Pauline reached across the island to grab one of my wrists. "This is all conjecture. He's going to be pissed at you. And it's his dinner time."

The women's footfalls came on the staircase. I abandoned Pauline for the moment to greet them in the foyer and wish them a good dinner. They were all teary-eyed, including Zadie and Yola. Nobody appeared capable of murder. Doubts sluiced through me, shredding any confidence I had in the theory Pauline and I had just discussed.

With the women gone, Lucky Harbor joined Pauline and me. He was eager for attention and his fake "fudge" treats. Seeing him reminded me that Brecht had gone earlier to meet Mercy. I was surprised he hadn't called yet. Pauline and I ate toasted cheddar cheese sandwiches with tomato soup in my kitchen. The clock was moving toward seven in the evening.

When Dillon came through my back door, I fell into his arms, reveling in landing against his sturdy frame. His hair was still wet from a shower and he had a pleasant manly soap aura about him. He wore a Green Bay Packer sweatshirt, denim jeans, and running shoes.

He said, "Hey, Sweetie, what's going on? What have those women done now?"

"Nothing, really," I said, releasing him. "That's the problem."

Lucky Harbor bounced at Dillon's feet, smiling and wagging his tail.

Dillon slung a hip onto a stool next to Pauline. "Hey, teach, you must have better things to do than solve murders with this girlfriend."

Pauline twisted her hair into a bun in back. "We have a theory." She told him about the boat and the killer liking the boat for some reason.

"My parents own a boat. A lot of people own boats."

"Do the Elliott's?"

"Yeah. Mom's mentioned going with them several times for excursions along Chicago's lakefront. Where is this line of questions about boats leading?"

"Kim, Yola, and Eliza don't appear to have enough cash to own a boat. Is it possible one or all of them are jealous of the Valentines, or mad at them?"

"Mad enough for murder?" Dillon snatched up a piece of fudge, his mouth working it. "This is great. Just needs some grape jelly with it."

"I was thinking the same thing!" I reached for a jar in the refrigerator. "Pauline, I was hoping your butterflies might taste-test the combo soon."

"We could feature it at Saturday's filming!"

My phone rang in my pocket. It was Brecht. He'd visited Mercy and her father and wanted to talk. Within a few minutes he came through the back door to the kitchen to join us.

I asked, "What'd you find out from Mercy?"

Brecht stood at the end of the island. "She tried to feed me meatloaf. Did you know she makes it using marshmallows instead of eggs to make it hang together?"

We all nodded.

I said, "Sorry about that. Even Lucky Harbor knows about it. He ate one of her meatloaves last fall. It didn't stay down."

Lucky Harbor wagged his tail at Brecht, who said, "But even stranger than the meatloaf, she said she found a white glove next to a trash can near Erik's bar on Saturday night."

I fell against the counter in shock. "She found a glove? Why didn't she tell me? She knows full well that Kim Olkowski sells those gloves. Did she call the sheriff about it?"

"Not yet. She asked me what she should do with it. I had told her I was part of Army special operations, so I guess she thought I would know what to do next. I told her she should talk with the sheriff."

So Al hadn't found any white gloves in the garbage bins around town, but Mercy had. I simmered. "I can't believe that woman has had a white glove in her possession all this time. She very well knows that Kim sells those."

Brecht offered, "Is Kim capable of dumping a woman in the harbor?"

I said, "With help, maybe. Yes. I think." Why wasn't I feeling sure? Because everything about this murder depended on supposition. But now maybe it didn't because Mercy had found a glove in an odd place.

Dillon slathered jelly onto a piece of peanut butter fudge. "Any of those women could have stolen Kim's cleaning gloves and worn them when doing the deed. Or they might have tossed one there purposely to mislead the sheriff. If the killer had any smarts at all, she or he would lay false clues."

"Exactly," Brecht said. "False leads are stock-in-trade for calculating murderers."

I nodded. "There seem to be plenty of these false leads around."

Pauline told Dillon and Brecht about our list that included the hammer, dresses, receipts, and of course my knock on the head. The bump only hurt now if I touched it. My headaches and dizziness had gone away.

I fed the men sandwiches and soup, then they left. "Lucky Harbor was sniffing something unusual outside last night."

Pauline was clearing the kitchen island. "So a stranger could have been lurking about. Someone spying on the women? Or on you? Sounds like Mercy, if you ask me."

I hadn't thought of that. "Mercy usually just bangs on the door and affronts me. She's not all that sneaky. Dillon made me promise to keep my apartment locked when I retired for the night."

"Good idea."

The fudge divas came back around ten. Cathy said good night to me and returned to her own condo in the village.

While brushing my teeth, a knock sounded at my apartment door.

Pepper Elliott stood in the large parlor in a lovely pink blouse, black slacks and pink Cinderella slippers.

She said, "We need to talk. I need to tell you something that may be the reason Jackie was murdered. I'm dying."

Chapter 20

Pepper Elliott stepped into my apartment with hesitation, scrutinizing all directions as if waiting for somebody to jump her.

I closed the door and locked it, spooked. "Maybe I didn't hear you right." She was dying?

In her pink blouse, with her blond bob with nary a hair out of place, she appeared doll-like, perfect as always though her cherub face wore strain.

I invited her to sit on the loveseat. "Can I get you something to drink?"

"No, thank you. Please sit."

I did, across from her in the matching chair.

"I'm dying of cancer. Breast cancer. The doctors have said it's gone into my bones and only a miracle will save me."

"Ask for a miracle." Shame came to me with such a quick, flippant response. Pauline was so right--I needed to practice restraint. "I'm sorry I said that so quickly. You must be praying for miracles. I'm so sorry."

"It's a second recurrence. I beat it the first time for fifteen years. A good run, don't you think?" A wan smile ebbed across her face.

"You're a strong woman, Pepper. There's nothing they can do this time?"

She shook her head, then straightened something invisible on her black slacks before folding her hands, resting them on her knees. "I'm part of every experiment known to scientists at the moment, but I know where this is headed."

"There's always hope."

She grimaced. "I guess. Thank you. My hair? Fake. An expensive wig. I bet you wondered why my hair was always so neat." She smiled again. "But I didn't come here to talk about my diagnosis. My daughter doesn't know about this latest one."

My heart went out to them both. "Maybe she should know?" It had to be excruciating to keep this a secret from those who loved her.

"I'll tell her in due time. I wanted to enjoy this fudge frolic retreat with friends without her feeling sorry for me and making me feel like an invalid. That girl goes overboard on everything. As you know. She's a shopaholic. She loves pretty things. Always has. I find it hard to turn her down."

"She certainly seems to have done her share of shopping." I recalled the receipts under Pepper's car seat and pushed myself to be nosy. "Did you buy all those clothes for her on this trip?"

Pepper blinked in clear confusion. "Heaven's no. She's a shopper, but I believe my friends sneaked a few gifts in there. My daughter is a model, after all. They all adore her. It's like dressing a doll when you're a girl. You can't help but buy your doll new outfits every time you go to the store."

I got the feeling Pepper had no idea a big ball of receipts was under the passenger seat in her car. "Yes, your daughter's very pretty."

Another thought sprouted like a spring bud on a maple tree. "Yola doesn't seem to mind at all that her friend receives all those gifts."

"Yola is earthy. Like Eliza. You know how farm and garden women are. They'll put up with old clothes longer than the rest of us."

That felt like a subtle slam, considering my mother was a farm woman and I had been raised on a farm. I wore the same sort of jeans and blouse every day of my life.

I asked, "Are Eliza and Zadie close?"

Pepper wiggled as a slight disturbance rippled across her face.

I added, "I saw them hugging in the kitchen."

"That surprises me, but I guess that's good. Zadie doesn't ordinarily like to hang out with my friends." She chuckled. "We're considered old fogies in our fifties. But she does know who holds the purse strings."

"You mean she needs money to help expand your boutique business and her friend Yola's garden stores. She's made no secret of those things."

"Yes. Young people are all entrepreneurs these days, filled with more ideas and goals than we had in our twenties." Her "we" seemed to refer to the fudge divas.

"Do you think Jackie would have invested in Yola's business if Jackie had lived?"

"I don't believe so. For some reason she was hesitating. I still can't put my finger on it. She didn't talk about Yola in private. I guess she had dismissed Yola."

"You said something about Jackie's death minutes ago before you came in."

"Yes. Her death. She's the only one I told about the cancer recurrence. I couldn't help myself. I told her earlier on Saturday. It's hard keeping such things inside, and she'd been so bossy all week and the others were so fed up with her that I thought telling her about my diagnosis would make her soften her obnoxious tone and save them all from her."

"So she knew your diagnosis when you all went to dinner Saturday night."

Pepper nodded. "Could I take you up on that offer for a drink of water?"

"Of course." I trotted into the kitchen area and came back with her water.

While I settled in my chair, she drank half the glass. "Medications," she said. "They can make you thirsty."

I nodded, again feeling profoundly sorry for her. Life was not fair. Not at all. "I still don't understand how your cancer has anything to do with Jackie's drowning somewhere."

"She was upset about my diagnosis. Oh, she pretended to be her old self in front of the others, but Jackie was a caring person. She wanted to quit the fudge retreat right then and go back to Chicago and pay the researchers all her money to find a cure for cancer. She was very upset. That's why she went for a walk. And unfortunately was murdered."

I launched from my chair to sit beside her and hug her. "This was a horrible thing that happened, but your news did not cause her death."

"You're so naïve, Ava."

I let go of her. "What do you mean?"

"Jackie hated it when she couldn't solve a problem. Jackie was a know-it-all and with her money, she could solve anything. Except her marriage problems."

Victor appeared to adore his wife, but I could understand how difficult Jackie might be. "Victor loved her."

"Yes, he did." She finished the water and set the glass aside on the nearby end table. "But I believe Jackie might have been seeing somebody on the side. Here."

"Here? In Fishers' Harbor? How'd she have time? All of you were together most of the time, maybe all of the time."

"I think she sneaked out at night. I heard doors open and close quietly every night, as soon as we arrived on Wednesday. I can't sleep very well. I didn't dare look, but one night I ventured out and knocked on her door. There was no answer."

"What night was that?" As if that mattered now.

"Friday."

"Did you see her?"

"No. I was too scared to wait and take a chance of her seeing me. Jackie would have awakened the entire inn if she thought I was following her at midnight." Pepper sighed. "That's all."

"Does Zadie know anybody here in Fishers' Harbor?"

"Not that I know of. Why?"

Agitation roiled within me, beating like the drum of a washing machine. I had to get up. I went to the back of my chair and leaned against it. "Zadie and Yola are always out jogging or shopping, and they went out late at night every night they've been here. Maybe they met somebody or saw Jackie with a man and just didn't say anything."

"I doubt that. Zadie would tell me. My daughter and I are very close."

I sat in my chair again, needing support for my next comment. "There were reports long ago that you had an affair with the vice chancellor of the university and that Zadie isn't your husband's daughter."

She guffawed. "Zadie and I are close because we've endured those rumors. I did have an affair with the man. I was young and foolish. That was before I married my husband. I was scared and getting cold feet. It was a fling. But Zadie belongs to me and my husband."

"What about that fire in the vice chancellor's house?"

"You've been digging for dirt on me?" She began to rise.

"Please stay. The Madison reporter, Jeremy Stone, says that they thought the vice chancellor's wife may have set it. Another rumor?"

Pepper eased back down, now worrying one hand with the other. "It was ruled accidental."

I waited. She kept looking at her hands.

"That's true?" I said, feeling like a creep to press her.

Tears began to glisten in her eyes. "We don't know."

"You say 'we'." I muttered, "Oh, no. One of you..."

Pepper nodded. "We forgot the candles in our hurry to leave. Jackie was in charge." She sniffled.

I found her a tissue.

She dabbed at her eyes. "Please, please, that happened so many years ago."

Thirty-some.

She said, "Jackie is, was a perfectionist. That fire has plagued her all these years. Maybe that's why she was always so loud. She was always talking above the sound of the fire in her head."

I didn't know what to say. This was their secret. Jackie had caused the fire that burned down a mansion. Or at least she thought she did.

I said, "Now I realize that this reunion seemed to be a big deal because you were all nervous about this secret resurfacing. You didn't get together, all of you, much, did you? Because of that fire?"

Pepper nodded. Now Jackie was gone, and Pepper was stricken with a horrible disease, which was her secret. But she'd shared it with Jackie, and now Jackie was dead. The bad luck had affected Pepper. Her skin was gossamer, as if she were a ghost waiting to evaporate from my apartment.

I shivered. "Maybe all of you should talk about this, with a therapist. Group therapy. Or alone. It just seems like a very heavy burden, Pepper. Maybe you should tell the rest of them about your cancer. It's not good to keep these things inside."

"How would you know? You're so young and you're struggling to pull things together yourself."

As slaps on the face go, it was a mild one. "You're right, Pepper."

She rose. "I'm sorry. That was truly rude of me to insinuate any struggle on your part is a failure. The fudge shop is beautiful, and this inn is like heaven perched up here on the cliff. When it's surrounded by fog, I feel like we're sitting on a cloud."

"Thank you. I never thought of it that way."

"I get poetic when I'm tired. You're a good person and you've been a gracious hostess, Ava. Thank you. I felt I needed to tell you the truth, too, because your grandfather is so nice and we surely gave him a lot of trouble over the past few days."

I smiled. "Yeah, you did."

"Please don't tell anyone any of this, especially Victor. It would devastate him to know about Jackie's possible role in the fire, and the affair."

After she left, it struck me she meant Jackie's supposed affair, not Pepper's own from ages ago.

It horrified me that my grandfather and I had already been knocked out by somebody, probably Jackie's killer. The killer may have dumped us in the lake if not for others coming to the shop. Was the killer concerned that Grandpa or I had learned of the affair and the cause of that fire, and that the knowledge would somehow ruin something for somebody if we told?

A chill came to me that said I was on the verge of knowing who committed the murder. The danger of it, though, made me call Pauline. I asked her to come over.

"Why?" she asked. "I have my pajamas on."

"Put some clothes on. We have some spy work to do in the dark."

Pauline was acting pissy about being up at eleven at night. We were in my apartment in the inn, sitting at my tiny dining room table for two, waiting to hear footfalls on the staircase. My door was cracked.

Pauline wore dark clothes, as I'd instructed her, with black ballet slip-on shoes.

She huffed for the tenth time. "This is stupid. So what if somebody goes out and we follow them to that condo. What does that prove except that they're dating somebody on the sly that they met here last week."

Pauline had a point. I put my glass of water on the counter, then came back to the table. I had told her everything Pepper had revealed an hour ago. "These women are all hiding things. It's insidious with them all."

"Including your ex-mother-in-law?"

"She's the exception."

"You hope."

"Now don't be nasty. Cathy is nice."

"I have to teach in the morning." Pauline dug into her giant purse. "Crap. I forgot my phone. I have to go home."

"You're lying. You're staying here and helping me."

A creak on the stairs brought us alert. I doused my lights.

We didn't hear the front door, which always stuck. I whispered to Pauline that maybe whoever it was going out now had gone through the kitchen to avoid making noise.

We went across the parlor where Dillon had installed the new, additional door that led to the new covered verandah at the side of the building.

Keeping our distance, we followed behind a figure trotting down the hill. The figure obviously wasn't Pepper, though she was petite.

It didn't take us long to see that Zadie was headed for the condos where we'd seen her previously that day.

Pauline and I ducked for a time behind a bush next to a house. The night was black, the village asleep. One streetlight remained on behind us at the intersection that everybody slid through instead of stopping. Far off, a dog barked, probably asking to go in for the night. The barking stopped soon after. A soft breeze through the cedars perfumed the air.

We scuttled along the block, turning right, then left just as we'd done before. One of the condos had a light to the left of its front door. Zadie hustled to the golden glow where she appeared to be removing her coat.

Pauline and I took advantage of her distraction to sneak to the front of a car parked across the street in a condo driveway. I dipped to the ground to peek around the tire to watch.

Zadie was wearing the colorful sundress with the tulip-shaped skirt. She exchanged her flat shoes for high heels. The flats went into the coat pockets. She let her hair down as if she were Rapunzel; a golden shimmer swung about her back all the way to her waist. She had to be sporting hair extensions.

She lifted an arm. Her knock was so quiet I couldn't hear it from across the street. She had chosen not to use the doorbell.

The door eased open. A person was backlit by the lights within. A man?

Zadie leaped into his arms.

They kissed each other so madly that I held my breath in shock.

Then the man's words floated in the night to me. "You're beautiful. I can't get enough of you. We're going to be good together." As the door was closing, he said, "I get the ashes tomorrow. We can finally go back to Chicago."

The door clicked, then the outside light went off.

Pauline and I stayed frozen in our crouch, hidden by the neighbor's car.

I whispered to Pauline, "That's Victor. Victor killed his wife? With Zadie's help?"

"Apparently."

"But he was so charming, so sincere over the past few days. So kind to the ladies. To me. He even took Dillon's dog to lunch with them."

Chills overwhelmed me. My teeth chattered.

Pauline stood, giving me a hand up. "You don't believe he did it, even with proof of a motive right in front of our eyes?"

"He's having an affair with Zadie, but that doesn't prove he killed his wife. This is an older man having an affair with a younger woman. He should be tied up by his gonads for it, but does it mean he killed his wife? No." He looked guilty, though. I didn't want to believe what I'd seen. Had Zadie helped him move Jackie's body?

Pauline hefted her purse up from the concrete driveway. She checked her phone. "It's eleven-thirty. I need to get home so I can teach tomorrow."

"You can't teach. You have to help me. Call in sick."

"I already did that once this week."

"Jackie could have been drowned in the tub in that condo. We have to find out if that really happened."

"No, we don't. Call the sheriff. Let him check out the tub."

"I can't do that. What if I'm wrong? All of the women will hate me and I'll hate me. Those women are my guests. They came here because they wanted to help my fudge business. They like me."

Pauline reached over and pulled my hair.

"Ouch."

"Do you know how ridiculous you sound? Call the sheriff. I'm not getting involved with you in tracking down a killer yet again. I still have nightmares from last autumn."

I pulled her long hair right back. "Ouch."

"Pauline, Victor has to have drowned her in the tub."

"And he stuffed her in a garbage bag, then pretended he was taking out the trash late on Saturday night. Anybody out and about didn't notice. He then took the bag to the water and dumped her, then came back. Maybe Zadie was the lookout. That's what you think?"

"Damn, you're good."

"I just want to go home."

"We need to talk to Mercy Fogg. She was seen out late on Saturday night, acting a little weird according to what Erik told us. And Brecht told me she found a white glove. Zadie had to have planted that. She stole it from Kim at the inn."

"Or Kim helped Zadie and Victor."

"Holy moly. I thought maybe they could all be in on this together and maybe I'm right. All except Cathy of course."

I trotted across the street to take down the number of Victor's condo, then Pauline and I hurried to our respective homes.

I called Jordy at five a.m. He swore words I hadn't said since high school, but agreed to meet me at the fudge shop that morning.

Chapter 21

Before meeting Jordy that Thursday morning, I decided on a hunch to go outside at five a.m. to lurk about. Knowing what Pauline and I had witnessed last night around midnight a few blocks from the inn, I hid behind the trunk of one of the big old maple trees and kept watch. A jacket kept the damp morning out of my bones.

Sure enough, around six o'clock Zadie came bounding up Main Street and then the steep hill to the inn wearing running shoes and clothes.

The sticky front door creaked as she opened it, then to my surprise she pushed it back and forth to make it screech even longer. She was likely doing that on purpose to make sure I heard her coming back from her so-called run, her cover.

Zadie had done this routine from the first morning she'd been here in Fishers' Harbor and at my inn. We'd all heard her, seen her in her jogging outfit.

Next, I puzzled about Victor. Had he been ensconced in the condo since a week ago yesterday? Had he lied to us about his arrival in town? Had he and Zadie planned the murder to coincide with the fudge divas' retreat?

I scrambled away from the maple tree and ran before any of my guests might see me--most particularly Zadie.

As my shoes echoed on the empty streets, mist off the bay prickled my cheeks and forehead. The fresh smell of spring-tickled grass greening up woke me to a myriad of thoughts--all shocking and sad.

My grandfather and Lucky Harbor were not at the shop yet. I made coffee in Grandpa's pot. I wondered how the knot felt on his head. Mine was a hard marble and shot needles down my neck if touched.

I greeted Jordy at the shop door, flinging it open as soon as he pulled into the harbor's parking lot around six-thirty. The cowbell clanged, almost a rude sound in the peaceful morning. Sunrise was turning the edges of buildings pink.

Jordy wore his brown leather uniform jacket with the big badge. He'd left his hat in his vehicle. The short, dark hair had been combed with meaning.

"Coffee?" I asked. "It's Grandpa's formula."

"I'm in."

He sat on Grandpa's stool by the register counter on the bait side of the shared shop.

After a sip of the dark roast laced with Belgian chocolate, he said, "Victor's alibis seem to pan out. He insists he loved his wife. So far, I don't believe he could have murdered Jackie."

I wasn't surprised by his pronouncement. I'd told Pauline I was uneasy about blaming Victor. "But he'd have the tub where she was probably drowned. It seems logical. It's not an extraordinary walk from here either."

"He's been under suspicion all along, being the husband, of course. I have to keep him under suspicion because that's logical and wise."

I set down my coffee next to my register. To think, I began taking inventory of the fudge left in the glass cases. "I don't suppose you're going to tell me what you found out?"

"No, I'm not. You make fudge; I investigate felonies."

I scoffed. "No felonious fudge this time."

He laughed. "That case was a year ago."

"Are you going to question Zadie again?"

"Why? Because you saw her go see Victor last night? No. I've already questioned all of your guests a couple of times."

Hmm. So he dismissed Zadie? I couldn't read him today, which was unusual. I touched the bump on the back of my head. It still hurt. What had happened to me was real. I handed Jordy a piece of maple fudge, the last from its tray. "If not Victor and Zadie, then who murdered Jackie?"

"Everybody's under suspicion yet." He munched on the fudge, his eyes sparking with the sugary sensation. "Even Gil."

Pink rays from the sunrise sneaked through the bay windows now, bringing to life the pink purses, aprons, dishes, and more on the shelving. Even the shiny fishing lures seemed to dance like pink fairies.

"So, Jordy, why did you come when I called?" I shivered, thinking back to what Pauline had hinted at--that Jordy had feelings for me that went beyond professional. I rephrased my question. "What's your theory, Sheriff Tollefson?"

"While there's no proof that Victor or Zadie did anything," he said, staring into his coffee cup, before lifting his wide, dark eyes to gaze across at me, "there must be others involved and I'm always curious about your theories. A woman is dead, after all. If something you say can help me, I figure it's my job to come see you."

"Do you think strangers did it?"

"A random killing here in Fishers' Harbor on a quiet Saturday night? No. I'm wondering about Jane Goodland."

"Jane?" I almost fell off my stool. "She was out with Sam Peterson."

"You were engaged to him once for five minutes." Jordy got off his stool, still carrying his coffee. He slurped in a big gulp, taking his time, which always drove me nuts and he knew it. "No, I don't think Sam or Jane did it. But they could have been the inadvertent cover for the murderer."

"How do you mean?"

"They came back from a night out. Sam said they'd gone to a theater production over in Green Bay."

"About an hour or so from here," I said.

"Sam said when they got back they'd noticed raccoons had gotten into the garbage cans set out on the street near the bookstore. They saw Al and told him about it. They were all busy with that issue. Whoever may have taken the body down to the harbor could have easily done so without too much notice. Especially if the body were in a garbage bag."

"Jane never mentioned that garbage and raccoon thing when I talked with her."

"She likely didn't think much of it. They were just cleaning up after a raccoon, after all."

After mulling this over, I savored more coffee to help kick my brain into a higher gear. "Victor doesn't strike me as the kind who could sneak around. Or haul garbage bags, even with a body inside of it that he might want to get rid of. He's a good-sized guy and walks with grace. He's impeccable. Everything is measured. He'd hire it done maybe."

Jordy raised an appraising eyebrow.

A tingle went up the back of my neck. Yola needed money for her garden pop-up stores. Kim needed money for her glove business. Two women with big dreams.

Jordy stood in the center of the shop, staring into his coffee. "It had to be somebody strong, who also knew the environment and its layout and knew exactly how to get to the harbor fast and disappear. A stranger probably would hesitate here and there along the route, or stumble over unseen holes in the sidewalks or street that the village never had enough money to patch. Sam or Jane or Al would have noticed such a person."

"What time did you decide she was killed?" I went to the glass case and chose a piece of mint chocolate fudge. It jolted my brain.

"Not long after their dinner together. Her food wasn't digested."

"What type of water was in her lungs?" I sat down again on my stool behind the register, grabbing a notepad.

"You already know. Fresh tap water, tub water."

"I don't think that's entirely correct."

Jordy put down his mug on Grandpa's counter. "What do you mean?" He took out his own notepad.

"Did you find lavender bubble bath or lavender soap in her lungs with the water? You could match that with the products around the tub."

He eyed me carefully. "How did you guess there were lavender soaps and bubble bath? We found those essences in her lungs."

His information made me sink within myself. "The fudge divas all bought that stuff on a trip to the lavender farm on Washington Island."

Jordy grabbed a bright orange bobber from a shelf and toyed with it, rolling it about in his long fingers of one hand. "Victor probably didn't buy the bubble bath. What's your theory?"

"Let's say Zadie did it. It makes sense. As soon as Victor arrived in Fishers' Harbor and at the inn on Sunday, I noticed Zadie had rushed to help him. Looking back on it, I believe this affair has been going on a long time and she was eager to be Number One in his sphere of attention, even with all the other ladies looking on, even with her mother there. This affair had to have started before this retreat."

He rolled the bright bobber around in his hand. "But what if the other women knew? Or at least Jackie knew what was going on under her nose?"

"Maybe. But nobody let on about it. Jackie was loud and boisterous, and maybe that wasn't about being bossy. Maybe she was mad, especially with Zadie. But she didn't say anything because she felt sorry for Pepper. Pepper told Jackie on Saturday she had cancer but Jackie may have guessed something was wrong before that. Zadie had to have guessed her mother's not been feeling well. She could have mentioned that to Jackie."

I gave Jordy the rest of my conversation with Pepper. "Please keep the cancer a secret," I said. "She wants to tell the others on her own timetable."

Jordy set the orange bobber back in place and took up his notepad he'd laid aside.

I said, "There's something missing in all this, Jordy."

He peered at me with his penetrating eyes. "What's that?"

"Do you know when that condo was rented and to whom? If Victor didn't come until Sunday, as he said to us, then he didn't stay there Saturday night."

"Or did he?" Jordy walked to the coffeepot on the ledge and poured more of the dark chocolate-laced thinking brew.

"Victor is definitely our loose end. He could have stayed secretly in that condo during the entire retreat, having sex with Zadie right under his wife's nose."

"Easy enough to find out. I'll check to see when it was rented and who rented it."

A realization made me drop the pen on the pad of paper in front of me at my counter. "Cathy Rivers and her husband managed the reconstruction on those units. Dillon did carpentry in the homes. Cathy would know the manager's name. Dillon is around there now and then. Maybe he's aware of something that can help."

As Jordy headed to the door, I followed, saying, "You questioned Victor. He denies any involvement. Did he seem innocent?"

"He denies having anything to do with it. He says he came to town on Sunday, after her death. Is there a chance she was drowned at a tub at your place?"

If I hadn't been hanging onto the door latch to let him out, I might have fainted. "You think she may have been murdered at the inn?"

Jordy opened the door for me.

The cowbell clanged, punctuating the weighty silence.

His face glowed in the morning sunlight. "I need to stay open to possibilities. So do you."

With that, he strolled to Grandpa's boat, stripped off the crime scene tape, balled it up, and without looking my way he headed for his squad car.

After Jordy left, I began hauling fudge ingredients out to the copper kettles. Had Jackie somehow been killed in the inn? Luckily, before I could get too upset, my grandfather showed up. It was almost seven, late for him.

"That darn sheriff gone for good?" Grandpa asked, scooting over to the ledge near his coffeepot but grabbing his tin of bolts soaking in oil. "Gotta get back to work on that boat before those darn divas get a whiff of me. Sophie made bacon and chocolate chip pancakes and I can't get the smells off me."

He noticed I wasn't laughing as usual. He put down his bolts on his counter, then motioned for me to sit. "What's going on, A.M.?"

"The sheriff just asked if the murder could have happened in one of the tubs in the inn."

"Poppycock."

Grandpa's warm hands held mine.

"He could be right, Grandpa. The women made their share of noise that night. I went to bed, but they were up. They said that Jackie went back outside for a walk."

"You betchya. She got on the boat and started arguin' with me."

"But she could have gone back inside and amid all the hubbub of the women going to bed, nobody would've paid attention to her being loud or even quiet. The women wanted to ignore her. The killer used that. Maybe Jackie passed out and one of those women pushed her into the brand new jetted tub that Dillon and the plumber installed in that refurbished room."

I was lost in the mess in my head. Could it be? Another murder at the inn involving me? Could my luck be this bad?

Grandpa waved his hands in the air. "Bah. I know what you're thinkin' and you just stop it. Nobody was killed in your shiny new tub."

"After she left the boat, after your argument with her, did you see which direction she went?"

"No. Sorry, A.M." Grandpa did an about-face and headed into an aisle mumbling something about needing a screwdriver.

The dread squirmed inside me like spiders crawling about. So maybe Jackie had headed back toward the inn from the harbor. She could have come all the way back up the hill on Saturday night. Grandpa wouldn't have seen her from the boat in the harbor. The shop and cabins would have blocked his sight. Or she could have changed direction and headed for Victor's condo. Which brought me back to Zadie and Yola doing the deed.

I got back off the stool to continue creating Cinderella Pink Fudge by rote. Cream. Sugar. Vanilla. Pink coloring. Dried cherries from the Door County orchards. The copper kettle appeared to me in the form of a bathtub. A woman drowning.

Gasping, I backed away.

In horror, I realized I couldn't face making fudge. My life was unraveling. I wanted to run away. Panic beat at me like cold rain.

Grandpa was sloshing bolts around in the oil with a bare hand but noticed me standing frozen. "You better call Cody and get him here to help you. Maybe you should come help me on the boat instead today."

"I can't. I need to come up with a new fudge flavor for Saturday's celebration at my inn. And the ladies will be here later today checking in on me." I went back to stirring, turning the burner up underneath the kettle. Giving into my fear, I said, "The body could have been taken down the back stairway easily enough at the inn."

"Bah," Grandpa said, setting his rattling tin of bolts down on his register to grab his toolbox from under the counter. He opened it to take out a hammer.

That jogged me. "We found a hammer at the inn, hidden in Jackie's bed. But I don't believe Jackie was hit over the head with it. I haven't heard anything about the autopsy saying she was hit. She was drowned."

I kept busy stirring the cream and sugar and chocolate in the copper kettle. "Let's say Victor killed her, and if Zadie were there, they likely would have handled her together easily enough." Doubts niggled me.

"Somebody pushed a passed out woman under the tub water, but I'm not going to believe it happened in your inn."

"Maybe one of the women thought about using the hammer to kill her. Pepper was hit on the head somehow. Allegedly by Kim, but she denied it." Or had Pepper been shoved against the door handle where I found blood?

I needed to talk with Kim.

I stirred the fudge like crazy, wishing the crystals would hurry.

Grandpa took his greasy, stinky bolts and his toolbox out to the boat. He walked with a certain jauntiness, obviously glad the sheriff's crime scene tape was gone.

Jordy's next move would likely be inspecting every room at the inn, collecting all the lavender products he could find, and interviewing all the guests again.

Meanwhile, today was when Jackie's body would be released-- finally after several delays for re-examination at the request of the sheriff, I assumed--and the funeral home would cremate it. The ladies would likely want to do something together on such an emotional day, but Grandpa wasn't about to cart them anywhere with his boat or otherwise.

At around nine that morning, Mercy showed up driving a trolley, of all things. She swung into the harbor parking lot with the rig, dinging the bell several times. The trolley was painted red and green. It got liberal usage by tourists during our holiday season. People could take the trolley up and down the entire upper half of the county visiting shops, bars, restaurants, and skating rinks and more.

"Ain't she a beaut?" Mercy strutted into the shop, pointing back out the window.

"It says 'Happy Holidays' on the side." I had just finished loafing another batch of fudge, this time the Rapunzel Raspberry Rapture Fudge. I was looking across the white marble table and out the window.

"I was thinking I'd do what you do to get her painted a summery color." Mercy poked a finger in the middle of the loaf of fudge and slapped the smidge into her mouth.

I ignored the rudeness. "What do you mean?"

"Hold a contest. Maybe get your friend Pauline to have her kindergarten girls use paints. I heard they're gonna be famous doing a TV show. I could be on that show, too."

Oh, no. Mercy on John's show? This did not bode well at all for my life. Mercy would lord her television fame over me, especially since I'd failed miserably as a television writer in Los Angeles and Mercy knew that.

"Maybe, Mercy, those little girls will be too busy to paint your trolley. They're filming that show this Saturday. As part of the festival."

"So? I could be the one picking up the girls and taking them to that big house out there south of town."

Oh, no, again. She sounded as if she knew where that house was.

I offered her another gooey piece of pink raspberry-flavored fudge. She smacked her lips.

"Maybe," I ventured, going back behind the glass case to put a different batch of fresh fudge on display, "you could get the fudge divas involved in helping you paint it. Especially Zadie and Yola. They love colorful things. And Kim could use her white gloves to help you clean the inside. And Eliza loves machinery.

Let her give it a test drive and check the engine for you. Cathy can probably donate paint from her construction company. You could get that trolley re-painted today in any color you want, and all for free."

"Free?"

"Of course. The fudge divas would donate their time and elbow grease to honor their friend Jackie. It's a donation to the community, really. And it'd be all your idea. You'd look good, I have to admit. What do you think?"

I handed Mercy another piece of pink fudge.

She savored the fudge, chewing. She smiled at me across the top of the glass case. "I feel like you're tricking me into this for some reason but I can't figure out why."

I smiled back. "We know each other well, don't we, Mercy?"

"Damn, you're good. I'll take the trolley up the hill and see if those women will help me clean it up and repaint it before Saturday. But once I find out what you're up to, there will be hell to pay."

"Like with the dog?"

Her face flushed. "Queenie is pregnant. I concede it's not the fault of Lucky Harbor. But it's somebody's dog. If I can't be village president, I might become the self-appointed dog catcher."

She left, her blond mop of curls bouncing about in the spring breeze. I sighed with relief. And with a new plan. I called Pauline.

"Pauline, get over here right now."

"I'm teaching. It's nine-thirty in the morning."

"I thought you were going to call in sick today."

"I told you I couldn't do that. The kindergarten day is done at two-thirty. I can come then."

I popped fudge in my mouth to help me calm down. "Some friend you are, choosing thirteen cute little girls over me and the new clues I've stumbled upon concerning Jackie Valentine's death. I'll just have to solve this murder on my own."

"I guess you will." She hung up.

I stared at my phone. And smiled. Pauline would be watching the clock, aching to get out of school to join me.

When she met me that afternoon in the kitchen of the inn at around three, the women were with Mercy on a trolley trip around the county, stopping at the wineries they had missed. They had taken Victor along so he could visit more of Jackie's favorite places. Later in the afternoon, around five, he was to meet the funeral home director to accept Jackie's ashes. All of this panicked me.

Pauline plopped her billowing purse on the countertop. "I don't see why you're so concerned. It's a silly tour, and an appropriate way to honor their friend."

I finished wrapping plastic wrap over a plate of fresh sandwiches I'd made for my guests for whenever they returned. My hands were shaking. "One or more in that group are killers, Pauline."

"So who murdered Jackie Valentine?"

"The sheriff and I think a good clue might be the lavender products the women bought. The autopsy revealed lavender bubble bath or oils in the water in her lungs."

"You and Jordy, huh?"

"Stop matchmaking. Stay focused, Pauline."

She scoffed. "So what is the plan?"

"We have to count everybody's bubble bath and lavender oils. They all bought products on their shopping trip. It might be that if we find no products in their room or suitcase, that's the person who may have messed with Jackie."

"You know how far-fetched you sound? We have no idea how much stuff they bought, so if some is missing we won't know."

I took the plate of sandwiches into the dining room. "The thing is, Pauline, you complain, but I bet you're going to follow me up the stairs because you'd love to know, too, who's missing their lavender bubble bath. They could be the culprit."

"Grrrr."

We hurried up the staircase.

Chapter 22

Every one of my guests had some form of lavender products in their rooms from their sojourn to Washington Island. Pauline and I found bath bombs, sachets, bubble bath, shampoo--all could create lovely, killing bath water.

Pauline said, "This is just a dead end. Any of them could have used the products here, but I don't believe they'd drown Jackie here. There's no way they could sneak her down the back staircase without people knowing."

"They could if all of them were in on it."

Pauline flipped her hair off her shoulders in disagreement.

I said, "So, one of them could have taken the lavender bubble bath with them to Victor's place, used it, then brought it back. We women travel with our favorite soaps and lotions. We don't leave them behind."

Finding nothing out of the ordinary in the rooms, I checked the time. "Let's go over to the Troubled Trout. We can have a conversation with Erik and Piers before the group returns. Victor is supposed to pick up Jackie's ashes at the funeral home at five." It was after four o'clock now.

We headed down the carpeted stairs.

Pauline said, "What can Erik or Piers possibly tell us that's new?"

I grabbed a jacket off a hook in the front entryway. "Piers was the cook on Saturday night. He had to have gone out to the garbage bins and set them onto the street for Al to pick up. Don't you find it odd that Piers has not come forward in this mess?"

"I doubt that Piers feels obligated to tell you anything." Pauline looked down her nose at me. "The sheriff likely interrogated him already."

Pauline opened the door. A cool breeze pushed at us. "Can't you let Jordy handle his case? Why does Jordy intrigue you so much?"

Pauline's words reminded me of the time I was six and it was my first day of school in Brussels, near our farm. An older boy was playing in the sandbox with toy road graders and bulldozers creating roads and hills. I wanted to jump into the middle of it, but the boy's intensity made me pause. I was fascinated by his focus, his perfection and precision in everything he was doing. He had a mastery I admired. I wanted to be like him. The next day I had worked extra hard in our art period, drawing a horse. I used every crayon in the box to make my horse the most colorful of all in the entire first grade class. I showed my hard work to the boy, and he said, "Cool. You wanna play in the sand with me?" I glowed for days after that.

"Pauline, Jordy intrigues me because... He's invited me into his grownup sandbox and that's all that needs to be said."

"Pffft," she said. "You're going to get sand kicked in your face."

To my dismay, Jeremy Stone was at the bar of the Troubled Trout having a beer and talking with Erik and Piers. Seeing him reminded me he hadn't reported back to me as we'd previously agreed upon. Not that I expected him to be my best buddy.

Pauline and I had no choice but to join the conversation. We took seats on the corner of the bar to the right of Jeremy, with me closest to the reporter.

He offered to pay for our drinks. I accepted in the spirit of getting information. Erik served me a new Belgian ale that made Door County famous. It'd probably be a winner at Saturday's festivities. Pauline asked for a locally made root beer.

With beefy forearms braced behind the bar top, Piers faced Jeremy. Piers' brown hair stuck up every which way in the air; he'd removed a toque or hair net before coming out to greet us.

I said, "Piers, just the man I wanted to talk to."

"Already told the reporter here everything." He pointed with emphasis at Jeremy.

Jeremy patted an electronic notebook on the bar while swigging his beer. "Piers had interesting things to say."

Erik laughed. "Quit teasing the women." He left us to ferry a couple of drinks to a table by the window.

"Piers," I said, "all I want to know is if you saw anybody unusual on Saturday night."

Jeremy leaped in. "He saw your ladies that night having fun. Mercy Fogg came and went. Couldn't miss her loud voice even back in the kitchen."

"That's not news." I asked Piers, "Did she meet up with anybody?"

Piers grabbed a towel to wipe his hands in a distracted way. He nodded toward Jeremy. "Told him just now she met with Al. Behind the Troubled Trout."

"Al Kvalheim?" The back of the place opened onto a patio and beach onto the bay. "Doing what?"

Piers' beefy face wrinkled and bloomed red.

I said, "I hope it wasn't more than just kissing."

Piers waved his hands. "Oh, no. None of that. Didn't mean to imply that. They were sneaking a cigarette together."

Pauline burst out laughing.

I chuckled, too.

Jeremy put down his beer glass. "That's not the best thing Piers saw."

Piers looked about as if to make sure we were alone, then leaned toward me. "It was later, past midnight. Erik and I were going to close up when we heard wheels outside. Creaking. But tiny creaks."

Jeremy leaned in. "It was somebody pulling a big ol' suitcase. One of those big ones you take on a two-week vacation and check in the belly of a plane."

Pauline gasped.

I stared at Jeremy for a moment, then at Piers. "Big enough to hold a body."

Jeremy and Piers nodded.

Piers added, "The person went around a corner up the street."

Which corner? When he explained exactly, I gasped. "A woman?" I guessed it had to be Zadie.

"Nope. A man," Piers said.

By the time we left the Troubled Trout, it had become crowded with early dinner customers, tourists eager for their fried cheese curds and other Wisconsin specialties. The sidewalks bore more people, too, and vehicles cruised down Main Street in clusters. Tourists had begun to filter in for the weekend's Sweets, Suds and Buds Festival. A lot of Illinois license plates made me wonder about Victor Valentine.

Pauline and I took the turn down Duck Marsh Street where I'd parked my yellow truck in front of Dillon's cabin.

Pauline said, "I don't think we should meet the women and Victor at that funeral home. You're going to blurt out something about him murdering his wife."

"I will not. There is no proof he did it."

"Except that Piers Molinsky saw a man rolling a big suitcase around midnight on Saturday night."

"It could've been any man with a suitcase. Victor's too smart to roll a big suitcase around with his dead wife in it."

When we got to Dillon's place, I rapped on his door.

I'd barely said hi when he swept me into his arms and kissed me, then swung me around for the world to see. It was a delicious feeling.

He said, "Glad to see you. You, too, Pauline. I'm making a big batch of homemade chili to take to the work site tomorrow. Want to do some taste-testing?"

The enticing mix of spices tempted me. "Sounds great, but Pauline and I are on our way to the funeral home."

He closed the door behind us. "Are you sure you should go to that? That's going to be intense. One of them could be the culprit."

"That's just it. I need to be there. I might notice something significant."

His frown was instant. "You know you get involved in too many things at once. You promised me, us, last fall, that you'd slow down."

"You're right. But they're my guests. Maybe you could come with?"

"I'll bring some of this chili up the hill and watch over your place. That's my role."

"Okay." I swallowed my disappointment. "Did you have time to check with your mother on the rentals for the condos?"

He kissed me on the lips again. "Mom's manager said a man called to rent the condo last Wednesday for Victor Valentine."

"A man? But not Victor?"

He nodded. "Brace yourself. Victor was definitely there, in secret, it seems. I already called the sheriff to tell him what I found out. You won't have to contact him."

"Thanks." I felt hollowed out. This was so sudden. Wow. Had Victor killed his wife? Had Dillon just solved it? With reluctance, I kissed Dillon. "You're wonderful."

"I know," he crowed.

Pauline and I hurried back to my truck. I climbed in behind the wheel. I pulled a U-y in the street, and headed out of town and on the highway toward the funeral home.

Pauline said, "Maybe we shouldn't go. I have a bad feeling. If what Dillon said is true, Victor Valentine is a murderer, or at least he hired it done. It gives me the creeps."

"Me, too, P.M. But I want to be there to watch Jordy arrest him. And I want to be there for my guests, Jackie's friends, including Dillon's mother."

In Sturgeon Bay, we took a side trip to the Justice Center. Jordy was not pleased to find us outside the safety glass showing our identification to the uniformed receptionist.

We followed him to his office where Pauline and I sat in maroon plastic chairs opposite him. Always neat, his desk had two computer screens, a pile of folders, and a big soft pretzel on a napkin and a tall apple juice bottle. The clock on his wall said it was past five in the afternoon. We'd need to hurry to make it over to the funeral home.

I couldn't help but ask, "Is that dinner?"

With a curt nod he withdrew the food and drink from his desk, swiveled and set it all on the credenza behind him. Then he faced us. "So you have proof it's Victor for sure?"

I'd called ahead and left that message. "Don't you? We both know by now he's been in town since last Wednesday and didn't tell anybody. He had somebody rent the condo for him, an obvious cover."

"I know. Now why are you here?" Jordy's dark eyes regarded each of us one at a time before he landed back on me with a steady gaze. "So he came up from Chicago with the intent to kill? That's what you think?"

"Well, we didn't ask him yet personally."

"Don't." Jordy's face grew intense. "We're close to having something substantial about the murder. Don't mess it up. As usual."

Pauline elbowed me, hinting we should leave.

I couldn't. "My grandfather and I were hit over the head. Somebody hit Pepper over the head. I think that hit was some kind of distraction, though, to make us think Kim Olkowski and her white gloves might be at fault. But Kim could never kill anybody or get her white gloves dirty, at least not that kind of dirty. Kim would hate blood."

Jordy raised a hand to stop me. "Are you going to waste my time now running through the entire list of your guests and half of Fishers' Harbor to tell me who is not suspicious? Didn't you just say Victor Valentine killed his wife?"

Pauline elbowed me again. She nodded toward the door.

I eased forward toward Jordy, leaning an arm on his desk's edge. "I'm not thinking it's Victor. I think somebody wanted it to look like that and that's why the person invited him to come up on Wednesday."

Jordy leaned back, grabbed his soft pretzel and bit into it. "I have to eat and run. You understand."

He didn't believe me. "Listen to me, Jordy, I mean, Sheriff. Pauline and I saw Zadie Elliott going into Victor's condo. She wanted Victor's money to expand her women's products shop in Milwaukee. She also knew the fudge retreat would be her perfect cover to get rid of Jackie. And if Jackie were out of the picture, Zadie probably thinks Victor will help sponsor Yola's dreams, too."

Jordy finished the soft pretzel. My confidence kept draining as his nonchalance kept up. "There's only one problem. Zadie told me she was at his place and she said she didn't kill Jackie."

Pauline's big purse dropped to the floor with a loud *thunk*. "She confessed?"

"She didn't confess. She only said she was at his place." Jordy wadded up the napkin and then tossed it to a basket behind him. "That's all I can tell you."

I said, "So she's under suspicion yet. There's something about the dresses that is still vexing us." I told him about the receipts under Pepper's car's passenger seat. "I don't think Pepper put them there. Somebody else did to mess with her or implicate Pepper. Maybe Yola did that, to protect Zadie."

Pauline said, "I don't know about that. Why would they want to get Zadie's mother Pepper arrested?" She paused, then said a knowing "Oh."

Jordy came to attention. "What do you mean?"

I had to confess my secret. "Pepper has cancer. She believes she hasn't long to live. She didn't want any of her friends to know. But I think they might know. Lucky Harbor has been sticking with her, protecting her. He senses something's wrong. I think he might be one of those dogs that can smell diseases in people."

Jordy looked from me to Pauline and back to me again. "I'm not tracking on any of this. As usual."

"Jordy, let me help you. Witnesses at the Troubled Trout saw a man with a roller suitcase. It could've held a body. Let's say Victor did not kill his wife. He just got the suitcase from his car perhaps, and unknown to him, the killer used the suitcase a bit later. After he went to bed."

Now Jordy sat back in his chair, crossing his arms. "Go on."

"If Zadie had a key and was at his condo, she may have drawn Jackie there by telling her about the affair. So while Victor was out getting his suitcase from his car, perhaps, Zadie had faked taking a bath in the big jet tub but what was really going on was that she'd killed Jackie in the tub and was hiding the body. Victor went to bed, using the other bathroom in the condo. He fell asleep. Zadie--maybe with her friend Yola's help--got Jackie stuffed into the suitcase and off they went to dump her in the harbor. Yola goes back to my inn while Zadie heads back to be with Victor as if nothing happened."

Pauline cleared her throat. "Wow. That was eloquent. Totally believable, which is a switch for you. With me anyway."

Jordy had taken out a pad of paper and was making notes. Then he escorted Pauline and me out the doors. All the way to the outside.

"Thanks," was all he said.

When the two of us were alone, I said to Pauline, "Did he believe me?"

"Totally." Pauline dug around in her purse. She handed me a paper star, the kind kids receive on a bulletin board as a reward. "It's yours."

"Thanks."

As we walked to the yellow truck, my intuition reared into control. I halted.

Pauline said, "Now what's wrong?"

"Don't you think that all went way too smoothly and too fast? Jordy was just trying to get rid of us."

She wiggled her lips about. "So?"

"He wasn't buying into anything I was talking about. He let me talk on and entertain him with theories."

Pauline sighed. "He always does that. You do entertain each other quite well. If Jordy doesn't think Zadie or Victor killed Jackie, then who did it?"

We arrived at the truck. I opened my driver's door. "Maybe we'll never know. Maybe this was the perfect crime after all."

Chapter 23

Fontana called as Pauline and I left the Justice Center in Sturgeon Bay. We decided it was best not to go to the funeral home. Victor needed privacy to receive the ashes, and it was enough for him to possibly be accompanied by Jackie's women friends. After talking with the sheriff, it seemed I was all wrong about one of them being a murderer. Pauline and I were outsiders in this deal. I had to let it go.

I was driving up Highway 42 in the yellow pickup. Traffic was heavy. Tourists were filtering in for the weekend's Sweets, Suds and Buds Festival. It reminded me that I hadn't checked social media for a while to see what the church ladies had stirred up for the Oosterlings' fudge shop and the Blue Heron Inn on Saturday.

Panic flared again. What fudge flavor would I introduce on Saturday at my own open house? What fairy tale would it be named after? My brain felt like one of the ice chunks that still floated about in the coves along the bays of Door County.

Pauline put Fontana on speakerphone. Fontana said, "The doctor said I need to do stuff to stimulate me. The baby is ready and I say it needs to get out of this body right now. My feet don't like being pregnant."

"So how is that my problem, Fontana?" The truck was breezing along with winter-weary brown cattails waving from the ditches.

Pauline said to Fontana, "Do you need to borrow Ava's sturdy work shoes?"

Fontana screamed over the phone. "I wouldn't be caught dead in anything Ava wore."

I said, "You know I'm listening, right?"

"Of course. Maybe I should take you shopping. Seeing you in a dress might shock me so much it'll make my water break."

"I really need to get back to the shop and work on my fudge flavors for Saturday."

Fontana screeched, "Fudge?! No. I thought we could decorate the house out in the country with Pauline's kindergarten girls instead of us doing it ourselves. The excitement will help speed up the birth."

Pauline said, "But John isn't around. He wanted to direct the decorating for his film set."

That prompted me. "For goodness sake, Pauline, three women and thirteen little girls know how to hang a few balloons." I thought of what today still held for us. "We'll have to do this tomorrow, Fontana. Okay?"

And so it was set. It felt good to be planning something fun. I was even looking forward to going home now to make a new batch of Cinderella Pink Fairy Tale Fudge. Its sparkles would look yummy on camera. John would have to list the food donation credits, which could translate into sales for me. I imagined the mortgage on the inn paid off sooner than expected. Grandpa would get paid off. He could buy out Dillon for his half of the boat.

When I got back to the inn, though, chaos was underway of the kind I had never expected.

The women were in a flurry of loading their cars when I pulled the yellow truck to a stop outside the inn at around six-thirty.

Cathy was following Pepper, who carried her makeup case to her sports car, "Honey, please don't leave. Not like this. Let's not make it another thirty years before we all get together."

Pepper, with Lucky Harbor by her side, snapped back, "How dare you act so innocent, Cathy. You were always the one we protected. You never knew what really happened in that vice chancellor's house. So what if I had an affair with him? I didn't burn down his damn house!"

She tossed her case into the car, then hurried as fast as her frail body could take her up the steps to the verandah and into the inn.

Brushing past her with a suitcase was Eliza. She stomped down the stairs. When she saw me, she lurched to a momentary stop, scowled, then went on to her car.

I called after her, "What's going on?"

Cathy answered, "Him."

Jeremy Stone stepped from the front door. He wore a crooked grin on his smug mug.

Pauline grabbed my arm. "Don't kill him here. Too many witnesses."

I charged up the steps. "What did you do? Why are you here? Who let you in?"

"The door was ajar," he said. "You should get that uneven floor fixed."

"Never mind that. What are you doing here?" But I knew. I could tell he must have told them every scrap of information about the fire long ago and everything he knew about the current investigation.

He tried to get around me to leave.

I blocked him. "What was your purpose coming here to make accusations? Isn't that the sheriff's job?"

"And where were you just now?"

I narrowed my eyes at him. "How did you know I was at the sheriff's office?"

"The women said you never showed up at the funeral home, but I checked in with your boyfriend. He told me he suspected you were dishing with the sheriff."

"Leave Dillon out of this."

"But he's very quotable and makes for a great sidebar story. A bigamist, gambler, Vegas hotshot, in jail once and now he's back pretending he's just a construction worker." His eyebrows had risen along with a salivating smile.

"People can change." I held fists tight against my thighs. "You were supposed to help me, not make me the story."

"Hey, I'm a reporter. Just doing my job."

Eliza stomped by us and into the inn. Out came Yola and Zadie with a bag each.

Cathy rushed after them, repeating, "Stay, just until the weekend."

Cathy was trying to salvage something here, but for the life of me I wasn't sure what it was. I wasn't sure of anything anymore. I'd lost all confidence in myself and what I was doing.

I hissed again at Jeremy. "So the secrets are out. You have the ladies mad at each other. They're afraid you're going to make public Pepper's affair as well as their probable part in the chancellor's house burning down, his divorce, and you're going to end up ruining all their lives for what?"

Jeremy stuffed his hands in his pockets. "Ava, Jackie had threatened to tell all in a book."

"What book?"

"She has a manuscript at the Wisconsin State Historical Society Press. I know one of the editors. In doing the research that you asked me to do, the publisher happened to mention the manuscript."

"Is it slated to be published soon?"

"The marketing campaign kicks in later in summer, but they hadn't decided on a publish date. I told them they might hold off and add a new chapter set in Door County at a certain inn."

I wanted to toss him off the veranda. "They can't publish this, Jeremy. I'm sure Victor must have hated learning about this from you, but he can't say anything, can he? To make a fuss about it might make him look guilty as hell in murdering his wife. And if he cares about his wife and didn't murder her, then he just has to swallow this turn of events in his life. What is wrong with your ethics?"

"Aren't you in the least wondering where Victor is?" Jeremy's hooked nose sniffed and wrinkled, taunting me.

"On his way down to Madison to kill that book deal?"

Jeremy laughed. "He'll try, I assume. Did you know he filed for divorce a couple of weeks ago?"

I flinched.

Pauline stepped onto the veranda beside me. "But he's been here acting as if nothing's wrong. Where is he?"

Jeremy shrugged. "I suspect he took the ashes back to his condo to pack and leave. And get away with snuffing out a wife that was about to destroy his business."

Jeremy Stone had apparently solved the murder. Or at least he thought he had. My competitive spirit didn't like it, but what mattered more were my guests. These were friends of Cathy Rivers. I couldn't let them race away feeling that all their friendships had frayed and fallen apart because of their fudge retreat at the Blue Heron Inn.

I rushed about begging all the women to stay at least long enough to hear what I had to say.

In the foyer, watching women traipse up and down the blue-carpeted stairs, Pauline whispered to me, "What exactly are you going to say?"

"How the heck do I know?"

"How are you going to make them stay?"

"My secret weapon. Grandpa."

Grandpa was on his boat. It was now after seven. Pauline and I raced aboard. He was upside down behind the toilet stool again.

Grandpa explained, "My head must be pretty strong. Whoever clocked me the other day made me do more damage than I thought on the connections. Big water leak."

"Sorry to hear that, Gilpa. We need your help."

He came up for air, giving me a look that reminded me of a fox that had just spent an hour chasing a rabbit and missed the creature after all. His silver hair was tousled and wet on one side. "What's going on, A.M. and P.M.?"

I explained the mess at the inn. "They can't leave, Gilpa. They're all angry at each other and that reporter. He's my fault. It's all my fault."

Pauline dropped her purse to the floor of the boat. "What she's trying to say is that she doesn't know how to fix this without your help. She won't listen to me. If it were me, I'd let them all go home. Good riddance."

"Jordy is depending on me."

Grandpa settled his butt down on the closed toilet lid. "The sheriff?"

"Jordy knows who did it, but he doesn't have enough proof yet. Jeremy Stone thinks Victor murdered Jackie. But if everybody leaves now, Jordy will have one heck of a time solving this because they're likely lawyering up and won't be nearby anymore."

Grandpa said, "I can't take them for a boat ride with this leak. May have to have a tow down to Sturgeon Bay's repair shop."

"That's the solution. There's always some multi-million-dollar yacht from Chicago or some other place around the world getting new paint or repairs in Sturgeon Bay. You can take the ladies there tomorrow. You know the guys down there. We could let on that the owner of the yacht is an investor who supports women's businesses in particular."

Pauline elbowed me. "You think they'll really unpack for this?"

"They will if Grandpa asks them personally, as a goodbye gesture to honor their friend Jackie. And if enough money is dangled in front of them all."

Grandpa guffawed. "I need a stiff drink. I know I hid some booze on this boat somewhere. If those darn divas didn't find it already."

By seven-thirty that evening Grandpa was at the inn with the women hugging and kissing him and agreeing they would stay just one more day to see the multi-millionaire investor's yacht down at the canal zone in Sturgeon Bay. They had unpacked their cars. I made pizzas, including a fudge dessert pizza, and we poured wine.

Later, after the others had trundled up the stairs to bed and Cathy had left for her home, Eliza paused in the dining room to thank me. I was collecting dishes from the table.

"You have a way about you, a real Door County neighborly way. Your grandpa, too," she said. "It would have been sad to part with all of us upset. That's not how we want to remember each other or Jackie. Jackie kept us together."

The candles I'd lit on the table shimmered reflections into her teary eyes.

I offered, "She was certainly a force."

Eliza nodded. "Do you think Victor will get arrested soon?"

The question created discomfort inside me. "You think he killed her?"

Eliza nodded. "Now I do. Now that I found out about the divorce from that reporter. And that book."

I picked up a stack of saucers. "Did you know about this book before tonight?"

She shook her head. "Not hearing about it feels like a betrayal, but I guess each of us has a right to write a book in secret." She swiped at tears. "I just wish she had trusted us enough to tell us about these things. We were supposed to be friends. Why couldn't she trust us to tell us about her divorce happening? Or the book?"

Her words brought me pain, because they made me think about how I treated Pauline sometimes. I put down the stack of china plates on the table so I wouldn't drop them. I vowed silently to help Pauline in a full-throttle way. I'd acquiesced about John's plan to surprise her with a proposal on Saturday, but that's what it was in my heart--acquiescence. I hadn't been excited for her. Now, in talking with Eliza, I realized my allegiance was to Pauline, not others.

I picked up the plates again. "Eliza, maybe Jackie was going to tell all of you during your fudge retreat and she just didn't get enough time. She was loud and pushing you women friends to do too much while she was here, but I wonder if she was just nervous and didn't know how to tell you everything because she felt she'd let you down."

"How could she have let us down? She was successful, a leader. We depended on her. We loved her."

I walked the plates to the kitchen. Eliza followed, holding open the swinging door for me as I said, "She valued your friendship. She obviously knew that all of you looked up to her. But she was likely afraid she'd lose your respect if she failed by getting her divorce and doing that book. Maybe she was afraid to tell you about the book because she knew that would mean a new era for you all."

Eliza shrugged. "I suppose. We're getting older. Being fifty is a big deal for us women. If the truth about those parties at the vice chancellor's house hit the social media now, we'll all certainly have to grow up. No more innocence. We're way past our cheerleader days."

We walked back to the foyer, where she turned to mount the stairs.

I said, "I'm sorry about all this. I suppose, if he's not arrested, Victor will just leave for Chicago tomorrow with Jackie's ashes. If he hasn't already left."

Eliza sighed, nodding. She said good night and went up the stairs. I listened for the squeak on the last step, and then her door closing.

I thought that if anybody might know Victor's schedule, it would be Zadie. I mounted the stairs myself for a discussion long in coming.

Chapter 24

It was after nine that Thursday evening when I knocked on the door of the room in the inn occupied by Zadie and Yola. As I suspected, they were getting dressed to go out. I no longer had any patience concerning Zadie's shenanigans, so I asked, "Going to wish Victor goodbye?"

Zadie--blond, petite perfection in one of the cute dresses found in a local shop--sat down on the bed with a bounce.

Yola lounged in the stuffed chair.

Zadie said, "Everybody's wrong. Victor didn't kill his wife."

I leaned against the back of her door, arms crossed. "To be determined. You visited him a few times. You were having an affair."

"No."

Yola nodded. "She's telling the truth."

The room smelled of lavender perfume. It made me shiver. Was I in the room with the killer or killers? Two young women could've wrestled Jackie over to the harbor.

I mused, "I heard that a man was seen with a big suitcase. The sheriff probably has the suitcase by now. Do you know anything about that? Did you see anybody Saturday night with a big suitcase?"

Zadie said, "I didn't see a man."

"Any of the nights you went to Victor's condo?"

"No. And I wasn't having an affair. Not really. I was coming on to Victor, but we never had sex."

"So you were going over there repeatedly for what reason?"

Zadie looked at Yola, then at me. Yola had paled. Zadie's slim shoulders shrugged. "My mother and all her friends, they're so tight. They're all rich. Yola and I just have each other and not much really. I was trying to get money from Victor for our businesses. We both want to relocate to Chicago."

"It's sad the only way you know how to get a loan is through a man's pants. But have you ever heard of a bank?"

Yola grumbled, "That was mean."

"No, it wasn't. It's what normal adults do. They go to a bank or credit union for a loan, or their own parents. Zadie, why didn't you just ask your mother for a loan?"

Zadie tipped her head down, her blond hair swishing over her face. Tears flowed. "My mother is dying."

My heart went out to her. I sat down next to her on the bed and put an arm around her. "Maybe not. She's on chemo. She has a long journey, but doctors might be more positive than you think about her diagnosis. Have you asked to accompany her to her appointments?"

She shook her head.

"Maybe your mom would like that. Ask her if you can go along."

Zadie looked up at me, pushing hair from her teary face. "Just like that? I should ask her?"

I remember how lost I was in my early twenties, too. I nodded. "Sure."

Yola said, "I'll go with you, if you want."

Zadie nodded. "Thanks, Yola. I'm glad I have you."

Yola handed Zadie a tissue. I stayed beside Zadie on the bed. "Why did Jackie shower you with all those dresses? It felt like the entire trip was orchestrated to gift you. I found several receipts, by the way, under the passenger's side seat in your mother's car."

Zadie winced. "Jackie bought the stuff to get rid of me. I sensed she knew I had been sucking up to her husband in the past. That's why I couldn't tell her that he was in town on Wednesday night. I was sucking up to him."

"And you liked the new clothes."

She shrugged an assent.

Yola winced.

Zadie offered, "My mom tried to stop Jackie from buying me stuff. Mom has her pride. She even asked Kim to make me stop the affair that wasn't really an affair."

I rose from the bed. "Kim? What was Kim supposed to do?"

"Kim talked to me, but I told her it wasn't her business and to leave me and Victor alone."

"That was a dangerous game you were playing."

This girl really wanted his money. I shook my head in derision. "Cathy Rivers told me Kim was seen going into your mother's room down the hall about the time your mother was hit over the head. What do you know about that?"

"Nothing, but Kim would never do that. When Kim talked to me about leaving Victor alone, I told her that I'd talk with my mother again about a loan to help her get her white gloves on television."

"And did you do that?"

"No."

"Another lie. Do you ever do anything the right way?"

That made Yola yelp in her throat. I had my answer. I wasn't sure I could trust anything they'd told me just now, but I ventured one more question. "Who do you think hit Pepper over the head? And why?"

The young women hesitated just enough to make me suspicious.

Zadie finally said, "Who's left on your list? We didn't do it. Kim didn't do it. Cathy didn't. That leaves Eliza."

Her deduction skills were so smooth I couldn't trust them, but I hung in there. "Why would Eliza want to harm your mother?"

Zadie shrugged. "She's jealous? My mom is really cute and rich and is married to my handsome father. Eliza lost her husband, and from what I heard this past week her tractor place is going belly up. She's going to be dirt poor. The manufacturers own the tractors for sale at her dealership. She owns nothing but a rundown farmhouse." A nervous chuckle threaded from her throat. "Dirt poor. Get it? Farmers dig around in the dirt with their tractors. I told her that."

"That she's dirt poor?" I was aghast.

"No. I said she should stop digging around in dirt if she wanted my mom's help. It's a social class thing."

I left wondering if Zadie had just played me. I didn't trust anything she'd said. Especially the snobbery. My parents were farmers, after all. And my mom loved to vacuum. My family liked dirt.

After I said good night to Dillon over the phone and locked my suite's door for the night, I listened for Zadie's footfalls. It was after eleven. I was positive she would go to Victor's condo, if he hadn't already left town.

The doorbell rang, startling me.

I threw on clothes and headed through the parlor for the front door. To my surprise, it was the sheriff.

"Jordy? What's going on?"

The blue-and-red lights were rotating on top of the squad car, strafing the leafless oaks and maples.

Jordy was in full uniform, hat on. "It's your grandfather. I have him under arrest."

"What for? Is he in your squad now?"

"Yes. He tried to break into a condo not far from here. Do you know anything about that?"

"You must mean Victor Valentine's condo. Where I saw Zadie Elliott go in the door." I shivered. The night air was damp. A fog was whispering around us and I only wore a sweatshirt and jeans and slippers. "Was he really breaking in?"

"No. He pushed through the front door as bold as ever when it opened. The woman with Victor called us."

"Zadie Elliott?"

"No. Another one of your guests. Eliza Stefansson. She was returning a necklace that belonged to Jackie Valentine."

I looked about. "Where is she?"

"Still with Victor."

"What about my grandfather?"

"He's going to jail. He broke in."

"Aren't you stretching things?"

"He was also threatening Mr. Valentine. Your grandfather said that he was going to sue Victor Valentine for bringing all this trouble to his granddaughter."

"Do I need to come with you to bail him out?"

"No. He's in for the night. Accusing somebody of murder and breaking into their house aren't things I can take lightly."

I was trembling. I looked about. "Where's Eliza?"

"Mrs. Stefansson is still with Victor Valentine as far as I know. She was crying and pretty upset by the whole deal. She may not want to come back here. Gil is your grandfather, after all. She said something about suing Gil."

"I guess I better put on a jacket and go down to Duck Marsh Street. My grandmother's not going to be pleased about this."

Jordy touched the brim of his hat in a nod goodbye, then took off with my grandfather inside the caged back seat of the squad. I waved at him. Oddly, though, Gilpa wore a huge smile. What was he up to?

Grandma was not pleased about Grandpa's midnight arrest.

In a long pink nightgown, she was racing about their small house gathering up things to take Grandpa in the morning. His watch. His billfold he'd left behind. Caramel candies he loved. Everything was going into a shaving kit.

Her white hair floated behind her like a ghost on the loose.

I trailed after her. "Grandma, slow down. You can't bail him out tonight anyway. You need to get a good night's sleep. I'll drive you down to the jail tomorrow. Dad will meet us there and Grandpa will come home."

"I have to do something or I'll go nuts. Why does he always do this? You're just like him, you know." She chucked a pair of sunglasses into the shaving kit.

I'd long ago gotten over the fact that Grandpa and I could get into trouble without trying. Though this time, Grandpa had tried. "Why do you think he smiled like that at me?"

She put the shaving kit down on the couch. "He knows something you're supposed to know."

"Like what?"

"Like who the murderer is? That darn Gil would not have gone out at midnight to break into that condo unless he knew something valuable to help you. Everything he does is about helping you, my dear. You're his favorite granddaughter."

"I'm his only granddaughter."

"That helps." She zipped the shaving kit and took it to the TV tray that sat next to the front door as a catchall for keys.

I gave Grandma a hug. "Go to bed now. Don't worry about a thing."

"I'm not worried. He's safe in jail. What makes me mad is that he thought he could walk right into that condo and face a killer. Victor Valentine is a dangerous man. Gil might have been hurt."

"So you think he murdered his wife?"

"Absolutely. Somehow you have to prove he carried his wife's body in that suitcase and dumped her in the harbor in front of your fudge shop and next to my husband's boat. He chose us for a reason. What's his motivation for doing that? I don't know. You have to find out."

On my way back up the street and the hill in the brackish night, I swallowed my pride and called Jeremy Stone. "I have a couple of favors to ask of you."

"What's in it for me?" He sounded groggy. Probably woke from a deep sleep. I envied him.

"A story. My grandfather's in jail."

"Again?"

"This time, I believe he's caught the killer. Well, actually, the killer is free and my grandfather is the one caught, but you and I can reverse the roles."

"How?"

"I need you to do some more digging."

"My pleasure."

"And I have a second thing I need your help with, too."

Friday came with a great swell of support for my grandfather around the table at the Blue Heron Inn. To my astonishment, Victor came for breakfast with the group. Victor was adamant about his innocence. He apologized to me and everyone.

He said, "I'm sorry we had to call the sheriff, but we heard Gil pounding and so we called. By the time your grandfather had barged in and was yelling at me, the sheriff arrived and they were gone."

Cathy Rivers was at breakfast, too. Dillon was there for support, helping me serve the group. As soon as I'd called him last night he'd come up the hill to spend the night. He slept on one of the sofas in the parlor. This morning he'd donned a long bibbed apron and was serving peanut butter fudge pancakes. He fried the bacon, too.

Eliza was shook by last night, apologizing for threatening to sue Grandpa. "I was returning the necklace I had borrowed from Jackie." She looked up at me as I poured coffee for Cathy across from her. "Ava and I were talking yesterday, and I was reminded of Jackie's clothes and jewelry. Jackie was as bright as an Amazon parrot and we loved her for it."

Zadie, sitting next to Pepper, said, "If it's okay with you, Victor, I'll give the dresses she bought me to Goodwill. Would that be okay?"

Victor was impeccably dressed in a suit, with his hair perfect. "That's probably a good idea." He gave me another look. "I'll be happy to go down to Sturgeon Bay and cover the bail for your grandfather. This was my fault. I panicked. I'm so upset about Jackie's death. Of course I'll drop the charges."

With some hesitation, I said, "But you let him get taken away."

Eliza said, "It was after midnight. It was scary."

"My grandfather can be scary," I said, pouring coffee for her, "but he means well."

"Because he loves you," Eliza said. "It's a lesson for all of us. Don't you think, gals? What would our world be like if we could all protect and support each other in the way Gilsen Oosterling loves his family?"

Several of them muttered, "So true."

I exchanged a look with Dillon, who had just set down another plate of bacon in front of the ladies. Zadie and Yola reached for pieces immediately. Had my grandfather's arrest been one more thing to deflect suspicion from them?

In the kitchen with Dillon, we discussed my odd mix of guests while we prepared hot cocoa made with Belgian chocolate for the special chocolate serving cups.

Dillon gave me a kiss then stirred the chocolate on the stove. "Let Jordy worry about all this. John and I are taking Lucky Harbor back to the woods today. John is determined to find that ring."

Concern blew through me. "Is he really going to propose tomorrow? He won't do it on the air will he?"

Dillon put down his spoon for a moment to come to me. He took one of my hands and kissed my knuckles, sending a zippy tingle up my arms and across every inch of my skin. "What if you and I focus on the fun we'll have tomorrow during the Sweets, Suds, and Buds Festival?" He gave me a searching look.

"Fun. I haven't had fun for a while, have I?"

He shook his head.

"And I promised to get better about not trying to do too many things at once and to remember to have fun."

"Yup." He went back to stirring the dark chocolate that had begun to bubble. He turned off the burner. "Honey, I'm trying my best to change. But are you? Do we have a chance?"

My heart broke. I rushed to him and hugged him. "Of course we do."

After breakfast, Victor did as he promised and drove down to Sturgeon Bay to spring my grandfather.

I wondered if Grandpa had gotten jailed on purpose so that he could avoid taking the women on his tour with Mercy today, who would be driving them down in the trolley.

My dad had driven up from Brussels to pick up Grandma and take her to the Justice Center.

I went to the fudge shop around ten. Cody was there. So was Brecht Rousseau with the twins. Several customers were buying fudge as well as items from the sports equipment side of the store. Everybody cooed over the twins. I told Brecht to come more often; it helped sales.

"Hey," Brecht said, selling a fishing pole to a father and son, "this gives me a great place to go. Beats just walking the streets."

I felt for him in his quest to find a real job. "I'm sure something will turn up. With the tourists coming back, a lot of part-time seasonal jobs open up."

Cody called out, "Miss Oosterling, maybe you'll have to hire Brecht if I quit."

In shock, I turned to him as he wrapped bright pink crinkly cellophane around a fudge purchase. "You're not quitting, are you?"

"Not now. But what happens when I get my badge? What happens when I become a park ranger? You gotta get used to change, Miss Oosterling. Even hard dolomite rock here in Door County changes."

"Yeah. We usually have to blast it here to build a basement."

"But not if it has cracks in it. Acidic rainwater gets in, and pretty soon you get caves and sink holes forming out of the hardest rock ever. Strong bonds in rock can be broken by simple water."

"This is your geology studies talking."

"I'm trying to tell you I'm changing--faster than when the climate here melted the glaciers ten thousand years ago. I'm growing up, in case you haven't noticed."

"You're nineteen."

"Going on twenty, then twenty-one and then thirty-three like you."

"Don't say it like that. You make me feel old."

"You better be thinking about getting married if you feel old." He nodded toward the baby carriage in the middle of the shop.

"You should be having kids someday. Name one after me. Ranger."

I giggled. Cody always had a way to make me smile and take my mind off my worries. "You still have a couple of years of training and college work, so let's not think about you quitting just yet."

"Yes, Miss Oosterling-who-denies-reality-in-her-fudge-shop because she lives in fairly-tale land like her fudge."

Customers chortled. A woman asked, "What's the new flavor for tomorrow's festival?"

Oh, crap. I hadn't a clue. It made me think about the thirteen kindergartners I'd be seeing just after lunchtime. I said, "I have a research team working on it."

A lady with a little girl in tow said, "We'll be back. We're collecting all of your fairy tale fudge flavors and the matching aprons and purses. My little one can't wait to pick up the new flavor and tell all her friends."

Somehow her comment buoyed me. This was where I belonged--in my fudge shop.

Minutes later, Fontana and I headed for the palatial house south of town in her red Mustang convertible.

My mom drove up from the farm and brought along her vacuum cleaner. One of the school bus drivers delivered Pauline's class of thirteen girls to the house. A couple of the parents also came along to chaperone.

By one o'clock we were thick in the middle of decorating every inch of the beautiful house with all manner of pink and purple crepe paper streamers, balloons, sparkling decorated stars the girls hung on strings in doorways. Glitter seemed to multiply worse than a springtime ant hatch and cover the floors.

Fontana, determined to make her baby come early, kept up with the bouncy group as best she could, even stepping up and down a ladder.

At one point I hadn't seen Pauline for a while, so I went looking for her. She was out front, sitting on the bench near the little angel statue in the front yard. She sat ramrod straight, staring out in the sunshine, though cobalt-colored cauliflower clouds were budding to the west.

I sat down next to her. From inside, the whir of my mother's vacuuming continued as she tried to keep up with the glitter on the floor.

"Hey, friend, what's wrong?"

"I'm happy."

I laughed, draping an arm around her for a quick hug. "Sure beats the alternative."

"This is going to be perfect for John. It's beautiful inside. He's going to be famous. Everybody's going to love his show. The girls will be making fudge and having a tea party in this place and it'll look so cute on camera that advertisers won't be able to resist it."

"All good. What's really wrong?"

"I'm happy for him. But I can't be with him as his life grows. He'll move away to New York or Chicago. I can't move away from those girls. I can't move away from Fontana or Laura, or Door County. Or you. You're my friend. You're all I have for family."

I gulped. Did this mean what I thought it might mean? Crap. John was planning to propose to her tomorrow.

I ventured, "It's okay to be sad about being happy. Change is good, Pauline. You told me that many times. And maybe John won't become famous. He'll just be his usual miserable lout and stay here."

Pauline chuckled. "I sound stupid, I know. I'm a teacher. I always wanted to be a teacher. Right here. I know what I want."

"You could make new friends if you moved away with John. Teach at a new school."

"Don't you see what your women guests showed us? After thirty years they had to get together because they missed each other. I don't want to be away from you for thirty years. We were apart for eight years while you lived in California and it was too much, even with social media. Facetime isn't the real thing. As much as I hate all the trouble you get into, I don't want to be stupid and not be with you. At least, if I'm going to be stupid, I want to be doing it with you."

I had to swallow the lump in my throat. "I guess that's a compliment. And maybe some wisdom I hadn't thought too much about."

She gave me a pleading, soulful look as she gathered her long hair with one hand. "Tell me you returned to Door County after eight years because you missed me. Truth. Did you miss me?"

I tossed my arms around her and hugged her tight, sniffing back tears. "Grandma and Grandpa gave me a good excuse to come back so I could help Grandma with her broken leg last spring, but I was ecstatic that I'd be with you again. I missed you. I'm glad I'm back."

We interlocked pinkie fingers for a shake on it.

But as we went back into the house, I realized tomorrow could be a huge disaster for my best friend and I had no control over that. The knot on the back of my head pulsated, as if forcing me to think of better ways to help Pauline, to stop being such a knothead myself.

Chapter 25

At the fudge shop later that afternoon, after I got back from decorating the house with Pauline's kindergarten class, Grandpa stormed in and out of the shop working on his boat. He was happy he'd evidently interceded with the murder case.

The problem, though, which I didn't voice to Grandpa, was that it seemed whoever murdered Jackie was going to get away with it. The chilling truth in my gut said one or more of my guests had something to do with it. Maybe Victor, too. Grandma Sophie taught me that we women have intuition and gut instinct, and when things feel rotten in our gut, listen to it and heed it.

Cody was helping me, thank goodness. The church ladies had left--after leaving me with two card tables in the center of the shop filled with their homemade quilts for sale. I couldn't complain. They were busy now with a Facebook campaign to encourage sales of my fudge at tomorrow's festival. One of the messages on Facebook said, "Beer and Belgian Fudge for Breakfast."

I looked around to see if Dotty Klubertanz or Lois Forbes had created a new fudge recipe under Cody's guidance, but nothing new waited for me on the marble table or in the glass cases.

Cody was stirring a batch of dark Belgian chocolate fudge in a copper kettle. "Miss Oosterling, nobody would ever think of making a new fairy tale flavor without you. You're the queen of fudge. You have the magic wand."

He always forced a smile from me. "Thanks, Cody, for your confidence. But my head just won't wrap itself around a new recipe for this event."

"That's because you're worried about everybody else. Too bad."

That stopped me from cleaning the clutter atop the register counter. "What do you mean?"

"You're a nice person. You worry about everybody. Your grandpa, your grandma, your guests, Mercy Fogg, Dillon and John, the sheriff, Pauline, Fontana, Bethany, Sam, Brecht and Laura, me, and Lucky Harbor, Dotty and Lois..."

His list sank into me like a summer sunburn, warm at first but then hurting.

"You're insinuating that I shouldn't worry."

"You shouldn't quite so much. You know, we can live our lives without you."

I gaped at my red-haired employee. "That wasn't very nice to say."

"Sam told me that. About me. I'm just sharing it with you now. If it helps. I used to worry, too, about everybody staring at me and being concerned I might do something odd just because I deal with Asperger's. Sam said worrying so much about others when you can't control them or their feelings is like trying to empty Lake Michigan with a cup. It might help you pass the time to be scooping with that cup all the time, but it doesn't get you much. It's like Niagara Falls--it'll disappear in fifty thousand years or so, scientists say, but why worry about that now? Worrying just becomes a habit. Another habit you have to break. A vicious cycle for humans."

I put the papers down, then grabbed a pink apron to put on over my shirt and jeans.

"Sam said all that?"

Cody's face became so red it almost covered up his freckles and matched the color of his hair. "Some of it. A lot of the words are mine. Stuff I learned in my geology class and in our group sessions."

"Seems those sessions brought you a lot of wisdom."

The shop was taking on the heavenly aroma of the dark, rich, imported Belgian chocolate. "Thanks, Miss Oosterling. I like being wise." He winked at me.

"I appreciate your wisdom. Thank you." I went to the kitchen for cream and sugar and came back, setting the ingredients next to another copper kettle. "Dillon said several months ago I needed to work on how involved I am with everybody's business. He didn't say it that way, but I got the message. Pauline tells me I have no restraint because I don't trust anybody, not even myself at times. I guess I interfere in things." I poured the cream into the copper kettle. "Do I interfere?"

He focused on stirring faster with the wood paddle. I had my answer.

I said, "I remember when we first met I didn't exactly trust you because I just didn't know you. It seems I'm no better. After a whole year."

"Oh, you're better!" He practically shouted in my ear. "You trust me now, mostly."

"What do you mean 'mostly'?"

"You panicked when I broke up with Bethany. Sure, I didn't do it smoothly, but you also never asked why I broke up with her. Instead, you had Brecht ask me for you."

It was my turn to flush. "Okay, why?" I poured a bag of sugar into the kettle in front of me.

"She wants to study in Europe. I don't want to go to Europe. I like Door County."

"Because it has great dolomite rock and sea caves still carved into our cliffs."

Cody chuckled. "I suppose. But I think Bethany needs to be free to explore relationships. We're too young to be tied down right now."

"Sheesh. You must have taken wisdom pills."

"Is there such a thing?"

"No, Cody."

He laughed. "With the amount of pills I've taken in my life, I always think there must be a pill for everything. Whew."

"The wisdom is all your own." Something happy and warm was rising within me as we talked and as I began making fudge. "What do you think I should do, Cody, to make my life better? You have a good handle on yours, it seems. How do I get some of your mojo?"

He smiled so big the gesture wiggled his ears. "Make fudge? I have an idea for a new flavor. Want to hear it?"

Once I heard his idea, I knew it would be perfect for tomorrow's Sweets, Suds and Buds Festival. It would also be photogenic for the television taping in what I now called the "Pink Palace" after we'd decorated it earlier that afternoon.

Grandpa came stomping in covered in oil. It dripped off his silver hair and slid down the side of his face. The words coming out of his mouth could have blistered wallpaper.

Cody and I stared at him as he tromped, grumbling, over to his register counter and grabbed a rag. Grandpa found another can of bolts soaking in oil, then headed back outside. The door banged shut, setting the cowbell off a half-dozen times before it settled back in place with a dying thud.

Cody said, "Seems like things might be getting back to normal."

"Except..."

"You still think one of your guests killed Mrs. Valentine."

"Let's not talk about it. Leave it to the sheriff."

"Miss Oosterling, those women tried to make you believe their friendship is as solid as dolomite rock, but remember what I said about acid rain?"

"It creates cracks in the solid rock."

"Cracks big enough for some of the rock to fall away. Just like those women maybe. The cracks among them might be growing wider." Cody shut off the burner under his copper kettle. He hauled the kettle of fudge over to the window loafing table. "I know how you can find out if one of them killed Mrs. Valentine."

I came over to help him haul the kettle over to the marble table. "How?"

"You should let all of your guests go home. Send them away."

We watched the sweet, hot lava ooze onto the white marble. "Go home? Let them get away with it?"

"No. In my psychology class we learned that people who are guilty might hang around, trying to not look guilty. They try to be your friend. Guilty people show up at funerals, for example."

"I don't think your idea will work. They're all going home soon. There's no reason to test them. And no funeral."

Cody picked up a wood loafing paddle and moved it in and out of the fudge. "You could create a life celebration and see who stays."

"See who's solid rock? And who's going to crack up?"

Cody smiled. "You could be a geologist."

Dillon insisted I come to dinner at his place that evening. He baked salmon that he'd caught in the waters off Door County last year and had flash-frozen. With a little maple syrup on top to form a crunchy glaze in the oven, it was a heavenly treat.

Afterward, we sat in each other's arms on the sofa in front of the lit fireplace. Rain splattered against the windows. One of my ears listened to Dillon's heartbeat.

The only thing missing was Lucky Harbor. He insisted on protecting Pepper Elliott and had stayed at the inn with her.

Earlier in the day the hunting dog had gone to the woods down near Brussels with Dillon and John to look for Pauline's purse and the ring. They'd still had no luck.

Dillon said, "Maybe it's just not to be."

I had told him about Pauline's new feeling about moving on without John. "I feel sad for Pauline."

Dillon kissed me on the top of my head. "She'll be fine. She's got you."

"Thank you, Dillon, for saying that." I kissed his chin, then lay my head back atop his heartbeat. "But what about...Jackie?"

"How do you help her? You leave the murder case to Jordy Tollefson. You've got enough to worry about tomorrow."

I leaped off Dillon and off the sofa. "That's it!"

"What? Come back here. I'm cold without you."

I snuggled in beside him again, threading his luscious dark hair with my fingers. "You're brilliant. So is Cody. Do you think your mother can convince all her friends and Victor to stay through tomorrow's festival?"

"I doubt it. They're eager to go home."

"Not if we suggest that Jackie would want a proper sendoff, and what better way to do that than having them be together at the festival where I'll offer a new fudge flavor in her honor."

I got up to toss another piece of cherry wood on the fire. "There are five women to watch. We don't need to watch your mother, obviously."

"What are we watching and why?"

"Cody says that we might be able to tell who committed the crime if we watch how they act, that guilty people often attend a funeral. The guilty party might stick around longer, or act weird."

"This is nutty, you realize."

I folded my arms on that. "You could be right. The sheriff's going to be busy with the traffic tomorrow at the field where the tractor pull will happen. Some of us can form our own posse and mill about watching the women."

"Who will be doing nothing but drinking great Door County beers and eating your new fudge flavor, which is what?"

I came over and climbed into his lap. "You'll have to bribe me to get that information out of me, Mr. Rivers."

"I know just how to bribe you."

The fireplace snapped and crackled.

Chapter 26

I'd worked until almost midnight making batches of Cinderella Pink Fairy Tale Fudge and the new flavor to accommodate both the festival tourists plus the television shoot for John in the early afternoon at the "pink palace".

I also had to have plenty left for the crowd I hoped for at the inn's open house later on Saturday.

My guests got into the excitement of the hubbub. They bought into the idea of enjoying one last big fling with fudge in honor of Jackie. They were even excited about the morning's tractor pull, especially since Eliza had volunteered some of her equipment at her farm implement store.

"It's just sitting there and I have to sell the equipment anyway. This is free advertising for me," she conceded. "Maybe somebody will take pity on me and buy the building, too."

I felt sorry for her, though I wondered if her visit with Victor at midnight on Thursday had little to do with a necklace and more to do with begging for him to buy her business.

A tractor pull happened in a big field where various drivers with all kinds of tractors with varying horsepower would test their ability to pull heavy objects certain distances within timed races. Some events also included tractor drivers showing off skills using plows and disks--the tools that cultivated and turned over the soil and readied it for planting with corn or soybeans. How a driver navigated turning in the corners of a field was valued as well. Making pretty designs with the disks didn't necessarily add points, but the crowd loved the artistry. The events even sold framed photos taken by drone cameras of the accomplishments.

Fishers' Harbor was bustling by eight o'clock. The Troubled Trout had a special breakfast planned with my fudge pancakes featured.

Jane's bookstore was filled with books by several authors who would be doing signings on tables set up on the sidewalk in front of the shop. She was giving away free fudge samples for me.

Various stores had "Sweets, Suds and Buds" specials. The grocery was selling baskets filled with cherry everything, including a six-pack of a new cherry beer brewed in Bailey's Harbor by a bar that had rebuilt after a fire last year. Dillon had stocked the brew at the inn for the celebration later.

Flyers on windows advertised the "cow bingo" later at the grounds outside of town where the tractor pull would be. My dad was bringing two Holsteins for the event. A large pen was always set up for the bingo. Dad and other farmers created a grid on the ground using lime--not the fruit but ground limestone, a white granular substance the consistency of sand. Each section of the grid had a number and you could put down a bet on which square would get pooped on. This year, the flyer said the lavender farm on Washington Island was donating big baskets of sweet-smelling items for the bed, bath, and laundry, which seemed appropriate. But there was also local beer, wines, and vodka at stake, and I had put in a free weekend for two at the Blue Heron Inn as part of the cow bingo prize.

Grandma and her flower committee had managed to fill every merchant's window flowerbox with early-blooming geraniums grown in local homes and nurseries. Marigolds grown in nurseries decorated the street terraces in bunches. By the official start of the tourist season in May the entire Main Street would be lined on both sides by continuous marigolds.

The air was sweet with the breeze off the bay.

Adventurous yellow daffodils and white narcissus poked through the ground here and there, ignoring frost warnings for next week.

By nine o'clock, my shop was mobbed. Stacks of Fairy Tale Fudge shrank piece by piece.

The Fisherman's Tall Tale Fudge packaged in beer cartons sold so well Grandpa had to make several runs over to the Troubled Trout to get extra cartons.

All six copper kettles remained steamy and aromatic with Belgian chocolate swirling into a tasty thermometer range below the hard boil stage.

Customers egged me on to reveal my new flavor early. I said "no." I didn't mind the grousing. It was all in good fun. They said they'd be at the tractor pull south of town later, where I'd unveil the flavor as one of the prizes for the winner of the pull.

Cody was beaming. The flavor was his idea. He'd stayed late at the shop after closing time last night to help make several kettles' worth of the new Fairy Tale Fudge flavor.

I left Cody in charge of the shop. Brecht would relieve him at the time of the tractor pull. Cody was eager to play detective, equating such a thing with being a forest ranger trying to solve a poaching crime. Somehow he was going to get extra credit for a college class with this effort, he said.

The fudge divas fluttered about the inn. I kept my own detective eyes on them as they chose clothes to wear, changed outfits a couple of times, tried on jewelry, packed and re-packed. They hugged a lot. This was going to be their day for the official goodbye to each other. They all made vows about the future.

Eliza wanted to sell her dealership in earnest now. She seemed happier now than when she'd first arrived at the fudge retreat with her friends.

Yola and Zadie were determined to head for Chicago, but I hoped Zadie would stick around in Milwaukee for her mother, Pepper Elliott.

Kim Olkowski would probably give up her white glove business if she couldn't find an investor to push it further. She seemed ambitious enough to succeed at something.

Victor had called to say he'd meet us at the tractor pull. If he were the killer, he was sure acting cool about things.

At the inn, where I was in the kitchen wrapping fudge that I'd made there, Pauline came through the back door dressed in an elegant pink blouse and matching slim pink jeans that made her look like a model. I was envious. I mucked about in the kitchen in my usual white blouse and denims.

I was nervous for her. Would John's proposal today please her? Or send her into a depression? I wasn't sure. I was afraid for her either way.

She plunked down a big, new pink purse about the size of a beanbag chair. "This is a special day for me. Couldn't you dress up just a little?"

"This is a new blouse."

"White. All you ever wear is white. Wear something for the festival mood."

"Apple blossoms are white."

"The apple trees won't be in bloom until later." She hissed at me. "This plan of yours and Cody's is not going to reveal anything. We'll follow those women around for no good reason. And they're going to be suspicious."

"You're assigned Eliza. She's the easiest one. She's got a couple of tractors in the tractor pull. I've got Zadie and Yola, two guilty parties if there ever was a pair."

"What about Pepper?"

"Sam is watching her."

The doorbell rang several times. Before I could even leave the kitchen, Mercy Fogg lumbered into the kitchen. Her blond curls bounced about as usual, but she had a sparkly comb pulling them back on each side. Her stout frame was sheathed in a gray bus driver's uniform, but she had tucked a pink handkerchief into the pocket. Most shocking of all--she wore lipstick. Pink and shiny.

Pauline elbowed me. I closed my gaping mouth.

Mercy said, "Yeah, shocker, isn't it? I clean up good. Reporting for duty. Is Vic here or do I follow him starting somewhere else?"

Pauline widened her eyes at me. "You asked Mercy to tail Victor?"

I shrugged.

Mercy made fists in a playful way. "If he makes any moves, I can bring him down."

Pauline shook her head into her hands, then came up for air. "You both are nuts. You're not going to catch a murderer at a tractor pull."

Mercy nodded, her curls flopping about. "Who cares! This is fun. And from what I hear, ol' Vic is filthy rich and I'm single."

"You're making a play for Victor?" Pauline spit out the obvious.

I said, "It's part of her cover."

Mercy primped her hair. "Maybe it's more than that."

I was amused. I'd never seen Mercy act coquettish. She evidently wasn't serious about Al Kvalheim, despite the liplock they'd had on Saturday night.

Pauline shook her head. "And Al Kvalheim is tailing Kim Olkowski?"

"I figured they both like clean things. Al will be there anyway taking care of the garbage cans. He might find out more than any of us."

"If anybody can find dirt, it's Kim," Pauline said.

I said, "Nice pun."

Mercy used her trolley to drive the women to the make-shift fairgrounds in a farm field outside of Fishers' Harbor. Victor passed on joining them, saying he'd go in his own car. I thought that suspicious, but Mercy thought we should give him some slack. He had a long drive back to Chicago coming at him and he'd be able to get an earlier start leaving from the fairgrounds.

About a couple thousand people converged on the festival grounds--a very good number. The beer tent was busy. Grandma Sophie was busy with several of her friends from various charities selling Belgian pies, cookies, and bars. Chocolate perfumed the air, along with notes of malty beers.

My mom and dad ran about helping with registration for the events, including the tractor pull.

Nothing much seemed suspicious on the surface. The women enjoyed beers and wandered about in a group. The first events were for kids--sack races, egg races where they raced with fresh eggs balanced on spoons, and corn bag toss games.

Mercy was chatting up Victor. If he were going to make a quick getaway, well, good luck. Mercy liked to best me in everything, and holding onto a killer or an accomplice, at least, would please her to no end. Gut instinct told me Victor played a role in his wife's murder, though I couldn't articulate exactly how yet.

Zadie and Yola parted the group to go to the beer tent.

I kept a watchful eye on both of them.

Pauline brought me a piece of pie. "I told you this was stupid. You should worry about your fudge announcement. Did you make enough fudge for this crowd? And I don't see any TV cameras. Or Jeremy Stone. Now that's suspicious."

"Don't worry. We have plenty of time." I felt in control. The new fudge flavor was going to be announced as a prize for the tractor pull winner. Then I'd host the open house at the Blue

Heron Inn during the later afternoon. I also felt that our murderer--or two--would be found out. I'd eliminated Cathy and Pepper as suspects. That left Kim and Eliza, along with the suspicious roles presented by Zadie and Yola, along with Victor.

John was supposed to show up for the tractor pull announcements with his camera crew. From there we'd segue to the decorated house and the kindergartners for taping his show. My new fudge flavor would be used by the little girls in their tea party.

As I wandered the grounds, I began to relax. Several of my high school classmates were there. It was fun to hear about college, marriages, kids or not, and travels. Their stories felt innocent compared to what I'd been living through in the past week with the fudge divas--alleged friends.

It was minutes before the tractor pull when I realized I'd lost track of Pauline. I found her in the beer tent with Sam.

"You're supposed to be watching your fudge diva," I said. "Where's Eliza?"

Pauline raised her beer in a toast. "Relax. Most of your guests are getting something to eat at the food tents. Eliza and Zadie took off to get the tractors at the implement dealer."

"Eliza should've had those hauled here before this."

Pauline shrugged. "Eliza said the flatbed truck had arrived late at her dealership. He'd had a tire problem."

"Where's Yola?" A dark worry stabbed through me. I saw her over at the dessert tent talking with Ruby and hustled over. "Yola, can I interrupt? I have a question."

"Sure." She was sunshiny and bright, dressed in a blue-flowered peasant dress, innocent-looking for sure. She held a napkin with a brownie on top of it.

"Did Zadie go with Eliza to get the tractors?"

"Yeah. Not my kind of thing. Driving a garden tractor around my shop's sales yard is the most I can handle. The farming tractors are monsters these days."

"Why did Zadie go along? She's a city girl." A possible murderer. Was Eliza in trouble?

Yola stared into her brownie. "Eliza said maybe she could go in with Zadie on the Chicago shops we want to set up. But Eliza said she'd have to have Zadie sign papers right away, maybe turn over the ownership of a tractor to her. Do you know how much those things are worth? Eliza's dealership has one that costs over a hundred thousand, she said."

The darkness within me turned to panic. "Yola, nobody signs over a tractor like that. This is all wrong."

I raced back to Pauline. "Come with me now."

I was already calling Jordy on my phone. He didn't answer. I left a message. I called 911.

I called my father. He was stuck in tourist traffic, probably just like Jordy. Sometimes two-lane Highway 42 could be bumper-to-bumper with our big events.

Pauline trotted at my side as we wove helter-skelter against the tide of people coming through the main entrance from the parking area roped off in the hay field. "What's the matter?"

"Zadie's in trouble. Or Eliza is. I don't know which."

"How?"

"I think one of them is about to do in the other."

I called both their numbers. I always had the phone numbers of guests handy. There was no answer from either.

Now we were running down the grassy aisle between vehicles to get to my truck. "Zadie and Eliza were using each other and one of them or both of them murdered Jackie. My bet is on Eliza killing Jackie. Eliza is bigger and can pass as a man. She knew Zadie was trying to have the affair with Victor, and had been following her. When Jackie took off on Saturday night, Eliza saw her chance."

"Chance for what?"

We were out of breath as we hopped into my yellow pickup. As I was backing out of my parking spot, I said, "Chance to get revenge, chance to suck up to Victor after Jackie's death. Chance to get him to save her implement dealership or just save her from being poor. I still don't know why she had to drag Jackie next to Grandpa's boat, but I'm going to ask her."

My phone buzzed in my pocket. I got it out and tossed it to Pauline.

She said, "Jordy texted back. A traffic accident down in Sturgeon Bay and his deputy Maria is up in Sister Bay. He says, 'Stop causing trouble.'"

I muttered, "Crap. Text him that it's urgent, that a murder is about to occur. Tell him I've caught Jackie's murderer. Then call Dillon. Please." My whole body was engaged with pushing my yellow pickup around cars, taking to the gravel shoulders and a ditch or two to get out of the crowd coming in for events.

I careened down Highway 42. The south lane became clearer.

I took a sharp left turn after several miles to follow a lonely country road that led inland in the county and into farm country.

It took us a good half hour to see the implement dealership up ahead.

After I skidded to a stop in the gravel parking lot amid hay rakes and plows, I leaped out.

Pauline shadowed me in her pink finery. "There's nobody here. Maybe they left already? Took another route to the tractor pull and festival."

"Let's be sure they're not around."

My nerves fizzed. The back of my head throbbed. I headed for the office and shop, but before we got there I heard a low rumble behind the implement dealership.

About fifteen acres was freshly plowed in the demonstration field. In the far distance, a huge tractor with an equally giant disk behind it crawled along. A disk was a piece of equipment about twenty feet across with rows of metal disks that sliced through dirt clods to break them up in preparation for planting.

Pauline said, "Just a farmer."

A chill strangled me. "That's Eliza."

"Eliza? You sure?"

"It's her. Her car is over here behind the building where nobody can see it from the road."

"Maybe she's just trying her equipment out before she brings it to the fairgrounds."

"Where's Zadie?"

We shouted her name and got no response.

I squinted again at the tractor lumbering along. It was maybe a quarter mile from us. The tractor and disk were approaching a fence line and slowing down. The sudden flash of colors on the ground behind the giant machinery flagged my attention. "No! Oh no!"

"What?" Pauline asked.

"Zadie's being dragged behind the disk. Eliza's trying to kill her."

Pauline screamed.

I rushed back to my truck. "Come on. When Eliza makes the turn, all she has to do is back up and that disk will make mincemeat of Zadie. She'll be buried in pieces in the field."

Chapter 27

I put my pickup truck in four-wheel drive. I hit the gas.

Through the windshield Pauline and I watched with terror as Eliza's huge set of machinery dragged Zadie through the thick loam as if she were a hated doll.

My pickup bucked hard when it met the plowed field. The engine growled louder. Wheels spun, tossing dirt, sinking some. I put the engine in "snow mode". The engine geared down, the wheels gnawing at the loam.

Pauline and I jerked in our seatbelts, thrashing about while clods of dirt flew over the hood and past our windows. A sickness erupted within me. Zadie could be dead already, but I hoped we could somehow make Eliza stop and save Zadie.

Pauline yelled, "We're going to get stuck!"

"Like hell we will."

We lurched at a crawl toward the tractor and disk.

Eliza was steering the tractor and disk back around, whipping poor Zadie through the dirt as if she were a ragdoll. It dawned on me the young woman might be dead already.

I hung on tight to the steering wheel and kept pushing the accelerator.

Pauline yelped before I did when the giant tractor turned, facing us. It charged, grinding over the uneven plowed earth.

When I tried to swerve, the pickup truck bucked and leaned, tipping. We rose again over a row of dirt. Then the pickup stopped. The sudden jolt snapped our heads back against the headrests. The goose egg on my head felt cracked, so painful it blinded me.

I pushed at the gas pedal anyway.

The truck engine roared. Wheels spun--in place.

The giant tractor was bearing down right for us.

Pauline screamed again. "Get out!"

Eliza's giant machinery kept coming.

Pauline leaped out. I was still seeing stars and fumbling with my seat belt.

The tractor coming straight at me was a story tall and looming taller by the second.

I leaped out. My feet sank into the loam at first, as if I'd plummeted into a vat of mud. I couldn't move.

With my hands grabbing at the soft piles of dirt around me, I climbed over one row of loam, then another. In slow motion.

Eliza rammed right through the pickup truck. Yellow metal groaned, popped, buckled.

I dug with my hands and crawled through the dirt.

Then an explosion behind me hurt my ears. My truck's gas tank must have split open. I turned to see crumpled yellow metal fly into the air.

Fire shot up in front of the giant tractor. My truck was entangled with the tractor.

The flames jetted alongside the tractor's engine compartment.

Pauline and I stood ankle-deep in dirt, frozen at first, in shock. Just as we started toward Zadie still tethered behind the huge disk, a fire exploded inside the enclosed tractor cab, swallowing Eliza.

"Get to Zadie!" I yelled. "I'll take Eliza."

Eliza leaped from the cab on her own, clothes and hair on fire. "Help me! Help me!"

She stumbled and sank into the furrows.

I fell twice trying to reach her, the foot-tall rows of loam tripping me. Once I got to her, I rolled her in the dirt and scooped dirt on her head.

Eliza thrashed about. "Get away from me, Ava! Get away! Run! This is none of your damn business!"

I slugged her in the jaw.

She dropped back onto the cushion of loam.

My hand was killing me. It felt broken.

Despite the pain in my head and hand, I scrabbled up out of the loam to help Pauline. She had untied Zadie and moved her several yards from the disk and the tractor fire.

To my relief, Zadie was alive. She'd been tied to the disk by her hands. Her wrists were red and bloody. Her legs had also been tied and she'd been gagged. Her clothes were bloody rags. Freed to talk, she said Eliza had hit her over the head with a wrench.

I said, "A wrench, a hammer, a knife, a pink pistol--or a giant tractor and disk. That woman uses whatever is handy."

Every inch of Zadie appeared to be bleeding. As soon as we got her to her feet, she collapsed in our arms.

Tears overwhelmed her. "Thank God you found me. I'm so sorry this happened, Ava. I'm sorry. I am. I really am."

A siren bleated in the distance, a heavenly sound.

I wiped her muddy, wet cheeks with the sleeve of my once-white blouse. "It's all over, Zadie."

"No, it's not. This is all my fault. I was so stupid."

"Because you made Eliza jealous of you by trying to curry favors from Victor when she couldn't? Pauline and I figured that out."

"No. I knew too much. I knew all along she did it. But she threatened me with killing Yola if I interfered. She said she'd go over to Green Bay and Yola would have an accident at her garden shop." Zadie bawled against my chest.

I rubbed her back while exchanging a knowing look with Pauline.

I said to Zadie in a calm voice, "You love Yola, don't you?"

She nodded against my chest. "I just wanted to get the money so that Yola and I could live in Chicago together. If only I hadn't tried to get the money from Jackie and Victor, but I thought it would be easy. Jackie was a friend of my mother's. I didn't want to get money from my mom. I wanted to do all of this on my own, show her I wasn't just a stupid blond model who could only run a business if mommy did it for her. That's what they say about me, you know."

My definition of a friend was far different than Zadie's. Friends didn't "use" friends for selfish gain. Zadie had tried to use her own mother and Pepper's friends.

Pauline and I switched our attention to the noises coming from across the field near the implement dealership. My truck was still burning. So was the big expensive tractor worth more than many homes in Door County.

The sheriff's squad had stopped in the field where it sank up to its bumpers. Jordy was doing his best to lumber over the furrows in his fancy cowboy boots he liked to wear as part of his uniform on festival days. He had his gun drawn.

As he punched closer, I said, "Hi, Jordy."

He took a look at us and the destruction in the field. "You are one scary woman."

"No 'thank you, Ava, for solving the case'?"

"None." He pushed through the mounds of loose dirt to get to Eliza, who was coming to.

I cradled my sore hand.

My dad wasn't far behind Jordy. He swept his long arms around Pauline and me. His hug was tight, as if he'd never let us go again. I felt him sobbing, so uncharacteristic of him that it made me cry in response. I heard his whispers. "Thank God, thank God, you're both all right."

By the time we got to the gravel parking lot and on level ground, Mercy's trolley pulled in and my grandpa leaped out, growling, "What the hell happened, A.M. and P.M.?"

"We solved a murder, Gilpa, and saved Zadie's life."

"Is that all?"

He took over hugging us. I'm pretty sure I heard him swallow a sob in relief.

Pauline and I went to Sturgeon Bay to the Justice Center to give statements. Since Jordy had sunk his squad car into the muddy field and couldn't get out, all of us were driven the several miles down Highway 42 in Mercy Fogg's trolley. She was grinning the entire time. She loved rescuing me.

Pauline and I washed up at the Justice Center. We didn't have a change of clothes of course, so we sat in Jordy's office in our mud-stained, torn attire. I felt sorry for Pauline's once-pretty pink outfit meant to impress John. We smelled of smoke and tractor oil and maybe organic stuff from the cows that farmers put on their fields.

Jordy handed us forms and pens. We sat in chairs opposite him. "Write everything down you can think of, start to finish from this morning on."

I asked, "Even the worry about my new fudge flavor?"

Jordy's eyelids narrowed.

"Okay," I said. "You're invited to the inn later, you know."

Pauline poked me with an elbow. "Will you please just write and hurry up? We have to get to the taping at the house in only forty minutes. And we have to change clothes and shower yet."

"Okay, okay."

We scribbled away, then handed the forms to Jordy.

He perused them. "Looks good." He laid the forms aside. "That'll be all."

Pauline launched from her seat, but I pulled her back down.

To Jordy, I said, "Don't you want to hear about the motive and how it all unfolded this past week?"

"I don't need to know that from you. I'll talk to all the women again. Maria is getting Zadie's version now. Eliza lawyered up pretty fast."

Pauline got up again, her face scrunched at me. "I'll wait outside."

She left. I pointed a thumb in her direction, saying to Jordy, "She has a big television taping her boyfriend is doing. Actually, she says he's not her boyfriend now. She's over him. Just like that."

Jordy sighed, his eyes narrowing again. "I care about this why?"

"You care about her, Jordy, because she's my friend. Don't you have any friends?"

He blinked. Several times.

I was shocked by his discomfort. "You don't have friends?"

"I have friends."

"But not like best buddies? Who are your best buddies?"

"This is not why you're here." He grabbed a file, fumbled with it, then put it aside and picked up a pen and pad of paper. "What else do you want to tell me about what happened?"

I explained to Jordy this all started thirty-five years ago with a fire.

The tale drew him in. He took notes.

I said, "They had never resolved that and blamed each other for the fire. And Pepper had the affair, but they all kept it hush-hush. Cathy Rivers wasn't there, so she never knew about it and the group liked it that way."

"They protected Cathy?"

"Yeah. She's low-key, smart. I think they respected that about her and left her out of what had happened. Friends do that sort of thing for each other."

"Friendship at work."

"Sort of. I think they were afraid if she knew about what they did, she would have reported them. Cathy does everything the right way. She would have confessed it to somebody. Of course, that would have broken up the friendship, too. They knew that, I suspect."

"What about Victor's role? You spent a lot of time with him."

"I don't know what to make of Victor, Jordy. He evidently had no idea his wife was filing for divorce. Allegedly he was draining their accounts. But I suspect Jackie was on to him giving money to every pretty young woman who came along asking for investment funds."

"Any indication he hired Eliza to kill his wife?"

I sat back again. I'd never thought about that. "I don't know. I don't think so."

Jordy made another note.

I said, "But I'm afraid Zadie knew all along who killed Jackie. I saw her help pack Jackie's things because Zadie wanted them all to go home as soon as possible so we wouldn't dig deeper and blame them. Zadie would've been happy if a stranger had been blamed."

"A stranger come to town and then be gone, never to be found."

"To her naïve mind, that seemed to be the solution to it all."

Jordy got up to grab an old coffee cup from his credenza behind the desk. He appeared troubled by it being empty but didn't seem to know what to do.

I said, "I suppose I should go. Pauline--"

"Ava, why do you think the body was taken all the way from Victor's condo to the harbor in front of your shop?"

A chill sullied my body. My clothes felt heavy with mud and Zadie's dried tears. "It probably has something to do with boats, but I don't know why. The placement of the body was a definite statement."

Jordy came back to his desk, still standing, putting the cup down. "We'll certainly be trying to find that out from Eliza, but I doubt she'll be talking now."

He kept staring at me in a meaningful way.

A warmth spread inside of me that I recognized from months before when another murder had happened. "You can't ask me out loud or officially, right? But you want my help?"

Jordy tilted his head. A version of a nod.

I stood. "I'm intrigued by the boat. I'll see what I can find out."

I was about to leave when I remembered something else. "This is just a hunch, but about all those weapons, like the bloody hammer I found in Jackie's room, and the pistol under her mattress, I believe Cathy when she said she saw Kim cross over to Pepper's room. I think Eliza threatened Kim, and Kim was supposed to hit Pepper over the head, but Pepper did it to herself to distract us and to cover for Zadie."

Taking a breath, feeling connections finally, I continued. "Pepper probably knew all along Zadie was in some kind of trouble. What mother wouldn't have noticed her daughter coming in every morning early after a night out? Pepper had to have put two and two together. Pepper bought her a pretty dress to try and make her stop seeing Victor, and Jackie bought Zadie even more clothes for the same reason. Kim was cleaning everything like crazy because she was going crazy with what was going on in my inn."

"They all sensed things were wrong but didn't quite know what to do?"

I nodded. "Sometimes that happens with friends."

"Like this thing with Pauline?" Jordy's voice had gone low and tender.

I was surprised by his emotion. "Yeah. John's going to ask her on national television to marry him, but she's decided she's going to say 'no'."

"No changing her mind?"

"I'm not like the deadly fudge divas. Buying Pauline a dress or a gift won't distract her or solve it. I'm going to stay out of it. I tend to mess things up when I interfere."

"Indeed." Jordy smiled.

I conceded with a smile, too. I started for the door.

"Ava?"

I turned back to Jordy standing behind his desk yet. "Yeah, Sheriff?"

He ran a hand over his neatly clipped hair. "Nothing, I guess. Thanks maybe. Maybe..."

"Maybe?"

"Yeah. Nothing definite. Just maybe." His eyes didn't blink.

"We're talking about the case, right?"

"Of course. What else would I be talking about with you?"

"Well, we were talking about the women and their friendship. Weren't we talking about you not having friends?"

"Maybe. Do I have you?"

An emotion bloomed inside me that had me relaxing for the first time in over a week. I was oddly at peace, comfortable with Jordy in some new way that felt soft as spring fog. "Yeah. As a friend."

"As a friend. That's what I meant to say. We're friends. Maybe."

He sat down. Sweat had brought a sheen to his forehead.

I left.

Maybe...?

Chapter 28

B y the time I finished up talking with Jordy, I realized I was somewhat alone except for the trolley with Mercy Fogg standing next to its door.

"Mercy, where's Pauline? And my grandpa?"

"Pauline called Fontana. They loaded up in her convertible to head back to the festival. Your grandpa said he had to see Sophie and tell her about this in person." She chewed at a fingernail. "That sheriff is cute, isn't he?"

"None of your business, Mercy." I boarded the trolley. "We need to hurry."

I took out my phone and hit Pauline's number. I texted: Do not let John ask you on-air.

I called Fontana as Mercy drove the trolley away from the Justice Center.

Fontana answered amid screaming girls. "Where's Pauline? Everybody's here. You should see these lights. John says my hair looks like it's on fire. Maybe you should have dyed your hair red, Ava. We'd match."

"I'm not going to be on camera. Listen, Fontana, when Pauline gets there, distract John somehow. Delay the taping."

"How?"

"You're pregnant. Pretend you're fainting. Pour water on the floor and say it's yours."

"Why am I doing this again?"

I wasn't sure. "Pauline and John need time together in private before the taping begins."

As I talked with her, a message popped up from Dillon. "Ring found."

Oh no. John had to be over the moon. Pauline would not be.

"Fontana, I have to go." I clicked off. "Mercy, go faster."

"I can't. Not with this line of cars ahead of me going into Fishers' Harbor for the festival."

"Take the back roads."

"Maybe you should include me in on the big secret, sis."

"You're not my sis. You realize you're older than my mother."

"Humpf. You're only as old as you feel."

"Then I'm about eighty at the moment. Please hurry."

We had to park the trolley out on the road in front of the fancy house. Cars were parked up and down both sides of the lane next to the white board fence.

As I ran up the driveway, Lucky Harbor came loping at me from the house. He halted, obviously shocked by my appearance. I'd forgotten I was in muddy rags. It didn't matter. I had to find John or Pauline, whomever I saw first.

Inside the house, camera and lighting people where trotting everywhere. Little girls in pink fairy outfits flitted and bounced with wands. Chatter and shrieks of laughter scored the air, echoing off the high ceilings. My eardrums pulsated.

I looked every which way for Pauline and didn't see her.

I ran to the restrooms. Maybe she was cleaning up. She was nowhere.

Dillon loped from the entertainment room on the other side of the kitchen. He picked me up in a hug, ignoring my mud, swinging me about. "Isn't it great? We found the ring."

"How? Where?"

"Actually, Lucky Harbor found it. It must have been carried half a mile from where you and Pauline were tied up in that ravine last fall. The purse was wedged between a couple of big rocks. Probably a raccoon dragged it that far and--"

"Dillon, stop. Where's Pauline? And John?"

Dillon put me down. A camera guy rushed past us in the kitchen, chasing a kindergarten girl carrying a yellow cat wearing a tiny tiara.

I shook my head against the chaos of cats, pink streamers, cherry cake smells, and the aroma of my Cinderella Pink Fairy Tale Fudge sitting on the counter next to us, its top glistening with pink sprinkles. Cody had obviously made it, which made me wistful to get back to what I loved to do most.

Dillon whispered. "John's putting on a tux. He's back in one of the bedrooms on the other side of the house. What's Pauline wearing?"

"A ripped blouse and slacks and mud. Heck, she must be home showering." I fought to catch my breath. "Dillon, we have to stop John. This will embarrass both of them. She's going to say 'no' to his proposal."

"You don't know that."

"I know my friend. We have our secrets, too."

Dillon shook his head. "Look at this place. It's beautiful. Pauline will love this. Pauline never gets dreamy stuff in her life like this. Look what John has done just for her. Maybe they're having ups and downs like we've had, but they love each other, just like you and I love each other."

Something in my bone marrow shifted.

What did I know at all? Why was I so presumptuous to think I knew what was best for John and Pauline when I may not even know my own heart? How does one tell if it's love versus just a good friendship?

Dillon was right. Pauline never received dreamy stuff. Was I lacking my usual restraint in trying to prevent her engagement? Was I jealous? Sad? What?

I had to let her experience this and take care of herself. Maybe she really needed and wanted to say "yes" to John. Maybe I had been interfering with her thinking, her heart--her life.

Mercy Fogg breathed in my ear. "Hey, Oosterling, I get paid for rides, you know."

I found cash in one pocket and gave it to her. I was almost glad for the interruption. "Have you seen Pauline?"

"Nope, but saw the host of the show outside. He was cursing and looking all over in the lawn for something."

I looked to Dillon.

Dillon nodded. "I'm on it. He lost the ring."

After Dillon left, Mercy dug around in the breast pocket of her bus driver's uniform and came up with a shiny trinket.

My eyes popped wide. "You have the ring?"

I tried to snatch it from her, but she put it back into her pocket.

I said, "That's the ring John and Dillon found in the woods."

"Yada yada, lady. Pauline bought this ring last year in her deluded state of mind. There is no damn way I'm letting that man use this ring to get on his knees to your BFF Pauline. Don't you think that girlfriend deserves to have him bust out his own checkbook and lay out some proper cash if he wants to marry her?"

I dragged her over to a corner, away from the fray of little girls and camera people racing through the kitchen. "But he did go to the effort of finding it."

"No, he didn't. If it weren't for Dillon and his dog, this ring would not have been found in the woods. The dog found the purse." She patted her pocket. "Now you get along. What is it about you, Ava? Do I have to spell it out to you? I'm being a friend. If there's no ring, there's no proposal on camera with Pauline turning John down or John whining about how she has to say yes. If there's no ring, there's no embarrassment for both of them."

My mouth went dry. She was so dead-on right that I hugged her. Then I backed off real fast. "We haven't talked about this, okay?" I backed off another step. "I know nothing."

Mercy laughed. "You got it."

Later that Saturday afternoon, I hosted the open house at the inn with the debut of Goldilocks and the Three Bears Fairy Tale Fudge. It was a triple-layer fudge, a layer for each bear. Black bear dark chocolate on the bottom, a scrumptious cinnamon bear-like milk chocolate for the next layer, topped with white chocolate to honor polar bears and golden glitter for Goldilocks. Chocolate edible black bears made with imported Belgian chocolate lay snoozing atop each piece of fudge.

The inn was crowded with tourists galore as well as locals. The back yard was hopping, too. A band was playing country swing music in the gazebo, the music wafting through the open door in the parlor.

My guests had left of course, which gave me relief.

A white-haired couple perhaps in their early eighties squeezed through the crowd, waving their hands at me. The gentlemen came up to me with eyes sparkling. "Miss Oosterling, I want to thank you."

"For what?" I asked.

"We won the cow bingo prize, with a free weekend at the Blue Heron Inn. We're going to use it for our honeymoon."

"Congratulations! You just got married?"

"Last summer, but we haven't yet taken our honeymoon. I'm Ned. This is Darla. We lost our spouses some years ago. Darla and I went to high school together in Illinois. I met Darla again at our high school reunion last summer."

Darla said, "It was love again at first sight." Her face beamed. "And we visit Door County all the time. It's our favorite place. We're looking forward to coming back for our honeymoon now. And taking your fudge home to share with all our relatives and friends. Thank you for the wonderful prize."

They went on their way, hand in hand.

Tears came to my eyes because of their happiness. I felt honored to have played a small role in their lives. They were what an inn and my fudge were supposed to be about. Being sweet to each other. Spreading love.

Pride welled up inside of me for the first time in days.

Then I spotted Jeremy Stone, but he wasn't the only reporter lurking about.

The next several minutes ended up with me on the verandah fielding questions. I stuck to the topic of fudge and the history of the inn. Yes, it was built by Scandinavians and Belgian workers who had immigrated in the late 1800s. They bought land at a buck-twenty-five per acre. The Wisconsin territory government encouraged the immigration to settle land that had once belonged to Indiana and Michigan. Finally, the Door peninsula became a county within Wisconsin.

It wasn't long before it was discovered the soil was perfect for growing cherry and apple trees. Tourists followed from Chicago, enjoying the cool, fresh air and quiet backroads and beaches. A rich doctor needed a place to stay, and liked the area so well that he built the Blue Heron Inn. Its first guests were the local lumberjacks clearing the land. The hustle and bustle of those times created the commerce and the village of Fishers' Harbor.

Back inside, I spotted Pauline moving through the crowd, wearing a peacock-blue dress that gave her the aura of a princess. I worried about her.

She seemed stoic, though, about no marriage proposal coming from John during or after the television show's taping. John hadn't shown up at the inn, so I hoped everything had turned out the way he and Pauline had wanted for now. The taping had gone so well that it was the talk of the crowd. I could hear Pauline chatting about her "Butterflies", or students, and acknowledging "congratulations" from the crowd. Ned and Darla hugged her.

After six in the evening the open house was still going strong with people coming and going to see the infamous, felonious inn.

Jeremy Stone found me out in the gazebo where I had been giving a tour after the band took a break. He whispered, "She's here."

Tears came to my eyes. He and I had a secret. "You found--?"

"In the kitchen. I went through the back door like you suggested."

"Thanks, Jeremy. You've redeemed yourself with me."

"Hey, I'm here to get a great story, so don't make me out to be a saint."

I nodded, but appreciated him anyway.

I looked about for Pauline. Not seeing her outdoors on this warm, spring evening, I wended my way through the crowd and back inside the inn.

Pauline was in the crowded parlor.

"Pauline, I need to talk to you in the kitchen."

"Now?" She was definitely enjoying her television fame.

"Yes. It's important."

She looked down her nose at me for a second. "This better be good."

"Trust me. Come with me." My insides were tumbling. I wasn't sure this would be good at all. In fact, it could be awful. It could even make her mad.

I opened the door to the kitchen, then waved Pauline to go in ahead of me.

She stopped only a foot inside the room. "Mom?"

At the other end of the kitchen, leaning back against the wall and looking like she wanted to escape out the back door, was Pauline's mother.

Both women froze.

They hadn't seen each other for years.

I whispered to Pauline, "It's really her."

The women stared at each other. Her mother's hair had gone gray, but it was long like Pauline's, just as I remembered it. She was shorter than Pauline, skinny beyond what was healthy. I could see history and pain hanging on her like worn-out clothes that needed to be swapped for something nicer.

Pauline's mom cleared her throat. "I've missed you, Paulie."

That was all it took.

Pauline ran amid sobs to hug her mother...

...The mother who had been unkind at times.

...The woman Pauline had never wanted to see again.

...The woman who Pauline missed more than anything and needed.

My best friend needed to pour her heart out to her mother about John. I knew long ago that Pauline would never want to plan a wedding without her mother being here by her side. We best friends just know stuff like that. Secrets of the heart were what good friends shared.

I left, closing the door to the kitchen behind me.

Two weeks later, Fontana and I were in a birthing room at the hospital and she was gobbling my new Goldilocks fudge as well as the Cinderella and Rapunzel flavors.

"Sweet girlfriends," she repeated like a pain-killing mantra.

A nurse and doctor were doing their best to help the delivery along.

Fontana screamed in between gobbling fudge. "More fudge! More sugar! Now!"

It was just me and the doctor and a nurse in the room. Pauline and others were in the waiting room.

"What flavor do you want next?" I asked.

"Pink. Cherry. For Cherry." It was the nickname of the deceased man who had fathered this baby. "Dammit all, I thought sugar would dull the pain!"

"Here, try more of the Goldilocks."

She was munching away when the baby came bawling out.

"It's a girl, Fontana!"

"That quick?" Fontana looked between her legs at the baby. "This fudge really *does* work, Ava."

After the baby was given to Fontana to touch and cuddle, I asked, "What're you going to name her?"

"I haven't the foggiest idea."

"Fudge always makes me think more clearly. Want another piece?"

"Sure. Let's go through the alphabet."

We did. Along with Pauline, Mom, Grandma, Jonas Coppens who came to take her home with him, Fontana's relatives, and everybody else who showed up at the hospital. Everybody agreed that the name she'd chosen was perfect and "so Fontana."

A couple of days later, on a quiet Tuesday evening later in April, I joined Grandpa on the dock.

Jordy had been in touch with me several times, ironing out details of the case with Eliza Stefansson. He'd found the pink pistol in the burned tractor. Jordy said she confessed she'd stolen it from the hutch where Pauline and I had put it after finding it under the mattress in Jackie's room. Eliza had planted it there, hoping to cause trouble. Because I couldn't prove anything by finding it, I had returned it to the top of the hutch, intending to tell Pepper where it was, but when it was gone I assumed she'd retrieved it. My mistake was not following up with Pepper about her pistol. Eliza stole it later and intended to use it. I sweated now just thinking about what my decision could have wrought. I vowed to be more vigilant and wiser in the future, perhaps more caring. Being an innkeeper and having guests was indeed proving hard for me.

Eliza confessed to everything, Jordy told me. He'd driven out for a chat yesterday just before lunchtime, pulling his squad into the parking lot outside the Blue Heron Inn. As he removed his official hat, I said what I already had guessed, "Eliza drowned Jackie in the tub at her husband's condo. True?"

"Yes. She confessed. Eliza said it was easy enough. She knew about Pepper's daughter sneaking over to Victor's condo the minute he'd come to town. Eliza could never sleep, she said. Eliza told Jackie about Victor and Zadie. Jackie kept it a secret, but it cost her to keep from her friends what was happening right under everybody's noses. Eliza asked Jackie to meet at Victor's condo Saturday night after dinner, but Jackie refused and suggested they meet at the harbor. By that time, Jackie had too much to drink, and ended up very confused when she encountered your grandfather on the boat retrieving his keys."

"She was violent toward Grandpa. Now I realize that's because she was so upset at the world, and especially Eliza." I gave Jordy a questioning look. "But how did Eliza get Jackie's body back to the harbor without being noticed?"

The sheriff smirked, to my surprise. "Eliza's a strong woman, used to working on farms and around machinery. It was easy, she said. Victor had stepped outside for fresh air and a walk, he said, evidently with Zadie, so Jackie went into the condo--angry, I can assume, and inebriated, and was confronted by Eliza who'd followed Jackie to the boat and then back to the condo. Eliza dispatched Jackie in the tub quickly. The water had been drawn earlier by Zadie and left there when they went for a walk."

It seemed so simple. So foolproof. I was in awe, though in an awful way. "The two women were left alone and Eliza shoved Jackie under the lavender bath water."

Jordy nodded. "Eliza took one of Victor's big suitcases with wheels on it, stuffed Jackie in there, and then took off. In this town, with all the tourists, nobody would have thought a thing of a woman heading down a street with her bag, even at ten at night or midnight."

"Well, most people are asleep, so they wouldn't even hear such things. I recall Mercy had been sneaking around the bar that night, acting strange, as if she'd seen something. That's what Erik said."

"I've questioned her. She heard a strange noise. She probably heard the loud wheels going across the concrete a block away maybe, but before she could investigate, she saw Al dumping garbage and got distracted."

"Yeah, for a stolen smoke and kiss behind the garbage cans." I sighed. "So Eliza dumped Jackie in the lake. Did you find the suitcase?"

Jordy nodded. "Yeah. At the farm implement dealership. She said she took the empty suitcase of Victor's up to her room in the inn Saturday night, after everybody else went to bed. I called Victor, and he said he never got his suitcase back. He had assumed Zadie had taken it. He bought a new suitcase to pack for home."

I shook my head, thinking back. "There was commotion that night with all the women coming in after their big dinner and drinks. She could have left that bag outside in the dark easily enough, then retrieved it after I want to bed. I was so used to the front door squeaking that I must not have paid attention. Then she packed with it. It was almost the perfect crime." My insides felt empty. "This is all so sad."

"Yes. Very sad. Unfortunately, it's part of my job, too." Jordy turned to go.

"Jordy?"

He spun back to me, eyes mirthful, the corner of his mouth twitching. "Yeah?"

"Did she say what her motive was? Was it jealousy?"

He nodded. "You'd make a good cop."

I shivered in the spring day.

He said, "She was jealous of everybody and everything others had, even your grandfather's boat. She said Jackie and Victor had a boat, too. In jail, she won't shut up about how she hates boats because they're a symbol of all that is wrong in life, the haves and have nots."

"So putting the body there in the water wasn't a statement for Grandpa or me to take to heart. That was about her jealousy with everybody. It was about her grief, really, in missing her husband and losing all that they had built with the implement dealership. I remember one of the women said Eliza had cried out her husband's name at the dock one day."

Jordy sighed, settling his official hat back in place. "Her heart had turned cold. We humans are a frail bunch sometimes. Stay strong, Ava."

With that, he had climbed back into his squad car, leaving the hilltop overlooking the bay and the harbor below.

It was now two days later. The knot on the back of my head had finally disappeared and the hand I'd injured socking Eliza in the face was feeling up to pushing wood ladles in the copper kettles again.

I sat on the boards still warm from the day's sunshine, letting my legs dangle toward the water. Cool air feathered around Grandpa and me with the sun lowering to the west behind us.

Grandpa's boat--bathed in a pink hue from the sun--rocked in the harbor in front of us. Grandpa was on the boat putting tools away in a wooden toolbox. The plunk-plunk of his actions soothed me.

Lucky Harbor sat next to me, munching on fish-shaped crackers. In looking back on that time when Dillon and I followed the dog sniffing about the yard, I realized now that the dog had been following the trail of the suitcase Eliza had rolled about the yard of the inn on Saturday night. The suitcase had likely dripped lavender water that Jackie had been drowned in. Or maybe dogs can detect the smell of death.

Grandpa climbed off his boat, then stretched, releasing the day's kinks. "Whaddya think, A.M.?"

I tossed a cracker a few feet away and Lucky Harbor went after it.

Grandpa sat beside me with a grunt as he lowered himself to the boards. We stared at his boat.

"It's a beauty, Gilpa."

"But it's not mine."

The old frustration still weighed him down.

I said, "Now don't get down on Dillon for going in halvsies on this. You wouldn't have a boat if he hadn't pitched in to buy it."

He growled but didn't say anything.

I thought it best to change the subject. "You never did tell me why you dreamed of that dress."

"I saw the dress in the window of the shop a couple of days before those women bought it. Your grandma wore a dress with one of those tulip skirts when I met her."

"So the woman you saw in your dreams was Grandma? In the dress? Not Jackie?"

He turned red. Behind us the glow of the sun made his silver hair take on a pink tinge. "It was your grandma in the dress, but I also saw Zadie in the dream. And Jackie yelling at Zadie. I felt their invasion in my dream, how distressing it was interrupting me and your grandma."

"Grandma said you swore at them in the dream."

"I knew then that Zadie was no good."

"She didn't actually murder Jackie Valentine."

"Might as well have."

I patted his shoulder next to me. "It's over with now. Let's think happy thoughts."

He chuckled. "Happy. Your friend Fontana sure picked funny names for her baby, but I like them. Happy Cinderella Dahlgren."

"Yeah." I chuckled, too. "A kid called Happy Cinderella is destined to a happy life with some sparkle in it."

My phone rang in my pocket. I'd forgotten to shut it off. "Sorry."

"Who is it?"

"Mercy. A text. She's thanking me."

"Don't make friends with that woman. I've still got bets on her wanting to shut us down and build condos here. If she were ever village president again, we'd be in a helluva lot of trouble."

"She's not texting me about that. Cody told me about a new program for community paramedics in Door County. They're looking for veterans who can talk to other veterans, help them with PTSD and just about anything. I recommended it to Brecht Rousseau. He ended up being asked to visit older veterans, including Mercy's father. Mercy had told me months ago that her dad was lonely. I remembered that. That's why she's thanking me. There might be a job in this for Brecht. A job that matters to him."

"So you helped Mercy. My arch-enemy. Huh. But you helped Brecht Rousseau, a very nice guy. And you helped Pauline find her mother--though that was mighty risky considering how much Pauline always said she didn't want to see her again."

"Grandpa, she'd never want to get married without finding her mother. That's why she was going to say no to John. It was my gut instinct and I had to listen to it. Grandma taught me to listen to my gut, you know."

"I know. Sophie's a wise dame and all mine. But I thought Pauline wanted to get married come hell or high water."

"She only said that because she was scared. She didn't want to get married without first finding her mom, but Pauline was afraid to tell me. She wanted me to intuit it."

"I'll never understand women."

I chuckled. "She wasn't ready. But maybe she really does love John. And now that her mother is back, at least for a visit,

Pauline will be able to think more clearly in her heart. And I'm sure Mercy will find it in her heart to give John the ring eventually and do the honorable thing."

Grandpa patted my right knee. "You're a good person, Ava Mathilde Oosterling."

"I have you and Grandma as role models."

"Me?"

"You helped me with so much, the shop and the inn. I keep trying to make my life a good one, like yours."

He tossed an arm around me for a quick hug.

"Gilpa, I need your help with something."

"Shoot it at me, honey."

"I keep doing things backwards. Upside down even. I keep grabbing at too many things at once."

"It's okay to grab at life. It's okay to stumble through life, too. Just think how many great discoveries came about through pure accidents."

Lucky Harbor settled between us, puffing. He laid his head on my thigh. Grandpa and I each put an arm around the dog as we continued to stare at the boat and the bay beyond, where pink sunlight limned the gentle waves.

I said, "I made enough bookings during the festival to give us a cushion with the inn's mortgage. You could borrow against it to buy Dillon's half of the boat."

Grandpa stirred, glancing my way. "You'd be okay with me buying out your boyfriend? You and Dillon breaking up or something?"

I swallowed, hesitating.

Then my phone buzzed. I took it out of my pocket. It was the sheriff. I showed Grandpa the text.

Grandpa grunted. "The sheriff, huh? He wants to talk to you about something tomorrow night? At a fancy restaurant in Sister Bay? What kind of business requires a 'business' meeting at a fancy restaurant?"

My face was flaming hot. "Don't worry, Gilpa, I'm telling him no. We're just friends."

"And Dillon? How's that going?"

"It's going."

"You're friends, too?"

"Good friends."

Gilpa reached over the top of Lucky Harbor to pat my knee again. "Your grandmother is wondering about grandchildren."

"Only her?"

He guffawed.

Then he nudged Lucky Harbor to back off.

Grandpa scooted over to draw me into a two-armed hug as we sat by the water. "Ava Mathilde Oosterling, I just want you to be happy, and to be happy with your choices. That's all you need to give me, a promise that you'll be happy in life. You know that, don't ya?"

"I know, Gilpa. Thank you. I love you."

"I love you, too, Ava. I'm very, very proud of you."

Lucky Harbor's nose nudged between us, snuffling.

Grandpa and I laughed. We took turns tossing goldfish-shaped crackers into the air. We did that until the sun set and it was time to go home.

Goldilocks & the Three Bears Fairy-Tale Fudge

In the fairy tale, little lost Goldilocks wanders into the bear family's lair while they're away. She helps herself to their porridge bowls, sits in their chairs and breaks one, then tries all three of their beds to take a nap. By breaking chairs and sleeping indiscriminately in three beds, Goldilocks would be a dubious guest of Ava's at the Blue Heron Inn, but Ava might charm Goldilocks into better manners with this four-layer fudge that is easy and fun to make, particularly for children who can choose the layers--or the colors of bears. The golden layer on top is of course a symbol of Goldilocks herself.

Preparation time: 10 minutes

Cooking time: approximately 1 hour total because you have to wait for each layer of fudge to cool for about 10 minutes before adding the next layer. The cooking time for each fudge layer will be about 5 minutes using your microwave.

Before you cook: Prepare a 9x9-inch pan by either greasing it with butter on the bottom and sides, or lining it with wax paper so that the wax paper comes over the edges. Spray the paper lightly with nonstick vegetable cooking spray.

Use a small microwaveable bowl (washed between cooking each fudge layer) or four bowls for the mixing and cooking the ingredients.

Ingredients

1 cup dark chocolate chips
1 cup butterscotch chips
1 cup milk chocolate chips
1 cup white chocolate chips
2 cups sweetened condensed milk
Butter or nonstick spray for the pan
Optional: edible gold glitter for Goldilocks layer
Optional: Gummy bears or small chocolate bears for garnish

Directions

Line the pan with wax paper, spray, and set aside.

For the first layer (dark chocolate "bear"):

Combine 1 cup of dark chocolate chips, 1/2 cup of the sweetened condensed milk in microwave bowl. Cook at 70 percent power for 30 to 40 seconds, then stir vigorously. Return it to the microwave for another 40 seconds if needed, stir again. Repeat as needed until melted and smooth. Spread this "first bear" in his bed--your pan--and let stand for about 10 minutes or until firm to the touch.

Repeat that method for the butterscotch chip layer (second "bear") and the milk chocolate "bear" layer.

For the Goldilocks layer on top, combine white chocolate chips with 1/2 cup sweetened condensed milk, ½ teaspoon vanilla, and 2 or 3 drops of yellow food coloring. After cooking and pouring on top of the other three layers, add gold edible glitter.

Let the four-layer fudge set up and get firm--approximately three hours should do, or make this a day ahead for the next day's book club meeting discussing *Deadly Fudge Divas*.

Cut into one-inch squares or smaller. This is a rich fudge.

Candy chocolate bears can be poked into the top of each piece or served alongside the fudge for a bit of fun. Gummy-style candy bears create colorful, edible fun when sprinkled on a serving plate with the fudge pieces.

Tip: *Any flavor and color of fudge that matches the colors of bears can be used. Ava Oosterling encourages creativity!*

Copyright: Christine DeSmet

You can find ALL our books up at Amazon at:
https://www.amazon.com/shop/writers_exchange

or on our website at:
http://www.writers-exchange.com

All Christine's Books:
http://www.writers-exchange.com/christine-desmet/

All our mysteries:

https://www.writers-exchange.com/category/genres/mystery-thrillers-suspense/

About the Author

Christine DeSmet is an award-winning fiction writer and professional screenwriter. She is the author of the bestselling *Fudge Shop Mystery Series* and the popular novella series called *Mischief in Moonstone*.

She is a Distinguished Faculty Associate in Writing at University of Wisconsin-Madison where she teaches novel writing and screenwriting and directs the annual summer Write-by-the-Lake Writer's Workshop & Retreat. Through her master classes she has seen many of her adult students become published.

She is also a professional writing coach in the UW-Madison Writers' Institute conference's Pathway to Publication program.

Christine is a member of Mystery Writers of America, Sisters in Crime, Wisconsin Writers Association, Wisconsin Screenwriters Association, and other professional associations.

Christine is active on Facebook and you can also find her at http://www.ChristineDeSmet.com

Christine's author page at Writers Exchange E-Publishing is: http://www.writers-exchange.com/Christine-DeSmet/

If you enjoyed this author's book, then please place a review up at the site of purchase, and any social media sites you frequent!

If you want to read more about books by this author, they are listed on the following pages...

Fudge Shop Mystery Series

Deadly Fudge Divas

A taste of trouble is in the air when a group of well-heeled, fudge-loving women descend on Ava Oosterling's newly acquired and lovingly refurbished bed & breakfast inn for a chocolate lovers' getaway.

When one of the women turns up dead--and Ava's grandfather is a prime suspect--Ava plunges into the thick of a murder case stickier than her candy store's line of Fairy Tale fudge flavors and the chocolate facials the women adore at the local spa.

It's springtime and the start of the tourist season in Fishers' Harbor, Wisconsin. Ava has opened the Blue Heron Inn with the help of handsome construction worker Dillon Rivers. Unfortunately, Dillon's mother--Ava's ex-mother-in-law--is among the secretive divas who become suspects along with Grandpa.

Ava turns for help from her friends but they have troubles, too. One is eager for a wedding proposal to unfold on live television, while another friend is expecting her first baby and asks Ava to assist with the birth.

Everything and everybody Ava loves seems in chaos--her fudge shop, her inn, her family, and her own friendships... Until she uncovers a thirty-year-old secret of the "deadly fudge divas".
Publisher: http://www.writers-exchange.com/Deadly-Fudge-Divas/
Amazon: http://mybook.to/DeadlyFudgeDivas

Undercover Fudge (new cover coming soon!)

Candy shop owner Ava Oosterling has her hands full when her best friend Pauline Mertens takes a summer job as a wedding coordinator--

with the nuptials and reception scheduled in mere days in the back yard of Ava's Blue Heron Inn overlooking Lake Michigan's bay.

To help out her best friend, Ava is intent on making the table favors-- edible fudge lighthouses patterned after their county's 11 lighthouses.

Unfortunately, trying to finish the luscious ruby chocolate lighthouses becomes elusive. The sheriff informs Ava that a band of thieves storming the country may have targeted this wedding. And that's because there's proof Pauline's mother is associated with the thieves.

When the sheriff asks Ava to go undercover, she finds herself in an emotional quagmire. Pauline's mother only recently returned to Fishers' Harbor after years of estrangement from her daughter. And, Coletta Mertens now works as the housekeeper at Ava's inn. Has Ava's fudge-and-wine hospitality provided a hideout for a criminal?

Unfortunately, "until death do us part" takes a murderous twist involving Ava's Grandpa Gil, the dog Lucky Harbor, and Ava's own beau.

Publisher: http://www.writers-exchange.com/undercover-fudge/
Amazon: http://mybook.to/UndercoverFudge

Holly Jolly Fudge Folly

An early, deep snow has gifted Fishers' Harbor, Wisconsin, with a perfect setting for the holiday celebration. Unfortunately removing snow from Main Street for the parade reveals the dead tax assessor with a knife in him--containing Grandpa Gil's fingerprints.

It's clearly a setup and one that keeps Ava and Grandpa Gil under the watchful eyes of Sheriff Tollefson. Who wants Grandpa to miss playing Santa Claus in the Christmas parade and why? Who's being naughty instead of nice?

Grandpa doesn't help his case with talk of leaving town for good-- words that chill Ava worse than the weather. She can't imagine life without Grandpa's warm hugs and laughter.

When vandals strike the historic shop and someone leaves Ava and fiancé Dillon Rivers for dead in the snow, Ava wonders if she may need the magical help of Santa's elves to solve the holiday folly.

Publisher: http://www.writers-exchange.com/holly-jolly-fudge-folly/
Amazon: http://mybook.to/HollyJollyFudgeFolly

Mischief in Moonstone Series

  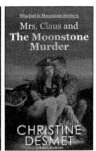 

This delightful series focuses on the humorous mystery and romantic adventures of the kind folks who live in the environs of a small village nestled on Lake Superior in northern Wisconsin. Along the way in the series, silkie chickens, a giant prehistoric beaver skeleton, a kidnapped reindeer, and other flora and fauna contribute to the amusing mischief and mayhem.

Novella 1: When Rudolf was Kidnapped

When her pet reindeer, Rudolph, is stolen from the live animal holiday display, first-grade teacher Crystal Hagan has a big problem on her hands. Her students fear that Christmas will be canceled. Ironically, the prime suspect is a man who lives in a mansion known as the "North Pole". And to her shock, Peter LeBarron admits to kidnapping Rudolph and he won't give him back without some romantic "negotiations".
Publisher: http://www.writers-exchange.com/When-Rudolph-was-Kidnapped/
Amazon: http://mybook.to/Moonstone1

Novella 2: Misbehavin' In Moonstone

When the men of Moonstone suddenly seem to be off fishing a lot in the evenings, thus cutting down on her new restaurant's business, chef Kirsten Peplinski becomes suspicious. She discovers a topless touring boat has set up business in Lake Superior, just outside the jurisdiction of Moonstone. She sets out to give a "dressing down" to the boat's owner, but Jonathon VanBrocklin kidnaps her, having "undressing" and marrying her on his mind.

Publisher: http://www.writers-exchange.com/Misbehavin-in-Moonstone/

Amazon: http://mybook.to/Moonstone2

Novella 3: Mrs. Claus and the Moonstone Murder

On her second day of duty, new county deputy Lily Schuster finds herself smack dab in the middle of Moonstone, Wisconsin, trouble. She arrests archeologist Marcus Linden for trespassing, then finds she needs his help in solving the murder of a pie contest judge. The suspects involve none other than the town's Santa, Henri LeBarron, an eighty-four-year-old man now cavorting with the sexy, mysterious newcomer, Felicity Starr, twenty-seven. But can Lily trust her trespassing prisoner, Marcus, who seems to be willing to exchange kisses for clemency?

Publisher: http://www.writers-exchange.com/Mrs-Claus-and-the-Moonstone-Murder/

Amazon: http://mybook.to/MoonstoneMurder

Novella 4: When the Dead People Brought a Dish-to-Pass

Three days before Halloween, Alyssa Swain finds a man dead in his car but, once she gets help, the body is gone. When scruffy, tall, dead man John Christopherson shows up alive on her doorstep, he insists she called him to help her get ready for a party. Now the crazy man won't leave her house or her heart. How can she keep him from crossing over into the afterlife at midnight on Halloween?

Publisher: http://www.writers-exchange.com/When-the-Dead-People-Brought-A-Dish-To-Pass/

Amazon: http://mybook.to/MoonstoneDish

Novella 5: A Moonstone Wedding

When grocery store owner Margie Mueller's fiancé--chef Tony Farina--sends her a "fertility rug" to stand on at their wedding, she panics. Margie's no spring chicken and she's not about to hatch a big brood for

the Farinas. Before she can call off the wedding, the Farina clan invades Moonstone for partying and interference in the wedding preparations. But Margie doesn't mind--behind the scenes she's got a murder to solve. A dead man has shown up wrapped in the fertility rug. And it looks like her fiancé may know more about it than he's letting on.
Publisher: http://www.writers-exchange.com/A-Moonstone-Wedding/
Amazon: http://mybook.to/MoonstoneWedding

Coming Soon:
Novella 6: The Moonstone Fire
Novella 7: All She Wore Was a Bow
Novella 8: Pest Control
Novella 9: The Big Love & Murder Shilly-Shally in Moonstone

You can find ALL our books up at Amazon at:
https://www.amazon.com/shop/writers_exchange

or on our website at:
http://www.writers-exchange.com

All Christine's Books:
http://www.writers-exchange.com/christine-desmet/

All our mysteries:

https://www.writers-exchange.com/category/genres/mystery-thrillers-suspense/

Made in the USA
Middletown, DE
19 September 2023

38768504R00215